A CAULEY MACKINNON

Novel

OTHER BOOKS BY KIT FRAZIER

Scoop
(A Cauley MacKinnon Novel)

Praise for the first
Cauley MacKinnon novel,
Scoop

Here's a new talent as big as the Lone Star State!
I've just added new author Kit Frazier to my
favorite things about Texas list…

—Laurie R. King, Mystery Guild

In her debut mystery, Frazier has created a sleuth
to be reckoned with. Cauley MacKinnon is a tough-
talking but vulnerable heroine who acts first and
asks questions later. This story has all the right
ingredients: zany characters, plenty of humor and
mayhem surrounded by a mystery
that engages from the start.

—Romantic Times Magazine

I suggest that you go to Kit Fraiser's Austin
for a heaping serving of down-home
chick-lit murder-mystery, Texas-style.
Scoop left me looking for seconds…

—Gumshoe Review

Kit Frazier has created a smart, independent,
strong-minded woman to be the heroine of her series,
and with *Scoop* has written a solid mystery
that should appeal to a wide range of readers.

—New Jersey Online

Kit Frazier

DEAD COPY

A CAULEY MACKINNON *Novel*

MIDNIGHT INK
WOODBURY, MINNESOTA

FIRST EDITION
First Printing, 2007

Cover design by Ellen L. Dahl
Cover photo © 2006 by Leo Tushaus

Midnight Ink, an imprint of Llewellyn Publications

Cover model(s) used for illustrative purposes only
and may not endorse or represent the book's subject

This is a work of fiction. Names, characters, places, and incidents are either the product of the author's imagination or are used fictitiously, and any resemblance to actual persons, living or dead, business establishments, events, or locales is entirely coincidental.

Library of Congress Cataloging-in-Publication Data
Frazier, Kit, 1965-
  Dead copy : a Cauley MacKinnon novel / Kit Frazier. —1st ed.
    p. cm.
  ISBN 978-0-7387-0959-8
  1. Women journalists—Fiction. 2. Austin (Tex.)—Fiction. I. Title.
PS3606.R428D43 2007
813'.6—dc22   2007005328

Midnight Ink
2143 Wooddale Drive, Dept. 978-0-7387-0959-8
Woodbury, MN 55125-2989

www.midnightinkbooks.com

Printed in the United States of America

For my father, Col. Stephen T. Frazier, USAF.
I miss you.

*A friend is someone who knows the song in your heart
and can sing it back to you
when you have forgotten the words…*

ONE

ANSWERING THE PHONE IS always a crapshoot ... it's usually the electric company checking to see if I'm dead because they haven't received a payment in two months or my mother calling to remind me that I'm on a swift approach to thirty and time's a-wasting.

It's never a good call, like my dream guy ringing from the driveway or Publishers Clearing House calling to tell me they're circling the block with a big fake check for a million dollars. Although if it was one of the guys from Publishers Clearing House, he would definitely be at the top of my Dream Guy list.

The phone trilled again. From the foot of the bed, Marlowe growled low in his husky-mutt throat. I cracked open one eye. Family or creditor, it was clear the phone was not going to stop ringing. My answering machine was broken, so, short of faking my own kidnapping, I was going to have to answer it. Searching through the tangle of sheets, I nearly knocked Muse's grouchy little calico butt off the bed. *Jeez, what time was it anyway?*

"Sorry, cat," I muttered, ferreting the cordless out from a pile of pillows.

"Cauley MacKinnon," I said into the receiver, my voice heavy with sleep and sounding a bit like Lauren Bacall.

I waited.

Nothing.

"Hel-loooo," I said into the silence, and there it was.

The unmistakable sound of heavy breathing. The little hairs on the back of my neck lifted, and I blinked myself awake. I'd been getting calls like this since word got out I was testifying in the upcoming federal trial of a beautiful, blond Argentinean gang leader who looked like Grace Kelly with fangs.

"Look, you big jerk," I said with a mix of fear and false bravado. I was about to blast the bozo with a string of anatomically impossible suggestions when a deep voice drawled, "I need somebody dead."

Aha! This time it really was my dream guy.

Grinning like an idiot, I wrapped my quilt around me and snuggled deep into my big, empty bed. "Somebody *already* dead, or somebody you want to *get* dead?" I said. Just for clarification.

"The latter."

I nuzzled the phone to my ear and could practically see Special Agent Tom Logan leaning against his battered gray bureau car, looking like a tall, dark-haired, square-jawed Eagle Scout on high-octane testosterone. "Is this going to be one of those things where I have to help save the world and I get stabbed in the ass and then I *don't* get to write a Pulitzer Prize-winning article when it's all over?"

After a long pause, he said, "Probably you won't get stabbed again."

"Tom Logan, how you talk. FBI agents are so mercurial."

"How many FBI agents do you know?" he said.

"Enough that you shouldn't leave town again anytime soon."

I could practically hear him smile over the line, and I wondered where things stood between us. The last time I'd seen Tom Logan, he'd thoroughly inspected my tonsils at the Fourth of July picnic and then disappeared into the night to go interrogate fugitives or use thumbscrews or whatever it was FBI agents did when they were called away in the line of duty.

"Yeah, sorry to leave in such a rush," he said, and he sounded like he really meant it. After a short pause, he said, "I need a favor."

"Right now?" I rolled my head to look at the little analog clock ticking away on the antique nightstand.

Four in the morning. It is my opinion that four o'clock should only come once a day, and it should come firmly entrenched in a happy hour.

In his deep Fort Worth drawl, Logan said, "I need an obituary."

I frowned. "An obituary?"

Anywhere else in the world, a request for an obituary in the middle of the night might seem crazy. But in Texas, we have a special affinity for crazy. I hear up North they lock their crazy people in the attic. Down here, we prop them up on the sofa and invite the neighbors over for iced tea. In Texas, crazy is relative.

Rubbing my eyes, I said, "An obituary for who?"

"I can't get into it on the phone," he said. "I just need to know if you can do it. If you can't, I can get somebody else … "

"Well, of course I can do it," I said irritably. "Besides. How many obituary writers do you know?"

"One is all I need," he said, and I blinked in the darkness. Was Tom Logan flirting with me at four in the morning?

"It needs to look authentic," he went on, "with the right wording and on newspaper, printed on both sides so it looks like the real deal.

And this has to be off the record. No files laying around. No ghost images floating in the hard drive."

I sighed. Not flirting. But then, that was Logan: all business.

"Well," I said. "The last part's no problem. We've got a Dead Copy file we use to obliterate information from confidential sources. The *Sentinel's* reaction to you feds tippytoeing all over the First Amendment."

"We never tippytoe," he said, and I smiled.

"So. Let me get this straight," I said. "You want a fake obituary on a tear sheet?" I said, wondering how I was going to pull that off. "And when would you need this real-looking fake obituary?"

"Now."

I bolted upright in bed. If Tom Logan said he needed something now, he wasn't kidding.

"Okay, just … give me a minute," I said.

Stumbling out of my old four-poster, I stepped on the sharp corner of a DVD case of *The Searchers*. "Ow!"

"You okay?"

"It's four o'clock in the morning," I growled, snatching up the DVD.

Logan had given me the flick right after my house had been burgled and my movie collection trashed, probably hoping to win over another John Wayne convert. The movie wasn't noir, my favorite, but it was pretty good—if you like endings where the hero wanders off into the sunset alone. Which I don't.

But wandering off into the sunset alone is something I seemed to be doing a lot more of since I met Tom Logan.

"Is this going to be a problem?" he said.

"No … I'm ready, sort of … " With the phone wedged between my shoulder and ear, I tossed the case onto the dresser and yanked open a drawer for a pair of jeans and a tee shirt, wishing I had time to find a killer summer sweater that fit so well it would make him think twice before leaving again.

I glanced in the mirror above the dresser and immediately wished I hadn't. Ordinarily, no self-respecting southern girl would be caught dead going out of the house with Stage Three Bed Head. But I have found that self-respect is often highly overrated. I swiped a brush through my hair and gave up.

"Cauley? You still there?"

"I said I'm ready," I huffed, juggling the phone as I hopped on one leg, wriggling into a pair of jeans. "Where do you want me to meet you?"

"No need for that," he said. "I'm in your driveway."

TWO

Tom Logan was in my driveway?

Shit, shit, shit!

My heart sprinted as I ran a toothbrush over my teeth, fed the cat, leashed the dog, and locked the front door of Aunt Kat's little Lake Austin bungalow. I skipped down the porch steps to where Logan's beat-up old bureau car was idling under the magnolia tree, headlights glowing against the warm, blue velvet sky. I couldn't help but smile.

The scents of fresh-cut grass and Mexican sage hung heavily in the pre-dawn air, and I wished I'd had time to pop an antihistamine. We were well into August, that torturous stretch of heat that puts teeth on edge.

Despite my endless-summer restlessness, getting that phone call from Logan made me happier than I'd been in a month. I stood outside Logan's dented passenger door, waiting for him to pop the lock as the dog made little warbling noises, leaping at the window like a hound from hell.

The dome light in the car was out, but the stars were bright in the August sky and I'd know that dark hair and those dark eyes anywhere, even in the dead of night. Men like Special Agent Tom Logan are the reason southern women get the vapors.

Logan grinned, his face illuminated from the blue glow of the dash lights. Leaning across the console, he opened the passenger door from the inside. "Hello, kid. Long time, no see."

My heart did a ridiculous little jazz riff and I felt my cheeks go red, despite the fact that it was four in the morning. He was wearing faded Levi's and a worn, white tee shirt. Both garments bulged in all the right places.

I slid into the tattered passenger seat after Marlowe, who was happily greeting Logan with a whole-body wag.

I knew how the dog felt.

Squinting at Logan, I said, "I am not a morning person."

"No kidding," he said, but he was smiling, scratching the dog's white, fuzzy muzzle as I buckled up. "You still putting him through his paces?"

Marlowe actually belongs to Logan, although I've been looking after the dog since Logan got called away on a big assignment. Or the dog's been looking after me—sometimes it's hard to tell.

"Yeah, we do the training thing every month," I said. "He's great at the agility stuff, but so far the only thing I've seen him search and rescue is a peanut butter sandwich."

Logan chuckled at that and handed me a trough-sized go-cup of iced tea. "We doing this downtown?"

I shook my head and gratefully swallowed a big gulp of undiluted caffeine. "We don't do print or production at the *Sentinel* satellite, but we do have Cronkite."

"Cronkite?"

"It's a working model of an old-fashioned printing press. We use it to make mockups when kids come for Career Day and that sort of thing."

"Mockups?"

"We take a stock story, plug kids' names in, and they get to take a personalized article home. Only we try not to use obituaries."

"Right," Logan said, a small streak of amusement in his voice. "You need to call anybody to make it happen?"

I shook my head. "It's early. The nightside crew rarely comes up front and we'll get there before dayside gets in. That way we don't have to explain anything."

Logan nodded and put the car in gear. "We've got to make a stop first," he said, and turned his attention to the big white dog who was straddling the console.

"Back," Logan ordered, and Marlowe leapt into the back seat.

Behind me, a nasally voice yelped, "What the hell? What's with the dog? I hate dogs!"

Startled, I jerked toward the back seat. As my eyes adjusted to the darkness, I saw a guy shielding himself from Marlowe with his forearm. He looked like one of those guys you see getting chased over a chainlink fence in a bad episode of *Cops*. His spiky black hair looked like it'd been hijacked off a hedgehog and moussed with so much product you could bounce a quarter off of it. The sleeves of his black tee shirt were rolled up to reveal biceps that didn't quite bulge. His features were straight and even, but there was something sort of vague about him that landed him on the ugly side of handsome. With his pointy nose and too-close eyes, he could very well have been a genetically altered weasel.

"Who's that?" I said to Logan, who was staring at the guy in his rear-view mirror.

"That," he said, "would be our obituary."

THREE

"Wylie Ray Puckett," the weasel said. "But everyone calls me Puck. My sister says it's somethin' about Shakespeare."

Oh, good. Shakespeare. Like a fake hit wasn't enough drama.

Puck lunged halfway over the front seat to shake my hand. The smell of stale beer and cheap aftershave oozed from his pores, and when he took my hand, I had to stop myself from flinching. The guy's palm was sweaty as he leered at me in the dim light.

Marlowe growled.

Puck sneered at the dog, then looked me up and down through the gap in the seats. "You're the Obituary Babe? *You're* the girl who's gonna kill me? You don't look like an obituary writer. You look like one of those blond Gap babes on TV."

He seemed entirely too excited at the prospect of reading his own obituary, but I got the distinct impression that Wylie Ray Puckett was the kind of guy who inspired lots of people to want to read his obituary.

"What kinda name is Collie, anyway? You named for a dog?"

I narrowed my eyes. Despite his butchering my name, there was something familiar about him, something I couldn't quite put my finger—or my foot—on...

"Sit back and shut up," Logan growled.

"What? I'm just talkin' to the girl," the weasel said, but he sulked into the shadows in the back seat.

Logan watched him in the mirror. "He's testifying at the Obregon trial, and apparently some of his buddies in El Patron would rather he didn't."

"*He's* with El Patron?" I shuddered and nearly broke into a sweat. The last time I'd had a run-in with Selena Obregon and her band of South American baddies, I'd been stabbed, run into the river, and very nearly had my heart broken.

"Puck's their numbers guy," Logan said. "Word on the street is there's a hit out on him."

My eyebrows shot up. "That guy's an accountant?" I said, sifting through which part of Logan's announcement surprised me most. "An accountant who needs protection?"

"Hey, blondie. I'm freakish good with numbers."

"Freakish," I said.

Logan shrugged and kept driving.

Puck leaned forward. "Look, babe, I'm a real asset to this investigation. And I need protection. Those El Patron freaks FedExed me a dead canary—a canary, get it? They don't want me singing in court. They're scared, 'cause I know where the money is made and laid."

"And some of that money came up missing," Logan said. "Seems our pal here has sticky fingers. He's agreed to dime out his buddies for a deal."

"It wasn't embezzling," Puck grumbled. "It was an investment. I'm producing a video. It's going to pay off in spades. They woulda got their money back and then some."

"How's that working out for you?" Logan said.

Puck folded his arms and sank back into the seat.

I shook my head. "So we're going to stage this guy's death? Am I allowed to do this?"

"We've been outsourcing some projects—we get more leeway through Homeland Security. You write obituaries for a living, so it makes sense to source it out to you."

"So, I'm like a contractor?"

"Unofficially."

"And do I get paid?"

Logan cleared his throat. "Yeah. That's what I thought."

I couldn't argue with his logic, but I was the tiniest bit disappointed that Logan hadn't dropped by just to see me, even at four in the morning.

Especially at four in the morning…

Puck poked his head over the console. "Hey, I thought we were hittin' Mickey D's."

"The one out here's not open yet," Logan said. "And sit back."

Puck sat back in the seat. "Yeah, well, I'm hungry. I want a couple of those egg muffins. And some of those hash browns that come in the little paper things and a big ol' thing of Diet Coke. Hey, I can hear my stomach growling back here."

"That's the dog," Logan said. "Keep it down. He hasn't had breakfast yet."

I grinned, shaking my head. "How long have you been babysitting?"

"Too long," Logan said. "The sooner we get this guy dead, the sooner I can get back to my real caseload."

"Hey. I got an idea about that," Puck said, leaning between the seats again so that his head was bobbing above the console between Logan and me. "So we're goin' to court, right? So we get to the courthouse, and see, I'm goin' up the steps to go make my statement, mindin' my own business, and then—*bam!*"

He was so excited he was frothing at the mouth. I leaned forward in my seat to avoid his flinging bodily fluids.

"These guys come out of nowhere," he went on, clearly caught up in his own criminal genius. "They come wheeling around the corner in a big, jacked-up 4 × 4 and they just—*bam-ba-bam-bam-bam*—gun me down, but they're really FBI guys, see? They're shootin' blanks! Only nobody knows it but you, me, and the Obituary Babe here. Pretty cool, huh?"

"Sit back," Logan said. "We're not staging a shootout. Hits don't go down like that."

"How do you know? You got statistics to back it up?" Puck grumped, sounding hurt.

"Logan's right," I agreed. "Hits *never* go down like that. Nobody knows there's even been a hit until the cops find a dead body in a deserted ditch in the boondocks."

"Oh, what d'you know, blondie?" Puck said, and I stared at him in the rear-view mirror. He really did look like a weasel.

My great aunt Kat says there are three kinds of men: the ones you play with, the ones you stay with, and the ones that just need killing.

I hadn't known Puck long, but I suspected he fit rather nicely into that last category.

"My dad was on the job," I said quietly, but Weasel didn't know when to quit.

"No shit?" he said. "I always wanted to be a cop. I figure I'd be a good cop. You know that show *CSI*? I figure it out. Every time. Way before those dickheads on the show figure it out."

"You know," I said. "My dad used to say it's better to keep your mouth shut and let everyone think you're an idiot than to open your mouth and prove it."

"Hey," Puck said. "What's that s'posed ta mean?"

"Sit back," Logan said. His voice was quiet but there was iron in it.

Puck sat back.

We dodged in and out of traffic and for a time I sat back too, watching the sliver of moon shine down on the rolling hills of Ranch Road 2222, the live oaks cast in shades of copper and blue in the early August morning. Big, beautiful houses cut jagged chunks out of the limestone cliffs, a reminder of Austin's relentless population boom. Even at that insane hour of the morning we were boxed in by traffic. The last of the big ranches were being devoured by a profusion of ever-present McMansions—enormous, ostentatious homes carving their carefully fenced half-acre out of the diminishing Hill Country. Lots of people visit Austin. No one ever leaves.

I turned from the window toward Logan. "So where are we heading?"

"To tie up some loose ends. What kind of shoes are you wearing?" he said, sliding a glance down my legs.

Each of my nerve endings pinged simultaneously. I cleared my throat. "Excuse me?"

"What kind of shoes?" he said, taking an abrupt right. "We're going off-road."

I gripped the dash as the car squealed onto Mount Bonnell Road. I glanced down at my Keds, glad for once that I'd forgone fabulous for functional.

"We're goin' up to Mount Bonnell?" Puck jammed his head over the console again, wiggling his shaggy, dark brows at me.

My upper lip curled into a grimace.

Mount Bonnell has one of the most spectacular views in Central Texas—miles and miles of rolling Hill Country to the west and the glittering Austin skyline to the east. It's also one of the hottest spots for the back-seat mambo in the four-county region.

"I never been up to Mount Bonnell. It's kind of a lover's leap, right?" Puck was all but bouncing at the edge of his seat. "The three of us are going up there? Really?"

I stared at him.

Logan's jaw muscle tensed, and for a minute I thought he was going to elbow the weasel right in his pointy nose.

"Three of us are going up," Logan said. "Two of us are coming back."

Puck's over-large Adam's apple bobbed as he swallowed hard and sat back in his seat.

"We're doing it here? I thought most of these things went down east of Austin," I said.

"Most of them do. But we're on a tight schedule. Today's the only day he won't be accounted for. We stage the obit today and postdate it for next week. He needs to be seen in public a couple of times this week, then we put the word on the street he's been snuffed, flash the right people the obit, and he's out of it until his court date."

"And then you're finished baby-sitting?"

"Until some other disaster blows in."

"Hey! You callin' me a disaster?" Puck said.

Logan ignored him.

It was harder for me. I stared out the window. I was going to help fake a death. It seemed surreal. But then, half the time I spent with Logan was surreal.

I shivered. There were people—bad people—who were going to think Puck was dead. But if Puck could help put Selena Obregon and El Patron—her malicious band of murderers—behind bars, it was worth it. Even after two months, the mere thought of Obregon still made my stomach twist into a big, oily knot.

Logan turned into the narrow lot at the foot of the enormous limestone cliff, parked, and got out of the car.

I took a deep breath and climbed out after him.

Marlowe bounded out of the passenger door after me, probably using Puck's lap as a springboard, judging from the way the weasel yelped.

Logan pointed at Marlowe. "Back."

The dog leapt back into the car and waited. I shook my head. One of these days, I was going to have to figure out how Logan did that.

I stood beside Logan at the back of the battered car, which probably had been a piñata in a former life. The scents of cedar and blue sage wafted on the warm breeze and the sky was brilliant with stars—not a scene conducive to murder. In the movies, murders take place in cold, dark alleys—not on warm, beautiful, tree-covered banks overlooking a moonlit river. But this was Austin, where anything could happen and usually did.

Logan rummaged through the trunk, which was jammed with a large duffle bag, two radio consoles, a plastic tool kit marked *Crime Scene*, a box of twist-tie handcuffs, three large flashlights and an assorted array of weaponry. He pulled a leather shoulder holster from beneath a blanket and slid it over his right arm.

"Jeez," I said. "You use all this stuff?"

"Not all at once," he said, and I grinned. The edginess I'd been feeling started to ease.

Puck stumbled out of the car and gawked at the one hundred steps that led straight up to the rocky point. Puck was probably in his mid-twenties, but his voice had a telltale smoker's rasp and his butt was shaped like it'd been acquainted with the tops of too many barstools.

At the foot of the stairs, he balked—probably afraid Logan wouldn't let him stop for a smoke break.

"That's a helluvalot of stairs." He turned back to Logan and pointed at the park sign. "Says here this place locks up at ten, right? Maybe we should just do this here—you know, we don't want to mess this up 'cause some neighbor calls on criminal mischief or something. I could get made."

"Yeah," Logan said. "I hear you're a real stickler for rules."

Logan shoved a clip into a huge .45.

Puck's eyes lit up. "Hey, is that the gun you're gonna shoot me with?

Logan stared at him.

"Can I see it?"

"No."

I shook my head. Texas men and their firearms—the final frontier.

Logan checked the clip and then handed me a Polaroid camera, hefted the duffle over his shoulder, placed his left hand at the small of my back, and guided me toward the stairs. Despite the warmth of his large hand, a cold chill skittered up my spine.

"You ready?" Logan said, and I blinked.

Ready? I wasn't sure. Me on an honest-to-God FBI mission. My heart pounded and I felt a little dizzy. But Logan was trusting me with this assignment, and I liked the way it felt.

As we headed up the stairs, I could feel Logan's presence behind me, solid and steady. I'd forgotten how tall he was. His hand was strong, and I could feel the heat of it through my tee shirt, spreading to some underused parts of my body...

I shook my head. *Good grief, Cauley—get a grip!*

"You okay?" Logan said, and I nodded.

To be fair, I hadn't seen him in more than a month, and I hadn't felt a hand on my back, not to mention any other part of my body, since Logan set off my fireworks and then left on the Fourth of July. I figured I was entitled to a little latent lust, even under the less-than-desirable circumstances.

The three of us trekked up the steps, with much wheezing and moaning from Puck, past the park rules sign at the top. *No one in after ten, no glass bottles, pick up your own trash, no throwing rocks off the cliff…*

Sounded reasonable. Mount Bonnell is the highest point in Austin. It's a small park but a spectacular one, with a narrow observation deck and a rustic pavilion at the top. Rock throwing used to be a real problem at the park, which is one of the reasons they'd set a curfew. Some of the high-dollar homes perched beneath the peak had holes the size of small craters in their expensive Spanish tile roofs because some nitwit downed a couple of beers and pitched golf-ball-sized rocks from the peak.

I gazed around in the tree-shrouded darkness. Puck had been right about one thing—the park definitely closed at ten. The place was deserted.

We were too high to hear the lake lapping the shoreline, but I could smell the fresh water, even at that distance. The only sounds were the rasp of rustling branches and a chirring chorus of cicadas.

"Stick close," Logan said, and I nodded.

Logan led us past the pavilion, where we picked our way along a crude deer path fifty feet straight down to an outcropping. Beyond that, the cliff dropped another seven hundred feet down to the lake.

"Stay away from the ledge," Logan said, setting the duffle on a waist-high boulder.

I looked down—way down.

My stomach lurched. "No problem," I said, edging back toward Logan.

Puck didn't seem impressed by the altitude. "This is it? This don't look so bad. Hey! You see those houses down there? Jeez! Talk about *la mansiones*."

I followed Puck's pointing finger. He was right. The homes tucked into the cliffside were multi-million-dollar estates—some I recognized from the ubiquitous two-page spreads Meggie in the *Sentinel's* Lifestyle section can't seem to stop covering.

Puck stood peering over the edge like he was deep in thought and unfamiliar with the process. He turned abruptly and shouted, "Hey, y'all. Watch this!"

He picked up a rock the size of a softball and heaved back to throw it over the cliff. Judging from the look on Logan's face, it could have been Puck's last act.

But the scree beneath Puck's boots gave way, and as though he'd seen it coming, Logan grabbed him by the back of his neck and jerked hard. Puck's life flashed before my eyes.

"Give me that," Logan growled, wrenching the rock from Puck's grip. "You keep that up and we're not going to have to fake your death."

Logan's voice was low and rough, and I had to give him an A-plus for not pitching Puck over the edge right then and there. Logan is a patient man, but I have found there are limits to his civility.

"Gimme a break," Puck said. "What are there, about fifty houses down there? Statistically, the odds of doing any real damage—"

Logan leveled a John Wayne gaze on Puck, and Puck stood down. His Adam's apple bobbed violently, and after a big swallow he said, "Jeez. Take a pill. I didn't mean nothin' by it."

"You never do. Just stay there and don't move," Logan said.

Puck settled in by the rock as Logan unzipped his duffle, extracting a trash bag, a shirt, and a squeeze bottle of catsup.

Logan twisted a silencer onto the barrel of the gun. "Take off your shirt."

Puck grinned at me.

"I think he meant you," I said.

"Oh, yeah, right," he said.

He hesitated, then yanked his shirt over his head. Puck had a red farmer's tan that ended abruptly at his neck and a tattoo on each arm— one of a Confederate flag and the other of an elaborate pot leaf behind a snake slithering up a dagger. He noticed me staring at the tattoos but obviously mistook my attention. "You like 'em? I can get you a good deal on 'em."

"A real renaissance man," I said. Logan grinned.

"How come you want my shirt?" Puck wanted to know.

Logan whipped Puck's shirt over a low-slung oak branch, stepped back, leveled his weapon, and shot the shirt.

The gun made three weird *thwip, thwip, thwip* sounds, the shirt jerked three times over the branch and the bullets pinged off a rock below.

Puck jumped. "Holy shit! What the hell are you doing?"

"Goin' for reality." Logan tossed Puck the shirt.

Catching the shirt, Puck poked his fingers through three holes. "This was a good shirt! Why didn't you shoot a hole in that other piece of shit shirt you just pulled out of the bag?"

"I told you to wear something old," Logan said.

"Well, yeah, but you didn't say you were going to shoot holes in it," Puck grumbled. He pulled the ruined shirt back over his head, careful not to muss his hair.

Ignoring him, Logan turned and leapt about eight feet down to the next rocky ledge. He shifted back and forth, checking for sturdiness.

He looked up at Puck. "Your turn."

Puck looked down, warily, watching Logan check the rock.

I waited.

Shrugging, Puck said "See ya" and jumped off the ledge to join Logan.

"Not if I see you first," I muttered.

"Hey, where do you want me?" I called down to Logan, dizzy at the height.

"Right where you are," he said. "Just point the camera down the incline when I get him in position."

He turned to Puck. "Roll up your sleeves so we can see your tats, then get on your stomach, face to the side so we can get it on film."

Puck hesitated, but he did as he was told.

Even at that distance, I could see a shift in Puck's demeanor. As he knelt down on the rock, his back slumped a little and he wavered. I didn't know him very well, but I thought he was getting spooked.

"Hey," I called down. "This seems like a lot of trouble. Why can't you just give the money back?"

Puck sneered. "Aside from the fact that I don't have the cash, they don't let you do that, blondie." I didn't say anything, but he looked up at me, agitated. "I was helping my sister out of a sort of contract, okay? She don't need any of this shit rainin' on her."

"All right, get down," Logan said, his hand at Puck's shoulder. "We gotta get this done before daylight."

Logan shook the bottle of catsup and squeezed it in short, sharp bursts so that it spattered the rock, then poured three big globs on the holes in Puck's shirt.

"Ugh, that feels disgustin'!" Puck yelped.

But I was still thinking about the sister. "Contract?"

I stood staring down at the bizarre scene unfolding. I knew the blood was fake and no one was hurt, but it felt creepy with Puck laying there in a crumpled heap halfway down the cliff, gaping red bullet holes in his shirt barely visible in the dawn's early light.

Unease prickled the back of my neck. Puck wasn't a likeable guy, but somebody out there wanted him dead. And he had a sister in trouble.

"Yeah," Puck called up, his voice muffled by his awkward position. "She's a singer and she's real good. All she needs is a video. We're this close."

He indicated with his fingers how close they were.

Ah, his sister was a musician. Anywhere else, that might have been news, but Austin bills itself as the Music Capital of the World. Half the waiters and most of the cab drivers in Austin are musicians waiting for their big break. The other half are writers, but I don't like to go there.

"Move your arm out by your head and hold still," Logan said to Puck. "You ready with the camera, Cauley?"

"Yeah," I said, aiming the Polaroid straight down. I snapped three shots, careful not to get the toes of my shoes in the frame, and placed the developing photos on the boulder as the camera spit them out.

I peered down at the white-framed window of black film. The image began to surface from the void, and there was Puck, broken and blood-soaked on a boulder. I grimaced, fighting back a sudden wave of nausea. I knew Logan knew what he was doing, so I fought the urge to call down to him, *I've got a really bad feeling about this*...

"We done here?" Puck said. "I gotta go shake the stick."

LOGAN TOSSED PUCK THE clean shirt and led the way back up the steep rock face as Puck wandered into a thicket of live oaks.

I grimaced. "He couldn't have waited?"

"He missed that chapter in Emily Post," Logan said. He brushed off a nearby bench so we could sit down.

I shook my head. "You've got the patience of a saint."

Logan shrugged. "He's a pain in the ass but he's a good informant. He testifies and we get Selena Obregon tied to El Patron, we got them all for organized crime, tax evasion, and all kinds of other good stuff."

I sat down beside him, suddenly very aware that we were alone. I smoothed out my hair, wishing I'd had time to do something that resembled an actual style before leaving the house. There ought to be a rule—a guy should give a girl at least an hour's notice before asking her to help fake a hit.

He was quiet, like he was edging around something he wasn't sure how to approach. He blew out a breath and said, "You heard from John Fiennes lately?"

I felt like I'd been sucker-punched. Of all the things that could have surprised me on a night like this, I wouldn't have guessed that's what Logan had on his mind.

John Fiennes was the missing piece in the El Patron trial—the one that got away. He was a darkly handsome, young Pierce Brosnan type: beautiful, mysterious, and with the soul of an assassin. He got away with a truckload of antique gold, a lot of my research on the Argentinean crime syndicate, and a chunk of my heart. While it is true that hell hath no fury like a woman scorned, I was trying to be a bigger person. Some days it works better than others.

I suspected Logan knew there was more to the Fiennes thing than I'd told him, but he hadn't pressed it. Until now.

Drawing in some air, I said, "No. Not since that last call. If I had heard from him, I'd have called you and Cantu and the United States Army."

Well. Maybe not the Army.

"No phone calls?" he said, and a streak of irritation ground up my spine like nails on a chalkboard.

"No," I said. "I've been getting some heavy breathers, but I assumed that's because I'm testifying at the trial or that it was one of the dorks that Mia and Brynn tried to set me up with—so no, I haven't heard from John."

I wondered if his interest in Fiennes was personal or professional. With Logan, I've found that it is sometimes both.

"Phone calls with heavy breathing?" he said, and I groaned.

"If you will recall," I said, "you yourself gave me a phone full of heavy breathing just this morning."

Logan chuckled. "That was different," he said, and the tension between us eased.

"So Puck is being pretty altruistic, considering he thinks his life is in danger," I said, and Logan looked out across the horizon.

"Yeah, funny, isn't it?"

I was quiet.

"Funny thing about a blabbermouth—they just can't keep a secret. Especially when there's a secret they're dying to tell."

That got my attention. Being a natural-born snoop, my ears were pricked. "You think there's more he's not telling, and you're hoping he'll crack at the trial or be so indebted to you for saving his life that he'll tell you when the time comes?"

Logan didn't say anything, but I could feel something inside him relax. Probably there weren't a lot of people he could talk to, and it made me feel like Queen of the Known Universe that I was one of those people.

The predawn air was heavy with quiet. We sat there, looking at the lake below, and I felt the small space between us begin to buzz with electricity.

I snuck a surreptitious glance at him. His dark hair was short, shorter than the last time I'd seen him. His chin was strong and his eyes were the color of warm chocolate. His nose was a little crooked, like he'd seen both sides of a bad punch and came out none the wiser. And we were on top of Mount Bonnell, the most romantic spot in Central Texas—if you weren't helping fake the murder of a guy who could be the poster child for celibacy.

Logan sat staring out over the skyline. He was quiet the way my stepfather, the Colonel, is quiet when he's got something to say.

I waited.

"After today, we're going to have to limit contact until the Obregon trial is over."

"Oh," I said, feeling like the breath got knocked out of my lungs. I hadn't seen that one coming. I tried to swallow my disappointment. "Because we're both witnesses in the Obregon trial?"

He nodded, and we sat there in silence.

"When you say limit contact, does that mean reduce contact or no contact at all?"

He smiled at that. "Let's try reduce and see how that works."

I felt a little better, but not much. Logan had finally waltzed back into my life, and now he was waltzing right back out.

We sat for what seemed like a very long time.

"Puck's sister's got a gig on Friday at the Pier. They're shooting some kind of music video there and it'll be Puck's last official public appearance. Maybe you could come and we can see how the reduce thing works out," he said, and I smiled with my whole body.

"Did you see that?" Logan said.

"Hmm?" The only thing I'd been looking at was Logan.

"There," he said, nodding toward the still-dark sky.

"What? I don't see anything—" but then I did see it. A shooting star. And then another. My breath caught, and I watched as bright stars streaked across the early morning sky. "Wow … " I whispered. "Shooting stars."

He smiled.

"It's incredible. They must be late this year," I said, watching as tiny bits of comet blitzed the sky. "I've always had a thing for stars. Daddy used to say you were never really lost because you could navigate by the stars. One time I asked him what happened when the stars fell, and he just smiled, and I'll never forget this: he said that the important stars didn't fall—that they were always in the same place in the sky, even when the sun came up. He said, *The stars are always there, Cauley Kat. You may not always see them, but they're always there … you just have to have a little faith.*"

My voice trailed off, and my cheeks warmed with color. I looked back at the sky. "I used to think it was magic."

"There are more things in heaven and earth than are dreamt of in your philosophy," Logan said, and I smiled.

"A philosophical fed."

"A literate one, anyway. This is one of my favorite things—the Perseid meteor shower. We won't see another Perseid this active in our lifetime." He nodded toward the sky. "One of the most beautiful sights in the world and it only lasts a little while," he said, but at that last part, he was looking at me.

Our gazes caught and I swear I could hear my heart pounding in my ears.

"There must be hundreds of shooting stars," I whispered. "I don't think I have that many wishes."

"You only need one good one." Logan smiled, and his eyes did that crinkle thing at the corners that made my stomach drop to my liver.

We were sitting close, so close I could smell the leather of his shoulder holster, his lips just a few inches from mine, and in that moment I thought he was going to kiss me.

I jumped when his cell phone rang.

He cleared his throat and went for his phone.

"Logan," he said by way of greeting. His voice sounded gruff, like he'd swallowed sandpaper.

He was quiet for a moment as he listened.

"About thirty minutes," he said and waited some more.

"Right," he said, and disconnected.

Logan blew out a breath and clipped his phone back on his belt next to his badge. "Well, kid, we gotta go."

That was *so* not my wish.

I gazed up at the stars still streaking across the sky, but I felt a lot less enthusiastic about it. *Somebody up there owes me a wish.*

He tucked the Polaroids in his pocket. "The obit needs to be dated for Tuesday. I've got a mug of Puck on a CD. Can you do this yourself or do you need me for anything?"

Did I need him for anything? Clearly he didn't understand the whole wish thing.

"Um, no," I said, trying not to stare at his lips. "Just his vitals—name, age, where he was born. I know you want the pub date marked Tuesday, but I'll need the time and day of death… "

Logan nodded, his eyes still intent on mine, and I felt like I was right back on the edge of the cliff, dizzy and about to fall.

The bushes behind us rustled, and Puck came tromping though the undergrowth. My heart dropped, and the reality—and the unreality— of what we'd done came flooding back.

And Logan was leaving. Again.

Puck came into the clearing, snapping his jeans as he walked. "Hey! Did y'all see all those stars?"

"Yeah, we saw 'em," Logan said. "We've got to go."

At that moment, an enormous star blazed through the sky, so close to the earth that it looked like it might set the trees on fire and plummet into the lake.

"Will you look at that?" Puck said, staring as the star flamed toward the earth. "Ain't that the shit?"

"Yeah," Logan said. "It is."

But he was looking at me.

FOUR

THE SUN HAD ALREADY begun its assault on the horizon as Logan dropped me off at the *Austin Sentinel's* West Austin satellite. It was a little after six and he sat idling in the parking lot, waiting for me to get inside the office safe and sound. I smiled. Luckily, some things don't change.

Part of me was jazzed at the idea of getting to work on official FBI business, and part of me—the bigger part—wanted Logan to take me home and see if we could instigate a little criminal mischief of our own...

I swiped my keycard through the security slot and turned and waved to Logan. Marlowe was sitting next to him in the freshly vacated passenger seat with his head out the window. Puck was in the back, his head bobbing over the console. I watched as Logan put the car in gear and the three of them pulled out of the parking lot, and I got that weird little pang I always feel when Logan leaves.

Logan said he'd take the dog and the weasel to the FBI field office, with the promise that he'd be back to pick me up when I was ready to go home. I was ready now.

But I'd made Logan a promise, and I intended to keep it.

For once I was glad I didn't work at the main office downtown, with all its bells and whistles and computers that don't require a sledgehammer to reboot. Despite all the hand-me-down equipment, the satellite had what I needed: the model printing press, a laid-back atmosphere, and an incredible lack of supervision.

To be honest, an office downtown at the *Sentinel* was my goal. It's a huge, Frank Lloyd Wright-style building that presides over the city on a bluff above Town Lake, where it watches over the capital city like a wise old uncle. Editors at the *Sentinel* take lobbyists to lunch, reporters have offices with walls, and all of the news that goes through the City Desk is the real thing—stories that matter. Stories that can change people's lives for the better. Not the fluff, filler, and birdcage liner we churn out at the satellite.

The satellite is the *Sentinel's* redheaded stepchild once removed. It's located west of Austin in a strip mall between a bank and meat market. It's a journalistic purgatory where reporters do time. Staffers at the satellite are either paying their dues on their way up or doing their time on their way out.

Unfortunately, I was doing time.

I'd been sentenced for life as an obituary writer for sins I'd committed when I accidentally slept with my boss at the *Austin Journal,* the *Sentinel's* bigger, better-funded rival newspaper. Okay, it wasn't so much an accident as a monumental mistake.

Sighing, I swung open the interior heavy glass door, trying not to think about Logan as he pulled out of the parking lot. In the lobby I badged Harold, the heavyset guard who hulked behind his big, round desk eating powdered-sugar donuts and watching an infomercial about a miracle weight-loss pill.

"Well, if it ain't the Obituary Babe," he mumbled around a mouthful of donut. He looked down over his considerable belly for a peek at his watch. "What are you doin' here so early? You're never early. Hell, you're never even on time."

I scowled, signing into the off-hours log. "I'm usually on time."

He stared at me.

Okay. I'm rarely on time. But I'm working on it.

"So what's got you chompin' at the bit?" he said, powdered sugar puffing from his ample lips.

"I have something on my desk that can't wait."

"A dead guy can't wait?"

"Not this time," I said and headed through the interior doors and down the main hall toward the Bull Pen, the maze of cubicles where budding young journalists pounded out filler and ferreted out mind-numbing research for the City Desk downtown.

At this time of day, the place was like a tomb. The nightside copy-editors were winding down, getting ready to go home, and the dayside shift hadn't even started smacking their snooze buttons. Perfect.

Tossing my purse under my desk, I booted up my computer and shook my head. Ethan Singer, the *Sentinel's* hard-drive jockey, had been messing with my system. I knew this because he'd changed my screen saver from "Shut up and write" to "I see dead pixels."

It really annoys me when he lurks in my hard drive.

Growling, I retrieved the CD and the note Logan had given me out of my back pocket and got to work. On the computer, I opened the obituary layout, popped in a photo of Puck, and wrote a generic cutline with Puck's name, date of birth, and supposed death.

Studying the notes Logan had given me with Puck's info, I settled in and began the obituary. I decided to post Puck's bogus demise as a family-placed obituary.

A family-placed obituary is different from the funeral home's generic, twenty-five-word death notices, in that they're longer and more elaborate because the family writes the obit and pays for the space through the Classified Department.

It annoyed me that the paper made the bereaved buy a few pitiful column inches to give their loved ones a decent sendoff.

My gaze dropped to Puck's photo flickering on the monitor, and I flinched. This obituary was different. I was writing a death notice for a person who was very much alive, and it gave me a big case of the creeps. Shoving back the jitters, I put my nose to the digital grindstone and got down to official FBI business.

There are some unwritten rules about writing obituaries. You use euphemisms. People don't *die* in obituaries; they pass away, pass on, get called to Jesus, or go to play the banjo in the All Boys Choir. But the euphemisms don't always stop there.

While it is true that sometimes a cigar is just a cigar, an obituary is often rife with euphemisms. If the dearly departed had an *ebullient personality*, he probably spent a lot of time staring at the bottom of a highball glass. A *confirmed bachelor* is code for gay. *Never met a stranger* means he screwed everything that moved. I leaned in and began tapping away at the euphemisms.

> Wylie Ray Puckett, 29, of Blackland, Texas, passed away after a tragic accident (mob hit) on Mount Bonnell on Tuesday, August 15. Puckett was an unusually successful accountant (an embezzler) and was a gifted storyteller who regaled friends and family with tales of adventure (a big fat liar).
>
> Puckett is survived by his mother, Kimberly Ray Ainsworth, stepfather Cullen Wallace Ainsworth II, sister Faith Milam Puckett, and stepbrother Cullen Wallace Ainsworth III.
>
> Puckett was preceded in death by his father, rodeo cowboy (flat broke loner) R. L. "Tuffy" Puckett and grandparents Joseph and Nellie Milam Puckett, who managed the family ranch until the day they died (were good, God-fearing, gun-toting, land-poor Texans).

I sat back, tapping my pen to my lips, mentally wording the kicker for a big finish. Leaning in, I tapped out:

The family has requested cremation (nobody wanted to spring for a funeral). In lieu of flowers, the family requests donations be made to Animal Friends of Austin.

I figured if a guy like Puck had any friends at all, they could use a dose of good karma.

Nodding after a quick re-read, I popped a generic article about the Texas legislature's non-progress on school finance for the backside of the obituary page and sent the whole shebang back to Cronkite.

Finished, I sat staring at Puck's freshly typed memoriam, tapping my pen to my lips.

There was something familiar about Wylie Ray Puckett that had been bugging me all morning. Not that we ran in the same circles—I prefer that my friends have opposable thumbs—but there was something familiar about the name...

I glanced up at the clock above the editor's office opposite my cubicle. Six thirty. Plenty of time. No harm in a little snooping. I Googled "Wylie Ray Puckett" and got what you usually get on the information highway—thirty-eight sites on sure-fire stock options, sixty-two sites guaranteeing amazing male enhancement, and an interesting site on honorary lesbianism.

There was also the obligatory bazillion hits that had nothing to do with Wylie Ray Puckett. I frowned. No matter who you are or how sheltered your life, you usually get at least one shout-out from Google.

Undaunted, I accessed the *Sentinel's* morgue—the archive of dead stories—and ran the same search.

Nothing.

Puckett. Wylie Ray Puckett. I could've sworn I'd heard that name before. I did a split screen and skimmed the obituary for relatives' names. Entering *Kimberly Ray Puckett Ainsworth* into the morgue, I got seven legitimate hits—three mentions in the society pages about charity balls she'd recently attended, three wedding announcements for previous and current marriages, and two for business-related articles about the sale of an old family ranch.

"The family ranch," I whispered to no one. *Bingo.*

I clicked the link and an archived article popped onto the screen. The photo at the top right of the article showed a crowd emerging from the Dawes County Courthouse.

I leaned forward for a better look. There, in crystal-clear clarity, was the youthful image of Wylie Ray Puckett. He was standing next to a beautiful, dark-haired waif who must have been his sister. I zoomed in on the photo and compared it to the photo in the fake obituary. The years had not been kind to Puck.

In the archived photo, Puck's face was sharp and square, his hair dark and glossy. I zoomed again. There was no network of boozer's veins criss-crossing his nose, no bloated cheeks, no unfocused, dilated eyes. His eyes were clear and gray, almost silver, the color of water in winter. I drew a quick breath. Wylie Ray Puckett had once been a hottie.

His sister was even more arresting. There was something about her—something quiet and haunting. She had large, dark eyes, high cheekbones, and long, dark hair—like Audrey Hepburn in *Roman Holiday.* I imagined the siblings got more than their share of cheek-pinching at the Puckett family reunions.

In the photo, Puck and his sister looked like they were loaded for bear and spoiling for a fight. Sometimes a photo really is worth a thousand words.

Family Feud Spurs Court Battle Over Old Blackland Ranch

By Rob Ryder
Austin Sentinel Staff

Two generations of the Puckett family duked it out in court yesterday over the fate of the Blackland Ranch, located northwest of Austin off County Road 241 near the fork in the clear, clean waters of Blackland Creek.

Wylie Ray Puckett, together with his sister, Faith, have taken up the family feud over the proposed sale of property and mineral rights at the Blackland Ranch, a struggling family-owned cattle ranch that has been passed down through generations of the Puckett family since the Texas Land Grants. Flanked by supporters, the Puckett siblings took on Ainsworth Enterprises, an acquisitions company owned by Cullen Ainsworth II and third wife Kimberly Ray Puckett Ainsworth, mother of Wylie Ray and Faith Puckett. Development plans submitted to the Dawes County Courthouse include a proposed surface mining permit to extract the coal, which could compromise the habitat of the endangered Texas Cave Beetle...

My eyes flicked back to the photo. In the background, protesters picketed the courthouse. I shook my head. You gotta love Austin. It's an enclave of bunny-kissing, bug-loving environmentalists right smack in the middle of gun-toting, oil-drilling, refinery-hugging Texas.

I zoomed the photo and grinned. A young woman in the background brandished a sign that read *Strip-Mining Stinks! Dethrone Kimmie the Cave Beetle Queen.*

In a town where gossip fuels society events like high-octane ethanol, my mother and her best friend, Clairee, got enough juice out of that scandal to power the Charity League's entire holiday season that year. Never mind that the ranch deal never went through, or that Kimmie Ray later became Cullen Ainsworth's third—and last—wife, or that the ranch never shed one ounce of coal, strip-mined or otherwise. Kimmie Ray had never been able to shed the nickname.

"Cave Beetle Queen," I snorted.

"You see a bug?"

My heart slammed into my throat, and I nearly fell out of my chair.

I spun around to find Ethan Singer peering over my shoulder. Ethan is a height-challenged geek with inquisitive, tawny eyes and a charming beak of a nose—cute in his own binary-code-writing, Jolt Cola-drinking, thermal-grease-smeared way. Today, he was wearing his favorite black *Resistance Is Futile* tee shirt and a pair of vintage Levi's.

He was known around the newsroom as Wonder Boy, and he could make computers do things God never intended. Ethan and I had developed a bond due to my tenuous relationship with my piece of crap computer. Ethan says I exude a magnetic field that causes computers and other mechanical devices to lose their will to live.

"Good grief, E, make a noise or something!"

My heart pounded, and I propelled my chair to the left to conceal the monitor.

Ethan eyed me with interest. "Hey, what are you doing here so early?"

"Why does everybody keep saying that?" I said irritably. "You'd think it's a wonder I show up for work at all."

After I caught my breath and got my heart rate below three hundred thirty, I said, "While we're on the subject, what are *you* doing here at this time of the morning?"

"I couldn't sleep, so I thought I'd come in and try out a program I've been working on. I made the finals in the Game Geeks Competition, and I might even get a contract."

"Game Geeks?" I said.

"Yeah, you'll have to play it. The prototype is *Hard Target*. Sharpens strategy and shooting skills."

There were lots of things you could get away with at the satellite that you didn't dare at the main office, but I wasn't buying it. Ethan didn't get much sleep anyway on account of him having an even more abysmal unsocial life than I did.

"Who is she this time?" I said.

"Doesn't matter." He sighed, plopping down in the swivel chair next to my desk.

I waited.

He pushed the wheeled chair back and forth with his feet. "Hey," he said, not meeting my gaze and trying to sound disinterested, "how come girls don't like me?"

"Oh, come on. Girls like you," I said. "I've tried to set you up twice with that girl in Web Design."

He toed the burgundy carpet with his ratty red Converses and twirled his chair. "Yeah, I know. But she's a geek."

I almost laughed out loud. This from the guy who had a *Star Fleet Academy* bumper sticker on his Volvo and the entire cast of *Star Wars III* action figures Velcroed to the back dash.

"*You* could go out with me," he said, and I smiled.

"Oh, Ethan. As flattering as that almost is, you say that every time you break up with someone."

"We don't have to go *out* out. We could talk on the phone."

"Every time we talk on the phone you ask me what I'm wearing."

He grinned. "Can't get slapped if you don't try."

"Well, E, maybe you need to meet people *outside* the office," I offered, but I had to question his judgment. He was asking *me* for relationship advice?

I was staring down the barrel of my twenty-eighth birthday, and I already had one disastrous marriage under my belt. And due to Logan's absence, I was fully engaged in situational celibacy, in deed if not in thought.

"I have a life outside the office," he said.

"Gaming conventions don't count."

Ignoring my comment, he spun the chair. "You working on an obituary?"

"Just trying to get caught up on some work."

"Who's the stiff?" he said, leaning toward my computer.

My first instinct was to leap forward and switch off the monitor, but I shrugged and said, "Just some guy. Actually, I'm, um, working on a new design layout, and this obit was at the top of my inbox."

Ethan's face lit up. "Let's see."

Oh, hell. Showing a new page design to a guy like Ethan is like dangling a rib roast in front of a rottweiler.

Logan had asked me to keep Puck's fake death notice under wraps. But it was an obituary, and I was an obituary writer. If I played it right, I could pass it off as just another part of my job, which was supposed to be the whole idea, anyway.

No time like the present to see if I could pull it off. Taking a deep breath, I rolled my chair out of the way and gave E full view of the screen.

"What's this?" he said, pointing at the archived article flickering on the screen.

"Just some background. You know. For the obituary." I was aiming for cool and casual, but my voice seemed unnaturally high.

Ethan's eyes narrowed as he skimmed the obit. "Dirt-poor widowed mother… Kimmie Ray Puckett… Cullen Ainsworth II… sale of the family ranch… surface mining for clay products… feline refuse pellets?" He shook his head. "Strip-mining for kitty litter? You going to include that little gem?"

"No," I said evenly. "I only get twelve inches a week for a lead obituary. I'm waiting to make sure we don't get a dead celebrity."

"Too bad." Ethan frowned and bumped me out of the way. His gaze flitted from the archived article back to the obit.

Double hell.

Ethan leaned more closely to the monitor. "If you really want to change the layout, you could always run wider gutters and use a different font." His long fingers zipped over my keyboard at warp speed, and I let out the breath I didn't know I'd been holding.

"There, see?" Ethan said with a *ta da!* in his voice. "Just run it to the printer and you can get a good look at it."

"It's great! I can see it from here—there's no need to run it to the printer," I stammered, reaching over him to close the archive page. I'd already printed a copy of the fake obit and it was laying in Cronkite's tray. I needed to get to the back office, get it off the printer, and call Logan to take it off my hands before anybody else got wind of the damn thing.

I was racking my brain for a way to get Ethan away from my computer and out of my cubicle when a bright voice beamed from a distance, "Hey, Cauley, what are you doing here so early?"

My left eye twitched—it was way too early for beaming. Ethan and I turned to see Marina Conchita Santiago bouncing into the pressroom, her ubiquitous Nikon bobbing from a neon strap around her neck. Mia was wearing eyeball-burning orange, from her short, swingy skirt to her strappy sandals. She looked like a dark elf disguised as a sunbeam.

"Why does everyone keep saying that? Y'all act like I've never been early in my life," I said.

Mia rolled her eyes and Ethan ignored me.

"Come look at this," he said to Mia, tugging her toward the monitor. "Cauley's doing a new style sheet for the Death Page."

"Oh!" Mia said. "I always thought that page could use a little pop."

I gritted my teeth. I was in serious danger of blowing it for Logan. Swinging around in my chair, I kicked the switch on the surge protector under my desk, inadvertently clobbering Ethan in the knee. The hard drive made a wilting noise and abruptly powered down.

"Yow!" Ethan howled.

"Oh, Ethan!" I said. "Jeez, I'm sorry! Are you okay?"

"Screw my knee! My knee is fine! You never, *ever* shut a computer down like that."

"It was an accident." Part of it was. And I really was sorry about his knee. "Probably lost the whole morning's work."

"You didn't back up your work?" he said. His voice was unnaturally high, and his eyes bulged dangerously.

I shrugged, and he stared at me with a look reserved only for the very young and the very stupid. I didn't care to venture a guess as to where I stood in that scenario.

He sighed and shook his head. "Well, don't worry about it," he said, turning to the hard drive and lowering his chin. "I can fix it."

"Yeah, I figured," I said, and as Ethan and Mia set to work getting my computer back online, I slipped out of the cubicle and down the hall, cell phone in hand. I had a fake obituary to save and an FBI agent to call. Life just didn't get any better than that.

FIVE

LOGAN MUST'VE HAD HIS hands full with Puck because he didn't answer his cell and I had to leave a message. After my third attempt at a message that sounded cool and breezy, I hit *send*.

Ethan had recovered Puck's obit, and I promptly dumped it into the unrecoverable Dead Copy file before anyone else laid their eyeballs on it. I folded the newsprint into a manageably sized square and shoved it into a manila envelope, along with the printouts of Logan's notes, Puck's pictures, and the CD Logan had given me. I shoved the whole thing under the teetering pile of detritus in my inbox. If anyone wanted to sneak a peek at that bad boy, they'd need a Sherpa and a GPS tracking unit.

With the fake obit done and tucked safely away, I turned back to my computer, presumably doing the job I get paid to do, when a wall of weariness hit me so hard I could have fallen asleep standing up.

I glanced up at the clock. Eight thirty. Great—no time to go home for a short nap.

The dayside crew was already trickling in, carrying big go-cups of coffee and wearing sleepy expressions on their faces.

I knew how they felt. I was daydreaming about snuggling back in my big four-poster bed and hitting the *snooze* button for the thirteenth time when a voice bellowed, "Cauley! What the hell are you doing here?"

I jumped and knocked a stack of funeral home death notices out of my inbox as Mike Tanner scowled over me, looking almost as intimidating as Hugh Grant with a head cold.

I shrugged. "Jeez, can't a girl come in early to get some work done without everyone acting like it's the first sign of Armageddon?"

Tanner eyed the blizzard of unfinished paperwork fluttering back down to my desk.

"See?" I pointed to the mess. "I'm getting caught up."

He grunted, heading into the glass-enclosed office we call the Cage.

He set his coffee precariously on his own pile of unfinished paperwork, turned, and crooked his finger at me. Oh, good. A summons from the home office.

Sighing, I trudged through the open door and said, "What?"

It came out a little crankier than I meant.

Tanner motioned for me to shut the door.

Great. I was about to get my ass handed to me on a silver platter.

He crossed his arms, leaned against his desk, and stared at me. The man couldn't possibly be old enough for the big purple vein that bulged on his forehead, and I wasn't in the mood to defend myself.

"All right. Give," he said.

I raised my eyebrows, trying to appear charming and innocent.

He narrowed his eyes. "You're here for a reason. Spill."

Apparently I need to work on my charm and innocence. I hedged, trying to come up with something that was close to the truth without spilling the beans about the fake obituary. Tanner looked tired, more tired than usual, and the dark circles under his eyes made him look far older than forty.

"Logan's back," I finally said.

Tanner's eyes rolled back in his head. While he hadn't officially met Logan, he knew I'd been involved with the FBI agent during the federal sting on Selena Obregon and El Patron, and that I'd been carjacked, kidnapped, robbed, and stabbed in the rear. But Tanner was a sharp guy, and I think he suspected there was more to the story with Tom Logan than me just horning in on a federal investigation.

Tanner pressed his thumb against his temple, dropped into his chair, and reached over the picture of his wife for his jar of licorice whips. "Am I going to have to start smoking over this?"

"I don't think so."

Gnawing on the red, rubbery stick, he fished through the paperwork on his desk. "I've got an assignment for you," he said and handed me a folder. "You see the front page of the *Journal* today?"

I winced. But then I always wince at the *Journal*. I learned everything I know about journalism during my brief stint at the *Journal*. I also learned what happens when you sleep with the boss.

I turned my nose up at the paper. "I avoid that rag like you avoid carbs."

"Yeah, yeah. Just look at this."

Scowling, I snatched the paper. The front page story—above the fold—had a byline "by Miranda Phillips." And *story* was the right word for it.

The headline read El Patron and Texas Syndicate: Gang War Imminent as Obregon Goes to Trial? in bold, fifty-point Helvetica type.

I skimmed the article and shook my head. "There's nothing new in this article, and we have no idea there's going to be a gang war. This is pure speculation."

Tanner nodded and took one of those profound breaths he takes when he's planning strategy. He looked out the wide window that framed the ever-spreading suburban sprawl devouring the Hill Country. He turned and leveled his gaze on me. "They still having you testify before the grand jury?"

"Next week," I said warily.

Tanner grunted. "You doing that demonstration thing tonight?"

I nodded. "The police department's hosting a demonstration of different branches; SWAT and forensics will be there. This is the first time search and rescue volunteers have been invited."

"Place'll be crawling with cops. Keep your eyes and ears open. See if there's anything they haven't released. The *Journal* may be all bleeds-'n-leads, but Mark Ramsey's no fool. There may be a gang war on the horizon, and if so, it's going to get bad."

Tanner booted up his computer and swiveled to look at me. He must not have liked what he saw. "I'm not asking you for state secrets—just find out what's going on. Keep track of it."

"*You're* giving *me* an assignment?" I said suspiciously.

"Research," he said. "Shiner's got the story."

"Of course he does," I said, trying not to grind the enamel off my back teeth. Paul Shiner is the tall, blond sports reporter climbing his way up the *Sentinel* ladder on the rungs of *my* story on El Patron.

"Come on, Cauley. You'll get your chance. He needs this now. He's downtown three days a week now and he's in over his head."

I felt little puffs of steam coming out of my ears. "I'll get right on it."

"One more thing."

I was already at boiling point, and Tanner always saves the big whammy for the finale. "What," I growled.

He fished a folder from his desk drawer. "Clear your schedule. You're going to a Press Association conference this summer."

My mood lifted about eleven feet. "Me? Going to a national conference?"

"It's for obituary writers."

I froze. If I attended a conference full of other Dead Beat reporters, it would be admitting that I'm probably going to be stuck writing obituaries until cobwebs grew over my cold, dead fingers.

"Tanner," I said, resisting the urge to kick him in the shin, "send somebody else. I hear there's an intern downtown *dying* to get on the Dead Beat."

He stared at me.

"You said I had a shot at City Desk. All I had to do was bide my time, pay my dues, and get in line. If I go to this conference, does this mean I'm stuck on Dead Beat?"

Tanner shook his head. "City Desk is still there, and you're still in line. But like it or not, you're on obits until it comes open."

He rubbed his eyes with more force than necessary. "Cauley, you're good at what you do. You get grieving families to open up. They talk to you—tell you stories they wouldn't tell Shiner or even me, for that matter. You've got a way of telling stories about stiffs that makes their lives seem like they really meant something."

Tanner was giving me a compliment? I eyed him suspiciously. "Tanner, are you okay? You don't have a twenty-four-hour brain tumor or anything?"

His face went ashen, and he reached for another licorice stick. "There's nothing wrong with me except insubordinate staff. Take the itinerary on the Dead Beat and Shiner's research, and go do the job you get paid to do."

I tried not to slam the door on my way out of the Cage, but I didn't try very hard, and the breeze from the sharp smack of door against frame felt good.

I was tired and getting crankier by the minute. I had the sum total of three hours of sleep, Logan was back in town and we couldn't see each other, I helped get a guy "dead," and now I was doing research for someone else's story that may or may not damage my relationship with the police department—the only tie I had left with my father. And to top it all off, I may or may not have just received a life sentence manning the desk on the Dead Beat.

The day was taking a definite nosedive.

But Tanner was right. The Dead Beat was my job, and I took it seriously. Last month I started a new series on Austin natives, people who were born here and died here—no easy feat, since more than half the population wasn't even here ten years ago. I'd actually started getting fan mail. The accolades were nice, but I really enjoyed listening to people talk about their loved ones and then telling those stories in the newspaper. I especially liked the little old ladies, who weren't "little old ladies" at all. Most of them were good old-fashioned tough Texas gals, the kind of women who could stave off attacking Apaches, plow their own fields, and make babies by the dozen. Many of them had been beauties in their day—not unlike my own mother and my great aunt Katherine. I smiled a little. The last of the big-shouldered broads; I hoped to take my place among them someday.

Resigned to doing Shiner's footwork—for now—I plopped down in my chair and glared at the folder, sending Shiner a legion of unkind thoughts. Flipping through the pages, an eight-by-ten shot of Selena Obregon stared back at me. I felt that familiar, nauseating jolt. She was preternaturally beautiful, with sleek blond hair, luminous blue eyes, and a fair, fine-boned face. She also had the heart of a rattlesnake.

She'd been the brains behind El Patron, an Argentinean smuggling ring notorious for settling disagreements by chopping off ears and shoving burning Bridgestones around shoulders. I'd spent a week in the hospital after a run-in with Obregon and her thugs.

While I was thinking about El Patron, I called the downtown cop shop and asked for Dan Soliz, the gang guy. I didn't know him but I'd seen him in passing, and he knew I was a friend of Cantu's. As credentials go, you can't get much better than Jim Cantu.

"Soliz," he said. His voice lilted with Latino accent so that even his name sounded like a song.

"Hello, Mr. Soliz. My name is Cauley MacKinnon, and I was wondering if you were going to be at the demonstration tonight?"

"The blond girl that hangs out with Cantu?"

I cringed a little at the "girl" part, but maintained my stiff upper lip. "That would be me," I said, all bright and sunny.

"The one that works for the newspaper?"

"And volunteers for Team Six."

"And why would you be wanting to know if I was going to be there?"

I thought about making up some preposterous story but decided to tell the truth. "Look," I said. "The *Journal's* been printing a lot of crap about some looming gang war, and I noticed you, the guy in charge of gang crimes in the whole county, weren't quoted. I want to know your thoughts on it."

"There's a reason for that. A lot of what I do is outreach," he said. "I try to get the kids before they've done something they can't take back. Some of it's not pretty, and the only way I can do my job successfully is if the people I'm working with trust me."

I was quiet. I knew the people he was talking about weren't his buddies on the force.

"I won't print anything you don't want me to print," I said. "And if you need some quals, you can talk to Cantu or anybody in his unit."

He was quiet.

"What are you doing after the demo?" he said, and I grinned a happy grin.

"Whatever you're doing after the demo," I said, and, smiling, I hung up the phone.

I stared down at the file I was going to have to eventually give to Paul Shiner, fair-haired boy of the *Sentinel's* up-and-coming News Boys.

"Top that, Sports Boy," I said, and happily got back to work.

I WAS PAGING THROUGH the file for background when a familiar female voice behind me coughed "Ahem."

I scowled, muttering a string of inventive swears in my head.

"Ahem," she coughed again, and I swung around to find Merrily March, the *Sentinel's* most annoying sales rep and resident busybody, staring down at me, clutching a clipboard to her pastel pink twin set. She couldn't have been much more than forty, but she was easily the oldest person at the satellite and acted like a study hall monitor with *The Big Book of Grammar* rammed up her rear.

"May I help you?" I snapped, slamming the folder shut, not really caring whether I could help her or not.

It had been Merrily's idea to slice the office into cubicles, which nearly caused an interoffice riot. She's the publisher's sister-in-law, and she'd been sent to the satellite to prevent the editorial staff downtown from pushing her out a fifth-story window. At the satellite, she's gone mad with power, and unfortunately for our editorial staff, it's a one-story building.

Merrily has platinum hair approximately the shape and consistency of a football helmet. She's short but she carries a big stick, and at this moment, her big stick was office supplies.

"You're over your allotment of Post-its," she said.

I stared at her. "There is no allotment of Post-its."

"There is now," she said, and ripped a page from her clipboard and slapped it on my desk. "The supply closet will be locked until further notice. Fill out a request form if you feel you need something."

"Great." I scowled. "Thanks for the update."

I turned back to the file, but Merrily didn't move.

"Is there something else you need?" I said, though I doubted anything short of something with a Y-chromosome with an incredibly low self-esteem was going to do her much good.

"Since you asked," she said, sliding another order form onto my increasing pile of paper, "my niece is selling meat for a fundraiser at her high school."

"Meat?"

"Yes. Meat."

"What happened to cookies and candy?"

"You get more money for sausage and jerky."

I shook my head and grudgingly picked up the order form. "What's the fundraiser for?"

"The flag team is going to Barbados—you know, for spring break."

"Barbados?" My jaw twitched. "That's not a fundraiser, that's panhandling," I said, but I figured any kid associated with Merrily was due at least a week for a mental health break. Sighing, I checked off a square for some smoked turkey.

I passed the sheet back to Merrily, but she just stood there. "The jerky is really tasty," she said. "You could get some for that non-existent guy you're always mooning over."

Merrily had been needling me about Logan since he'd left. It wasn't that I didn't date. I'd gone on the requisite setups from my friends and, God help me, my family, but I prefer men who don't already have girlfriends, reek of Metamucil, have pending charges, or be so charming that women all over town drop to their knees for him—at his house, at his office, in my driveway…

48

To be fair, I had been mooning a little and pretty much lost interest in mingling with the opposite sex since Logan left town.

Merrily cleared her throat and stood there, brow arched like a bat wing, waiting for me to sign over this month's paycheck for her niece's tropical retreat. I wondered if Logan would bail me out if I smacked her with a stapler—and if I'd have to fill out a requisition for a new one if it broke...

"Well, Merrily, I'd love to order the jerky, but it seems all my expendable income will now be going toward Post-it Notes," I said. "And I don't moon."

"What's this about mooning?"

Merrily made a bleating sound and every bit of air left the room when I turned to see Logan sauntering past the front desk with Mia, who was grinning a mile wide as she trotted along beside him.

"Look what I found!" Mia sing-songed, and then she leaned close to me and whispered, *"Interoffice Hottie Alert!"*

Logan grinned a little, looking at me.

Hottie Alert was right. Merrily was standing there with her mouth open, and the heads of copyeditors and junior staffers popped above partitions like a field of alarmed prairie dogs. Logan looked down at me, amused.

"Where's the dog?" I said, brushing the hair out of my eyes as I rose to meet him.

"In the car with his new best friend," Logan said. He looked at Merrily, who was still gaping at him. "Am I interrupting?"

"Not at all. Merrily here was just telling me I'm in danger of going over my Post-it quota."

Merrily made a gakking noise, and I grinned.

I shuffled the papers in my inbox and nonchalantly showed Logan the envelope with the fake obituary.

"Still on for Friday?" he said, and warmth rushed to my cheeks.

"What's Friday?" Mia wanted to know, and Logan said, "We're taking a mutual friend to the Pier for some live music."

"Oh!" Mia all but bounced on her toes. "I love the Pier! We should ask Ethan to go, too."

"We?" I said.

"Well, of course," Mia said. She turned to Logan and whispered, "He's having girl trouble."

"Lot of that going around," Logan said. "I heard you needed a ride home," he said to me. "You ready?"

That was a loaded question. I'd been ready for months. "Um, yeah," I said, reaching for my purse from beneath my desk.

"We're on a tight schedule," Logan said, and I sighed.

"Message received," I said, but I felt like somebody burst my balloon.

I glanced over at the Cage. Tanner was on the phone, rubbing the back of his neck as he went over the budget report. Probably worried about office supplies.

I smiled at Logan. "Yeah, I'm ready."

Merrily was still standing at the corner of my desk, mouth working like a catfish stranded in a low-water crossing.

I shouldered my purse, grabbed the file Tanner had given me to research, and turned to Merrily and whispered. "You're mooning," I said. "Don't wait up for me."

SIX

I slipped Logan the envelope with the fake obituary, and he dropped me and Marlowe off at my house, which left me with mixed emotions. I wanted to spend time with Logan, but Puck had gone way over his limit on egg muffins and the whole car smelled like fried eggs and Puck. Never a good combination.

Logan said he and Puck were going into lock-and-load mode to prep for the trial—the translation, as I took it, meant they'd be off the radar until Friday, when we would all meet at the Pier.

In the front yard, I let Marlowe off the leash, encouraged him to pee on my neighbor's rosemary bush, and then admired my little Lake Austin bungalow. Well, it's not really *my* little bungalow. I'm currently mortgaging my soul to my great aunt Katherine, a fabulously famous romance author who is as darkly beautiful as she is slightly crazy. But in Texas, we like crazy. In fact, we reward it. Just take a look at the legislature.

And as far as the soul-selling goes, Aunt Kat is a forgiving proprietor. All she asks is that I do my best to follow in her Manolo-clad footsteps and try not to burn her house down, which is sometimes easier said than done.

To that end, she's left me in charge of her Lake Austin bungalow crammed with bizarre antiques, many of questionable origin. My favorites are the old Wurlitzer jukebox, the Remington Scout typewriter, and a cranky old calico she calls Muse.

Despite my lack of sleep and a file full of research for a story I'd never write, I was in a pretty good mood. While I didn't have a date with Logan in the strictest sense of the word, I figured a Friday night hanging out with him and a couple of cold beers at the Pier was the next best thing.

Marlowe followed me up the steps onto the wide, white front porch. As I dug the key out of my purse, Marlowe bristled and growled low in his throat.

The little hairs on the back of my neck lifted.

"What's the matter, boy?" I said, pushing the key into the lock. The door gave without any pressure. I stopped inside the foyer and listened. Marlowe bristled, his growl deepening. The breath caught in my throat.

A sudden wave of déjà vu sent my heart plummeting to my stomach.

Not long ago, a bald, earless guy I called Van Gogh had terrorized me in my own home, but he was dead. I knew he was dead. I saw John Fiennes shoot him in the head right in front of me. He *had* to be dead ... didn't he?

My heart kicked up about ten beats, and I glanced around the room. The last time I had this feeling, Van Gogh had turned the place upside down, destroyed most of the furniture, and shoved my cat into the sofa along with a gift-wrapped package that contained a severed ear.

Something was wrong. I glanced around the house. The place was just as I'd left it. Not exactly ready for a photo spread in *Southern Homes*

& Gardens, but no overturned furniture, no gift boxes of chopped ears, no cat trapped in the sofa . . .

The cat!

Where in God's name was Muse?

"Muse!" I screamed, my heart thumping hard against my ribs. "Muse?"

Marlowe barked, something he rarely does, and lit out down the back hall to the bedroom, where he skidded to a stop in front of the closet. He circled three times and snarled—what he's supposed to do when we're running our search and rescue drills, but a whole lot meaner. My heart hammered in my throat.

Scrambling, I raced back to the bar that opens to the kitchen, reached over the counter and grabbed the cast-iron frying pan the Colonel had given me as a wedding present five years ago. I don't cook, but I've found that the pan does come in handy.

"Muse?" I hissed, creeping back down the hall, brandishing the frying pan like a baseball bat.

Sucking in a breath and a big dose of courage, I threw open the closet door.

"Muse?" I called again, panic blistering my insides, when something the size of a fat, fuzzy football with spikes leapt onto my head from the sweater shelf, screeching like a banshee.

Like a flash of silver lightning, Marlowe snarled and leapt past me into the closet, tearing the pile of shoes sprawled along the floor.

"Marlowe," I yelled, dropping the frying pan as I tried to peel Muse's claws out of my scalp. "Marlowe, no! Not the shoes!"

The frying pan clanged as it bounced on the floor, and I struggled to pull Muse's sharp nails out of my earlobe.

And then I heard it: a male voice. And he was yelling.

It's not often I hear a man yell in my bedroom, but there it was, and Marlowe came crashing out of the closet in pursuit of a man with slicked-back hair clad in camouflage, a red bandanna masking the lower half of his face. The man was flailing at the dog, scrambling to get away from Marlowe's snapping, snarling, spit-spewing jaws.

The breath left my body.

The man lunged at me, a long-bladed hunting knife glinting in the dim light. Marlowe chomped down on his right hand, barely missing the sharp blade.

The man howled in pain, trying to jerk his arm from Marlowe's death grip, but Marlowe bit down, hard.

"Holy hell!" I screamed, and Muse screamed, too.

The man landed on me, all greasy haired and smelling like three dollars' worth of bathroom Polo. Marlowe was still clamped on his hand, and we all fell in a writhing pile on the floor beside the bed—Marlowe snarling and biting, Muse whirling about the man's head, spitting and scratching like an angry badger.

Pinning me, he ground his pelvis against me, his dark eyes locked with mine in a terrifying embrace. I gulped and turned away, thinking about fresh air and a good dental hygienist.

I wriggled against the hard surface of the floor, struggling to get out from under the man, stretching my arm to reach the frying pan.

Wriggling, he dug his knee into my stomach so hard I saw stars flicker in front of my eyes.

Muse whirled about, bit him hard, and took a good chunk out of his ear. The fleshy chunk fell by my cheek in a shower of blood. The man howled.

"Get these animals off me, or I swear I'll cut out your heart and feed it to them!" the man yelled, glaring down at me with eyes so dark and empty it was like looking into the eyes of an East Texas alligator. The bandanna covered the lower part of his face.

For a split second I froze, his knee digging into my kidneys. I laid there, staring into his eyes like I'd been hypnotized. Muse screeched and slashed his cheek, tearing at the handkerchief.

The man's hand flew to his face, and we all rolled in a confused, furry, bloody jumble, bumping hard into the bed, where a small box had been perched at the bedside.

The box fell beside my head, and a small, yellow bird rolled out, right beside my face. I stared at the stiff body of the bird, its black eyes open, its tiny feet stiff, curled in death.

I screamed.

Marlowe let go of the man's arm and went for his neck.

The man made a horrible gurgling sound, and I reached for the frying pan, rolled out from under him, reared back, and hit him right on top of the head.

The man didn't keel over, passed out, like they do in the movies. He wobbled a moment, shook his head, then glared at me with a hatred I've only seen in ex-husbands.

"This isn't over, blondie," he said, and leapt to his feet, racing for the hall, Marlowe hot on his heels, his fuzzy white muzzle dripping with blood.

"Marlowe, no!" I yelled, but the dog was in pursuit mode, chasing the man into the foyer and out the front door. Marlowe stopped on the porch, still bristling and barking, as the man disappeared into the brushy back of my neighbor's yard.

I stood in the doorway, holding my stomach where the man had kneed me, panting and staring around the yard, hoping he had come alone.

"Good boy, Marlowe. Good dog," I panted, dropping to my knees to kiss him on the head, careful to avoid the bloody muzzle. "Come on," I said, staggering into the house. "We gotta call the cavalry."

I WAS SITTING, WRAPPED in a purple chenille throw that smelled like lavender, at my neighbors' house. Beckett and Jenks have been partners as long as I can remember and are a source of friendship, support, and a steady supply of sample sale shoes.

On the sofa, Marlowe pressed against me as Muse made a fool of herself, purring until she slobbered, wrapped around Jenks' neck.

"A dead bird? Somebody broke into your house, attacked you, and left you a dead bird?" Beckett said, bringing me a tall glass of bourbon and Diet Coke. "Oh, honey, you have the worst luck with men."

Red lights flashed outside the large living room window, and both Beckett and Jenks swiveled toward the window.

"Is that your FBI agent?" Jenks said breathlessly as a heavy knock sounded at the door.

"That would be him," I said, trying not to stumble over Marlowe in the entryway.

"Logan," I said, swinging open the door.

"Are you hurt?" he said, and I shook my head, even though my whole body felt like it'd been run over by a bulldozer.

Logan stood there, looking tall and dark and dangerous on the front porch as he did a visual checklist of bumps, bruises, and scratches on my body. Beckett and Jenks went into a simultaneous swoon. Logan nodded to them and said, "Thanks, guys. I'll take her from here."

"Will you keep the cat until forensics gets through with the house?" I asked Jenks, and he grinned.

"Is the agent going to come back for the cat?"

Logan actually blushed as he ushered me out the door. "I'll be back," he said, and then turned to me. "Come on, kid. We got a lot of work to do, and not a lot of time to do it."

Inside the house, I led Logan back to the ransacked bedroom and unmade bed.

"He toss your room?" Logan said, and I said, "Um, yeah," like the room wasn't always a mess.

Marlowe scowled at me, the traitor.

"What happened?" he said, his gaze sweeping the room from the roof to the floorboards and probably places I couldn't even see.

I told him, trying not to leave out any details, from the guy's empty reptilian eyes to the red bandanna and camouflage clothing.

"Red bandanna?" he said, and I nodded.

"What?"

He shook his head, but his jaw was set as we moved toward the bed. Marlowe followed him, bristling, obviously in on the investigation.

"And the bird?"

I pointed under the bed, where the box lay next to the pitiful pile of yellow feathers. A lone bullet casing rolled around in the box. Logan knelt and cocked his head for a better look, and I sidled in next to him. His large body felt solid beside me, and my frenetic heartbeat began to slow.

A steak knife impaled a note on the small white box.

The note was one line, written in big, boxy letters with a red marker.

KNOW WHAT HAPPENS TO BIRDS WHO SING? I DO.

My heart slammed into my throat.

"Come on," Logan said, rising to his feet. "Let's go sit on the porch. Crime scene techs are on the way."

On the porch, we waited. I sat on the porch swing. Logan stood on the porch, eyes sweeping the street, Marlowe at his side.

"Didn't someone send a bird to Puck, too?"

Logan nodded, his jaw working. He looked like he wanted to break something.

"Speaking of the devil, where is Puck?" I said, in a feeble attempt to change the subject.

"Left him at the field office. He hit the dirt when he heard you had a visitor," Logan said, looking over my shoulder as the cop cars began to pull in. "You call Cantu?"

"What? No," I said, following his gaze.

Cantu was climbing out of his ten-year-old station wagon, which had the entire cast of *Dora the Explorer* dolls strewn about the dash. As he exited the car, he looked like he was ready to spit nails.

"Oh, hell," I muttered.

Behind him, the forensics van jumped the curb, the driver overjoyed at the opportunity to use the lights.

Cantu's eyes sparked dark and angry as he stormed up the walk, a look he'd sported only once before.

"What the hell is going on?" Cantu snarled. He squared off on Logan, which was pretty ballsy, considering that Logan had almost five inches on him. "You have anything to do with this?"

Logan took a step toward Cantu. Life as I knew it flashed before my eyes.

My friendship with Cantu was complicated. He was about ten years older than me, and once upon a time I'd had a terrible crush on him. I was eight, and he was a dashing young beat cop when my dad was a detective. When my father died, Cantu stepped up to fill in some of the empty spaces.

"It's the Obregon trial," I stammered. "Just some nut trying to spook me. Whoever it was didn't take anything, and they didn't do any real damage."

Except attack me, kill a poor, innocent bird, ruin one of my steak knives, leave a creepy note in red magic marker, and make me be afraid in my own home…

Cantu took a deep breath like he was counting to ten, and Logan did, too.

"You take prints?" Cantu said, and Logan said, "Waiting on the geeks."

Cantu nodded.

Then they both turned toward the van, where the crime scene techs were tumbling out the doors, big black toolboxes in tow.

"You take the kitchen, and I'll do the bedroom?" Logan said.

Cantu nodded, and the two of them headed into the house like they'd been best friends for life.

I stood on the front porch, bewildered.

"What just happened?" I said to the forensic photographer who trotted up the stairs and dropped to one knee, taking shots of the doorjamb.

"War buddies," he said, and then he shouldered his camera and headed through the front door.

"Fine. Now I'm a war zone. This was *so* not on my list of five-year goals." I sighed. "Come on, Marlowe," I said, and realized he'd followed Logan into the house.

Marlowe had defected.

Months of male drought, and now I had a veritable battlefield of men marching down the driveway to ransack my house.

THE CRIME SCENE TECHS left my house a wreck. Cantu set up increased patrols in the area and put a guy on my house. The boys in blue were out making the city safe for civilians, so I felt marginally better.

Turned out my lock was broken, so Logan made a call to have one of his buddies come change my locks, and Cantu said Marlowe and I could be excused from the demonstration, but I didn't think that was fair. If Marlowe and I were going to really do this search and rescue thing, people were going to be counting on us, no matter what was going on at home.

Plus, Marlowe had actually found Muse. Okay, so she was just in the closet, but still… it was a glimmer of hope, and I intended to grab it with both hands.

Logan fetched Muse from Beckett and Jenks' house right before he left. I glanced up at the clock. I had time to clean the print dust off every imaginable surface, and a little time to look into the file Tanner had given me. I set about getting rid of the graphite with my mother's lemon-scented industrial cleanser and mopped up the footprints the boys left all over the hardwoods, stopping periodically to take a peek through the curtains to make sure there were no ear-chopping maniacs circling the block. The only thing out of the ordinary was a couple of young cops circling the block. They were in an unmarked car, but they were easy to spot. The only cars that make that many rounds are soccer moms looking for their wayward offspring, not two grown-up Boy Scouts in dark sunglasses.

With the fingerprint surfaces newly fresh and shiny, I was caught up in a full-on, adrenaline-inspired cleaning blitz. I tackled the shower and then buckled down to battle the dust bunnies behind the fridge, but it turned out they were armed to their fuzzy little teeth, so I settled for making a pot of tea and going over the paperwork in Tanner's file.

Mama had taught me that busywork was the best way to forget about my problems.

I settled in on the sofa and flipped open the file Tanner had given me, wondering where in the world I should begin and what questions I should ask Soliz about this evening.

"Well, Marlowe," I told the dog. "We can add today's little adventure with ear-chopping maniacs to our stack of research."

The dog didn't say anything.

"Fine," I said. "I'll work on this myself."

Legal pad in hand, I scribbled possibilities—turf wars, disrespect, anything that could be a link between El Patron and Texas Syndicate. Muse hopped up on the sofa, leering at the pristine pages like a juvenile delinquent looking at a sidewalk of fresh wet cement.

Because I always think better with the black-and-white clarity of noir rolling in the background, I zapped on the Turner Classic Movie channel and found a Charles Vidor director's marathon. To my delight, *Gilda* was showing—a flick about a sultry, if somewhat tainted, night-club singer, her horrible husband, and the man who loved her. It's a story about a doomed triangle of a woman and two men, complicated by love, lust, and the danger of obsessive desire.

It was a study in greed, cunning, and the age-old question of honor among thieves—the perfect backdrop to looking for clues in an escalation between El Patron and Texas Syndicate. Plus, I could get a few tips on the art of stripping without taking anything off—something I planned to take notes on.

I spread out the pages Tanner had given me on the coffee table and narrowed my eyes. A lot of the info on El Patron was stuff I'd dug up over the summer.

And Tanner thought I couldn't handle working downtown. As I flipped through the file, I made three piles—one for El Patron, one for the Syndicate, and one for anything that looked like it might connect the two. Muse, meanwhile, made a concerted effort to stomp on every sheet of paper until she found the one I was trying to read, at which point she turned around three times and settled in on the paragraph I'd been studying.

"Muse," I growled, fixing to move her fat little calico butt off my research, when she blinked her big yellow eyes at me.

She sat there, wide-eyed, staring at me. In that moment, my lack of sleep hit me like a loaded cattle car. I'd had a restless night followed by an adrenaline-packed morning of faking an obituary, interrupting a breaking and entering in my home, and having an unattractive man wrestle me to the floor. To top it off, he left me a nasty note meant to discourage me from testifying at the trial.

I stared at the cat, who sat staring back at me, and I realized I was so tired I couldn't have kept my eyes open with a crowbar.

"You can take a nap without me," I told the cat, who blinked very slowly back at me and jumped to the coffee table.

I sighed. "Fine," I said. "Just a short nap."

I pulled the quilt from underneath Marlowe, who'd already staked out his end of the sofa, and wriggled beneath the soft patchwork, worn smooth as silk from generations of MacKinnons snuggling beneath it.

Marlowe opened one eye.

"I'm just going to lay down for a minute," I said to the dog. "There's plenty of time to take a shower and get us a sandwich..."

Marlowe eyed me skeptically. Then he sighed and laid his head on my feet. Muse leapt from the coffee table and slipped beneath the quilt, turned around twice and settled beneath my chin. Within moments, her loud, rusty purr vibrated against my chest.

"All right," I yawned. "But just for a minute."

And then I closed my eyes and dreamed of Logan.

THE PHONE TRILLED, JOLTING me out of a truly excellent PG-13 dream that started with Logan bare-chested on the banks of the Pedernales River. I'd had this dream before, but it never got past that mind-numbing, pulse-pounding kiss we'd shared at the Fourth of July picnic.

In the dream, my heart was hammering and I was about to ask him a question when Marlowe grumbled low in his throat.

A real growl punctured the dream, and it was not the sound of a heart pounding.

With one eye twitching, I fished through the sofa cushions in search of the phone. One of these days I'm going to get organized. But probably not today.

"This better be good," I snarled into the phone.

"Hey *chica, qué pasa?*" chirped Mia's cheerful voice.

I grimaced. I was not in the mood for cheerful.

"What am I doing?" I said, blinking at the pile of paperwork that had spilled over the coffee table and onto the Turkish rug. "Committing career suicide."

"Oh, good. Then I didn't disturb you," she went on. "Want me to come by and pick you up?"

"Why would I..." I glanced at the clock blinking on the DVD player and then down at Marlowe.

"Oh, holy hell!" I hissed.

"If you're ready to go, I could come get you," Mia said, and I shook my head, stumbling out from beneath the quilt, which caught under my foot, and I fell flat on my ass.

"Ouch!" I yelped.

"Are you okay?" Mia said.

"No... yes... I mean, just go on without me. I've got a meeting with Dan Soliz after the rally anyway."

"You know it's media night..."

A primal scream bubbled up in my throat, and I pounded it back with a great deal of effort. "Yes, I know that, Mia. Thank you for the reminder."

"I'm just saying…"

I wedged the phone between my shoulder and ear and staggered to the bathroom for a look in the mirror—and immediately wished I hadn't.

Cantu had decided that since we still hadn't passed our test, Marlowe and I would be the communications team for Team Six. Hopping around and wrestling with the phone, I struggled into my black SAR gear, scrunched my hair into a ponytail and slapped on the black SAR baseball cap.

"Want to go out after?" Mia said, and I sighed.

"I would, but I'm interviewing Soliz, and Tanner dumped a bunch of research on me and I gotta get it done before the grand jury thing."

Plus, there was some house-breaking, woman-attacking, bird-killing maniac running loose in the city who now had an up-close-and-personal visual of the floor plan of my house…

There was a silence over the line in which I knew I was being disapproved of, but life is like that sometimes. "*Está bien, chica*, see you at the rally," she said.

"Right," I said, and disconnected.

"Crap, crap, crap," I growled, scrambling through the leaving routine, trying to be on time for a change, which Muse made nearly impossible by yowling and doing figure eights around my shins.

I freshened the water in her champagne glass—a little compulsion my aunt started years ago—grabbed my purse, leashed the dog, and skipped down the steps and hopped into the Jeep.

I looked at my reflection in the rear-view mirror and groaned. There is nothing like trying to weasel information out of a cop while dressed in black Army surplus gear.

Sighing, I cranked up the engine. Nothing.

"Shit!" I swore.

I cranked again and got rusty, metallic ratcheting from under the hood. It was a little after five and still hotter than hell, and I was beginning to sweat.

Marlowe watched with something that bordered on interest as I jumped out of the Jeep, hustled to the back cargo area, and grabbed the hammer I keep behind the spare tire.

I jogged around to pop the hood, where I proceeded to beat the starter within an inch of its measly little metallic life.

A big *wham* sounded near the front fender, and I jerked up to find the obnoxious neighbor kid staring at me over the fence.

I wiped my forehead and glared at him. He was about nine, and worse, he was one of the notorious neighborhood Bobs. I like most of my neighbors, especially Beckett and Jenks, the guys who cohabitate in the bungalow on the left.

The Bobs are a different story.

Bob, Mrs. Bob, and the baby Bobs routinely steal my newspaper, let their dog crap on my porch, and generally remind me why abstinence can be a good thing.

"What?" I said irritably as the kid looked me up and down.

"You're scary," he said.

Narrowing my eyes, I marched around to the driver's side, leaned in over the seat, and cranked the key again. The engine stuttered twice, thumped, then grudgingly engaged.

I threw the hammer in between the seats and stalked back around to slam the hood.

"Kid," I said, bending over to lob his ball over the fence. "You don't know the half of it."

SEVEN

A TWINGE OF FOREBODING sprinted up my spine as I pulled into Fiesta Gardens and slid into a parking space behind a familiar white van that was hogging three parking spots. My sense of foreboding had been correct.

"*Miranda,*" I swore.

Miranda Phillips was issuing orders to her television crew, her perfect platinum hair oblivious to the humidity, her perfect body oblivious to gravity. Her boob job had taken nicely, I guess, if you like breasts you could eat hors d'oeuvres off of. Apparently she'd skipped the silicone and gone straight for helium.

I cast a quick glance into my rear-view mirror and sighed. Standard SAR gear isn't my most flattering look. In addition to the unfashionably high-necked, black long-sleeved tee shirt, I had on black jeans and black hiking boots, which were neatly accessorized with a whistle, webbed utility belt, black nylon gym bag, and a fanny pack—not exactly a *Chic Magazine* Glamour Girl moment.

Miranda, on the other hand, looked flawless. Miranda is the Martha Stewart of journalism but with better shoes. She has her own wildly successful syndicated column at the *Austin Journal,* the *Sentinel's* bigger, better-funded rival newspaper, and it is rumored that she landed the television gig by letting KFXX's big fat producer snack on her mackerel in the middle of Interstate 35 during a live shot of a hostage stand-off. The rumor might have been hard to believe, except that I'd caught her doing the very same thing with my ex-husband, Dr. Frank Peters, aka Dr. Dick, in the middle of my living room sofa. Same ho, different hoedown.

Today her ho-ish charms were cranked up to "obliterate" and aimed at detective Jim Cantu, who was waiting for her to set up the shot. Cantu had taken over SAR training right after Amy Bracken left because her burgeoning pregnancy had finally forced her to quit scaling fences and rooting around in drainage ditches.

My main job for the evening would be to explain how search and rescue worked and let people see the kinds of tools we take into the field. But mostly it was to let little kids pet Marlowe.

I lugged the bag out of the Jeep's back cargo area and was passing between my Jeep and the cop car when a giant brown shark with legs threw himself at the car's rear passenger window, snarling and scrabbling and looking for blood.

"Jeez!" I yelled, yanking hard on Marlowe's lead as he bristled, looking to return the favor. "Hey, Napalm, take a Milk Bone! It's just me and Marlowe!"

The dog settled, and his snarl spread into a big, dopey doggie smile. I looked around, wondering where his equally dopey owner was. It was entirely too hot to leave a dog in a car for even a few minutes.

Shaking my head, I tried the door. Since it was unlocked, I undid my fanny pack and hooked it on Napalm's collar. The dog capered about like a giant set of jaws on four legs. Trying to get both the dogs under control, I let Marlowe drag us to the staging area, where we hurriedly signed in with Olivia Johnson, the team's operation leader, at base camp, which consisted of a card table lined with ID tags and clipboards and a big white RV outfitted with first-aid supplies, radios, a satellite dish, a generator, and enough maps to wallpaper my entire house.

"I'm sorry, I'm sorry, I'm sorry," I whispered as Olivia handed me my ID badge. Her eyes were nearly as dark as her skin, and she gave me a look she reserved for criminals and people who don't pay their parking tickets.

She shook her head. "Girl, you better get your act together. All the other units are here."

"I'm working on it," I said, looking around. She was right, of course. The gang unit was there passing out tee shirts, SWAT had the big black van, and the forensics guys were laying out a practice crime scene, complete with yellow tape and chalk marks.

Olivia looked at me. "What're you doin' with Hollis's dog?"

"He left him in the car, windows rolled up. Will you take him?"

"Hollis," Olivia growled and muttered a string of very inventive curses as she fished an extra lead from a large plastic box under the table. "Tryin' to train a Malinois fuckin' attack dog to search and rescue people … that dog ever manage to find somebody to rescue, they prob'ly die of a heart attack at the sight of those big ol' teeth." She attached the lead, brought him around to the other side of the table, and poured him a bowl of water. "You can't help it, can you, baby?"

"Thanks, Olivia. I owe you," I said over my shoulder as I hurried over to the staging area.

"You owe me nothin'," she said, petting the dog. "You see Junior Hollis, you tell him *he* owes me an explanation."

I'd sure hate to be Hollis after Olivia got ahold of him. And he thought his dog was scary.

Gazing around at the crowd, I recognized some of the police officers and one of the SWAT guys, and spotted a tall Texas Ranger with salt-and-pepper hair that I'd have to tell Mama's friend Clairee about.

Dan Soliz was already onstage, giving out awards to kids who'd made a difference in the community. I watched him for a moment. He may be the head of the gang unit, but you'd never know it if you met him on the street. He was wiry, but it was a tough wiry, and he wore his usual uniform of ostrich boots and worn Wrangler jeans that fit him well. For the occasion, he wore a black DARE tee shirt and his trademark grin that had been known to make women take their clothes off.

There was an area cordoned off for media, where a posse of reporters from the tri-county area were enjoying overstuffed Thundercloud subs and chocolate brownies so good they made your eyes water. I smiled. I'd told Cantu the way to get the Fourth Estate interested in a press outing was free food.

Behind the lines, camera crews were setting up, and Mia, who'd been chatting up the guy from *Live at Five*, caught my eye and waved both hands, fingers crossed. I smiled and nodded.

Cantu was giving Miranda the short explanation of Team Six Search and Rescue for the enquiring minds of Miranda's viewing audience. For the most part, I doubted anyone in TV Land was listening. Most of Miranda's core viewership was simply waiting for her cleavage to pop out of her low-cut Versace blouse—again.

Miranda seemed captivated with Cantu, which wasn't surprising. Women often had that reaction to Cantu.

I watched as he charmed her, and I remembered why I'd had a crush on him when I was a kid. The years had sharpened his features and defined his body. He was a couple inches taller than me—just under six feet—with skin the color of a double latte and the body of a runner, probably from chasing around the three small reprobates he calls his children.

He was wearing his black SAR gear, neatly accessorized with a silver whistle on a lanyard around his neck. On him, the getup looked dangerously appealing. On me, it looked like I was early for Halloween.

John Moreno and his black Shiloh, Gandalf, were already there, demonstrating a perfectly executed climbing rescue on a portable rockwall.

Meanwhile, the cameras rolled as Cantu spoke. "Team Six is a team of volunteers with specially trained dogs who search for missing people and evidence," Cantu said in his trademark laid-back style. I watched, wondering when the guy who used to be a beat cop when my dad was a detective had become so cool. "The team is partially funded by a grant from Homeland Security, but the volunteers provide their own dogs, their own training, their own uniforms and gear. Team members and their dogs are available 24/7 to respond to missing persons cases."

Cantu motioned for me and Marlowe to come closer.

"Cauley MacKinnon and her dog Marlowe are a prime example of how to become a search and rescue team member. Cauley has a day job, but she regularly trains with her dog to become part of the team."

I smiled weakly. Marlowe practically took a bow.

And it was at that moment that Marlowe decided there was something to search and rescue. He jerked his leash out of my hand and leapt over the park's cross-tie fence, taking off for the wooded area behind the park.

I stood there, dumbfounded, while Miranda had her cameras rolling. Climbing the fence, I scrambled through the woods, listening for sounds in the brush.

I was pretty sure this wasn't the best way to represent the SAR team. To my surprise and consternation, I found bent twigs and dog prints in the sun-scorched foliage and over another fence, one of barbed wire.

"Marlowe!" I shouted. "Get back here! Marlowe!"

I waited, listening for him.

"Great," I grumbled. I followed the fence line for about sixty feet, but there was no end in sight. I was going to have to climb that sucker. The barbwire fence was an old model from back when they knew how to build fences, with mean-looking, rusty, jagged points every five inches. Five strands of wire were evenly spaced on thick cedar poles, stretched tight and about six feet apart. One of the big no-nos in SAR, or anything else for that matter, is cutting fences. There was a time in Texas when the cattle kings ruled the range and you could be horse-whipped for cutting a fence. Now it's just illegal and not very nice.

Sighing, I sidled in as close to the rough cedar pole as I could get and stepped on the third rung of wire with my left foot, holding tightly to the top of the fence post so I could get some leverage. I swung my right leg over the top of the fence and pivoted so I could replace my right foot with my left on the rung of wire when the pole cracked. I slipped and fell hard on the wire, twisting as I dropped, and the prongs of the barbed wire caught me squarely in the crotch. I did the only thing a sane person would do: I screamed bloody murder.

"Ow, ow, ow!" I yelled.

While yelling didn't help, it did make me feel marginally better. I took a deep breath and rotated carefully back the direction I'd fallen to try to pry the barb out of my inner thigh and yelled again as the barb dug past the seam of my jeans and into flesh, tearing it as it went. The hot sting of blood trickled along the inside of my thigh.

"Ahhh!" I winced, and then I heard a familiar woofing noise.

Marlowe bounded out of the underbrush and stood beneath me at the bottom of the fence. He turned twice and woofed again—his "alert" signal—his sign he'd made a find.

I grimaced. The find was me.

"I know, you big jerk, and now I'm stuck and it's all your fault for taking off."

He woofed again and leapt over the fence with ease, and then back again, as if to show me what a piece of cake it was. All it did was piss me off.

"Just give me a minute," I said, trying to steady myself to get a look at my watch.

"We're supposed to meet Dan Soliz and try to get some information on El Patron and the Syndicate tonight, which is going to be hard to do if I'm stuck on a fence," I growled at the dog.

And then I saw it.

Marlowe dropped an old red bandanna beneath me.

"Holy hell," I said, glancing around in the woods, panic bubbling up inside me.

"He's here?" I whispered. Marlowe woofed twice.

Marlowe sat, ears pricked, waiting. I tried to balance so I could use both hands to free my jeans from the barbs that stabbed near my panty line when my foot slipped off the wire and I fell, twisting sharply. My head swooped as I plunged downward and the wire gouged deeper into my jeans and caught me.

And there I was. Suspended upside down, trapped on the fence.

Marlowe woofed at me and glanced back over his shoulder toward base camp.

"Oh, *now* you want to play Lassie," I said, and Marlowe woofed again.

He barked twice, turned tail and galloped back to base.

"Marlowe," I screamed. "No!"

But he was already gone.

The blood was rushing to my head as I hung upside down, wildly grabbing for the fence post so I could get some leverage, but each move I made dug the barbs deeper into my leg until I thought I was going to gouge my initials into my own thigh bone.

Within moments, I heard the sound of woofing and branches cracking, and Marlowe came crashing through the mesquite thicket, Cantu, Moreno and Gandalf hot on his heels.

"Jesus, Cauley, are you okay?" Cantu said.

"Yeah, I'm just … stuck."

And humiliated.

He chuckled then, the traitor.

A commotion crashed behind him, and from out of the bushes came Miranda with her camera crew.

"Great," I growled, but beggars can't be choosers, especially when they are hanging upside down by their ass, impaled on a barbwire fence.

Cantu slipped a knife from an ankle holster and sliced the barbed wire out of my jeans, then extracted the razor-sharp spikes from my now-bare upper thigh.

I winced as he righted me, and I tried not to whine about the stinging pain from the barbs that ran from my butt to my inner thigh. I had a distinct jolt of déjà vu.

I reached down for the handkerchief, which sent Marlowe into a woofy frenzy.

Cantu's eyes narrowed. "Where'd you get that?"

"Ask Marlowe the Wonder Dog."

He tucked the handkerchief into his back pocket as news crews stormed the scene.

Miranda cleared her throat. "We're here live at the Police Roundup, where they have just rescued a search and rescue team member," Miranda was saying as she rushed toward me. Mia skipped ahead of her, Nikon bouncing, where she settled between me and Miranda's cameraman.

"You're in my shot!" Miranda shrilled, and Mia said, "Oh, gee, I'm sorry," and then Mia stuck her foot out and tripped Miranda, who tumbled head over high heels, landing right in front of Cantu, skirt yanked up, exposing her Pretty Me figure-correcting undergarments. Well, who knew Ms. Perfect and her tiny little butt had a little help from her friends at the Lycra factory?

Flash! Mia snapped a picture.

Miranda made a bleating sound worthy of the goats that were wandering up to the fence to get a look at the commotion. At that moment, Dan Soliz and some of Austin's finest were crashing through the bushes.

"Jeez," he said with his million-watt grin as he stared at me and my bloody, torn jeans and then over to Miranda, who was yanking her skirt down over her undies. He shook his head. "I hope to God you and that mutt never have to rescue me."

DESPITE OR MAYBE BECAUSE of the demonstration catastrophe, Dan Soliz bought me dinner at Sandy's Hamburger Hut off Ranch Road 620, west of Austin and just south of the dam. We sat outside on the small, grassy lawn under a sprawling live oak. We had monster-sized hamburgers and fried jalapeños on a picnic table, with Marlowe standing guard lest any food be wasted.

The EMTs at the demonstration had made good use of their Bactine and bandages, which itched and burned as I sat on the old wooden bench.

"Thanks for meeting me," I said, cutting my burger in half and slipping the larger portion to Marlowe, who'd repositioned himself under the table for maximum begging capacity.

Soliz grinned at me. "Looks like you had a tough day."

"Yeah, bleeding always makes me hungry."

The smell of the freshly watered lawn mingled with the scents of good hamburgers and engine exhaust from passing traffic still winding down from rush hour.

I shook my head. "I think maybe I'm not cut out for this stuff."

"Give yourself a chance. You'll get the hang of it." He tore off a big bite of burger and ate it ravenously. "So what is it you been dyin' to talk to me about?"

We both had to talk a little louder than usual because of the steady stream of traffic muttering by.

"You know the *Journal's* making a big deal out of El Patron and the Syndicate and some kind of looming gang war."

Soliz took a long draw on his beer and looked at me with dark eyes that were charming, bordering on dangerous.

"Organized crime isn't what people think it is here," he said. "Or at least it wasn't. For a long time, Austin was a free city. In the seventies, a couple of gangs came in and tried to get organized, but the silicone city's like Teflon—they all failed to stick."

He looked out over the traffic clogging 620, moving and stopping for no apparent reason. "Remember when this road used to be two lanes and you actually had to drive over the dam?"

I nodded. "I was a little girl, but yes, I remember."

"Things change. Now there's a couple of gangs dividing up the city—Northside Posse's got Rundberg through Cameron, Brotherhood of the Cross's got the south end, and Texas Syndicate takes up most of the East Side. There's a white-collar crew running out of Lakeway, and a few others, but those are the big three. Syndicate's the most organized."

"So how does this happen?" I said.

"Syndicate started as a prison gang back in the seventies at Folsom—"

"California?" I said around a little bite of burger.

"Yeah. Tejano prisoners formed the gang to protect themselves from California Mexicans called the Mexican Mafia."

I raised my eyebrows. "Racial unrest among Mexican Americans?" I said. "I thought prison gangs broke off by race—Mexican against black, black against white…"

Soliz smiled. "That's what a lot of white people think. But there's all kinds of Mexicans, so the government or whoever the hell it is that labels stuff came up with Hispanic.

"But most Hispanics don't see themselves that way. You got Hispanics from Mexico, Guatemala, Columbia, Peru, all over the damn place. And we don't lump ourselves into one category any more than white people in the United States would lump themselves in with Canadians or Brits."

I nodded. "My friend Mia has mentioned this to me before," I said.

"Well, makes it hard to get organized," he said. "Different nationalities, different dialects—in some cases, different languages."

Soliz took another bite of hamburger, chewed, and swallowed. "Until about eight years ago, when Texas Syndicate opened up and started street recruiting. Now their population isn't just inmates."

"I didn't know that."

He shrugged. "Most people don't. But they also did something else. The Syndicate used to be Tejano—Mexican Texans. Now they've opened the ranks to all so-called Hispanics, and they've even moved outside Texas, like Florida and California."

I frowned. "So how do you tell one gang from another?"

"At first glance you can tell by tattoos. Most Syndicate members ink 'TS' somewhere—usually upper arm, sometimes on the bulge of the calf. They're getting clever about it—hidden in some sort of intricate tattoo. The more brazen have something like a cross with a ribbon or a sword with a snake, that sort of thing. And they have colors and sign."

I raised a brow. "Colors?"

"Yeah," Soliz said. "Syndicate is burnt orange."

"Like the University of Texas?"

"Unfortunately, yeah," Soliz said. "And their sign is the hook 'em sign—thumb, middle and third finger folded. That way, if they're caught throwing sign or wearing colors, they can just say they're students."

I shook my head and gave Marlowe another bite of burger when he put his head on my lap. "Does it work?"

"No. But it makes them feel smart," Soliz said.

I thought about Marlowe and his little "gift" at the fence, and about the man who'd broken into my house and the shadowy look Logan had given me when I'd told him about the red bandanna. "So what does a red bandanna mean?"

Soliz stopped chewing and stared at me. "Where did you see a red bandanna?"

"The guy who broke into my house, assaulted me, and left a dead canary. He was wearing a red bandanna over his face. And when Marlowe took off this afternoon, he brought me an old red bandanna."

Soliz's eyes got that cop look, like still waters over a riptide.

"You tell this to Cantu and your FBI buddy?"

I nodded. "Cantu has the bandanna now."

"What did Cantu say?"

I shook my head. "Nothing really. Just got the same look you just did."

Soliz nodded. "You afraid?" he said.

"No. I'm used to having people break into my house. Of course I'm scared."

Soliz's dark eyes narrowed. "You should be. Red is El Patron."

"But they nearly killed me this summer, and I never saw one single red anything—except blood."

"They're reorganizing," he said.

I nodded. "And El Patron and the Syndicate—they're all Hispanic, then?" I said, thinking of John Fiennes and his international citizenship.

He shook his head. "Opened the gates. Hell, they're even recruiting white people."

"How progressive of them."

Soliz smiled. "It makes them dangerous. And that's why Syndicate is so interested in El Patron. El Patron came in from Argentina fully organized when they hit the ground. They had inroads—smuggling through legitimate transport—so at first, they weren't stepping on the Syndicate's boots. *That* happened when Patron started gobbling up strip clubs."

"But strip clubs are legal," I said.

"Yeah, but a lot of the activity that goes with them isn't," Soliz said. "And El Patron started specializing in young girls."

I just about lost my lunch. "But Syndicate does all kinds of illegal stuff, too. Are you telling me they are morally opposed to young girls stripping?"

Soliz laughed a bitter laugh. "No. Syndicate opposes anything that draws the attention of the police department. El Patron was catching interest into all gang activity every time they hooked a young girl, lopped off some dude's ear, or set some poor *vato* ablaze in a burning tire."

"Syndicate doesn't like attention," I said, nodding.

"It's not good for business."

"I had dinner a few months ago with an old acquaintance from school," I said, handing Marlowe a fry. "Diego DeLeon. Do you know where he is in all this?"

Soliz grimaced. "Diego is Syndicate. His uncle was what they call a Chairman, or the leader, but he's been off the radar since El Patron's leadership got sent to the slammer. My guess is your friend Diego is either a Second or maybe even Chairman in receivership to the Syndicate."

"Receivership," I said. "That sounds like a legitimate business."

"Some of it is. Strip clubs, bars, that sort of thing. But the drugs, gambling, whores, and the underage girls are a whole other ballgame."

I leveled my gaze on his. "Do you think there's going to be a war?"

Soliz smiled a wry smile. "Word on the street is there ain't enough El Patron left to start a war. And DeLeon's a practical character. He's probably trying to assimilate what's left."

"What if they don't want to assimilate?"

Soliz shrugged. "Blood in, blood out," he said and took another big bite of burger.

And suddenly, sitting under a shade tree on an August evening, I wasn't hungry anymore.

EIGHT

I was bruised and scratched from my botched search and rescue presentation, not to mention thoroughly humiliated and totally spooked by the red bandanna. I seriously considered calling in dead the next morning, but there's a point when your embarrassment level bottoms out and just stays there. I was going to have to face the office some time, and I wanted to get it over with before my pseudo date with Logan at the Pier. As I'd suspected, I'd been plastered all over the five o'clock news, hanging upside down from my undies. Of course, Miranda's butt shot hadn't made the cut.

When I got to work, my voice mail light was blinking like a strobe, and someone had hung a Jessica Alba *Fantastic Four* action figure upside down by her spandex superhero costume, caught in a barbed-wire fence made of paper clips. Knowing his affection for action figures, I'd bet this month's 401(k) deduction Jessica was one of Ethan's dastardly deeds.

I left her hanging by her spandex. I figure I've earned every single scar on my body and will probably have a hell of a lot more by the time it's over with. Truthfully, I was a little proud of my scars.

"Cauley. In my office. Now," Tanner said when he made it into the office.

Sighing, I trudged into his office.

He nodded, meaning I should close the door.

"What the hell is this?" He shoved a copy of the *Journal* under my nose.

"Miranda," I swore.

"That's not Miranda hanging upside down by her underwear," Tanner growled, and I rolled my eyes.

"I notice the *Journal* left off the part where Miranda fell head over high heels, leaving little to the imagination."

"This isn't about Miranda," Tanner said, reaching for a licorice stick from the clear jar on his desk. "Shiner said you were the star of the cop squawk box yesterday."

Damn that Shiner and his stupid scanner. That boy needed a life.

"What?" I said, trying to look innocent. It was not my best look.

He eyed the scratch on my cheek, courtesy of Muse and our tussle with the latest El Patron foot soldier. "What happened?" Tanner sat with his arms crossed, gnawing on the licorice.

I sighed. "All right. I had a visitor yesterday afternoon. The police have been out, the forensics guys have been through my house—it seems someone doesn't want me testifying against El Patron."

Cantu asked that I leave the part about the dead bird out—something about using that fact in interrogation when they caught the guy.

Tanner sighed heavily. "Cauley, you collect stalkers the way other people collect postage stamps."

I wasn't sure what to say to that, so I chose discretion—a new experience for me. "I've got round-the-clock cops patrolling the block. There's nothing to worry about," I said, wishing I believed my own words.

Tanner rubbed his palms over his eyes. "You okay?"

"Yeah. Just banged up a little."

He stared across the room and out the window, which overlooked the last few acres of the Flintrock Ranch that hadn't been bulldozed down to put up the prolific tract houses that were popping up like a plague.

"We done?" I said, heading for the door.

"That FBI agent still around?"

"Um, yeah," I stammered.

He grunted his approval.

Relieved, I swung open the door, ready to leave this train wreck behind.

"Cauley," he called after me, and I turned.

He scratched the back of his neck like he was trying to say something and wasn't sure how to say it.

I waited.

"If it was El Patron behind your break-in, it's nothing to play around with."

"I know that," I said. "I'm the one who got stabbed and nearly killed this summer."

"I'm just saying—if you need help, ask for it."

I nodded. "That would be the sensible thing to do."

Tanner snorted. "My point exactly."

I headed back to my desk. It'd been so long since I'd done anything sensible I'd forgotten what it looked like.

My phone rang, and I answered.

"I got news." It was Cantu, and he didn't sound happy.

"Let me have it," I said, bracing myself.

"That bird—the one with the note?" he said. "It was a canary. Came from the same place as that Puckett guy's."

I sat, staring at nothing. *A dead canary.*

"You understand what this means, right?" he said, and I sighed.

"Yes, Cantu," I said. "The subtlety is not lost on me."

I MANAGED TO MAKE it through the day without any further catastrophes. I wrote three obituaries and avoided my mother's increasingly agitated phone calls. Apparently she'd seen the local news last night and no doubt was calling to chide me about my profession and my new "little hobby," as she referred to search and rescue. I'd have to face her sooner or later, but like most good procrastinators, I believe if something was really worth doing it would have been done already.

Other than that, I'd spent a lot of the day in the ladies' room avoiding my boss and Merrily. My mind was preoccupied with other things. People breaking into my house. Dead birds. Special Agent Logan. And my pseudo date at the Pier.

NINE

I was busy receiving an Extreme Makeover at Beckett and Jenks' house when a horn blared outside the living-room picture window.

"Ah, Cinderella's pumpkin has arrived," Jenks said, swishing back the curtains. Mia and Ethan had hitched a ride with Brynn, our PR buddy with a hot convertible courtesy of her ritzy PR firm.

"Are you sure about this?" I said to Beckett, staring into the door mirror at a woman who looked like me, only better.

Beckett had swathed me in an embroidered, nearly sheer camisole the color of late summer magnolias he'd picked up at Market in Dallas. On impulse, he'd ripped the bottom of my favorite jean shorts until they barely covered my bottom.

The camisole was soft, made of silk, and the hem floated just above my navel, the fabric skimming my breasts like a whisper. The camisole looked as good as it felt, and I had to look twice to make sure you couldn't see right through it, which I supposed was the point. Color rose in my cheeks, and my gaze drifted down to my newly altered shorts. The denim was soft and worn and fit my rear snuggly. The frayed edges were now about half an inch short of a Class A misdemeanor.

"They're awfully short," I said, making a futile attempt to tug the back of the recently sheared shorts a little farther down my thighs.

"They're perfect," Beckett said, smacking my hand away from my behind. "And stop tugging."

Beckett and Jenks escorted me to the door and stood watching out of the picture window like two proud parents.

As I stepped out on the porch, Mia, Brynn, and Ethan whooped like a crowd of downtown construction workers. I tugged at my shorts, and my cell phone beeped.

"Hello?" I said, tottering on my new Kate Spade wedges.

"Stop tugging!" Beckett and Jenks yelled over the phone. I glared back at them, snapping the phone shut, then took a deep breath and sashayed to the passenger seat in my friend Brynn's black convertible BMW.

"Wow," Ethan said, nearly choking on his tongue.

I looked back at the window, where Beckett and Jenks stood grinning and giving me the thumbs-up.

I smiled sheepishly back at them.

"Too much?" I said to Brynn as she put the car in gear.

"Honey," she said, "Captain America's not going to know what hit him."

EASY FOR BRYNN TO say. She looked like a knockout no matter what she wore, and tonight she was doing her signature bronze—bronze-streaked hair, bronze skin, bronze nails, and a bronze bandeau bikini top accented with a tasteful bronze sarong.

"Here," Brynn said and spritzed me with a bottle of something that smelled like the south end of a northbound skunk.

"Jeez, Brynn, what are you trying to do? Kill me?"

"It's a pheromone-based perfume we're doing a marketing campaign for. You'll have scads of men falling all over you."

"One will do," I said, and Mia said, "Ooooh."

Mia was doing a short, flouncy, strapless number the color of fruit salad, which barely covered what her *abuelita* called her "ya yas" to her "cha cha."

Ethan was sporting a black tee shirt with 0s and 1s.

I frowned. "I thought you were looking for a girlfriend, and you're wearing that?"

"Hey, this is a brand-new tee shirt," he said.

"How can anyone tell? It's just a bunch of binary code that nobody but you understands."

Ethan grinned at me. "When I find the girl who can read it, I'll marry her."

"Ah," I said, thinking of Beckett and Jenks. "The geek version of Cinderella."

BRYNN NAVIGATED THE NARROW tunnel of moss-bearded oaks along River Hills Road. She steered down the Pier's steep caliche driveway, which was already packed to near capacity with vehicles. She wedged her BMW into a tiny crevice between a Porsche and an old pickup. We piled out of the car, careful not to ding the truck.

The sun was on a slow slide into the lake, and the air was hot and wet, carrying with it the sweet scent of the river, fried jalapeños, and beer. The driveway bottle-necked into an admission area and then flung outward into nearly five rolling acres of river-green grass, a scattering of picnic tables, and a ramshackle stage, complete with a dance floor fashioned from packed red dirt. At the bottom of the hillside, the river rolled through Austin, where it eventually poured into Matagorda Bay, some 200 miles away.

When I was a little girl, I used to stand on the southernmost finger of the small marina and squint toward the horizon, imagining that I could see the palm trees swaying in the Gulf's tropical breeze. In twenty years, not much had changed.

There were still rusty old fishing boats bobbing beside million-dollar yachts in the marina and a wide backyard-style amphitheater. South of the stage was a sandy volleyball pit where a collection of children tumbled about, batting a colorful beach ball over the sagging net.

The Pier's small, white clapboard shack presided over it all like a gentle, if somewhat disreputable, old uncle with a wink and a nod.

Logan was already there—I knew it. Not because I saw him, but because my nerve endings started to sizzle and pop. I flashed my invitation to the big side of beef manning the admission gate. A band was busily jamming to the beat of a different drummer—from the sound of it, probably from a different planet. But what they lacked in talent they made up for in volume so that we had to shout to be heard.

"Holy shit," Brynn hollered into my ear as she peered over my shoulder.

I followed her gaze, and suddenly I couldn't hear one note of the deafening music. *Holy shit* was right.

Tom Logan was lounging against a picnic table near the lakeshore sipping a long neck and looking like six and a half feet of walking sin. His Levi's were worn and faded in all the right places, and his black tee shirt revealed the fact that he worked out. A lot.

His gaze met mine and the earth seemed to tilt beneath my Kate Spades. He looked at me like he might eat me alive and I'd be glad he took the trouble.

I moved toward him, trying to look calm and collected, a woman about town, all the while being careful not to topple face-first off my nifty new wedges.

"Hello, kid," he said, and he sent me one of his bone-melting grins.

"Sorry we're late," I said, resisting the urge to tug at my shorts. "You remember Mia and Brynn. This is Ethan Singer."

Logan nodded to Mia and Brynn and shook hands with Ethan.

"I thought you were shooting a video," I said.

Logan shook his head. "Hitchcock's over there." He motioned with his beer toward the stage, and sure enough, there was Puck, holding a beer in one hand and what looked like some sort of high-tech hybrid video camera in the other. He was chattering warp speed to a scantily clad blond who was doing her best to ignore him.

He saw us and grinned, giddy as a carload of eighth-grade girls.

Suddenly, I felt like someone kicked me in the stomach. This was the last time I would see Puck "alive."

Forty-eight hours from now, Logan was going to shove Puck's obituary under some shooter's nose and tell him Puck had made the big beer run to the great hereafter, a ruse to keep some El Patron thug from chopping off Puck's ear and setting him ablaze.

My breath caught and my hand flew involuntarily to my own ear. I was going to testify at the same grand jury. Until some nut job broke into my house and attempted to clobber me with a dead canary, I hadn't realized just how dangerous putting Selena Obregon behind bars could get.

"Hey! You came!" Puck yelled over the racket. He trotted across the sandy volleyball pit, careful not to drop the camera or spill his beer.

"This," Logan said to my friends, "is Wylie Ray Puckett."

I thought there was a note of apology in his voice.

"Whoa," Puck said, jabbing me with his elbow as he jogged to a stop beside me, wheezing for air. "Your friends are hot. Did you tell them I'm a producer?"

"Must have slipped my mind," I said.

"Hey, y'all could be in my music video," he said to Mia and Brynn. He leered through the lens, panning from my rear end to Mia's and then on to Brynn's. "Can y'all just, you know, give us a little goose?"

Mia rolled her eyes, but Brynn's expression barely moved. "If you point that thing at me again, you will pull back a bloody stump," Brynn said, and Puck swallowed hard.

"Hey, I didn't mean nothin' by it," he said, glancing nervously at Logan. "You're supposed to be protecting me, right?"

Logan shrugged. "You're on your own with this one."

Shaking my head, I slid onto the picnic bench, and Logan sat beside me, close enough that I could feel the heat of the afternoon on him. He took a long pull on his Shiner Bock long neck and looked at me, and I could practically feel his gaze skim my bare midriff and below. "Nice shorts."

Blood rushed to my cheeks, and a wave of pure pleasure washed over me.

"Told ya," Mia whispered.

"Y'all gotta be in the video," Puck said, and his camera was pointing down my shirt. He started to sit down beside me when Logan gave him a look.

"Right," Puck said. "I think I'm going to take a break." He slouched around the table to the opposite bench.

The small band was ranting on the elevated stage. The words *Phoenix and the Firebirds* were carefully painted across the width of the big drum.

Logan's gaze swept the crowd as usual, but flickered over the sound and light guys gathered around the console. I watched as they milled about, a small group of *vatos* who seemed to be jittering in place.

"Racial profiling?" I said.

"Troubleshooting," he said, his gaze not leaving the small group.

As Logan and I spoke, the man at the console caught my eye. He stared at me, a dead-eyed stare, and a sickening jolt slithered up my spine.

The man had slicked-back hair and wore headphones as he adjusted the levers on the console.

"Logan," I said. "I think that's him. The guy who attacked me."

"Guy with the headphones?" he said, his eyes narrowing in like a gun sight.

I nodded, my voice stuck in my throat.

He made his way through the crowd, people parting around him like he exuded some sort of force field.

The *cholo* saw us coming and tried to give Logan a dead-eye stare. It chilled me to the bones but bounced right off of Logan.

Logan badged him. "Wanna take off those headphones," he said to the guy. It wasn't a question.

He and Jitters looked at me, a pair of slimy looks that had me crossing my arms over my chest. Still looking at me, he slid the headphones off to reveal two rather small ears the approximate shape of turnips. No scratch marks on his face. No big cat-sized chunks out of his ear.

"Want the shirt off too?" he said.

"Not today," Logan said. "You ever see this woman before?" nodding toward me.

A slow smile slid over his thin lips.

"Now, don't you think I'd remember seein' something like that, *jefe*."

"Just answer the question. I wanna get wise, I'll visit your boss."

The *cholo* shrugged. "No. I never seen her."

"You?" he said to Jitters, scanning the skinny guy for scratch marks.

"*No hablo inglés*," he said with a twitch in his top lip.

Logan stared at him. The moment stretched uncomfortably, and Jitters was vibrating so hard he was in danger of wearing out his jeans from the inside out.

"No," Jitters said, his voice rising with his nerves. "No, I never seen her."

Logan stared at both of them, and I swear I heard his cop radar pinging somewhere near his spinal cord.

"You okay?" he said, and I shook my head.

"I'm sorry, Logan. I thought it was him."

"Don't worry about it, kid. Better safe than sorry."

I followed him back to the table, where my heart rate slowed below three hundred thirty, very glad that Logan was there. And very glad that Logan was Logan.

"Hey!" Ethan chimed in, breaking my trance. He spoke to Puck, who had lowered the video camera.

Ethan pointed. "Is that one of those new Tribeca mini DVD recorders?"

"Yep. Nothin' but the best for Faith's video," Puck said, slipping back into the present. "Quality all the way, baby."

"Can I see it?" Ethan said.

Puck gave him an appraising look. "Your friends are total babes," Puck said. "Maybe we could set something up."

"Right," Brynn said. She shook her mane of bronze hair. "Where do I get one of those?" she said to Logan. She was either pointing at his long neck or his long fellow. With Brynn, you could never tell.

Logan started to get the waitress's attention when Brynn purred, "Well, hello, Orange County…"

She nudged Mia, pointing toward two sandy-haired, prepubescent surf boys scarfing down Jell-O shots like they'd just hit legal age.

Mia snorted. "Brynn, you have underwear older than that boy."

Brynn smiled like a puma on the prowl. "Leave my undies out of this—for now."

And with that, Brynn stalked toward the bar, Mia in tow.

"Direct," Logan said, and I sighed.

"Yeah, you never have to guess what's on Brynn's mind," I said.

"Nothing wrong with that." He smiled and thrust my hormones into overdrive.

Logan caught the attention of a waitress as she wound her way through the crowd to take our drink orders. She had a forty-something face atop a twenty-something body, with bottle-blond hair and more hip sway than a waffle-house waitress. She wore a small denim skirt slung low on her hips, showing off an elaborate tattoo that spelled out the lyrics to "Dixie." She'd topped off the ensemble with a cropped baby tee that said *Keep Austin Weird*.

The Pier was a place where that advice was taken to heart. In the dance area, a creepy-looking guy wearing a battered Scala cowboy hat, tropical shorts, and a football jersey with a large blue "81" across the chest was doing a snappy little two-step all by his lonesome.

"What'll you have, honey?" the waitress said, leering at Logan.

Puck aimed the camera at the waitress's tattoo. "Reading material from top to bottom. Ya gotta love Austin."

Shaking his head, Logan turned to me. "What'll you have, kid?"

"Bourbon and Diet Coke," I told him.

His jaw muscle twitched. He repeated my request to the waitress, and to his credit, he didn't flinch. He indicated another Shiner Bock, and the waitress hustled off, bootie bustling, to get our drinks.

Near the stage, six very young girls danced with each other and seemed to be enjoying it. Puck shook his head and said, "Strippers."

"Aren't they a little young?" I said. "They don't even look old enough for training bras."

Puck looked down at his beer like the answers to the mystery of life were lying at the bottom of the bottle.

"How do you know they're strippers?" I said.

"You watch. They'll have more and more drinks, and then they'll start slithering all over each other." I stared at him. Puck, who seemed ready to pounce on anything in panties, didn't seem pleased about the strippers.

As it turned out, Puck was right. I tried not to seem scandalized when the girls started pantomiming sex acts that were probably illegal in at least twenty states.

The song changed, and the preteen stripper girls moved like a herd of gazelles toward the bar to ply drinks off of unsuspecting alligators. Who says women are the weaker sex?

"So what are we doing here?" I said to Puck, who had the viewfinder out, reviewing footage he'd taken throughout the afternoon.

"Shootin' a video for the CD my sister's cutting. We figure she'll get better media coverage if she's got a video."

I frowned. "Aren't videos expensive to make?"

"Yeah, how 'bout that, blondie," he said. "Now everything make sense? I needed that money to—hey! Ow!" Puck flinched and grabbed his leg under the table, scowling at Logan.

Ethan turned to me. "Actually, it's not so expensive to shoot films now. Some indie producers are shooting films on small-format cameras and they're good enough to get into Sundance."

"I figure I can get this whole thing shot for around ten large," Puck said, aiming the camera at the cleavage of a passing reveler. "I've been shooting atmosphere all afternoon." He turned to Logan. "You know, being a producer isn't such a bad gig. I'm thinkin' after all this trial stuff is over with, I might just go legit and be a producer."

"Yeah. I'll hold my breath," Logan said, just before his phone went off. "I'll be right back," he said to me, and then he disappeared into the crowd.

The waitress came back with our drinks, and I sat back and got a good look at the band. The balding guy on guitar looked like he'd slipped down the backside of forty about ten years ago, and he was wearing a short kilt and a tank top. Most men teetering on middle age buy a convertible and leer at girls half their age. This guy settled for dressing like girls half his age.

The drummer had long, stringy hair and a dull, burned-out look in his eyes, like he'd been sucking on glue sticks since the second grade.

The girl was a pixie-haired blond bouncing around the stage in hot-pink spandex looking like a radioactive raspberry. Her voice was so shrill she should have had us sign waivers for high-range hearing loss. The crowd milled about, some daring to dance, but most were laughing and joking as though there was no music at all.

I shook my head and downed the rest of my drink. If Puck really had absconded with El Patron's money to invest in his sister's career, he could kiss that cash goodbye. No way was this girl going to get a contract, no matter how cute she was. There's bad and there's really bad, and Puck's sister was *really* bad. On a scale of one to ten, she was in double-digit deficit.

"So what do you think?" Puck said.

Ethan was playing with Puck's camera, zooming in on the band.

"Your sister's band is, um, unique," I said to Puck.

"What?" Puck said, frowning, then looked toward the stage. "Oh, hell no! That's not Faith. Phoenix wanted a public gig, so I let her open for Faith." He shook his head. "No, you'd know Faith when you heard her. She's great. Terrific. And not only that, she's really good, too."

"Right," I said, looking around. "Where'd all these people come from?"

"I invited some of the regulars and some friends to pack the audience. The rest are atmosphere."

"Atmosphere," I repeated.

"Yeah, you know, eye candy. For the video."

"You paid these people to be here?" I said.

"Only the hot ones."

"What hot ones?" a female voice said over the din, and Puck's face softened. I turned to see what caught his attention, and I had to stifle a gasp.

"Hey, sukie," Puck said, his voice soft as he pressed a kiss to the girl's forehead. He looked up like a proud papa. "Cauley, Ethan, this is Faith."

Ethan dropped the camera.

"Hey, watch the equipment," Puck said, lacing his arm around his sister.

Nearby, I saw that men were noticing Faith the way that men sometimes do, and for the life of me, I couldn't see why.

Faith looked young. I did some quick math in my head—never a good thing—but from the articles I'd seen earlier, I surmised she was close to eighteen.

But with her slight stature, her small breasts, and nonexistent waist, she looked for all the world like she hadn't even blown out the candles on her fourteenth birthday cake.

She was petite, about five two and ninety pounds with all her jewelry. Her black eyes were almond shaped and had a haunting, empty quality that made it hard to look away. She had long, dark lashes and the kind of pouty kitten's mouth that would knock the style editors at *Chic Magazine* right off their pointy little Jimmy Choos.

She also had piercings on every surface of her body I could see and probably more that I couldn't. Her hair was very black and buzz cut, and it might have been pretty if you couldn't see huge patches of pink scalp between dark little islands of hair. Inky green tendrils of tattoos crept from beneath a worn John Deere tee shirt strategically cut to bare a lot of pale skin. On her left arm, the tattoos were interrupted by a sporty little nicotine patch and a square of unnaturally smooth skin, like she'd had one of her tattoos recently removed.

She looked like a preteen Audrey Hepburn, if Audrey Hepburn had been tattooed, pierced, and stricken with mange.

"So," she said. "You Wylie's new fuck?"

I blinked and, for once, was struck speechless.

Ethan, who'd been scrambling to pick up the camera, sat openmouthed. He couldn't take his eyes off of Faith.

She eyed Ethan with interest, her gaze skimming over the binary code on his tee shirt. "*You are dumb,* huh?"

My eyes widened. "Excuse me?" I said. Ethan may be a lot of things, but he certainly wasn't dumb.

"His shirt," she said. "Code for *You are dumb.*"

I stared at Ethan, but he was still staring at Faith.

"You know code?" I said, not meaning to sound as incredulous as I did.

She shrugged. "A lot of geeks come into the bar where I work. They like to talk."

"Oh," I said, trying to recover. "Where do you work?"

"Boners," she said like it was no big deal. "You know. Strip joint out by the county line."

Ethan choked on his tongue.

The girl dropped backward onto the bench like a rag doll and leaned bonelessly against the table. "I need a fucking drink," she said.

She seemed to relish the profanity, toying with the feel of it as it rolled off the tip of her pierced tongue.

I thought of the photo I'd seen of her in the *Sentinel's* archives and shook my head. This could not be the same girl. But then, ten years is a long time when you're eighteen—and even longer when you've lived a rough life.

Puck had the good grace to look uncomfortable. "Faith . . . we're rolling film on you tonight—"

"You're not my fucking dad," she snarled and pulled a pack of cigarettes from inside her combat boot and lit a match on the table. I guessed she wouldn't be getting many advertising endorsements from the nicotine patch company.

Puck looked like she'd kicked him in the stomach.

The Firebirds took that moment to go on break. I knew this because the decibel level plummeted and I lost the desire to puncture my own eardrums.

Puck shook his head and motioned to the creepy guy at the console who I'd mistaken for my bird guy.

"Chino," Puck called over the music. "You ready?"

Ready for what? I wondered.

Chino nodded and said something to Jitters, who nodded back. Or it might have been an epileptic fit. It was hard to tell.

Puck looked back at Faith, who was staring down at the table.

"I never said I was trying to be Dad," Puck said quietly, and for a moment, Faith's bravado faltered. She leaned toward him like she was going to apologize, but stopped. With her scruffy, half-bald head, she looked like a baby bird that had fallen from the nest, lost and confused, and I realized Puck had that same sense of being stranded and alone. I knew they'd lost their father early. So had I.

With a slight shock, I wondered if I looked a little lost, too.

Faith smiled then. It was just a kiss of a smile, and it flashed a single dimple in her left cheek. It lasted a split second, but it could have warmed the polar ice cap.

I heard Ethan's heart flip in his chest.

Her smile was short-lived.

"Angel Baby! Who's your friends?" A middle-aged man in a cowboy hat who looked and acted like an aging frosted-blond frat boy in search of his glory days slid in between Puck and Faith, slipping an arm jovially around their shoulders as he flashed me a lopsided grin. He had to be pushing forty, but he was fighting it hard. His face was long and lean, but it was shiny, like he'd just had a dermabrasion. He had an even, tanning-bed tan, and his hair was a longish George Michael man bob that was immobilized with enough product to make anothe hole in the ozone. His forehead had that telltale Botox immobility. He looked like one of those creepy guys who dress too young and sit outside the über-hip Be Be's at the mall leering at the teenyboppers as they trot around the racks in their undies.

Puck's gaze dropped to his lap. The man snickered and his shoulders shook with it. Faith shifted in her seat. The guy reached over, took Puck's beer, and slugged it back. Clearly a man who took what he wanted. Faith motioned to the waitress and pointed to the place where Puck's beer had been.

Two men the size and shape of water buffalo trailed the guy at a respectful distance. They were both buzz-cut and wore black, paramilitary-style pants. They took turns flexing their muscles. I wondered if they took turns performing other tasks, like thinking.

The man took Faith's arm and examined the square lasered scar. "Looks good," he said. "Another couple of treatments, you won't even know it was there. Now if we could just do somethin' about your hair."

Faith's eyes went cold as he ran his hand over her nearly bald head. "You know, sometimes we want something so bad we make it impossible to have."

I stared at him. I wasn't sure if he was talking about Faith and her music career or something else.

Faith pulled her arm away and stared down at her lap.

Ethan leapt to his feet, his thin chest puffed. If I didn't know any better I'd think he was being protective. "Ethan Singer," he said. "And this is Cauley MacKinnon. We're friends of Faith."

"Well, good to know you. Damn good," the guy said, his head bobbing like one of the yachts moored at the pier. "Any friend of the angel is a friend of mine." He snickered again, and I worked hard to keep my lip from curling. "Cullen Wallace Ainsworth the Third," he said, jutting his hand, offering Ethan a shake. "My friends call me Tres."

Ethan stood his ground.

Tres Ainsworth had longish hair that nearly pageboyed around his face. He was maybe five foot six, but he wore expensive, stacked-heel cowboy boots that added at least three inches, and a full beaver felt cowboy hat that nearly covered his dark eyes. I shook my head. Nobody wears felt in the summer—it's too hot. Like my daddy used to say, "All buckle and no belt."

With those irritating snickers and stacked heels, I guessed him for a mama's boy trying to be a daddy's boy. Probably pledged his daddy's fraternity. Probably pulled the wings off butterflies.

"Pleased to meet you," he said, turning to me. He produced a card from his shirt pocket and handed it to me with a flourish, then leaned in for a shake—one of those that start with the hand and end with a squeeze to the upper arm.

"Buzz and Bud," Tres said, using his thumb to point back to the buffalo.

Something about him cranked Ethan up to hard boil, and I swear I saw little puffs of steam blowing out of the little geek's ears. Trying to defuse the situation, I reached up and put my hand on E's elbow. He grudgingly returned to the bench, but he was still glaring at Tres.

"Well, if it isn't Little Miss Barbed Wire," a familiar voice said, and I looked back to see Junior Hollis sucking on a long neck, grinning like an insurance salesman. A very young blond in half a month's salary in makeup hung on his arm. She wore a cut-off camouflage shirt and shorts that could have fit my three-year-old niece.

"Hey, Tres! You doing an after party?" She brushed her fingertips along the tops of his shoulders. It was the kind of thing you see on *Good Girls Gone Bad* late-night infomercials.

"Ah, Junior and Baby Chick!" Tres flashed her a shark's smile. She giggled and leaned down for a kiss. "You ever known me to miss an opportunity for a party?" He pulled a wad of bills out of his wallet and handed her a fifty, nodding toward the bar. "Let's go ahead and get 'er started now."

Miss Preteen Tractor Pull took the money and towed Hollis to the bar.

"What's Hollis doing here?" I said.

Tres grinned. "Junior Hollis is a friend of mine. Matter of fact, I helped him get elected to sheriff."

Love, money, and politics. The Texas love triangle.

I looked down at Tres's card. It was expensive, the kind that real estate jocks carry, with a picture of his face taking up most of the space. There wasn't much room for words, which seemed to be okay, because there were only four of them:

INCUBUS

Tres Ainsworth, Owner

Tres's picture on the card had been touched up—no pockmarks, and the Photoshop artist had generously removed some of the ingratiating smirk.

"Incubus?" I recoiled, not even bothering to hide the grimace that spread across my face. "Like the demon that rapes women when they're asleep?"

"Well, now, rape. That's an ugly word," Tres said. He took the second beer the waitress brought for Puck and slugged half of it down. He wiped his mouth with the back of his hand, his pupils constricting, like a smart bomb in search of a target. "More like a seduction."

My eyes snapped to tiny little slits. "Calling rape a seduction is like hitting someone with a frying pan and calling it cooking."

Tres looked at me, and for a moment, I thought I saw past Tres the good ol' boy and into something else.

He laughed then, and I looked twice to make sure his teeth weren't pointed.

"I'm in the music business," he went on. "I find talent and nurture it. Grow it to its full potential. This girl's got a million-dollar set of pipes."

Tres Ainsworth had a company named after a misogynist demon. I bet his nurturing skills ranked right up there with serial killers and hot check writers.

"How long have you been nurturing talent?" I said out of sheer, morbid curiosity.

"Oh, we just started. It's a family business, right, Faith?"

Faith was still staring at her hands. Ethan was watching her the way Marlowe watches the Jeep when I run into the store for groceries.

Puck didn't say anything.

"Oh, now, we got no secrets here," Tres said. "Angel Baby and the Puckster are my sister and brother."

"Step," growled Puck. "Our *step*brother."

There was a powerful, unpleasant undercurrent flowing between and around them, and it was spilling over toward me.

I glanced nervously around, looking for an escape hatch.

"Looks like you're ready for another round," a low voice drawled, and I turned to find Logan standing behind me with a freshened libation for me and a cold beer for himself. I smiled with relief as he lowered himself onto the bench beside me.

My escape hatch had arrived.

"Hello, Faith," Logan said, "You're looking lovely this evening."

To my amazement, the girl ducked her patchy head and actually blushed. But then Logan could send Condoleezza Rice into a full-fledged swoon. He sat with his back wedged toward Lake Austin so that he had a view of the Pier. Logan seemed relaxed and at ease, but I knew from past experience that he was aware of everything going on around us and probably some stuff that hadn't even happened yet.

Tres's eyes rested on Logan for a moment, and then he smirked. "Well, I'll let you kids catch up." Tres handed Puck his empty beer bottle and waved at a group of co-eds doing body shots at the bar. He winked at me. "No rest for the wicked."

As he left, I let out a breath I hadn't realized I was holding.

"You okay?" Logan said, and I nodded, shaking off the bad juju that'd been rolling around the amphitheater.

"Long line?" I said to him, accepting the drink.

"Got a call from the office."

I got that feeling you get when they read the lottery numbers and you've got five of the winning six. "Do you have to leave?"

"Not just yet," he said. His eyes were warm, the color of melted chocolate, as he looked down at me. All the discomfort I'd felt between Puck and his sister began to soften around the edges.

A woman who looked like a garden gnome appeared behind Puck and cleared her throat. "It's time," she said, tapping her watch.

"Oh. Right. Faith, come on. You're up…" Puck said. He slid over and hugged his sister hard, and they stayed that way for a long moment. I thought of something the forensic guy said to me earlier… *war buddies.*

Faith took a deep breath and rose bonelessly from the bench.

"Well. This ought to be good," I said to Logan, taking a long sip of the drink he'd given me.

"A cynic underneath it all," Logan said, and I smiled, feeling my body relax.

Ethan was still gaping at Faith as she made her way through the noisy crowd toward the stage. The horde of people surrounding the stage was restless and rowdy, no doubt due to a combination of bad music and a full bar.

Not far from our table, a man I hadn't noticed before staggered over to Faith as she moved. A boy, really. His face was handsome the way farm boys are, boyish, with big blue eyes, chiseled cheek bones, and a cleft chin. He was tall and wiry and wore a starched, long-sleeved shirt over faded Wranglers with a tell-tale faded round rim of a Copenhagen can at the right rear pocket. His John Deere gimme cap matched Faith's tee shirt.

"Oh, hell," Puck muttered.

"What's going on?" I said.

"Josh Lambert. We all grew up together, and he still thinks Faith is that same girl he used to take fishin' at the quarry."

"Is he her boyfriend?" I said, and Puck shook his head.

"It's complicated."

Josh gently took her arm and looked down at the laser scar. From where we sat, I could see a tear slide down Faith's face. She rose to her tiptoes and kissed his cheek.

A goodbye kiss, I thought.

At that moment, Tres came barreling through the crowd.

"Who the hell invited you?" Tres snarled, and Faith's eyes went wide.

"Tres, don't. I invited him," Faith stammered.

Tres nodded, then smiled—right before he swung a long, slow right fist that connected hard to the left side of the farm boy's face.

Sucker-punched and under the influence of enough alcohol to run a hybrid Honda, the kid staggered and toppled.

The kid came up mad, swinging a hard left, and caught Tres under the chin. Tres went down like a sack of wet cement. The buffalo, who'd been at the bar with the strippers, peeled themselves off their barstools and barreled toward Tres.

"You leave her alone!" Josh stood over Tres, fist clenched. Then he turned and scooped Faith into his arms. Faith's eyes were wide in surprise, not fear, and she said, "Josh, don't do this—"

"I had enough o' this bullshit!" he growled. "You're mine. You're parta me and I'm parta you, and if I can't protect you, nobody can."

Both the buffalo flanked Josh, chests out, chins down. Josh set Faith aside and squared off on the steroid studs, not caring that he was fixing to get a serious ass-kicking. Fumbling his cowboy hat back onto his head with more force than necessary, Tres climbed to his feet, anger etching deep lines in his shiny face.

"Excuse me a minute," Logan said and handed me his beer.

One of the buffalo caught sight of Logan and he elbowed the other. Together, they squared off, crossing their arms over their chests, biceps flexed, legs braced in a pose meant to scare the pants off of unsuspecting bystanders and anyone looking to get interested in Tres.

Logan seemed to have tunnel vision, his attention trained on Tres.

Beside me, Ethan pushed up his short tee shirt sleeves and said, "That doesn't look fair."

"Which way do you mean?" I said, watching Logan move effortlessly through the crowd.

"Now, there's no need for violence," Tres said, reaching a hand out to Logan for a friendly shake.

I thought this skirmish was over but then Tres kicked out, hard, in some kind of karate move and caught Josh in the stomach, knocking him backward, where he sprawled at Faith's feet.

Several men near the stage noticed and turned to watch as Logan stepped between the hired muscle. Buffalo One grabbed Logan's left arm. Without a word, Logan turned the other way, driving a knee into Buffalo Two's groin. Buffalo Two didn't move, and the only reaction I could see were his eyes crossing, chin dropping. One seemed surprised, but not as surprised as he looked when Logan jerked his arm away and threw an elbow into One's crooked nose. One dropped, blood spurting through his fingers as he gripped his broken nose.

Two regrouped; Logan swung and drove three punches, catching Two with a left, a right, and a left in his already slack jaw. Two's head snapped at each blow, and he dropped like his oversized partner.

In a move so swift I barely saw it, both buffalo were face-down in the dust, and Logan squared off on Tres.

Without his henchmen, Tres looked like the emperor caught without clothes.

Tres glared at Logan, but he was breathing so hard his chest looked like someone was beating his ribs from the inside out. He opened his mouth to say something and then closed it. Clearly a man not used to having the odds evened.

Chino, the creepy tattooed deejay, leaned on the console, grinning in slitty-eyed amusement. His hand slipped under his loose shirt. I froze.

"Logan!" I screamed, but he was already on it.

Logan turned toward the deejay and shot him a look worthy of John Wayne. Chino shrugged and put his hands up, palms out, grinning a toothy grin.

Logan stepped over Two's big, prone body, backing out of the circle of onlookers that formed around Faith and the men. Ethan made it halfway through the crowd, chest out and spoiling for a fight, but it was over before it even started.

The crowd roared, juiced on whatever it is that gets people pumped at the sight of bloodshed. Faith knelt, Josh's head in her lap as he grinned up at her. "I knew you'd come to," he said.

Logan reached for Josh, checking his pulse as Ethan plowed through the throng of people. When he reached Faith, he looked at her for a long moment. Gently, he put his arms around her, pulled her up, and lifted her onto the stage.

I stood there, stunned.

With Tres bested, something came alive in Puck, and like a rejuvenated ringmaster, he motioned to Chino and the jittery lighting guy. At his cue, a warm spotlight surrounded Faith, sparking interesting glints off her bazillion piercings.

No one seemed to notice Faith as she stood alone in the spotlight, hitching her guitar strap over her neck.

Two big middle-aged bouncers parted the crowd, scanning the onlookers, assessing who'd done what to whom. Logan flashed his badge. The bouncers nodded. The older one persuaded Tres's buffalo it was closing time. The other stuffed something into Josh's nose to stanch the blood and led him off the dance floor.

Mission accomplished, Logan came to reclaim his beer.

I blinked. "Are you all right?"

Logan grinned.

"That's it? You're going to sit here like nothing happened?"

Logan shrugged. "It was over before it started," he said and took a long pull on his beer.

I sighed and shook my head, bewildered, my adrenaline pumping a strange mixture of fear, excitement, and something else I wasn't ready to explore.

Ethan made his way back to our table, shoulders squared, chin up. He picked up his beer and downed the rest of it in one gulp.

I rolled my eyes. "Easy, killer, you don't want to strain your ego."

WITH THE STAGE LIGHTS situated and the sound in check, Puck adjusted his camera and yelled, "Roll 'em!"

"Roll 'em?" I said to Logan.

"Movie talk," he said. "He's a producer."

"Everyone in Austin is a producer," I said, and Logan grinned.

"Oh, yeah? What do you produce?" he said, and I blushed.

Logan was sitting close to me, his hand next to mine, and I wondered what it would be like to be on a real date with him. Just him and me—no fake obituaries, no loud crowds, no beating up bad guys. No reason to be together except that we wanted to be.

From the stage, Faith began to strum her acoustic guitar, and I frowned. I hadn't figured her for an unplugged act. As I sat, listening, the rich sounds of the guitar swelled out from the stage, engulfing the crowd. It had a sad quality, but strong, too, and then she opened her pierced lips and began to sing.

Like Ethan, I sat there with my mouth open.

Her eyes were large and dark, her skin pale, and despite her outward appearance, she had a kind of innocence about her.

As she sang, her voice was clear and strong and somehow vulnerable. The words seemed to rush out of her from someplace deep and urgent:

"Alone in the dark, she fades in the night
Remembering sunshine and music and flight
There was a season she knew how to fly
But even birds with broken wings
Still long to sing
She just needs to remember how…"

The crowd went dead quiet.

Under the hot, dark sky, we all watched and listened, as though we were all witnessing a shared miracle.

I turned to Logan. "Did she write this?"

He took a long pull on his beer and said, "Yep."

"Wow," I said, and turned to Ethan, who was still sitting there, eyes fixed on Faith, mouth slack, looking like he'd been hit in the stomach.

"Ethan," I said. "Are you okay?"

And then I heard it.

The loud *plop* of Ethan's heart as it hit the dirt.

I shook my head.

Ethan, it seemed, was a goner.

"COME ON," LOGAN SAID, and I frowned.

"We're leaving? Aren't you working?"

"So impatient," he said, leading me toward the small dock area. The last mooring was empty, and we walked along the weathered planks, our footfalls sounding hollow, the way wood sounds over water.

At the edge of the pier, we stood for a long moment surrounded by earth and sky and water, the music softly enveloping us as though there had never been a fight.

Standing next to Logan, I closed my eyes. In that moment, it felt like we were at the end of the world, looking back.

"How are you getting home?" he said, breaking my trance. I looked toward the bar, where Mia was reading Orange County Two's palm while Brynn appeared to be examining OC-1's esophagus.

"I came with Brynn, but she looks a little busy."

Logan grinned, "Yeah, I hate it when that happens. I'll take you home."

My breath caught, and all of my nerve endings went on red alert.

He eyed me suspiciously. "You okay? No more gangbangers hiding between your hangers?"

I shook my head. "You set Boy Scouts all up and down the street."

He chuckled at that, and I sighed.

"I need to talk to you," I said. "I think I may be involved in a co-dependent relationship with your dog."

"Ah, the dog."

"Yes, the dog. Logan, I know you asked me to keep up with the search and rescue thing, but I don't know if I'm cut out for it."

"Marlowe's got the best nose in Central Texas," Logan said, spiking my frustration.

"Everyone keeps saying that, but I don't see it. It's like he gets some kind of personal satisfaction from making an idiot out of me."

Logan laughed, and I hit him with my elbow. "It's not funny."

"You're right. It's not funny. It's hilarious."

"Logan!"

After his bout with hilarity subsided, he looked at me with those eyes the color of melted sin. We were standing at the end of the farthest pier, and he tipped my chin up so he could see my face. "Cauley, you're doing fine. Most rescue dogs have one handler. Marlowe's had three. He'll get there, and so will you. It just takes time, and you have to show him you're serious."

"Marlowe's had three handlers?" I said, doing the mental countdown. Me and Logan and who else?

Logan heard the unasked question and blew out a breath. "She was my partner," he said. The silence that followed had a weight to it that I could feel all the way to my bones. I wanted to ask him who she was and if she mattered as much to him as I imagined she did, but I could sense the wall there.

I sat down on the dock, and Logan sat beside me. The water lapped the pilings beneath the pier, and around us reeds and cattails rustled like old petticoats in the warm, wet breeze. I felt like I'd drifted into a lost piece of my past.

Behind us, Faith played on, slipping into a throaty old Etta James song.

"*I do believe it's time for a change,*" I sang along. "Aunt Kat used to sing this song to me when I was a little girl."

Logan gently brushed my hair out of my face. "I bet you were a cute little girl," he said, and heat lingered where he'd touched me. He gazed down at me intently. "What else did you do when you were a little girl?"

Despite the excitement of the evening, a wave of warmth and pleasure swelled over me like the waves gently lapping the pilings below us. "Actually," I said, slipping off my shoes, "I used to come here with my dad. He taught me and my sister to swim not far from here." I looked at him, assessing. "Do you have siblings? I bet you're the oldest."

"One younger brother—John. He's a cop in Dallas."

"Ohhhh," I said, smiling. "Big shock."

110

"You have a sister?"

"Yes, Suzanne the Splendiferous."

Logan grinned. "Do I detect some sibling rivalry?"

I blushed. "She's my big sister and what my mother aspires for me—former beauty queen, married Mr. Perfect, has three equally perfect kids and can single-handedly bake a cake, plan a dinner party, and refinish the bedroom furniture."

"Right," he said, "No sibling rivalry whatsoever."

I gave him a shot to the ribs with my elbow.

"Jeez, killer, take it easy," he laughed. "I'm just kidding."

He was quiet. "Is that what you really want? To be like your sister?"

I was uncomfortable with the turn of conversation. Of course there were parts of Suzanne's life I envied. But not now.

I shrugged. "Maybe someday," I said.

I slid my bare feet into the water and did a whole-body cringe.

"No matter how often I've done this, the chill of the water is a surprise—like a cold, hard slap."

Logan smiled, and he was close. I inhaled the scent of good soap and leather and something else that was pure Logan, and I felt something inside me open and bloom.

The music was quiet and sweet and sad, and he slid his arm around me, large and strong and warm. The awkwardness I'd been so worried about melted into a distant memory.

I laid my head on his shoulder and sighed. "What about you?" I said, suddenly feeling drowsy. "I bet you were a hellion."

He chuckled. "Actually, I was."

"So what turned you from your wicked ways?"

"My father died when I was very young. After he died, it was just my mom and me and my brother. We were a handful. And then along came the man who became my stepfather. There aren't many men like Jack Kinley. My mother lucked out and found two of them."

My soul went very still. Logan had given me this gift of his confidence, and I held it close to my heart like an unexpected treasure. I had questions, but they would wait. "Like the Colonel," I said, thinking of my own stepfather.

We were both quiet. The stars shone bright in the night sky, reflecting their other worlds onto the slick, black surface of the lake.

"When this is all over, I'd like to bring you back here," he said.

My whole body sighed. "I have a confession to make."

I wanted to tell him I remembered everything about him—the way he looked, the way he smelled, the feel of his hands in my hair, the feel of his body pressed against mine when he kissed me early in the summer—and that maybe I did believe in love at first sight...

"I missed you, Logan."

A night bird called from across the lake. It was a stark, lonely sound and hung in the air like a question.

And then it came. A clear, high answer, plaintive and sweet, calling back.

"I missed you too, kid," Logan said, and I felt him relax against me even as his arm tightened.

And in that moment, there, with Logan's arm around me, the water lapping the pier, and night insects chirring their late summer songs, everything was right with the world.

TEN

THE NEXT WEEK, I spent a disproportionate number of nights jolting awake in a cold sweat, desperately feeling around in the dark for my ears, which, happily, were still attached to my head. The night sweats were on account of the dreams I'd been having, which all featured Van Gogh, the El Patron enforcer, alive and well and in widescreen MGM Technicolor, making a miraculous recovery from the .45 caliber bullet wound between his eyes. These nightmares were invariably followed by the frenzied throwing open of closet doors, swishing back of shower curtains, and peeking under the bed, making sure the maniac had not somehow reanimated and come to spend his afterlife in my living room and that no dead birds roosted beneath my bed.

Of course, the only thing I found out of the ordinary was the rotating shift of young cops who'd drawn the short straw and got what they called "Pussy Patrol," the opportunity to spend the night camping out on my corner in an undercover car, making sure both of my ears stayed intact—at least long enough so that I could testify against Selena Obregon and El Patron.

I hadn't heard from Logan since the Pier, but then he'd told me we wouldn't see each other again until the trial, and I wondered how Puck's fake obituary had gone over with the shooter. Logan was right: Puck was like a fungus. Give him long enough and he'd start to grow on you.

Yes, he was annoying and he was a thief, but he clearly loved his sister and was willing to put his life on the line to get her out of her deal with Tres the Boy King. Of course, there were probably better ways to accomplish the task than stealing money from a bunch of mobsters, but then to guys like Puck, risk was relative.

I worried about Logan, but since he hadn't wound up in my inbox, I assumed he was still alive. I suppose there are some perks to being an obituary writer.

Tanner was still busting my butt for information about a gang war that may or may not be brewing in our backyard. I'd asked Logan and Cantu if they'd had any hot tips on gangland turf battles and been told *no* and to *stay out of it*, respectively.

To be honest, I wasn't trying that hard. There were other people I could ask and other hornets' nests into which I could poke my little stick, like my old buddy Diego DeLeon, one of the *jefes* in the Texas Syndicate. But the last time I'd seen Diego, I'd left him in the middle of dinner at the prestigious Shoreline Grill with a bad temper and a half-mast hard-on. I'm pretty sure even Hallmark doesn't make an "I'm Sorry" card for that particular occasion.

So I was left to my own devices—almost never a good thing—worrying about the upcoming El Patron trial, along with the things I always worry about—things like how I'm going to pay my bills, global warming, and what I would do with my hair if Logan and I ever got the opportunity to go out on a *date* date.

By the time the grand jury date rolled around, I felt restless and edgy and ready to jump right out of my skin. Truth be told, I was a big scaredy cat. Not only had I never testified in a trial before, I was going to be eyeball to eyeball with Selena Obregon. The woman had nearly killed me, and there was a pretty good chance she and one of her minions was behind the dead bird and the visit from the masked maniac I'd received the week before.

The morning before the trial, I woke up early, let the dog out, fed the cat, and showered. Dressed in a towel and a turban, I poured myself a bowl of frosted shredded wheat, careful to point the sugary side up and out of the milk so as not to disturb all that frosty goodness.

Like I do every morning when I'm not being hauled out of bed by a federal agent, I took the bowl and a spoon into my small home office to answer email before blasting my hair, getting dressed, and writing my daily to-do list. First I gave my Magic 8 Ball a good shake and said, "Is this going to be a good day?"

Turning the ball over in my hands, I read the message. *OUTLOOK NOT SO GOOD.*

I put the ball down in a huff. "Stupid 8 Ball. What do you know?"

I had approximately 330 emails encouraging me to enlarge my penis and 200 offering me the opportunity to place all of my money in an offshore account, guaranteeing to quadruple it by next week. Since I had a sum total of twelve dollars and fifty cents to my name, I did the math and decided it probably wasn't worth the postage.

I had two emails from Tanner wanting to know how I was doing on the gang research, and four from Mia regarding my daily horoscope, personal feng shui, and something about cleansing the karma of my past lives.

As I deleted my digital detritus, I scooped up spoonfuls of frosted wheat squares. Who says I'm not a multitasker?

I was about to enjoy another frosty bite when I scrolled down and found an email from my work address. I frowned. It wasn't from the umbrella *Sentinel* account, it was from my personal account, as though I'd emailed myself.

"Hmm," I said to no one. I shoveled the bite I'd been holding and double-clicked the message.

It blinked into view:

Like Your Panties?
I Do.

Under the email was a photo of my Jeep in front of my house. My breath went out with a whoosh.

"My Jeep!" I yelped, scrambling down the hall and out the front door, where Marlowe was sniffing around the Jeep. When he saw me, he turned around three times, then sat and woofed. The oldest of the Baby Bobs was sprawled across the hood, reaching for a familiar pink scrap of silk lodged beneath the wiper. When he saw me, the kid jerked his hand like he'd hit a hot poker. Without one hint of remorse, he jumped down from the Jeep.

"Oh, hell," I muttered, lurching to the other side of the vehicle, where I grabbed my brand-new Victoria's Secret wonder undies. I was about to stuff them under my towel when I noticed the fabric had a large, jagged rip where the crotch used to be.

"Cool," the kid said. He was about thirteen, and he was grinning, happy as a tick on a coon dog. I shoved the vandalized panties behind my back.

"El Patron," I whispered, staring down the street, looking for the cops that should have been there. My stomach pitched, and I got a severe hit of déjà vu. Several months ago, someone broke into my house and altered all my undies—not a crotch in sight.

The kid shrugged and made a face. "It's no big deal," he said. "Mom says I'm wise beyond my years. Besides, we've got cable."

I narrowed my eyes. "Aren't you supposed to be in school or something?"

"Waiting for the bus."

I sighed. "Did you see who did this?"

"No," he said. "But I could help you find out. You could leave them with me. You know, like a clue."

Right. He'd pull them out while he was in the lunch line. Show and tell courtesy of the desperate ex-housewife on Arroyo Trail.

I heard the distinct sound of hydraulic brakes, and the school bus rounded the corner, coming up the hill.

"You better go get your books or something," I growled, and he leapt over the fence, squashing the flowerbed of antique roses that'd gone wild and rangy in Aunt Kat's absence.

"You wearing that to your job?" he said, shouldering his backpack. I glanced down at my towel, which wasn't nearly as big as one would hope for, given the circumstances.

The bus was coming, and I could see the whites of the eyes of the balding bus driver as he got a good look at me. The driver must have made a noise because the bus suddenly swerved and then lurched as all the kids rushed to the right side, pressing their faces and hands on the windows for a better look.

I glared at the kid. "Didn't your mom get one of those television parental control boxes?" I growled.

He grinned.

"Sure," he yelled, jogging for the bus. "My parents are the only ones in the house who don't know how to use it."

Back in the house, I called Cantu, and he came and took my statement. His face was set in a grim scowl as he followed me into the house to look at the emailed note.

"You get anything on that red bandanna?" I asked.

"Not a single strand of DNA," Cantu said.

He asked me to print the email and whipped an evidence bag from his utility belt. "I'm going to have to take the note and the, uh… underthings back to the lab geeks," he said.

"Yeah," I said. "I heard they might be a clue."

TRUTH BE TOLD, I was spooked all the way down to my undies, crotchless or otherwise.

Cantu doubled up on the cop patrols, and Mia agreed to stay the night with me so we would drive to the courthouse together.

The plan sounded like a good idea at the time, but in reality, neither one of us could sleep. The evening wound up including a midnight margarita binge and singing along to Aretha Franklin on the Wurlitzer to stave off the fear. Okay, there was some dancing involved, but you can't hear *R-E-S-P-E-C-T* without sliding around in jammies and socks, no matter what kind of evil lurks in your flowerbed.

The following morning made me regret that choice.

The phone rang, and I resisted the urge to answer it with the business end of a baseball bat. "What?" I growled into the receiver.

"I hope you had a peaceful night." It was Logan, and I suddenly felt much better.

"Yeah," I said. "Like that's going to happen anytime soon. I thought we weren't supposed to be talking."

"We're not talking. I'm reminding you of your duty to the justice system and telling you that parking on Eighth Street is impossible. Park in that alley on Eleventh."

I stared at the phone. "You're already there?"

"Some people like to be early," Logan said. "I'm heading out in a few minutes to pick up Puck. They don't want him here until right before the grand jury convenes. Maybe media will clear before we bring in witnesses."

My stomach knotted.

"Hey," Logan said. "You okay?"

I blew out a breath. "Yeah. I'll just be glad when all this is over."

"I know. You're going to be okay, kid," he said, and his voice was calm and strong and sure. Then I had a thought.

"Logan?"

"Yeah?"

"Were you here late last night? You know, after the panty snatching?"

He snorted. "What, you think I spent the rest of the night parked outside your house?"

As he spoke, I looked out the wide front window at the street beyond, where a new kid in an unmarked car was taking up watch. And as he hung up the phone, I knew that he had.

LOGAN HAD BEEN RIGHT about one thing.

Parking was a mess. His hopes of the media getting bored and clearing out had been optimistic. News crews clogged every available spot with vans, cars, and cameras. I noticed two national crews jockeying for prime spots in the melee. The place was a madhouse. As Logan had directed, I found an empty spot on Eleventh, and Mia and I climbed out of the Jeep and headed to the federal courthouse on Eighth. The parking crisis had been averted, but I couldn't shake the creepy feeling skittering along my nerve endings.

A warm breeze ruffled my hair and whipped at my skirt. "Something's wrong," I told Mia, scanning the parked cars, looking for anything unusual.

"Of course something's wrong," Mia said, giving me her best *tsk tsk* voice, which makes her sound just like her grandmother. "We're testifying in front of a jury about a bunch of murderers."

"I know, but something doesn't seem right."

Mia shrugged. "This place is crawling with cops. What could go wrong?"

She hiked up her skirt, a neat trick since it was already so short you could almost see daylight.

"Do I look like a reliable witness?" Mia said, changing the subject. I glanced over at her short, bright blue fitted skirt and ruffled white blouse accented with her big digital Nikon. Her wild, dark hair was clipped back in a ponytail that cascaded down her back—conservative for Mia, but she still looked like she'd shimmied out of an MTV video about naughty teachers.

"They're probably not going to let you take the camera in," I said, and she shrugged.

"We been kicked out of better places than this," Mia said and smiled.

"Yes, but probably not some place that could handcuff us and put us away for life," I said, straightening my own skirt, which was black and hit me about mid-thigh. I wore a white boyfriend shirt and the thin gold chain my father had given me when I'd been christened. My only real concession to fashion were killer red stilettos. I hadn't seen Logan in almost a week, and I wanted to make sure he remembered it.

We walked up the alley and onto Eighth. From that angle, I could see the front of the gray granite courthouse with its wide front steps and solemn entrance—a good thing, since I was beginning to remember why I called these heels my killer shoes.

The shadow of the building provided a bit of blessed coolness, and the alkaline smell of polished granite pitched me back in time. I'd been to the courthouse as a little girl when my father testified against some thug or another he'd arrested, and the sheer enormity and grandeur of the building always took my breath away.

Alex "Live-at-Five" Salazar was setting up his crew with the rest of the local News Boys crowded around, buzzing like a bunch of vultures. Miranda was front row-center, as usual, her camera guy holding a mirror for her as she yanked up her bra to ensure maximum cleavage. Miranda would get a scoop out of this. She always did. The only difference between Miranda and a pit bull was a tube of murder-red lipstick.

Two dozen people hurried up the stone steps. Mia and I worked our way through the crowd. As we reached the double doors, the furious sound of clicking cameras clattered over us like a wave. I turned to see a black Suburban pull up to the curb, stopping about twenty feet behind an old yellow cab, when Logan unfolded himself from the back seat.

Flash! Mia snapped a picture.

Logan's eyes darted to the flash, then to me. He nodded at me as he continued to sweep the crowd. His gaze lingered on the cab and a couple of guys standing next to the driver's door. They were dressed in typical gangsta chic—baggy jeans and plaid shirts—which must have felt stifling in the early morning sun.

Watching carefully, Logan nodded, and Puck climbed out of the Suburban behind him. Mia flashed a string of shots.

With Puck in tow, Logan started up the steps. My breath caught the way it does when I'm around Logan and I stopped, watching him maneuver Puck through the reporters.

"Wow," Mia said. *Wow* was right.

Logan was dressed in a dark suit with a crisp white shirt and blood-red tie. While he always looked like a fed, today he looked like a fed on supercharged testosterone. My heart did a little two-step around my rib cage.

I navigated the steps with Mia. Logan turned toward the movement and our eyes caught. He raised a brow, and I felt his gaze skim my body like a physical thing.

Two U.S. Marshals had worked their way down through the crowd, flanking Logan and Puck.

Faith climbed the stairs at the right, along with Tres and a couple of suits who looked like lawyers. Between them, Faith seemed even smaller than I remembered. She wore a vintage black linen dress—probably her grandmother's—and it looked like it'd seen its fair share of funerals.

Her eyes darted toward Puck, then out over the crowd, nervous and jittery, like a caged bird before a storm.

Across the small distance, Logan smiled at me. It was a reassuring smile, and I smiled back, trying to calm my nerves.

Then I saw them.

The two gangbangers from the cab. They'd covered their lower faces with red bandannas, but it was them, I knew it all the way down to my bones. They moved quickly and quietly, coming up behind Logan. My heart jammed in my chest, and my voice caught in my throat.

I wanted to scream, to shout a warning, to do something, but I couldn't even breathe. Logan looked at me hard. I don't know what he saw in my face, but it was enough.

His jaw muscle snapped, his eyes narrowed, and his left hand darted under his coat, where I knew he kept his gun.

In the slow motion that accompanies trauma, the bangers brandished square, automatic pistols, pointing straight at Logan and Puck.

Crack-cra-cra-cra-crack!

A deafening hail of bullets rained through the morning. The air filled with the acrid smell of cordite and fear, and I stared, horrified, at Logan. Bullets riddled the stairs around him, but he didn't seem to notice.

He jerked his weapon level and fired short, sharp bursts in response. Puck lurched forward, and Logan shoved him down on the steps, pushing out in front of Puck as a second burst of automatic weapon fire blasted into the stunned silence.

Faith stood, frozen. She didn't move, never made a noise. She stood there staring down at her brother, who was motionless on the cold, hard stone.

Logan squeezed out a rain of bullets as he crouched over Puck.

I made myself as small as I could, my heart galloping. My ears rang in the bullet shower, but I couldn't break loose of the trance.

The marshal next to Logan made a terrible noise and then dropped, a circle of blood blooming near his badge.

All around me, bullets made terrible *thud-thud* sounds, the sound of metal against flesh. The bangers jerked and fell, one on top of the other, in a bloody heap.

Behind me, the cab's tires squealed, tortured rubber against pavement. Logan slammed a second magazine into his pistol. He sighted in on the car, but people were running, screaming—a colorful blur of civilian chaos—too many to make the shot.

A sharp shove smacked me in the middle of my back and I fell forward onto the concrete steps, twisting my ankle and getting a pretty good cut on my knee. A woman with a badge yelled, "Stay down!"

Uniformed officers swarmed around us, weapons drawn on the cab as it sped away.

Miranda tripped over her cameraman as she scrambled to safety. My heart stopped, and I could hear my own breath going in and out.

"Hey!" a familiar voice yelled.

Mia.

She'd fallen beside me, and we lay there together in the middle of the massacre.

"You get this?" I whispered, and she wrestled her Nikon out from under her.

"I think so," she said. "Is everyone all right?"

In the distance, a voice whispered *"Faith ... "*

The voice was soft and gurgling, trying to hold on.

My breath caught.

Puck.

"I don't think everyone's all right," I said to Mia. From the concrete, I stared over at Puck. He was facing me about fifteen feet away, blood pooling beneath him.

His eyes went lifeless and his face was still. He looked different—younger somehow, the way he'd looked in that old archive photo. I had seen death before, and some people say you get used to it. I don't think I ever will.

Logan pressed his fingers to Puck's neck, checking for a pulse. With a pained expression, Logan laid him over on his stomach, and in a flash, he went to one knee, tending to the wounded marshal.

I lurched to my feet, wobbling unsteadily on my heels, the red shoes now garish and out of place in this scene of bloodied bodies.

The doors to the courthouse flew open, and a dozen uniforms burst out. And there was Cantu.

His eyes met mine and he stopped, his gaze raking my body. I realized he was looking for bullet wounds.

I shook my head. "Go!" I shouted.

He nodded. Switching gears, he shouted something into his cell phone and moved down to Logan and the marshal. Cantu yanked off his jacket and bundled it under the marshal's head.

Sirens blared above the bedlam, and suddenly the steps were crawling with cops and paramedics.

Two of the medics stopped, giving Puck the once-over. Their eyes met over Puck's body, sending some sort of unspoken message to each other—*nothing we can do here*—and together they moved on to the wounded officer.

I wondered if this was what war looked like.

The paramedics flanked Logan, taking over on the wounded marshal, and Logan stood and looked down at Puck.

There was something in his dark eyes—grief and something else. And then he looked at Faith, who was still standing there, staring at her brother's lifeless body. Her stepbrother and the suits had ducked for cover and were now chatting warp speed on cell phones.

And then Logan turned to the two bloody bodies of the men he had just killed.

His face was still, his eyes hard. In that flicker of a moment, I wondered just how many men Logan had killed.

I decided then and there I would never ask him.

Unsteadily, I tottered down the steps and stopped abruptly. Pain, sharp and bright, shot from my ankle to my knee. Looking down at my shoes, I realized I'd broken a heel and twisted my ankle. I limped over to Logan and Cantu as the paramedics worked on the downed officer. We looked at each other, the three of us. No one said a word.

And then I looked more closely at Logan, and my heart stopped.

"Logan," I whispered. Visions of the day my father died whirled in my head.

Cantu frowned at me, and then followed my gaze.

The world swooped beneath me as Cantu grabbed Logan's sleeve and ripped. The white shirt beneath Logan's jacket was soaked in blood.

"He's been hit!" I said aloud to no one. "Logan's been shot!"

Even as I managed the words, a female deputy had me by the elbow, leading me out of the chaos. "Where's Mia? We need another ambulance!" I yelled. "Logan's been shot!"

ELEVEN

"It's only a flesh wound," Logan said, referring to the bandage around his upper right arm.

"Oh. Well. That makes me feel so much better," I said, still buzzing with fear and something that felt like a lingering, high-voltage shock. "Logan, you were shot."

"At least it was my right arm," he said, shrugging his left shoulder. "Still got my shooting arm."

I wanted to smack him.

He was sitting in an exam room at St. David's Hospital, his shirt stained with blood, his arm in a sling. He was waiting to be discharged, acting like it was just another day at the office. For him, it probably was. I wondered if this was how Mama felt when Daddy was on the job. I also wondered if this was how she felt about me now.

My mother had obviously seen the news and jammed my voice mail with 13,000 frantic phone calls, wondering where I was, who got shot, and how it was going to affect my love life.

When I finally got to a place and a state of mind where I could call her, she agreed to limit the phone calls for the rest of the day if I would come home for dinner. I'd get dessert if I brought Logan. Judging by the way things were going, I could kiss that banana pudding goodbye.

I'd been treated for some scratches, a big gash on my knee that would eventually be a beastly scar, and a nasty twisted ankle, and told that I'd probably have some hellacious bruises in the morning. In the middle of the mayhem, I hadn't realized I'd been hurt. From the ambulance, I texted Rob Ryder, assistant editor at the City Desk, the facts as I knew them and a description of what happened live on the scene. Ryder would clean it up and post it to the web. There's a real adrenaline rush that comes with news on demand, but it loses something, too. Today, I felt like it'd lost a lot.

Even with my own minor flesh wounds, none of what happened seemed real. I kept thinking I'd wake up and it would all be a nightmare. It was like tumbling back in time to that day my father died—the day he was shot in the back by a man who'd simply looked at me and grinned, then slipped into the shadowy night. And now, it'd happened again.

The techs let Mia go at the scene, and she raced back to the office to get the pictures up on the web. I wound up alone in triage, waiting for a shot of antibiotics and feeling numb.

Logan had been shot. Puck was dead. One of the marshals who'd been escorting them into the courthouse was in critical condition. The adrenaline that pumped through my system ebbed, and I felt cold and tired. And I was going to be sick. Again.

I kept seeing the look on Puck's face—that silent shock, that look of surprise, and then blood. So much blood.

I shook my head, trying to dislodge the image from my frontal lobe. But I just kept staring at the dressing on Logan's arm.

I swallowed at the lump in my throat. "I know this is probably no big deal for you, but I don't want anything to happen to you."

"I know," he said quietly.

We both stared at the floor, not knowing what to say.

"Did they ID the shooters?" I asked.

Logan nodded. "A couple of wannabe gangbangers, probably on contract, wanting to impress El Patron in the restructure."

I nodded, looking out the small window into the hall. The feds had taken the hospital full force, circling the wagons in the waiting room, ears glued to cell phones, faces set in grim resolve.

"So what happens now?" I said, and Logan shook his head.

"Too early to tell."

"And Puck?"

A darkness I hadn't seen before passed over his face, and I had to stifle the urge to take a step back. Logan was quiet.

I took a deep breath. "Logan, there wasn't anything you could do," I began, and he shook his head. This was a wound that no kiss would ever soothe. It was a guilt that I could never fathom. It was something encoded in his DNA, like his tall frame, dark eyes, and dark hair.

He moved toward the window, staring out at something I couldn't see.

"Where's the sister," he said, and I blinked.

"I don't know. I haven't seen her since the courthou—"

"Logan!" A woman in a suit with short, dark hair and no makeup stuck her head in the door. "Logan, there's a fire."

She stood staring at him, face grim. "And Logan, Selena Obregon and her marshal escort are missing."

A cold chill rushed from my stomach to my throat.

Logan grabbed his jacket. His gaze locked on mine. "You going to be okay?"

I blinked. "Yes, I—"

"I need a favor."

"Yeah, okay—" I stuttered, not quite believing he was leaving.

"Find Faith."

"Are you leaving again?"

"Most likely," he said.

"Seems to be a pattern," I said. "No one knows where you're going or when you'll be back?"

"Part of the job."

"Seems like a system that could be subject to abuse."

He smiled at me then, and stepped close to me in a move that sucked all the oxygen out of the room. And then he kissed me. Warm and soft, and then hard and urgent.

"I'll be back, kid," he said, and then he was gone.

I stood there feeling thoroughly kissed and in a state of shock. Puck was dead. Logan had been shot. Selena was in the wind. I stared at the sterile, empty room and wondered what in the hell had just happened.

SELENA HAD ESCAPED. I couldn't calm the fear of finding her in my closet, beautiful, blond, and brandishing a knife. I had to move or go crazy, so I started walking.

I found Faith huddled in the far corner of the waiting room, staring out of a window that looked out over a big black dumpster in the parking lot. The dumpster was overflowing with something green and oozing and I got the sinking feeling that might be the way this thing was heading.

"Faith?" I said, feeling awkward, searching for words. "Are you all right?"

She didn't look at me. She stared out the window, unseeing, her eyes dry and wide, her lips pale. Of course she wasn't all right. Her brother was shot to death right in front of her. I felt like I'd just stepped in the ooze.

She had more bald patches on her head, two of them were raw. There was a spray of elliptical blood spatter along the front of her dress. I was pretty sure it wasn't hers.

I sat down beside her and looked out the window, not sure what to say.

"You want to talk?" I said, and she drew back, eyes going even wider.

She was about ten years younger than me, but she seemed so small, like a little girl.

I blew out a breath. "I'm not going to say I know how you feel because I don't," I said carefully. "But I will tell you that I'm sorry."

"Yeah, right." She looked up at me. "You ever lose somebody?"

"Yes," I said quietly. "My father. A long time ago."

Her eyes went cold. "Yeah, but he didn't get shot in front of you."

"Actually," I said. "He did get shot in front of me. He was a policeman."

Faith sat, listening, so I swallowed the big lump that always clogs my throat when I think of it, and for Faith's sake, I went on. "I was a little girl, and he was home for the evening. My mother sent him out for milk. It was way after my bedtime, but I begged and pleaded and was a general pain in the ass until he agreed to take me with him. I stayed in the car while he ran into the store."

Faith was staring at me. "What happened?"

"He walked in on a robbery. Daddy took the guy down and cuffed him, but there was a second guy hiding in the beer cooler."

It was fifteen years ago, but I still felt the pain, sharp and bright.

"How did you know?" Faith said. "About the other guy?"

"Because he shot my dad in the back of the head while Daddy was securing the building."

"You saw it?"

I nodded.

She stared out the window, quiet for a long time. "You still miss him?"

"Every day."

Faith thought about that and was quiet.

She shook her patchy head and whispered, "I don't know what to do."

I took in some air. "You don't have to do anything right now," I said. "You just breathe in and breathe out. The rest comes when it comes."

Her voice caught, and for a moment I thought she might cry. "I feel like shit."

"I know," I said. "Is there someone you can talk to? Anyone I can call for you?"

She shook her head. "My brother is all I had in the whole world."

She was sitting right in front of me and life as she knew it was falling apart.

And there was nothing I could do about it.

I reached over and took her hand, and then it came to me. Not a solution, but the first step on what was going to be a long and treacherous road for her.

"Faith, have you eaten anything today?"

She stared at me.

"That's what I thought." I fished my cell out of my purse and hit the speed dial.

I couldn't solve her problems, but I could get her dinner.

"Mama?" I said into the phone. "Can you set another place for dinner?"

TWELVE

CHRISTIAN MORGENSTERN ONCE SAID that home isn't where you live, but where they understand you. I'd never been foolhardy enough to believe my mother understood me, but she was eccentric enough that she rarely went judgmental on anyone but me.

I wanted to get word to my mother about Faith—what had happened and the girl's unusual appearance—before Mama gaped or gasped or otherwise made things worse than they already were.

I was running on pure adrenaline—I'd hit that point where I was so tired and keyed up that I wouldn't have been able to sleep if I'd mainlined a truckload of Ambien.

Faith barely spoke as I took her to my house, changed clothes, and loaded Marlowe into the Jeep to go to my mother's. Faith refused to change clothes, and it had been a trial to get her wedged back into the Jeep.

Her face was still expressionless, and she still hadn't cried. Her only comments on the entire trip were that no, she didn't want to talk, and that she didn't like dogs—and that last comment was a response to Marlowe snuffling the back of her neck.

What kind of a person didn't like dogs? Her brother, for starters, but I wasn't sure what to say, so I heeded the angels of my better nature for a change and didn't say anything.

Despite Faith's hard-core appearance, Mama would know what to do. I was sure of it. I kept sneaking looks at the girl all the way down the winding, arbored path of Pedernales Trail. Faith stared straight out the windshield, not moving, not speaking, not crying, just sitting there in her blood-spattered dress.

Despite Faith's declaration of dislike for all things canine, Marlowe kept sticking his nose between the front seats, nuzzling Faith behind the ear. Trying to win converts is never an easy thing, but Marlowe was not a quitter.

I glanced down at my watch. Ten more minutes to Mama's house. But it wasn't the mile markers on the road that told me I was getting close to home, it was more like the prehensile umbilical cord with a quick-action spring.

Not to mention the pine-fresh scent of Lysol drifting over a two-mile area. My mother announces her presence with cleaning products like other people whip out business cards.

"This is it," I said to Faith as we turned into the driveway. Faith seemed to barely register the rambling white Victorian where I grew up.

The house had wide, Windex-clean windows accented with fluffy green ferns. I pulled past the big wraparound porch, turned the key, and leapt out of the driver's seat while the engine rattled to a halt. "Just come on in."

Marlowe did his speed-of-lightning thing, bounding out of the Jeep ahead of me.

Marlowe squeezed between me and the door jamb and galloped into the kitchen ahead of me, nails scrabbling along the hardwood, a giant streak of silver and white, warbling at the top of his lungs. Despite everything, I supposed it was a good day to be a dog.

Mama already had Marlowe's bowl brimming with his favorite doggy dinner. After enthusiastic greetings were exchanged between the two, he circled his bowl, dropped beside it, and began wolfing down chow, tail wagging like a metronome.

I slid in seconds behind the dog, trying to ward off the inevitable confrontation of the fright that was Faith. But Mama took one look at me and dropped the wet dishtowel she'd been using to wipe Marlowe spit. She sailed toward me, a woman on a mission. "Good gawd, Cauley, what have you done to yourself?"

"Mama," I said, catching my breath. "We're all right."

I must have looked a fright, too.

She proffered an elegant snort. "You don't look all right," she fussed, patting me down for open flesh wounds, broken bones, and hang nails. "Do you have any idea how worried we've been? You're giving me gray hair!"

"Mama, we're southern. We don't get grayer, we get blonder."

"Ahh!" she said, making the little puff of breath she always made, sounding exactly like someone stepped on her foot. "Let me look at you."

She pulled one of my eyelids open and put her forehead to mine for a closer look. "Good gawd, your pupils are dilated! Clairee!" she shouted, right in my ear. "Get me the VapoRub!"

Throughout my life, my mother put VapoRub on a wide variety of infirmities, from the episodic to epileptic fits. While I had never been stricken with either malady, Mama insists it was the mentholated wonder salve that warded off trouble.

"You better save the VapoRub," I said, thinking of Faith. "You're about to need all of it you can get."

"Don't be smart with me," Mama said, sweeping the damp dish-towel from the floor, and I said, "I wouldn't dare."

The screen door banged again, and in trudged Faith, all patchy haired and pink scalped, piercings and tattoos on every visible surface, and with blood spatter down the front of her dress. Mama dropped her dishtowel again.

Abruptly, Mama jerked to a stop like someone punched her in the stomach.

Too late for a warning.

Holding my breath, I waited for the other Ferragamo to drop.

Mama stood speechless but I could practically hear the gears churning in her pretty platinum head.

Calmly and with great purpose, she retrieved the dishtowel from the floor and folded it into four sections, like it had come fresh from the laundry, all disinfected and April fresh.

Placing it on the counter next to the old farmhouse sink, she turned to face Faith. "Well, hello!" she said, as bright and cheerful as if she was addressing a fellow member of the Charity League.

Faith frowned a little and put out her hand, but Mama had other plans. She pulled Faith close and hugged her tight.

The breath I'd been holding seeped slowly out of my lungs.

"It's so nice when Cauley's friends come to dinner. Are you all right, darlin' girl?"

Mama petted the girl's back in slow, rhythmic strokes, her perfectly manicured fingers brushing over the bristly patches of hair and down along the girl's back. Faith blinked and her throat moved hard, like she was swallowing tears she hadn't quite found yet.

I knew the feeling. There was magic in Mama's hands.

Growing up, I couldn't count the times I thought the world as I knew it was over, but Mama would get out her big silver brush and stroke my hair down my back in deep, rhythmic strokes until the earth tilted back into place and all was right with the world.

When Faith didn't answer, Mama said, "All right then, baby. You talk when you feel like it. And until then, let's get some dinner in you."

And then Mama set about filling glasses with iced tea. I watched her, blinking in amazement. She moved about the kitchen like nothing could be more normal, looking like the aging beauty queen that she was—just a little shorter than me, with a platinum pageboy of perfect hair. She'd always had a kindness to her, just below the surface, and it shined now like new spring sunshine as she retrieved the dishtowel and mopped up the counter.

All my life I've been told I look like my mother. This was one time I hoped that was true.

The sound of jangling bracelets rang around the corner, and I cringed as Mama's best friend, Clairee, came sailing in from the living room in a mist of gardenias and martinis. Her eyes went wide when she saw me.

"Good gawd, Cauley, we saw you on the news, what on earth—" She pulled up short when she got a good look at Faith.

"Look, Clairee, Cauley's brought a guest home for dinner," Mama hissed, throwing the dishtowel at her friend.

Clairee blustered, catching the dishtowel and shimmying out of her shock. "Well," she sputtered, screwing her hospitality firmly back in place. "Come pull up a chair. We're just going to have dinner." Her voice sounded tight and her faded blue eyes were strained, but I knew she was trying, and I loved her for it.

Mama and Clairee are old-school East Texas, more a time than a place. They're as true to their roots as hoop skirts, porch fans, and pearl-handled pistols.

The screen door banged open again and in poked the Colonel's handsome, silvering head. "Did I hear our Cauley Kat?"

A breeze caught the tail of his "Kiss the Cook" apron just as his gaze found Faith. A small shadow fleeted over his pale blue eyes, and then it was gone so that I had to look twice to make sure I'd seen it. He smiled and waved the long, stainless-steel spatula he'd been using to subdue a wayward rib roast. "Well, hello there. You must be Cauley's friend."

The Colonel slammed in through the mudroom, wiping his big hand on the apron, grinning like he'd just seen a long-lost friend. He was tall and strong, with a face that grew more handsome with each decade. "Well, then, welcome! Glad you could make it."

Uncertainly, Faith held out her hand and let him shake it.

My throat went tight.

I hadn't told Mama who I was bringing home for dinner, but Faith's blood-spattered, peculiar appearance didn't seem to startle them at all. But then I had a habit of dragging home strays.

I shouldn't have been surprised. I knew they'd seen the news. When I called Mama after her bazillion frantic voicemails, I'd told her I was fine, that Logan had been treated and was well onto the road to recovery, and that he had to leave to go brace some bad guys or grill some grifters or do whatever FBI agents did when they were called away, so God only knew what she was expecting me to bring home for dinner.

Faith's dark eyes were wide, and she looked like she'd been shell-shocked all over again.

I shook my head. Watching Mama and the Colonel and Clairee, something very tight inside me softened and began to unwind.

The house was filled with the sweet, tangy scents of barbecue; fresh, buttery cornbread biscuits; and the kind of calm that only comes with the chaos of family.

My stomach growled.

"Good heavens, girl," Mama declared. "You sound like you swallowed a boar hog on a bad day."

"It's been a while since either of us have eaten," I said sheepishly.

The day was closing in on me, and suddenly, I felt disoriented. It had only been eight hours since the world got knocked out from under us, but time had gone elastic, expanding and contracting until there was no time at all. I'd been sick twice since we'd been on those bloody courthouse steps; there was no telling what Faith had been through. I wouldn't have believed either of us could touch solid food for the next week and a half.

But there, with my family in the kitchen I'd grown up in, I felt the bloody abyss lessen a little.

The Colonel had been at the pit, and the platter he'd brought in moments earlier smelled like a little slice of marinated heaven. I noticed he'd also set out some chicken soup and a loaf of fragrant Fredericksburg bread. I smiled at the thoughtfulness of this simple act.

"All right, girls, go wash up," Mama said, swatting me on the rear with the dishtowel.

Faith stared at her.

"Go," she said, and then she swatted Faith, too. "Dinner's almost ready."

FRESHLY WASHED AND SEATED at the dinner table, I was so tired I could have fallen asleep face-down in the bowl of black-eyed peas. But manners prevailed and I gazed about, wondering what in the world we would talk about. There was, of course, a big white buffalo in the middle of the room, but we would vigorously avoid topics that included anything about the shooting, the trial, and anything else that might traumatize Faith. Those things they would lecture me about later.

And I knew Mama had to be hurting. I watched her as she unfolded the cloth napkin on her lap, her face subdued but strained.

She'd spent the day worrying about me and had probably done more than her fair share of reliving the night Daddy died. I remembered her sitting out on the front porch in her pale blue bathrobe as Cantu brought me home and broke the news. I don't know what he said, but he stayed with us long after sunup, letting Mama wail and pound and cry until her tears ran out.

Tonight, I watched Mama as she arranged her dinnerware. I should have known better than to worry about dinner conversation. Mama may have been tossed out of Miss Mona's School for Fine Young Ladies, but she could have taught those old biddies a thing or two about the ways of human kindness.

Despite her usual goading me about my work life, my un-social life, and the dubious state of my hair, Mama always knew just how to make people feel comfortable. Faith, there at the dinner table, covered in her dead brother's blood, was a perfect example.

"We don't usually have soup with barbecue, but I just had a craving for a little soup," Mama said sweetly to Faith, lying through her perfectly lined lips. Mama never had soup for dinner. Like most other Texans, she usually adhered to the four basic food groups—grease, fat, lard, and sugar. "Help yourself to whatever you like, dear."

Mama seemed calm, but there was an energy pulsing through the dining room so thick you could smell it. It was the same energy she'd put off in the emergency room that year I decided to channel Wonder Woman and jump off the roof.

Inside, I knew she was just waiting to get me alone and ask me what the hell I'd gotten myself into and how I planned to get myself out of it. But for now, she'd put that aside.

Mama set a glass of iced tea in front of Faith, and the Colonel placed another enormous plate of ribs and brisket between the corn and the potato salad. He took his place at the head of the table. Marlowe abandoned the dog food and took his place at the other end of the table, under Mama's feet. Dazed, Faith watched like she'd fallen face-forward onto a foreign planet.

We all held hands and the Colonel said grace, and then we tucked into our dinner.

"So, Cauley," Mama drawled.

I steeled myself.

Daintily, she selected a short rib from the platter, tore off a piece, and gave it to Marlowe, who took it carefully from her manicured nails. Faith watched with raised brows as Mama fed the dog from the table.

Mama turned her sweet gaze on me. "Clairee mentioned they have an opening for a receptionist over at her real estate office..."

I gaped for a moment. I figured if there was such a thing as a Get Out Of Jail Free card, it definitely would have come with nearly being shot to death on the courthouse steps.

I felt a headache tweak my left eye. "Yes," I said. "Clairee called to tell me that. Twice."

Mama pursed her lips. "Real estate is a perfectly respectable profession, and it wouldn't hurt to go down to her office and have a look around."

Faith listened with an expression that bordered on incredulous.

"And Faith, dear, what do you do?" Mama said, her voice lilting with moonlight and magnolias.

Holy hell. I scanned the table, looking for some way to start a diversion. Spill milk, dump salt in the peas, gouge out my own eye with a fork...

Seeing that Faith hadn't helped herself to the bounty of beef before us, Mama dished her up some soup and tore off a chunk of bread for her.

Faith shook her head like she was trying to break through a trance. "I'm, uh, a singer, but I wait tables and stuff to pay the bills," she said in a very small voice.

"Well, waiting tables is the training ground for Austin musicians," Mama beamed. "Where do you work, dear? We'll come by and see you."

Faith stared down at her soup like a suitable answer was floating among the noodles. She shrugged. "You probably won't know the place."

"Nonsense, dear, we love to try new places," Mama said.

Faith looked up, leveling her gaze to Mama's. "I work at Boners."

A hush fell over the table, and the Colonel choked on a big bite of barbecue.

"Isn't that the strip club out by the county line?" Clairee said, pointing a sauce-covered fork at Faith.

Mama's face didn't move, but I felt the swift breeze as she kicked Clairee under the table.

"Ouch!" Clairee yelped, rubbing her shin. "What? I'm just saying. I bet the money'd beat the hell outta sellin' real estate." She glanced down at her own abundant cleavage and grinned. "Talk about awesome tips."

MAMA AND I CLEARED the table while the Colonel and Clairee tended the grill.

With the food stowed away in half a ton of Tupperware marked with tape—half for me and half for Faith—Marlowe moved his attention to the back door, where he did a little tap dance on the hardwood.

"Faith, honey, would you mind taking the dog out?" Mama said.

Faith stared down at the dog uncertainly.

"Well, go on, dear, daylight's burning."

The girl rose and opened the screen door. Marlowe pranced ahead of her through the mudroom, and the door banged behind them as they went on their very first adventure out into the MacKinnon back forty.

I SETTLED BESIDE MAMA at the kitchen sink, grabbing a fresh dishtowel, and to my surprise, I toppled back in time as she washed and I dried.

We were both quiet. There was nothing but the sound of running water and the smell of lemon-fresh soap. Mama's hands darted in and out of the suds as they'd done so many times. I wondered why the floral pattern on the china hadn't rubbed off years ago.

She stared out the kitchen window, overlooking a kitchen garden in late summer bloom.

"You okay, Cauley Kat?" she finally said.

"Just some bumps and bruises."

"And your Agent Logan?"

"He's fine," I said, thinking of the cold look in his eyes when he'd left. "I think he's fine. He had to leave. Something about a fire. Mama, I'm worried."

"You love him?" she said, and I nearly burst into tears.

"I don't know. How can you really know what makes you love someone? I mean, we barely even know each other."

Mama shook her pretty platinum head and sighed. "Sometimes the heart just knows."

I nodded. "I don't know if I can take this kind of worrying—not knowing when or if he's coming home." I turned to her then. "Why, Mama? What made you put up with Daddy's job all those years?"

"Your father was a policeman." She rinsed the large, brown crock that'd held the potato salad, passed it to me, and dried her hands on her apron. "I was married to your father for ten years," she said. "You marry someone, you marry their family and their career, for better or worse."

I shook my head. "Does it ever get any better?"

She was staring out the window, looking beyond the rise, into the woods beyond the front pasture. "No," she finally said. "It gets worse. But that doesn't mean it's bad. I love the Colonel. As surely as there's a God in heaven, I do. But I wouldn't trade the time I had with your father for a living thing on earth. Cauley, darlin', the better was so much more than the worse."

"Do you still love him?"

"What a question. Of course I still love your father."

"Does the Colonel know that?"

"Cauley, honey, the Colonel is a good man with a big heart, and his heart is big enough for me and your daddy and your sister and her family and you and all the strays you drag home."

I stared out the window, wondering if I could stand the kind of life Mama had with my father. I leaned over the sink and studied the white-washed windowpane, chipped and worn from generations of MacKinnon women leaning forward as they watched through the frame of the kitchen and out onto the lives of the children they helped create.

On the horizon, Faith was sitting on the rise, the scorched grass beneath her, her arms wrapped around her knees as she rocked herself, trying to find some comfort in her aloneness. I wondered how many MacKinnon women had taken refuge, alone, on that rise.

And then I realized Faith wasn't alone. A large, silver figure crept along the hillock, ears flat, tail down.

"Marlowe," I whispered, and Mama smiled.

When the dog reached the girl he sat, hesitant, and stretched so that he could snuffle her neck.

Faith cringed at the contact, and then slowly, her shoulders rose and fell. She began heaving as the wave of grief finally washed over her. The tears came then and she collapsed, her tiny, birdlike frame leaning hard on Marlowe, and the dog leaned back, accepting her weight.

Tears burned the backs of my eyes as I watched. I shook my head in amazement. "Good dog," I whispered, and to my surprise, a tear slipped down my cheek. "I'm so proud of him."

Mama slid her arm around my shoulders and pushed a strand of hair behind my ear. She smiled. "I know the feeling, baby," she said. "I know the feeling."

THIRTEEN

MAMA HARANGUED FAITH AND me to spend the night, and I would've gladly conked out in my twin bed in my old bedroom, but Faith wasn't having any of it. Faith wanted to go home, she said. Get clean clothes, find a way to start her life over.

Reluctantly, I agreed to drive her.

Mama loaded us down with enough plastic-covered barbecue to get us through the next millennium. I promised Mama I'd call her when I got home and call her again in the morning to assure her that I had a five-year plan that did not include getting shot at. Never mind that the shooters weren't actually shooting at *me*.

The moon was high and Marlowe lay quietly, his chin on the console, the warm, late-summer wind whipping around us in the open Jeep. We were quiet as I drove the dark, flat county road, where the blacktop stretched toward the horizon and cars were fewer as we sped through the Dawes County night. I wondered where Selena Obregon was and if she would muster her troops and wage an all-out war over territory. I shivered.

"I thought your dad was dead," Faith finally said. She didn't look at me. Her eyes were locked on Marlowe, his white, whiskery brows moving as she spoke.

"The Colonel's my stepfather," I said. "But we don't think of him that way. He's more like the glue that holds our family together."

Faith stared out the windshield into the night. "You have a good family." There was a catch in her voice, and I knew she was thinking about the tattered shreds of her own family.

"Faith, are you sure I can't take you to your mother's house?"

"I don't have a mother," she said evenly, but her eyes were hard, and her voice was even harder. "She sent me away when I was thirteen. And those fuckers shot my brother. My family is gone."

Her mother sent her away? I tried not to gape. In my dealings with Selena Obregon, I'd learned that there are some mothers who eat their young.

"Most of my family's gone, too," I said. "My sister lives in Houston, my father's dead, Aunt Kat lives wherever her next romance novel is set, and Nana MacKinnon is crazier than bat shit.

"The Colonel is family by marriage and Clairee is family by proxy— what Mama calls *front-porch family*: you wander onto the front porch, you're family."

"That's not real family," she said.

"Maybe not. But when you hurt one MacKinnon, they're all there, locked and loaded and ready to roll."

A tear slid down Faith's cheek, and Marlowe edged over the console and put his head in her lap. She began to sob then—deep, wracking sobs that shook her body. Marlowe bumped her elbow with his white, pointy nose, and she began to stroke his velvety husky ears. As she stroked, her tears subsided.

"They're here for you, too, now," I said.

Faith sat quietly, petting Marlowe's ears. I didn't know what else to say, so I didn't say anything.

We pulled into the rutted, red dirt drive and bumped up to her house, which was actually a Jurassic mobile home that listed to the left, propped upright by a dozen cinder blocks and a prayer.

Marlowe and I walked her up the four wobbly aluminum steps, and Faith let us in the bent metal door.

The trailer floor creaked as I stepped inside behind her, and my heart did a quick thump. I wondered if ghosts haunted trailers or if they went for better real estate.

Somewhere in the darkness, I heard *screech!* and something small and sharp dug into the top of my head. It felt like I had been smacked on the scalp by a metal hairbrush. Marlowe went wild, leaping and growling.

Faith screamed and then something else screamed, and then I joined in.

Faith scrambled for the lights.

She flipped the switch, bringing garish yellow light into the room. The flying hairbrush hit me again, and Faith said, "Keates! Stop it!"

She shut the window the bird had flown in through, then held out her forefinger. A little yellow bird circled the ceiling fan, then landed on her finger, chittering at me angrily. Faith took the bird to a huge wrought-iron cage that took up most of the living room. The door was open, and Faith said, "Home."

The bird chided me again, then flitted into the cage.

"Aren't you going to close the cage door?" I said to Faith, touching my head. I looked at my fingers and realized I was bleeding—not a lot, but still…

Faith looked at me like I'd suggested we pluck the little darling and have it for dinner.

147

"He doesn't like the door closed," Faith said, and made a kissy noise at the bird.

My eyes widened, adjusting to the dim yellow light. Inside, the little trailer looked like décor by Disney: all pink and white and frothy frills. A row of beautiful, aging porcelain dolls lined a shelf along the ceiling. I half expected a host of fuzzy animal friends to burst from the hall closet and form a chorus line.

Pierced and tattooed, Faith trudged through the fairytale finery looking like a demon caught in Cinderella's castle.

"Does all this stuff belong to you?" I said, and Faith looked around like she was seeing her home for the first time.

"Yeah," she said. "My grandma left me her dolls. Some of them belonged to her grandmother."

I nodded but couldn't calm the feeling of dread that slipped up my spine. Marlowe and I checked under beds, behind curtains, and in the closets for latent signs of predators—which is to say that I checked while Marlowe sniffed out peanut butter cookies, stray Skittles, and anything else that seemed remotely edible.

"Is that it?" I asked Faith, and she shrugged.

"Well, there is a crawl space."

Of course there was a crawl space. Why did I have to open my big mouth?

Faith lifted a wooden door in the floor between the washer and dryer, and I wished then that I hadn't asked.

"What's down there?" I said.

"It's a tornado shelter, so there's canned goods, bottled water, and a year's supply of duct tape. I think there also might be a rat."

My breath caught, and I slammed the trap door.

"Well, I think we're done," I said. Faith looked relieved and very tired.

I knew the feeling.

I found no creepy earless guys and Marlowe found not one crumb of peanut butter cookie, so I watched as Faith slipped into a pair of pink Barbie pajamas and crawled into bed, then told her I'd call her in the morning and gave her my card in case she needed to get ahold of me before then.

Before pulling out of her driveway, I called the Dawes County Sheriff's Department and asked that they put a patrol on Faith's house, and then I headed home to my own little bungalow, tired all the way down to my bones.

At home, I gave half of Mama's barbecue to the freckle-faced rookie parked under the streetlight, tossed the rest of it in the fridge, and then checked my own house for rats, dead birds, and homicidal, nasty note writers.

Frankly, it would be pointless for Obregon or the masked bandit or anyone else, for that matter, to jump me now. They'd have to wake me up if they wanted to inflict any real kind of pain, and the chances of that were about even with the Democrats sweeping the state Senate.

I stripped, climbed into the shower, and nearly fell asleep as the water poured down on me. It wasn't until then that I noticed I was covered with bruises. My muscles were sore, and I felt like I'd been stricken with polio.

I had to get back to the gym.

I toweled off and fell into bed half wet and swathed in my bathrobe. I was too tired for a turf battle with the dog and cat, so I took the corner at the foot of the bed, determined to sleep for the next forty-eight hours or until I got hungry, whichever came first. I would, of course, have to get up in a few hours, head to work, and write Puck's obituary for the second time. The first obit was in the unrecoverable Dead Copy file. I felt sick all over again.

My brain was spinning, and I tried like hell to shut it off. Marlowe sprawled out on the pillow, taking up more than half the bed. He snored peacefully, probably just to piss me off.

Puck's second obituary would be different, but how? Puck's passing probably wouldn't be noticed by many, but for Faith and Logan and maybe even Puck's mother, I knew this bit of writing would mean a lot. What could I say about Puck that could soothe his sister and Logan? Who else had cared about him? Was there someone out there, other than Faith, whose life would be lessened because of his absence?

Marlowe grumbled in his sleep, and I reached up toward the pillow and scratched beneath his chin. Muse yawned and stretched and butted me with her little calico head so that I would lift the quilt and let her snuggle up under my chin.

I stroked her soft fur, and as she purred the tears came, quiet and steady. I would think about all that later. In the words of Margaret Mitchell, tomorrow was another day. The stars winked through my bedroom window, and as I drifted off to sleep, I wondered if Logan was somewhere watching those very same stars.

And then I said a little prayer for him and for Faith and for the soul of Wylie Ray Puckett.

THE MOON WAS SHINING through the window when I woke with a start.

Beside me, Marlowe growled low in his throat.

"What is it, boy?" I whispered, straining to listen. A floorboard creaked. One of the rafters settled. My breath lodged in my throat.

And then I heard it. Gravel crunching in the driveway. Marlowe leapt from the bed and was at the front door, leaping and jumping. I slid past the kitchen counter, slowing only enough to grab the cast-iron frying pan. I was using the frying pan twice in one week. Rachael Ray, eat your heart out.

Frying pan in hand, I scrambled past the front hall and into the foyer just as a knock sounded at the door. I peeked out the window, looking for the cop, and saw nothing. I took a deep breath and muttered, "If that's you, Selena Obregon, you should know that paybacks are hell."

I glanced back at the clock on the DVD player. Three AM. Who in the hell would be knocking on my door at three AM? Marlowe yipped and bounced and warbled at the door. No growling, no bristling, so it was someone we knew. That pissed me off even more.

Clutching my robe more tightly, I stormed to the door and flung it open, frying pan raised, swearing like a sailor.

"Somebody better be dead," I yelled, then immediately pulled back. "Logan?"

He stood there looking tall and dark in the night. He was also dirty and tired, with a big rip in his shirt, and he was holding a very large, very ugly, hissing, writhing orange demon of a cat. The cat was quite possibly the poorest excuse for an animal I'd ever seen. He left eye was sealed shut, one ear was missing, and one fang protruded from his thin, black lips.

"What on earth?" I sputtered, swinging the door wider. "Come in and put that thing down."

"I was hoping you'd say that," he said, with one of his sheepish Harrison Ford grins. He winced as the cat scrabbled at the bandages on his right shoulder.

As Logan stepped inside, he bumped the door closed and admonished Marlowe to leave the cat alone. I raced down the hall and slammed the bedroom door right in Muse's little tennis ball-shaped face.

Logan released the beast. The yellow demon bounced onto the hardwood, ricocheted off the chair, and began racing around the living room, yowling like a wounded banshee.

Brows raised, I stared at Logan.

"Puck's cat," he said. "It was Puck's trailer that caught fire. The cat was trapped in a burning shed near the trailer. It's the only thing that made it out of the fire."

"You went into a fire after Puck's cat?" I said, and my heart opened a little bit wider.

"Name is Tarrantino. I was, uh, hoping you could keep him a couple of days."

"As in *Quentin* Tarrantino?" I asked.

"You said it yourself: everyone's a producer."

"Any word on Obregon?" I said, and Logan said, "I'll find her," and I knew all the way to my heart that he would.

I looked over at Marlowe, who was watching the yowling cat with keen interest, ears pricked, the tip of his tongue sticking out of his mouth.

"You know," I said, nodding at the dog. "I'm kind of in the middle of the last favor you asked of me."

"Joint custody," Logan said, and grinned.

"I'm going by Faith's tomorrow to check on her. If she doesn't want the cat, I'll talk to Burt Buggess, the guy at the pet store. If anybody can love that cat, it'll be the Bug."

"Yeah, about that," Logan said. "If the sister doesn't want him, I'll take him."

I stared at him. "*You'll* take the cat?"

The cat had apparently finished racing around the room and settled down to extend his claws and make confetti out of my couch.

"Logan," I said. "Have you ever had a cat before?"

"Well, no."

I stared at the cat, who was growling and chewing his tail. "This isn't exactly a starter cat."

Logan rubbed the back of his neck, looking like the words coming out of his mouth were a surprise, even to him.

"Yeah, I just…" He blew out a breath and stared at the ceiling.

And in that moment, I knew. Silently, I thought, *This, Mama. This is why you put up with it.*

"Yeah." I went up on tiptoe to kiss Logan on his cheek. "I know."

LOGAN WAS GONE. MUSE was on a shelf in my bedroom closet plotting her revenge and Marlowe was sitting in the hallway, watching Quentin the Cat from Hell systematically destroy my living room. I was at the end of my rope.

"Quentin, no!" I shouted. The one-eared cat ripped a hole in the sofa and was yanking stuffing out of it like it was a box of Kleenex. I ducked into the kitchen and reached for the water pistol Mia had given me to stop Muse from peeing in the ficus. The gift that keeps on giving.

"No!" I yelled at Quentin, aiming straight for the demon cat's nose.

A small stream of water caught the cat by surprise, and he stopped and stared at me. Then he yowled, jumped straight into the air, did a one-eighty and scuttled under the sofa, muttering little cat swears from behind the Queen Anne legs.

"Wow," I said. "Muse usually just gives me a dirty look."

The beast growled an unholy growl, and a big yellow paw stretched out and began shredding the Turkish rug.

The phone rang and I bobbled it and the squirt gun, yelling at the cat. "Knock it off or I'll shoot you again!"

"Did I leave too early?" Logan's voice came over the receiver.

"You always leave too early," I said, sounding as grumpy as the latest addition to my menagerie.

"Yeah, I'm sorry about that," he said, and God help me, I believed him. "I just wanted to tell you you did good today."

Despite the cat, a smile curled my lips and spread all the way through my body. "Back at ya, Brown Eyes," I said in what I thought was a pretty good Bogart.

The cat seemed to calm down and I set the squirt gun on the counter, filling a small bowl of water to set it under the sofa in case the little beast was thirsty.

Logan said, "I mean it. It got ugly out there today, and you stood your ground. You're a helluva reporter, kid."

"Calling me a reporter is generous on your part." I sighed. "And I don't know how great a reporter I am. I have this terrible conflict of interest."

"Am I the interest?"

I grinned. "And the conflict."

"You'll figure it out," he said.

"I have a confession," I said into the phone, my heart kicking up a beat. "I think I have a terrible crush on you." My face flushed with heat, even as I said the words.

He chuckled at that and I said, "No, really, Logan, I feel like an eighth grader at a school dance or something. I get awkward whenever I'm within fifteen feet of you, and I'm telling you this now because it's killing me and I don't know when I'll see you again."

"Well, kid, I may have something like a crush on you, too."

My smile widened. "Every time I talk to you my heart pounds and my tongue gets tied and I don't know what to say."

There was a long silence, and then he said, "Would you know what to do?"

"You mean like kiss you until neither one of us remembers our own names?" I said, my cheeks going hotter at my own boldness.

"We could start there," he said, and lights flashed in my driveway just before a knock sounded at the door.

"Hold on," I said, frustration prickling my voice. "Someone's at the door, and the way my luck's been running he's probably earless and carting a dead canary."

"I doubt it," he said, and as I swung open the door, I found Logan, there in the moonlight, tall and dark and dangerous, even with his bandaged arm. His white shirt was open at the neck, his dark hair mussed, and I took a step back.

My breath caught and my heart pounded in my throat. "I thought you had to leave."

"Got someone else to cover the call."

In one long stride he was in the door.

He swept me into his arms and said, "What's this I hear about kissing me all over?"

My stomach swooped like I was on a roller coaster, and I reached around him and bumped his bandaged arm.

"Logan, your arm," I said.

He grinned a dangerous grin. "Totally worth it," he said, and he kissed me and the earth swayed beneath my feet.

Logan broke the kiss and looked at me, hungry, and heat rushed to my cheeks. I met his gaze, my breath coming hard, and every cell in my body pulsed. He leaned down, brushing his lips to the corner of my mouth, and a moan rose from somewhere deep inside me.

Without breaking his embrace, he kicked the door shut behind him and took the phone from my hand to toss it on the sofa.

"I want you, Cauley," he said against my cheek, and his voice was hard and fast and low. "I want all of you. I wanted you from the moment I saw you breech the police line at the Barnes ranch. I want you right here. Right now."

Well. When he put it that way.

I pressed into him with my whole body and kissed him back, and I felt the floor rush away when he scooped me up into his arms and carried me down the hallway, my heart hammering so hard I was sure he could feel it through the soft knit of my jersey.

He kissed me again, his eyes hard, and my breath went away. I don't know how he got the door open or how he got past Muse, but in the next moment I was on my bed, face flushed, lips tingling, my blood fizzing inside me like warm champagne.

He was over me then, shifting so that his cell phone didn't dig into my hip, and then his lips were on mine, kissing, harder, hotter, and I arched beneath him wanting more, wanting his whole body with my whole body.

"Logan," I whispered and he groaned, reaching beneath my jersey, his large hand, warm, cupping my breast. He smelled like soap and leather and fire and something that was pure Logan, and he moaned then and I moaned too, and my head said "Wait a minute!" but my body said "Yes, now, now, *now!*"

He kissed me again, softer this time, and then he rose, his arms caging me so that our faces were inches apart. He looked down at me with dark eyes the color of melted sin, and I felt myself fall a little more.

"This isn't just an adrenaline drop from the fire. I want you, Cauley," he whispered, his voice husky, and I whispered back, "Yes."

My breath came in small gasps and I leaned up and kissed him, hard, as he slid the soft fabric of my jersey up, over my breasts, off my shoulders, and over my head.

As he looked at me, he exhaled like the breath had been crushed from his body, and a low, gutteral noise came from somewhere deep inside him.

He rolled to his side then, his gaze raking my body as though he was going to eat me alive and I'd be the better for it. Heat flooded my cheeks and I went for the sheet, but his hand gripped my wrist.

"No," he said. "I want to see you."

He kissed me again, and I wanted him with everything inside me. "I want you," I whispered, and he said, "I know."

I went for the buttons on his shirt, needing to feel his warm skin, and his hand closed over mine.

"Patience is a virtue," he said.

"Virtue is overrated."

"Yeah," Logan grinned, "I like that about you."

And then he kissed me, hard, and his lips moved down, feathering over the pulse in my throat. I groaned and moved against him, feeling his hard heat, and he nipped my neck, gently, and moved lower, lower, to my breast, his lips warm as he grazed his teeth along my nipple.

I wanted to scream, but I held his head, his hair soft under my fingers, and he drew me into his mouth. My head fell back and I wondered if this was what it felt like to die happy. His lips trailed kisses down, down, raising chills along my skin, and he flicked his tongue against the soft silk edge of my panties. He looked up at me, his eyes hot with desire.

"What do you want?" he whispered.

A small noise came out of my throat, and I couldn't speak.

His tongue flicked again, up my exposed thigh, stopping at the silk edge. He looked up at me. "What do you want, Cauley?"

"I—I want you," I said, and then he slid my panties aside and his warm mouth covered me, his tongue hard inside me.

Heat pooled in my belly and shot through my veins like warm honey, and I arched up to meet him and he drove again and again and everything inside me seized, up and up, until I couldn't stand it anymore, and then I screamed a small, wild scream as my fists clenched and my body throbbed.

"Yes," he said, his voice hoarse, coming up beside me. He put his arms around me and held me tight as the waves washed over me. He looked down at me, smiling, and I smiled back, spent but wanting more. I went for the buttons on his shirt and he helped so that he was over me, bare chested, his body moving in a rhythm as ancient as time, and I reached for his belt and—*charrrrrring!*

I yelped and drew back like I'd touched a hot stove, and Logan swore a string of inventive swears.

He flipped open his phone, his chest still heaving, and he said "What?" and I was sorry for whoever was on the other end of that call.

His face changed, and he said, "When?"

He nodded then, closing his eyes.

"Yeah," he said. "I'll be right there."

He disconnected and his gaze fell on me, softer now, and I felt something inside me break.

"You have to go?" I said, and my voice sounded small.

"Yeah," he said, slipping back into his shirt. "The marshal that disappeared with Obregon? They found his cell phone."

"Is he okay?" I said, gathering the sheets around me to sit up.

"I don't know," he said, buttoning his shirt. "There was blood on the *send* button."

He buttoned his shirt, a pained look on his face. "I'll be back," he said, and I said, "I know."

He opened the bedroom door, and I heard his footfalls down the hall and then the front door softly click shut. Suddenly, I felt very naked and very alone.

Marlowe came to the edge of the bed and stared at me as I slipped the jersey back over my head.

"How did you get in here?" I said. He laid his head at the end of the pillow, his little white eyebrows moving like he was trying to figure out where Logan had gone.

I rolled over and petted him. "Is it always like this with him?" I asked the dog.

Marlowe whined. "That's what I was afraid of," I said. "So, tell me, puppy, is it worth it?"

The dog jumped up onto the bed and turned twice. He woofed and laid down.

"Yeah," I said, scratching behind his ear. "Me too."

FOURTEEN

"Is she okay?"

Ethan was perched on the corner of my desk, waiting for me the next morning. Just what I needed. I was tired and confused and a little embarrassed about my midnight tryst with Logan. I was more than a little pissed with Selena Obregon for ruining my love life.

I sighed. "I don't know. I called her this morning, and she didn't answer," I told him, moving his legs so I could sit down and log onto my computer. I Googled the Dawes County Sheriff's Department. "I'm calling right now to ask a deputy to go check on her."

I looked around my desk, which had been dusted, straightened, and rearranged. A small bowl of leaves and twigs was wedged between my *AP Style Guide* and the latest Robert Parker hardcover. I sniffed the bowl, which smelled like oranges and foot fungus. "What happened to my desk?"

"Mia and I came in early. She said your feng wasn't shui-ing so we did an extreme office makeover."

I growled. It was way too early in the morning for anyone to be messing with my shui.

"I can't believe you let Faith stay by herself last night," he said, and I put up my hand.

"Ethan, I am tired. I didn't get much sleep last night. I have a headache. I have a horrible ginger cat who hates me. If you keep bugging me, I'm going to give the little beast to you."

Ethan's face fell, and I relented. "Look. I tried to talk her into staying at my mother's or coming home with me, but she just wanted to go to her own house and sleep in her own bed, and that I can understand. She's a big girl, she can make her own decisions."

"I saw her on television," Ethan said. "She didn't look like she was in any shape to stay by herself." He stared at me, processing the information. "When have you had time to get a new cat?"

"It belonged to Puck. There was a fire at Puck's house yesterday, and Logan rescued the cat and now it needs a home."

"And you're taking it by Faith's?"

"I'm going to find Faith and ask her if she can handle it. If she can't, Logan's going to keep it."

Ethan blinked. "The FBI guy is going to keep a cat? The one who looks like John Wayne?"

"I've always thought he looks like Gregory Peck. And calling that big yellow monster a cat is pure charity. Last night it ate my sofa and made Muse so mad she peed in my ficus."

"And now you don't know where Faith is?"

I shook my head. "I found numbers for her mom and that stepbrother of hers, but neither one of them says they've seen her."

"Who's doing the memorial thing for her brother? Is there going to be a wake? You know press is going to want to be there."

I shrugged. "I figure Faith'll do the memorial. She said he was the only family she had, and I figure he felt the same way."

I reached behind Ethan's butt for the phone and called the Dawes County Sheriff's Department.

"Hollis," a familiar nasally voice drawled, and my heart dropped.

"Hey, how's it going?" I said, steeling myself. "This is Cauley Mac-Kinnon. From Team Six?"

"Oh, right. The Obituary Babe."

My eyes rolled back in my head, but I kept my voice steady. "I talked with the on-call guy last night to check on Faith Puckett, the girl whose brother was killed at the courthouse yesterday. I tried to call her this morning, and I didn't get an answer."

"You trying to drum up business for your little obit hobby?"

I ground my teeth. "I was hoping someone might drive by there and take a look. Make sure she's all right."

"The shooting at the courthouse?" he said, bloodlust in his voice. "You think she's involved?"

Not a lot happens in Dawes County, and on the rare occasion a traffic stop uncovers half a joint or a bottle of pain pills, every cop in a fifty-mile radius shows up for the bust. I could tell Hollis was getting a hard-on.

"Faith was there during the shooting, but so was I, and so were a lot of other people," I said patiently.

There was a disappointed silence over the line, and I said, "You think you could give me a call? Let me know if she's there and if she's okay?"

"Oh, sure. Can I get anything else for you? Wash your car? Change your tires?"

My eyes narrowed. "Thanks, but I've got Triple A. And I'd appreciate the call."

He disconnected, and I looked up at Ethan, who was still balanced on my inbox.

"Will he do it?" E said, and I shrugged.

"Probably he'll go check on her because he thinks she's involved with the shooting, but I doubt he'll call me back. Wouldn't want to look pussy-whipped in front of his fellow officers."

Ethan shifted, and my files crinkled beneath him.

"Is there something I can help you with, or have you and Mia decided that you're a necessary addition to my office feng shui?"

"I want to show you something."

He reached behind my computer and produced a video camera.

My brows shot up. "Is that what I think it is?"

Ethan nodded. "I told Puck I'd edit the video for him." He swung out the viewfinder and hit *play*.

I crowded in next to him, watching. The haunting strains of "Broken Wings" shimmered from the camera's speaker, and a tight shot of Faith's eyes, large and dark, swam onto the screen. A shot of her delicate fingers summoning music like magic from the guitar strings, and then a wide shot of Faith onstage, pouring her soul into the collective conscious of the crowd. A close-up of a woman in the audience, mesmerized, a single tear ready to fall, and then back to Faith.

I couldn't tell if I was watching a really good music video or a personal love letter to Faith.

"Did you do this?" I said.

Ethan blushed. "I put it together from Puck's shots."

The music swelled, and the screen faded to black.

Ethan sat quietly, his face strained, eyes ringed red. The boy had it bad.

Sighing, I closed the viewfinder and handed the camera back to Ethan. "I'm going by her place to check on her after work. Wanna tag along?"

With a renewed sense of purpose, Ethan headed back to the mother-ship to perform acts of God on errant computers, and I turned back to the digital grindstone to get some work done. It didn't go well.

The thought of writing Puck's real obituary made my stomach turn. I stared at the blank computer screen. Nothing happened. I kept thinking about Faith and how alone she seemed when Puck died.

When Daddy died, Mama's friends at the Charity League, the church ladies, and Daddy's cop buddies stormed the house with casseroles and kind words, offering to pick up mail, write thank-you notes, and take care of me and Suzanne during the five years that the wheels fell off of Mama's wagon. I thought about all of the ordinary angels who stepped up to the edge of hell and helped pull us through.

Faith didn't seem to have any of that.

I picked up the phone and dialed one of those angels.

"Dr. Toni Basset's office," a young, unfamiliar female voice drawled in a thick West Texas accent.

I smiled. Dr. Toni had obviously employed another stray.

The girl announced me and patched me through, and Dr. T said, "Well, hello, stranger."

"You got a new receptionist," I commented.

"Yeah, your buddy Cantu found her over on Eleventh Street. Needed a job and a place to stay."

I smiled. That was so Dr. T.

And so Cantu.

"I see you've had a rough coupla days. They find that fugitive?"

"Not yet, but they've got the best guy working on it."

I could see Dr. T sitting behind her sleek, black desk, dressed in a conservative gray suit. Her skin was the rich color of mahogany, her hair a closely cropped cap of autumn-tinted curls. Because she was talking to a family friend, she'd have her feet kicked up on her desk, revealing shoes that cost a month of my salary, accented with perfectly polished purple-tipped toes. God only knew how old she was, but I knew she was at least as old as my mama. She didn't look like a shrink, and she certainly didn't look like a former cop.

Her voice was still thick and sweet as dark molasses, even when chiding me.

"I'm sorry I haven't called," I said. "I've, uh, been super busy."

"I'll say. I've seen the news, baby girl," she said. "And I've spoken with your mother. In addition to being caught in the middle of a gunfight, it seems you may have a suitor."

My eyes rolled back in my head. "The jury's still out on that one," I said. "I need a favor."

"Of course you do."

"The informant who got shot… he has a sister, Faith," I said.

"Ah, the one who looked like she's been pulling her hair out?"

"That one. I think she's in real trouble."

"You want to bring her by?"

I grinned. "Thought I'd give her your number, but I wanted to ask you first."

"Mmm-hmm. And how you doin' in all this, Miss Thang?"

"I'm all right," I said. "Really."

"We're behind on lunch," she scolded, and I sighed.

"I know, and I've missed it."

"Well, girl, we're gonna have to do somethin' about that."

"Yes, ma'am," I said. "As soon as I'm finished with this Faith thing."

There was a silence over the line and finally she said, "Cauley, don't get tangled up in this. I know you're identifying with this girl, but remember, people experience trauma differently. This hair-pullin' thing could be a real problem. It could be a form of cutting."

"Cutting?"

"Self-mutilation. See if she'll come in, but don't be surprised if she resists help. And remember, a drownin' swimmer'll pull you under if you don't know what you're doing."

"I know," I said. "I just want to point her toward shore."

"Give her my number. I'll be looking for her call."

As I hung up, I felt like a ninety-five-pound weight lifted from my back, and I turned to my computer to work on Puck's obituary.

I PULLED UP A new Word document and sat staring at the screen, fingers poised over the keyboard, waiting for the words to come. Since nothing brilliant poured onto the screen, I checked my email, where funeral homes updated their death notices throughout the day. And there, among the octogenarians and untimely deaths, was Wylie Ray Puckett. I logged the stats—the bare skeleton of his life—and hit the *Sentinel* website to look at what Mia and I had posted.

I had done my job. The *Sentinel* got the story before anyone else, and because it was a shoot-out at a federal courthouse and an accused terrorist had escaped, the Associated Press was spreading my brief in every newspaper in the United States, but I found it hard to be proud.

I paged down, reading as I scrolled. Mia had captured Puck in a close shot, his cheek pressed to the granite step with that look of stunned silence. You could almost see the life slipping out of him. I swallowed, trying to quell the nausea pooling in my throat.

"FBI confidential informant Wylie Ray Puckett was gunned down in a gale of gunfire as he mounted the steps to the federal courthouse, where he was expected to testify in the trial of suspected Argentinean gang leader Selena Obregon, who managed to escape custody," the web article began, and I nodded. Not bad.

But I ground my teeth as I read on. "In what can only be described as an escalation toward a possible gang war …"

"That's not what I wrote," I said to no one and picked up the phone to dial the City Desk downtown and say it to someone.

"Metro," a familiar voice barked as I glared at the screen.

"What the hell happened to my story?" I growled.

"It needed some punching up," said Rob Ryder, the prototypical News Boy and heir apparent to the *Sentinel's* managing editor position.

"If anything needs punching up, it's you," I seethed.

"Wanna write my obituary, Cauley?" he said, and my eyes narrowed to slits.

"I would," I said, "but I can't think of a euphemism for *dickhead*."

"Now, now. Don't get a twist in your tube top. No need for hostility between friends."

"This isn't hostility. This is beyond hostility. Tanner's my editor, not you. Only predators and long, slimy tapeworms can screw with a story like you can. You keep your nasty little red pen away from my stories, you got it?"

"Let me take you to lunch, and I'll explain the way the big boys do it downtown," he said.

"Why don't you go fetch a newspaper in oncoming traffic?" I said.

I slammed the phone. And then I picked it up and slammed it again for good measure. That's why I don't use a cell phone at work. Slamming a flip phone lacks the brutality for a full-blown snit.

"Cauley," Tanner said, sticking his head out of his office.

The voice of doom, if doom was delivered by a man who looked like Hugh Grant. Sighing, I trudged into the Cage, which is conveniently located right across from my desk, where Tanner can hear every inappropriate snit that pops out of my mouth.

Tanner shut the door behind me, and I hopped up on his desk, scattering the copy he was editing, and crossed my arms, daring him to let me have it.

"Castrating Rob Ryder is probably not the best way to earn yourself a position on the City Desk," he said.

I wanted to say something witty and biting, but he was right and I knew it, so I sat on his inbox and sulked.

"You all right?" he said, studying my face, which was still scratched and bruised. I knew my eyes were bloodshot and probably a little hollow from the three hours of sleep I'd managed.

I smoothed my hair and said, "I'm fine. I'm just working on Puck's obituary."

"And Selena Obregon?"

"When Logan finds her, you'll be the first to know."

Tanner sank into his chair, his face drawn and tired, and reached over the photo of his wife for his jar of red licorice. "You did a good job yesterday. Real good."

"Thanks," I said, ambivalence clouding my judgment. I hadn't been doing this long, and I was creating my own code of ethics as I went.

I knew I'd done my job and I'd done it well. But I wondered if it wasn't chipping away at something inside me—something that needed to stay whole.

Tanner chewed the end of the licorice and then he nodded. "Give it to Shiner."

I stared at him. "What?"

"Give the shooting and Obregon's escape to Shiner."

"Tanner," I said, my voice going up two and a half octaves. "This is my story. *I* broke it. *I* was the one who got caught in the crossfire, *I'm* the one who's been working on it, *I'm* the one with the in."

"And that's why you're handing off to Shiner."

I shook my head, feeling the betrayal all the way down to my bones. "Is this because I'm a woman?"

"It's because you're becoming the story. Again."

"It's because of the burglarizing bird man," I countered.

"That too."

I wanted to scream. "I am an obituary writer. This is an obituary. If you take this away from me, you're taking away the job you gave me."

He rubbed his temple with the palm of his hand. "Writing obituaries is only part of your job, and this is no longer a straight obituary and you know it."

"No, it's a scoop that will get me on the front page, but that's not why I want to do it and you know it," I fumed, so mad I could feel blood boil behind my left eyeball.

"Isn't it?" he said.

And then he delivered the sucker punch. "How are you doing on that gang war research?" he said, and I cringed. I wasn't doing anything at all on the gang war research because I'd been busy trying not to get shot on the courthouse steps.

"I've been asking around," I hedged.

"Asking around and solid research are two different things," he said, and I scowled. But I knew he was right. At this rate, I was going to be stuck on the Dead Beat for the rest of my childbearing years.

Tanner turned back to his computer and logged on. "Give your file on Puckett to Shiner and email what you've got on your computer," he said. "Take the rest of the day off. You look like you've been rode hard and put up wet."

I was being dismissed. "Thanks a lot. You oughta volunteer for the self-esteem hotline. You'd be a real hoot."

I hopped down from his desk, resisting the sudden, violent urge to kick him in the leg. "I'll have solid intel on the gang war to you by the end of the week," I said, swinging the door shut behind me.

"Let the Puckett thing go," he called after me.

"Let the Puckett thing go, my ass," I growled, but I did it under my breath. I'd already sent my career into triage twice this week. I was afraid three times in as many days would send it permanently into the Dead Copy file.

I logged off my computer, grabbed my purse from under my desk, and speed-dialed Ethan's cell phone. "Hey, E? You wanna go see a girl about a video?"

FIFTEEN

"ARE WE GOING TO get the cat?" Ethan wanted to know. He sat in the passenger seat of the Jeep, the hot wind performing some kind of aerodynamic phenomenon off his gelled hair.

"You haven't seen that cat," I said. "Better to go find Faith and make sure she wants it."

I pointed the Jeep up Ranch Road 620, past the new flyover at 183, coughing and sneezing at the limestone and caliche dust the new roads kicked up. Traffic slowed as construction crews scattered about, jackhammering a foundation for future highways and spanking fresh strip malls out of the rugged cliffsides. Progress.

Beside me, Ethan rewound the tape and watched it again, pulling a pad and pen from his messenger bag.

I snuck a peek at his pad and smiled.

"Are you rehearsing?" I said, and Ethan blushed right up to his slightly overlarge ears.

"I just—I know she's upset, and I want to get this right."

After thirty minutes of full-contact driving, traffic diminished. Depressing, tightly packed tract houses slowly gave way to farms and fields pocked with thin, foraging cattle. The wide prairies north of

Austin unfolded into a vast, rolling grassland—or what used to be a vast, rolling grassland.

Despite the rains we'd had back in spring, the drought continued its two-year stranglehold on the state, and the once-green grass was dry and brittle. Hand-painted signs dotted barbed-wire fences, announcing "Horses for Sale." The sky wouldn't rain so hay didn't grow, and the progeny of family farms were making tough choices.

We bumped along Faith's driveway in a gritty cloud of red dust. I glanced down at the clock. A little past five. Yesterday I hadn't seen the barbed-wire fence that wrapped around a small patch of back yard or the sign nailed to a huge live oak that said *NO TRESPASSING: Protected by Smith & Wesson.*

I knew she lived on a fairly big spread, but I hadn't realized how isolated her home was. Several acres back, the remains of a burned-out, blue, two-story farmhouse cast a pyramid-shaped evening shadow that almost reached the trailer.

Daylight didn't do much to enhance my earlier assessment of Faith's home. It was a dingy singlewide that probably came from the factory white, but large colonies of aggressive orange rust ate away at the corners. Large smudges of grayish green mold streaked the metal siding at intervals between the single-paned aluminum windows. The windows themselves were neatly lined with pink and ivory frilly curtains, incongruous with the shabby metal trailer. It reminded me of a silk-lined steel coffin.

"She lives here?" Ethan said, staring at the crumbling, warped trailer. "Alone?"

I nodded. "Get your note cards ready."

I climbed out of the Jeep and Ethan scrambled out behind me, and we mounted the wobbly aluminum stairs.

I knocked.

No one answered.

We both knocked. Nothing.

I knocked again and yelled, "Faith! It's me, Cauley!"

I tried to peek in the peephole. I know you can't see squat from the wrong side of a peephole, but somehow, it never stops me from trying.

"What do we do?" Ethan said, leaning over the rusty railing for a peek in the window.

"I don't know. I've got a bad feeling about this." I bit my lip. "You see anything?"

"Do you count the huge rat sitting on the back of the sofa staring at me?" He grimaced. I would have grimaced, too, but I was five years older than Ethan, and I was trying to be a role model.

The evening air was hot and breezeless, thick with heat and dirt and the slight odor of skunk.

Ethan swallowed hard. "Maybe she's in there and can't answer the door?"

"Yeah," I said, studying the window latch. I climbed over the railing and pushed up hard on the window, grunting with the effort. "I think we're going to have to break it."

"Any problem with using the door?" Ethan said as he tried the knob and it gave.

I stared at him. "Well, sure," I said, climbing back over the railing. "If you want to take the easy way."

Through the open door, I could see that the doorjamb was slightly splintered. I was no expert, but I bet if the crime scene geeks compared this job with my own jimmied lock, they'd probably say it was done with the same type of tool and with the same strength behind it and the same skill set.

I glanced nervously around for Dead Canary Guy or Obregon the Maniac.

There are times to be brave—first one in the water, wearing white after Labor Day. And then there are times to call in the guys—kill the rat, squash the bug, armwrestle any stray homicidal earless guys.

Flipping out my cell phone, I dialed the Dawes County predator patrol. A bored-sounding woman answered the phone, and I identified myself and asked for Sheriff Hollis.

I could hear the theme song from *Desperate Housewives* playing in the background. The woman promptly put me on hold for ten minutes before coming back to inform me that Hollis was out of the office and not expected back.

"If he checks in, will you tell him I called?"

"Oh, sure. I got nothin' else to do."

"I'm checking in on a girl—Faith Puckett. I think she might be in trouble. Is there anybody else you can send over?" I said, and the women let out a beleaguered sigh.

"We're shorthanded right now. Is this an emergency?"

I stared at the splintered doorjamb and then around the rest of the crumbling structure. "I think maybe it is," I said and disconnected.

"Well, what now?" Ethan said, and I peeked inside. It still looked like someone went wild with Pepto-Bismol and a paintbrush, but there was nó sign of visible derelicts with daggers or of the rat.

"Faith?" I called.

No answer.

"Are you here? Are you all right?"

Hearing nothing, I stepped over the threshold and reached for a chair to prop the door open in case the need arose for a hasty escape.

Inside, I hesitated. The place smelled like baby powder and broken promises. It was empty of life, except for maybe the rat. We stepped onto the ivory shag carpet and I felt very much an interloper into a life where I didn't belong.

"Wow," Ethan said, studying the wide-eyed dolls that lined the shelf near the ceiling. "Creepy."

"It kind of is," I said, trying to quell the jitters. "Faith!" I called again.

The living room was even more dismal in daylight. It was small, maybe a hundred square feet, flanked by a short, pink Formica half-bar that separated it from the kitchen. To the left, a narrow hall led to the bedrooms and bath.

From out of nowhere, a little yellow rocket propelled right at my face. I ducked and Ethan said, "What the hell?"

"Shut the door!" I yelled. "That's Keates, Faith's bird!"

Too late. The bird was out, sitting in the tree, chiding me for all he was worth. After an hour-long attempt to catch him, we headed back into the trailer, making sure to crack the window of his "birdie door."

Back inside, Ethan scanned the pink and ivory panorama. "You don't think she's hurt or something, do you?"

"I suppose anything is possible," I said, but the moment I'd walked in, all the little hairs on the back of my neck lifted.

Ethan did a little hand gesture suggesting I go down the hall first.

I stared at him. "With a rat on the loose? If you're kidding, you don't know how to do it very well."

"What?" he said. "You think I should kill the rat?"

"Nobody's going to kill anything," I said. "I hope."

Ethan blew out a breath, ducked behind the small counter, and came back with a spatula.

"Planning on serving it pancakes?" I said.

"Only in self-defense."

We began creeping down the hall.

"Why are we creeping?" I said to Ethan, and he shrugged.

"It just feels like a situation that calls for creeping."

There was a door to the left. I knew from the brief search last night it was a bedroom, and I knocked and waited. Hearing nothing, I let us in through the flimsy door. "I'll take the bed, you take the closet," I said, and Ethan nodded.

The silence was heavy, and I could hear molecules bouncing around in my ears.

I looked behind the curtains and kneeled to pick up the bedspread, holding my breath.

"Did you hear that?" I said.

"Hear what?"

"A scratching noise, like something was moving underneath the floor…"

"I didn't hear—aaaaaahhhhh!"

From the closet floor, a huge, nasty rat stared at us, wide eyed, the very soul of beadiness.

Ethan screamed, and then I screamed too.

The rat leapt four feet in the air, flipped a three-sixty, landed, and scuttled over Ethan's sneakers, scrambling and squealing into the hallway.

"Ew, ew, ew!" he yelled. "I gotta go wash my hands."

"Did you touch it?"

"No, but still…"

"Give me that," I said, and confiscated the spatula from him and headed down the hall toward the bathroom, brandishing the spatula.

"Faith," I called, flinging back the shower curtain, watching carefully for the rat and hoping I didn't happen upon Obregon. The odds that I'd actually whack the rat were right up there at twelfth and never, but it made me feel marginally better.

I bumped into E as I backed out of the bathroom and yelped.

"Jesus, E! Make a noise or something!"

When my heart quit hammering next to my eyeballs, I took in a big breath and we hit the bedroom again, careful of the rat.

"Faith?" I said.

"This time I'll take the bed," Ethan said.

He lifted the old quilt and peeked.

I had opened the closet, checking behind the clothes, when there was another scratching noise. I slammed the door.

"Okay, I think we're done," I said.

"I thought you said there was a crawl space," Ethan said, and I did an inward groan.

"Of course there is," I said, and headed for the laundry area in the hall.

I turned to Ethan. "Hey, you have to come, too."

Ethan trailed along behind me and held open the trap door between the washer and dryer.

"Can you see?" he said.

"No." I dropped to all fours so I could get a closer look, and Ethan dropped too. We peered through the hole into the dry, dusty darkness.

And there it was. The scratching noise.

"The rat," Ethan hissed.

And then the closet door in the bedroom slammed.

"Not unless he learned to slam the door!" I yelled and scrambled to my feet, and Ethan scrambled too and bumped my head. I staggered backward, and we came face to face with a man in a ball cap.

"Shit!" I screamed, and the man screamed too, and he tried to clamber over us and fell, knocking the three of us into a big, struggling, swearing heap.

"Okay, everyone stop!" I yelled, and the struggling stopped. The smell of Jim Beam was so heavy in the air that I could practically see the fumes.

Someone in the pile was sobbing. I knew it wasn't me.

"E, are you all right?" I said, and Ethan stood, straightening his jeans and smoothing his short hair. We both stood staring at the man on the floor.

"Man" was overstating it. More like a kid with a bad beard, a bad hangover, and a bad case of the blues. The one Tres had sucker-punched at the Pier. The one who was deadly in love with Faith.

"Hey," I said to him. "Are you all right?"

He was clutching a photo of Faith. His eyes looked like a roadmap and his breath could choke a charging rhino.

Ethan got a gander at the photo of Faith and bristled. I was glad I'd taken the spatula away from him.

"Josh, what are you doing here?" I said. "Have you seen Faith?"

He shook his head and winced at the movement.

"I can't find her," he said.

Okay. Now I was concerned. "When was the last time you saw her?"

He hedged.

I waited.

"I came by last night. Just to check on her. I saw the news, and I wanted to see if she was okay. See if she needed me."

"Was she okay?" I said, and he shrugged.

I sighed. "You remember what time?"

"I saw you drive up," he mumbled. "You put her to bed."

"You were *stalking* her?" Ethan said. His fist clenched. His thumb was tucked inside his fingers so that if he ever did wind up hitting someone, he'd probably break his thumb. I shook my head.

A deep, guttural growl sounded at the front door. The hair on my neck lifted.

"Well, what have we here?" a familiar voice drawled. I looked up and found Junior Hollis tapping his palm with his billy club, Napalm bristling at his side.

"WE CAME BY TO check on Faith," I said, but my cheeks flushed. This was no time to back down. "Did you come check on her last night?"

"We're just lookin' for my girl," said Josh, and Ethan took a step forward to line up with him. I shook my head. War buddies.

We were all in the living room near the little pink coffee table, frozen like deer caught in headlights.

The big dog snarled and I put my hand out. He sniffed and wagged his tail, and it was Hollis's turn to snarl.

"Faith works at a titty bar and she does her li'l honky-tonk angel thing on the weekends. She's not missing. She's just got what you might call *other interests*." He smiled an ugly smile.

"Nothing so needs reforming like other people's habits," I said.

"You gettin' smart with me, blondie?" Hollis said, but Josh and Ethan looked like they were going to team up and pound the hell out of Junior Hollis. I stepped between them and the sheriff. There was no need to go to jail over this, and it was quickly heading that direction.

I glared at Hollis. "It doesn't worry you that her brother got shot less than twenty-four hours ago, and now no one's seen her since last night?"

"That happened in Travis County. We don't put up with that kinda shit here in Dawes County, and ever'body knows it. You do the crime in this county, you do twice the time. We got a reputation, and we like it that way."

"But you don't look for missing girls?"

"You said yourself you saw her at eleven o'clock last night. It's not even twenty-four hours. She ain't missing yet."

I ground my teeth. "You and I both know the longer you wait, the harder it's going to be to find her."

At that moment, Keates swooped through the window and dove into his open cage. Napalm went airborne after the bird.

Without blinking, Hollis swiveled and hit the dog on the nose with his club. The dog landed. He didn't whine but his eyes got a surprised, withdrawn look. Hollis went for the dog.

A small noise came from the back of my throat, and I extended my foot at the toe of his polished boot.

Ethan grabbed for my arm, but he was too late. Hollis tripped over my foot and he fell hard. His big, red-veined nose caught the coffee table on the way down, and he came up holding his face, blood oozing between his fingers.

He looked down at his bloody hand.

"You did that on purpose!" he sputtered.

"What?" I said. "It was an accident. I have witnesses."

The dog came and sat beside me. I scratched him behind the ear.

Hollis got to one knee and heaved himself up, a big vein throbbing on his forehead.

For a minute, I thought he was going to hit me. Ethan stepped between us.

The sheriff breathed hard, wiping his bloody nose on his sleeve. He stared at me, eyes bulging like they might pop right out of his crew-cut skull.

"That's it," Hollis growled, looking down at the blood dripping off his hand.

He grabbed my arm, yanking it away from Ethan, and before I knew it, I was cuffed and stuffed and in the back of the prowler, flanked by Ethan and Josh.

SIXTEEN

"He hit the dog?"

"In the head with a sap," I said.

Cantu nodded. "Even so, you can't go around tripping people."

"Can't or shouldn't?" I said. "And calling Hollis *people* is pushing it."

I was boiling mad and getting hotter. "And a Class A Misdemeanor?" I huffed as Cantu leaned over the back seat and handed me and Ethan our shoelaces. "I was just trying to help. I can't believe I have a *record*." I blew out a breath. "I bet Daddy is rolling in his grave."

"I expect he's proud right about now. It's your mother you got to worry about."

"Well, I vote that none of us tell her," I said, yanking my shoelaces into a double knot with a lot of unnecessary force.

Ethan still looked shell-shocked, so I laced his Converses for him.

"I expect you can get it expunged, if he even filed it at all," Cantu said.

"How come he's keeping Josh?" I said, giving E's laces a double knot, too.

Cantu shrugged. "Said he had to talk to him. Take care of some business."

"Can he do that?" I frowned, and Cantu nodded.

Resigned for now, I muttered, "Thanks for baling us out."

Cantu nodded. "You call Logan?" he said, and I blushed.

"Got his voice mail."

Cantu nodded. "You really think this girl is missing?"

"I don't know. It just doesn't seem right. And up until Hollis hand-cuffed us, he didn't seem to think checking on Faith was a big deal."

"What makes you think it is a big deal?"

"Well, let's see. Her brother got shot. Someone burned down his trailer. Nobody has seen or talked to her since last night...shall I go on?"

Cantu rubbed the back of his neck. "And this Josh character is stalking her?"

"I'm not sure he's actually stalking her. I think he's just worried about her," I said, and Cantu looked at me skeptically.

He pulled up in front of my Jeep, which was still in front of Faith's trailer.

"What does it take to put out a missing persons report?" Ethan asked. He'd been listening, quiet, so he didn't miss anything.

Cantu shrugged. "Usually a family member contacts the appropriate law enforcement agency to file an MPR. They get entered into the National Crime Information Center files by the agency who took the report," Cantu said.

"And in this case, the agency would be Hollis and his merry band of nitwits?" I said.

" 'Fraid so."

"Hollis said it hasn't been twenty-four hours yet," Ethan said, and Cantu nodded.

"Well, that's where it gets sticky," he said. "Doesn't matter how long it's been, but cops tend to take in the circumstances before they get excited about a missing person. With a kid, it's different, usually under the age of fifteen. They call the dogs and the 'copters and light a fire under the media. But with older kids and adults, it's wait and see."

"Why?" Ethan was leaning forward now, white-knuckling the console.

Cantu sighed. "Because some people say they've been abducted to explain a big chunk of time they were doing something they shouldn't have been doing."

Ethan looked scandalized.

Cantu shook his head. "Happens a lot more often than you think. Don't guess I could talk you into staying out of this," Cantu said. "Hollis isn't a good cop, but he's lead dog in his county. Probably not a good idea to start a war with him."

"I think I already did."

Cantu sighed. "What are you going to do now?" he said.

"I don't know. What kind of misdemeanor is stealing a dog?"

IT WAS LATE WHEN I got home, and I owed Ethan big-time for taking Tarrantino, the cat from hell, off my hands. I called Logan and left him a message telling him the cat was at Ethan's until he got back. I told him Faith was missing, conveniently leaving out the part about breaking and entering, then assaulting a police officer and getting fingerprinted at the Dawes County jail.

I fed Muse and took Marlowe for a short walk, too tired to encourage him to pee on the Bobs' rosemary bush. It was well past dark but still hot. Marlowe and I went through the garage and out the back to turn on the hose. Within moments, five deer peered from the shelter of the live oaks at the rim of the back canyon. I knew there were more that I couldn't see, waiting for the forward scouts to flash them their white-tailed *okay* sign. Two of the deer had thick necks and velvety antlers—

allies on the hunt for food. In two more months they'd be rivals, fighting for territory and females. I shook my head. Men.

I filled Daddy's battered old green Coleman cooler with water, then sat with Marlowe on the back porch, watching in the high blue light of the swollen moon. Muse sat in the windowsill, flicking her calico tail. She wanted to see the deer but declined coming outside, still in a snit over Puck's one-eyed orange cat.

I gazed out at the deer. The Bobs were always on me about watering them, blowing steam about survival of the fittest and all that crap. Who would have thought the Bible-thumping Bobs would be standard-bearers for Darwinism?

Watching the drought-stricken deer drink thirstily from the cooler, I thought about Puck and Josh. I thought about the way Logan had stood up for them. He'd made sticking up for the little guy his whole life. I smiled. Captain America incarnate.

Marlowe sat beside me, the moon glinting blue off his white face, his white chest puffed, the tip of his tongue showing as he watched the deer. There was no animosity between him and the foraging animals.

"All creatures great and small," I told him. He didn't have anything to say to that.

"Ya know, you're supposed to be search and rescue. We've got to do something about Faith and Sheriff Hollis's poor dog."

He bumped me with his pointy white nose, and I stroked his ears.

"People are saying Faith's not missing and that Hollis's dog is none of my business."

Marlowe stared at me without blinking.

"Well, buddy, I told Logan I'd watch out for Faith." I turned off the porch light. "I'm about to make it our business."

DESPITE THE FACT THAT I was so tired I thought my bones might fuse together, I couldn't sleep. Much to Muse's discontent, Marlowe and I sacked out on the sofa, numbing out in the black-and-white clarity of an Ingrid Bergman marathon on Turner Classics. *Gaslight* was playing, and obsessive Charles Boyer had Bergman trapped in her own home, convincing her she was a danger to herself and too crazy to leave him.

Marlowe took up more than his half of the sofa, his head on my legs, while Muse perched on the back of the sofa, tail twitching her displeasure. Marlowe grumbled, settling in.

"Don't worry," I said to Marlowe. "Ingrid Bergman always gets the right guy. Sometimes she gets two."

I watched as the movie flickered in the dark and realized that's not what I liked about the film. It was the fact that Bergman found a hidden strength—a courage she didn't realize she had. She stepped up to her abusive husband and made the final call.

Onscreen, Bergman and Cotten watched as the bobbies carted the crazed, evil husband off to get his just deserts.

I stared at the television. "You ever notice how Ingrid Bergman has guys falling all over her while the rest of us wind up sleeping on the sofa with a dog?"

Marlowe didn't answer, but Muse huffed. She leapt from the back of the sofa, landing on the hardwood floor like a horse. She shot me a pitying look that reminded me of the look Aunt Kat gives me when she's lecturing me on the ways of men.

"You scoff," I said to the cat as she sashayed down the back hall, heading for bed. "I have a man. Sort of. Somewhere.

"Maybe that's the book I should write," I said to Marlowe. "*Everything I Know About Men I Learned from My Aunt's Cat.*"

Marlowe snorted, and I sighed. "Everyone's a critic."

Annoyed, restless, and tired, I resorted to abusing Benadryl at approximately two in the morning and dreamed of Ingrid Bergman trapped by a man gone mad with obsession, power, and lust.

The phone rang and I woke with a yelp, snatching the sheet up to my chin. The phone rang again, and Marlowe growled. So it was with great displeasure and through a Benadryl-induced haze that I fished the phone from beneath his pillow.

"Somebody better be dead," I growled into the receiver.

"Close." Cantu's voice sounded tired and grim.

I waited.

"Cauley," he said. "There's been another fire."

SEVENTEEN

THE SMELL OF BURNING flesh is something you never forget.

When I was a little girl, not more than three, Daddy came home very late one night. I stood upstairs at the railing, quiet, watching as every light in the house blinked on. Mama hurried Daddy into the kitchen and sat him at the table and put some tea on to boil.

He was in uniform, but it was torn and charred. His handsome, dark head rested in his hands, his elbows braced on the table. Mama, dressed in a flowing white peignoir, had his cheek pressed to her breast, her pretty blond head resting lightly on his. She was crying and crooning something I couldn't hear. I crept down the stairs and into the archway, silent in my little pink footie pajamas, into the kitchen. And then it hit me.

A smell like nothing else on this earth. Sickening and strangely sweet, like burning hair and rotten pork, but worse, so much worse—something primal about it said *Danger here, stay away*.

I vomited all over my footie pajamas.

Climbing out of the Jeep in Faith's driveway, I felt that same awful urge as I stood next to Cantu. He watched as two Dawes County deputies roped off the perimeter. The trailer was barely identifiable. It looked more like an explosion than a fire. Twisted metal littered the charred grass like aluminum confetti.

"Marlowe, no!" I yelled as the dog dragged me toward the smoldering structure.

Four volunteer firefighters aimed a large hose at the blaze, doing little to douse the inferno.

Hair standing on his neck and tail out straight, Marlowe made a beeline for the area where the bedroom was, wound two tight circles, and made his peculiar little barking noise.

Oh, hell. His alert signal. I patted Marlowe on the head and did the *good dog* thing, but my heart was pounding. "Is she in there?" I said, and Cantu shrugged as he jogged forward to join us.

"Looks like your dog thinks she is," he said, staring down at Marlowe. "The guys are around back, looking. Keep a good hold on the dog."

Marlowe's ears were pricked, his body stiff as his eyes darted from me to the trailer and back.

"Easy, boy, they've got it under control," I said, the heat from the fire scorching my face.

The night was hot, made hotter by the flames and the acrid smell of death. The fire had moved beyond the building, unleashed like a wild beast on the dry acres of prairie behind the trailer.

My heart pounded as I craned to see into the flames. "You're not running the scene?" I said, and Cantu shook his head.

"Out of my jurisdiction."

"But you think it has something to do with Puck, who *is* in your jurisdiction."

"No such thing as coincidence."

The knot in my stomach tightened. "Sheriff Hollis is on the way?"

Cantu nodded. His eyes swept the horizon, watching for the seen and the unseen.

Marlowe shifted from paw to paw, waiting, listening.

The stench was getting worse. Salt pooled in my mouth, beads of sweat formed on my upper lip. I pulled the bottom of my tee shirt up to breathe through it, hoping I wouldn't throw up. An older man with a bushy mustache and a volunteer fire department uniform rolled another large hose from the rack of a second water truck, putting out brush fires that roared over the back pasture, which threatened the neighbors and, after that, the town.

The trailer itself was nearly unrecognizable, and in its place was a wet, smoldering shell spilling the charred, pink remnants of pillows and curtains like entrails. Little rivers of watery, black soot washed around fire-blackened china dolls that lay cracked and broken in the rubble, wide-eyed, as though in a state of permanent shock. A memory boiled up through the flames—Puck, lying on the courthouse steps, with that same look of shock.

I missed my footie pajamas.

Behind the remnants of the trailer, a battalion of volunteer firefighters and neighbors battled the fire as it raced across the dry grasslands, heading toward the old burned-out farmhouse and beyond.

Near a big, gnarled pear tree at the corner of the metal frame, a tall, lanky man stood alone, staring at the fiery mess. His shoulders slumped, and he clutched the tattered remains of a black notebook. His face was dark with soot, a streak of ruddy skin showing through the dirt. Had he been crying?

"Josh?" I said, and his head jerked up. His blue eyes were an ocean of grief, made bluer by the red-rimmed lids. "What are you doing?"

He stared down at the remains of the notebook. "Her music," he said, his voice rough, like he'd been chewing broken glass.

"Probably they're going to need that for evidence," I said. He nodded but didn't move.

A voice called from the smoking, twisted metal that was once a back bedroom. "We're bringing her out!"

Josh dropped the notebook and ran into the wet, smoldering dregs, leaping over bent metal and rubble.

Marlowe went wild as two EMTs dressed in fire gear picked their way through the wreckage. Marlowe circled and warbled, and through the smoke, the men carried a stretcher. Marlowe jerked hard against his leash, dragging me toward them, showing the full force of his husky heritage.

The EMTs settled the litter near the fire truck and knelt over a small, thin body as Josh rushed forward.

"Sir, this is a crime scene," the older man said, his voice firm but not unkind as he held an oxygen mask over her nose.

Josh didn't move. We stood staring, unable to look away. The fire had disintegrated most of the girl's clothing. The rest melted into the small islands of flesh that clung stubbornly to her bones. Her face seemed small and pinched, and what was left of it was pierced. Her dark hair was melted and charred, clinging like a Brillo pad to her scalp.

"Is she alive?" I said, panic twisting my insides.

"Barely," the EMT said, his voice jagged and brusque. "We're going to stabilize her and fly her to the burn unit at Brookes. Chopper's on the way."

Josh was quiet, staring at the girl on the stretcher.

I gagged at the smell and blinked back tears.

"It's not her," Josh whispered.

We turned to look at him.

Josh shook his head. "That's not Faith."

"You sure?" I said, and he nodded, gently touching the girl's damaged arm.

She stirred, but her swollen eyes were seared shut.

He pulled up his sleeve, revealing a tattoo of half a heart; inside, green letters spelled out *FAITH*.

"She has one just like this," he said.

"She had a scar there," I said, remembering the pink patch of skin and the fading letters that once spelled out her first love's name.

He nodded. The girl's skin was burned from her hands to her elbows, like she'd been shielding her face. There was enough fragile skin to show she hadn't been tattooed.

"Then who's this?" Cantu said, nodding toward the girl on the litter.

Josh shook his head. "I don't know, but it's not Faith."

Bare-faced and without breaking a sweat, Cantu looked more closely at the burned shape that used to be a girl.

And then he nodded. It was a short, sharp nod, and he hit the radio on his epaulet. "Base," he said. "It's Cantu. Call in the dogs."

THE FIRST RESPONDERS FOR Team Six arrived within thirty minutes. Olivia was first on the scene, armed with the base trailer, cases of bottled water, and two giant aluminum 100-cup coffee makers. The Army runs on its belly; SAR mainlines caffeine.

I watched as team leaders set up for the search with that odd, breathless sense I always get when I hear the National Anthem.

Olivia had already set up the recharge station, the area where handlers and dogs come to cool off. Even though the team would begin the procedure as a night search, temperatures wouldn't dip below eighty. The dogs would have to be rested and rehydrated more often, whether they liked it or not.

Olivia was busting out extra equipment. Apparently she thought we were going to be here a while.

A cold chill coiled in my stomach. "Whoever did this thought that was Faith, didn't they?"

"We don't know it's arson yet," Cantu said. "But the same thing happened to her brother's trailer two days ago, so that'd be my guess."

I followed Cantu to the staging area, where he barked orders into the controlled chaos as the number of responders swelled. Cantu had Rimmer and Moreno and their dogs out running preliminary searches, starting with the old farmhouse and then following the fence line and the creek as funnels, structures likely to influence a missing person's travel. The wind was picking up, blasting the heated air around like a convection oven. My skin was dry and gritty, and I could feel my lips chapping by the moment. I made a mental note to stock lip balm along with the sunscreen and bug repellent in my SAR fanny pack.

News crews roared onto the scene, hooking up satellite feeds in case we found a body or a clue or a map to Jimmy Hoffa.

Miranda's van slid into view. She stepped out, looking as flawless as ever. Journalist Barbie: comes with her own microphone and matching shoes. Probably had her own lip balm.

I watched Cantu as he watched her brush red dust off one of her bare legs. "Hey, are you going to be ops leader?"

He blinked and shook his head. "Dawes County jurisdiction. Six is here as a courtesy."

"Right," I grumbled. That was bad news for Faith.

Not knowing what else to do, I called Logan and left another message. It was nearly nine, and I looked up at the darkening sky and wondered where he was and if he was all right. I wondered whether he'd respond if I sent up the bat signal.

Beside me, Marlowe whined.

"Cauley," Cantu said, jarring me back to the task at hand. "You're still an apprentice. You gotta stay at base."

My heart dropped. "I'm not going to stand around to man communications and pass out Band-Aids," I said.

"You got training in media. We need you here for coms. Get photos of the girl and her stats out to every media outlet you can raise. We'll talk about the rest."

He pulled a compact digital camera from his fanny pack and tossed it to me.

"What's this for?"

"I want shots of all the volunteers and lookie-loos that show up. I'm having the geeks set you up a station at base."

"You think the person responsible for the fire will be in the crowd?"

"Almost always are."

I stared down at the small camera. "And you're choosing me for this duty because I'm nonthreatening and no one will ask why I'm taking pictures?"

"It's because you're cute and I trust you with the job."

I growled. I hate cute. Cute is for kittens and fuzzy bunnies.

But since I had no argument for that, I snapped a few wide shots of the assembled teams, then pocketed the camera and headed back for base with Marlowe in tow. He strained against the leash, eager to join the column of handlers and dogs. I knew how he felt.

I thought about my job at the newspaper—my quest to get off the obits and onto a real beat. Some things never change.

"Easy, killer," I told the dog. "We're on coffee and cookie patrol."

The dog whined.

I patted his head. "For now."

OLIVIA HAD ALREADY SET up the radio feed and was arranging maps and mission logs when a brown and white prowler screeched up the dirt driveway, spewing red dust and gravel as it spun to a stop. Hollis climbed out of his car, his dog clambering out after him. The dog snuffled about, probably looking for someone to bite. He should have considered taking a chunk out of his handler.

Hollis was dressed in full cop regalia, from trooper boots to big brown Stetson. His nose was still red where he'd miscalculated the proximity of my foot.

I smiled. Who says no good deed goes unpunished?

"Everything's under control," he announced to no one, which was okay because no one paid him any mind. He hiked up his belt and looked at Cantu. "Thanks, pal, I got it from here. Got deputies out doin' interviews, gatherin' intel. We'll meet back here at twenty-three hundred to brief the team leaders."

His gaze caught mine and he faltered, puffing his chest out. Animals do that when they're establishing territory. I wondered if Hollis was just going to get it over with and pee on my leg.

"What's she doing here?" Hollis growled, and Cantu stretched out to his full length, reminding me of a jungle cat, his tightly coiled muscles ready to spring.

"Cauley's assisting me on coms," he said.

"Not on my op she doesn't," Hollis sputtered, craning his reddening face at me. He was sucking on the ragged end of an old cigar and made a blatant attempt to blow the blue smoke in my face.

I smiled pleasantly, brought up the camera and snapped a photo.

Later I would make a to-do list, and at the top of it I would write *Annoy the hell out of Junior Hollis*, and then I would check it off with the satisfaction of a job well done.

Cantu squeezed the bridge of his nose like he had a headache coming on. "Hollis, she works at a newspaper. It makes sense she organizes the message."

"And speaking of message, here comes Miranda," I said. Hollis's head swiveled in her direction, and he sucked in his big stomach.

Men are so predictable.

"You know," I lied through my teeth, "she's an old friend of mine, and she'll be running the live feed for KFXX. Want me to introduce you?"

He rolled the cigar along his lower lip, and I almost felt sorry for Miranda. Then he grinned. "Let me get Napalm. Chicks dig dogs."

I thought about Faith, wondered where she was and if she was all right as I watched Hollis preen for Miranda.

Good to know his priorities were in order.

"WHAT GETS SAID IN here stays in this tent 'less I say so," Hollis announced, sucking on his cigar. He started the presentation twenty minutes late to reiterate that we were snuffling around in his territory. "Detective Cantu has agreed to sit in on this meeting as a consultant."

It was hot and dark and musty in the tent. The body heat from half a dozen hot, tired cops and team leaders made it that much worse.

My back was damp with sweat as we sat in rows of rickety metal chairs that reminded me of Sunday school.

A twentysomething, buzz-cut deputy I didn't recognize flicked on a PowerPoint presentation. The first slide spelled out "Operation Finding Faith" on the front wall of the tent. I wondered if Hollis was going to include theme music.

Hollis paced in front of the projected image, chewing his cigar, hands clasped behind his back, channeling General Patton. Napalm sat quietly near the speaker, eyes following as Hollis paced.

I leaned toward Cantu. "I am going to figure out a way to get that dog."

"Aren't you already in enough trouble with Hollis?" he whispered back.

Hollis pulled out an aluminum telescopic pointer, flicked it out to its extended length, and slapped it at the image on the makeshift screen. On cue, a photo of Faith appeared.

"We are here today in search of Faith Puckett," he announced.

It was an older photo of Faith. Long, dark hair; lovely, large eyes—Audrey Hepburn in another life.

Hollis cleared his throat. "Caucasian, eighteen years of age, small stature, 'bout ninety pounds. Last time she was seen, she was wearin' … " Hollis shuffled his notes, waiting for his deputy to switch screens. "Pink Barbie pajamas?"

Hollis looked at me, and I nodded.

Onscreen, the photo faded, and a new one took its place: Faith fronting a band that looked like a bunch of choir boys. Her hair was still long, but it was pulled back, and she wore the same green John Deere tee shirt I'd seen her in at the Pier. I pondered the significance.

"She smoked Camels, lit them with matches, so be on the lookout for butts and wooden matches. She was last seen at her home at approximately twenty-three-hundred hours yesterday. There's been no movement on her bank account or credit cards, no calls on her cell."

I noticed the way he spoke about her.

One of the main things I've learned since I began my gig on the Dead Beat is that most of the time, the deceased are still referred to in the present tense. Faith hadn't been gone an entire day yet and Hollis was already referring to her like she'd gone to smash guitars in that big punk band in the sky.

"Now," he said, slapping the canvas. A map flashed into view, a twenty-mile perimeter marked in red around the Point Last Seen.

"His perimeter's not wide enough, is it?" I whispered to Cantu. "And that was twenty-four hours ago. We got what, another twenty-four hours before we got a snow cone's chance in Hades of finding her?"

Cantu nodded. "You've been studying."

"I have a good teacher," I said. His dark skin went a little crimson, and I smiled.

"Now," Hollis said, whacking the pointer against his palm. "We've interviewed friends and family and have drawn some conclusions that should help narrow the search.

"As you know, the subject was involved in the shootout at the federal courthouse. Her brother was s'posed to testify against Selena Obregon, the leader of a gang who call themselves El Patron. Obregon is in the wind, and El Patron may be on the move."

Hollis rustled his stack of papers. "Other things to consider. The subject was in the middle of a record deal that could have made her a target, but..." He waited as the slide switched.

"The subject worked at an *establishment* called Boners," he said, and a series of masculine hoots went up around the dusty air.

"We supposed to go brace witnesses?" a young deputy quipped.

Next to me, Cantu's jaw muscle clenched.

Smiling, Hollis slapped the smirking deputy on the back. "Do what you feel you need to do, Willis, but the county don't pay for lap dances."

I raised my hand. "Why is this necessary?"

Hollis shot me a look reserved for the very young and the very stupid.

"Because, princess, we're attempting to establish a suspect, a motive, and an opportunity."

Nodding, I raised my hand again. "But she wasn't there that night. At the club, I mean."

"Far as we know," he said. "You got any idea what kind of perverts hang out at that kinda place? A girl works at a rundown strip joint, it widens the number of suspects."

My blood began to percolate, and he motioned the deputy manning the PowerPoint to continue.

"These are photos of the subject's room at her mama's house," he went on.

A wide shot of an expensive-looking Tuscan-style home shimmered against the tent wall.

"The subject's father died some time ago; the mother married Cullen Ainsworth II." The slide faded to a back yard shot of paradise, complete with an elaborate pool with a vanishing edge that appeared to fall into the main basin of Lake Austin.

"As you can see, the girl's mother married well."

Another chorus of snickers.

I have been around cops my whole life. I know that humor is a defense mechanism, but this humor showed no hint of defense. These guys were not taking Faith's disappearance seriously, even with a burned body. I got a sudden urge to kick Hollis in the leg and steal his dog right then and there.

Hollis cleared his throat. "We have not had a ransom call or any contact from anyone claiming to have kidnapped or harmed the girl."

The slide changed, and a beautifully appointed white and ecru room appeared, followed by a shot of a closet full of neatly aligned sweater sets on wooden hangers.

It had all the warmth and coziness of a nudist at the North Pole.

"This is the girl's room. You can see that she was provided every conceivable comfort... "

He motioned for a slide change. "Yet she chose to live here."

A digital shot I'd taken of the burned-out trailer.

"From what we figure, we got a number of possible scenarios," he went on, glancing over at Cantu for approval.

"One: a gangland payback based on the fact that her brother was on his way to testify against an up-and-coming gang moving in on Syndicate territory. Two: a boyfriend didn't like the fact she might be going big-time with her music and wanted to keep her all to himself. Three: some client at the club decided to pop his cork. Or four: she did it herself."

I sat stunned, forgetting the metal chair digging into my tailbone.

I looked over at Cantu, who was frowning.

I didn't bother to raise my hand this time.

"What do you mean *did it herself?* Her house is burned down, a woman who looks like her is burned beyond recognition, not to mention her brother, the only family she's got, is dead."

Hollis's voice rose. "She chose her burnout of a brother over her mother and a good life in a big house—a far cry from that run-down piece of shit she was living in." Crimson flushed Hollis's face, and I thought he might be heading for a stroke. "Maybe she found a way to get out of that hellhole she was in. We got to take that into consideration. This is America, Miz MacKinnon. You got a right to disappear if you want to." He drew in a lot of air and held it. "We're done here for now," he said. "See Olivia for assignments."

We were being dismissed.

"Cauley, can we talk a minute?" he said, giving me that cop-eyed stare meant to make me quiver in my undies.

All it did was make my lip curl.

Cantu hung back as the searchers and volunteers set about their tasks. Together, we waited for Hollis to get to the point.

Hollis squinted at Cantu, and I could see he wanted the detective to take a hike. I did an inward smile. Apparently, Hollis didn't know much about Cantu. Duty, honor, and damsels in distress were his specialty.

"Look," Hollis said. His voice rasped like he was having some control issues, and I knew it was some stupid guy thing about wanting to rip me a new one while maintaining Cantu's respect.

Ignoring me, he went straight to Cantu. "I'm giving her some latitude because she's a friend of yours. But don't think for a minute she gets special favors."

Cantu didn't move.

"And I swear to God any of this winds up in the papers without my say-so, I'm going to chicken-fry her liver for lunch."

Cantu said nothing. There was something bigger going on in the room that I wasn't privy to, and then Cantu said, "You ready?"

He was talking to me.

"Oh. Yeah," I stammered. "I just—yeah."

I retrieved Marlowe from Olivia, and Cantu walked me to my Jeep. At that moment, every ounce of adrenaline drained from my body, and my blood felt like cold sludge running through my veins.

"You okay?" he said, and I shook my head.

"I'm just really tired all of a sudden."

Marlowe and I climbed into the Jeep, and Cantu waited until the key in the ignition jarred the engine into gear.

He was quiet for a long time.

"I know he's got you pumped, but this isn't fun and games," he finally said. "People are dying. There's a federal witness dead, a girl burned, and a girl missing, and we don't know why."

I nodded, but I said, "Yet."

Cantu stared at me for a long time. He shook his head. "God, you remind me of your dad sometimes."

A slow smile spread over my face. I leaned out of the rattling Jeep and kissed his cheek. "That's the nicest thing you've ever said to me."

"You going home?" he said, and I smiled.

"Yes." It wasn't a total lie. I'd go home sometime, but not anytime soon. Cantu looked at me like he didn't believe me, but he didn't say anything.

I hit *reverse* and Marlowe braced himself as we backed up.

"Cantu?" I called over the engine noise.

He turned, moving slowly, like he was trudging through mud. His eyes were hooded and tired.

I smiled at him. "Thank you. And say hey to Arlene for me."

Cantu nodded and smiled. "I'm getting too old for this shit."

I gasped. "Say it isn't so."

He smiled. It was a small smile, but it was enough. I put the Jeep in gear and headed to Copy Mate.

I patted the little digital camera. I had some photos to print, a girl to find, and a dog to save. Life, sometimes, is complicated.

EIGHTEEN

I CALLED LOGAN ON his cell, prepared to leave him a message as I headed down I-35 toward the all-night Copy Mate near the university.

The phone clicked on, and instead of the standard hello, Logan said, "I heard you had an interesting night."

A couple of interesting nights, if you counted my midnight liason with Logan. My cheeks flushed, and I said, "Hello to you, too. How is it that you always seem to know what I'm doing?" I wasn't sure if I should be irritated or flattered. In truth, it made me feel safe.

"Where are you? Are you okay?" I said.

"I'm fine," he said, but he sounded tired.

I noticed he only answered the second part of my question but didn't press it.

"Any word on how the marshal's doing?"

"He's out of intensive care. He should be going home in about a week."

"That's great news. You find any leads on Obregon and her escort?" I said, and he blew out a breath.

"Running down some intel. What about you?"

"Faith. I'm heading to the copy place on campus. Cantu put me on cookie and Kool-Aid patrol, so I spent the evening handing out refreshments and taking pictures of other people searching and rescuing."

"You sure she's missing and not just gone?"

"Her trailer's burned down."

"There's that," he said.

"A girl who looks a lot like Faith got burned like a briquette in Faith's trailer."

"And the girl?"

I shivered; the beautiful girl's burned body, the smell..."She's on her way to Brookes. The EMTs are hopeful."

"Cauley, you gotta be careful," he said, frustration pulsing in his voice.

"I'm being careful," I said, and he was quiet.

"Still no word from Fiennes?" he said.

I was starting to get annoyed. "No, I haven't heard from Fiennes. You think he has something to do with this?"

Logan didn't say anything, and a flicker of fear sparked in my center.

With the phone shrugged to my ear, I rolled into the parking lot and climbed out of the Jeep, leash in hand, wincing as Marlowe nearly yanked my shoulder out of its socket, heading for the door. "Jeez—I feel like my whole body got beat with a ball bat."

"If you know what it feels like to have your whole body beat with a ball bat, then you've got bigger problems than I thought, kid."

"Yeah, I heard you're a funny guy."

"I've heard that, too. As far as the ball bat, it's the adrenaline drop. It'll pass. Eat a banana and take some aspirin. I'd say get some sleep, but I'm guessing that's out of the question. So what happened?"

I told him and he listened, and I knew he was putting the pieces together, looking for similarities, coincidences, and things that didn't belong.

"So what's next?" he said.

"Logan, Hollis is running that mission like a joke. If he was smart, he'd let Cantu lead."

Following the dog into the store, I nearly tripped through the automatic double doors, and I waved at the two night guys manning the register.

Marlowe was still in his bright orange SAR vest, and the guys grinned at the dog as we breezed through the fluorescent, artificially cooled air. That's one of the cool things about service dogs: you can take them almost anywhere. I took a place in the back row of cubicles and pulled the camera out of my purse.

"It's not Cantu's jurisdiction," Logan said.

"If I hear that one more time today I'm going to scream," I said, plugging the camera into the printer. "And Hollis couldn't find his dick with both hands and a flashlight."

"Wow," Logan said. "I'm scared of you."

"Got any advice?" I said, and Logan was quiet.

"Stay out of trouble."

I sighed. "I just feel like I'm not *doing* anything. I mean, Faith was counting on me. I'm the last person to see her before she disappeared." I thought about Josh watching me put her to bed in her Barbie pajamas. I got a very creepy feeling. "Well, I was the last one to *talk* to her. And you should have seen Marlowe. He was ready to roll."

The photo thumbnails popped onto the screen and I hit *print all*.

Logan said, "He'll get his chance and so will you."

The print machine spit photos into the tray, rolling and churning, then it choked and sputtered.

"Damn it! Hold on," I said to Logan. One of the photos wedged between the rollers. Growling, I popped open the front and wrenched at the corner of the photo. I tugged again and it ripped as I pulled. My breath caught.

I held the torn photo, staring down at the girl's burned body—or what was left of her. She had piercings and tattoos similar to Faith's.

I looked again at her charred body and wondered what she'd looked like before the fire. It occurred to me that every body is beautiful when it's healthy.

Staring at the photo, my mind flashed back to Daddy at the kitchen table, leaning on his hands, reeking of burned flesh and the cold, fragile edge of life.

My throat felt tight and tears gathered hot behind my eyes. It was suddenly very clear what I had to do next. I took in some air.

"Logan?"

"Yeah, kid?"

"I gotta go."

"You okay?"

I let my breath out slowly, staring at the torn photo and the broken life it captured.

"Logan?" I said. "I miss you." It came out as a whisper. I hadn't meant to say it, and I immediately wished I could take it back.

There was a long, soft silence, and then Logan said, "I miss you, too."

He was quiet for a moment, and then he said, "You're going to be okay, kid."

He disconnected, and I looked down at the dog, thinking of where we were going next, and sighed. "I wish I could be so sure."

CANTU HAD TAKEN THE bull by the balls and called out Team Six despite the fact that we were in Dawes County jurisdiction. Despite Hollis's participation in SAR training, he wasn't part of Team Six and seemed more interested in the SAR grant money and notoriety than in actually finding Faith. And he certainly wasn't interested in his own dog.

The window of time was closing. I was ready to take drastic measures.

With a very bad taste in my mouth, I called Information on my cell, got the address and number of Boners, and headed south on 183 toward the phallic-shaped neon light that jutted into the night sky, promising those that ventured in a "gentlemen's paradise."

I pulled off 183 at the Travis County line to the tiny, dying cotton town of Bates. My nerves went on red alert. The economic boom that boosted much of Central Texas had missed this area, and it was like a hurricane-struck island left to its own devices. The streets were darker here and covered in a kind of grit that blanketed the streets and windows and drifted like a silent menace in the hot, still air.

An absence of light passed over me, and I shivered despite the summer sun's heat stored in the asphalt. Nearly half the streetlights were broken or burned out, and slippery shadows of hollow-eyed people lurked in the darkness like ghosts of discontent. The houses grew shabbier as I turned down the offstreet, rolling by small clapboard affairs built in the early thirties and the late forties—before and after the great Dust Bowl. The white siding on most of the homes crumbled, and houses were patched together with plywood and waffled corrugated steel. Frayed sheets and duct-taped cardboard lined dirty windows. Iron bars kept family in and strangers out. The ragged remains of white picket fences lined front yards choked with waist-high weeds and the skeletons of long-discarded, rusting cars.

Inside my topless, doorless Jeep, I wished I'd taken the Colonel's advice and bought one of those police auction Impalas. Beside me, Marlowe stiffened.

The club was located on the county line, inside Travis County and about four inches away from Dawes, because Dawes was dry— no alcohol sold or served, which is not to say that people didn't drink. It's the same reason why the churches in Dawes don't allow sex standing up—it's too much like dancing.

Right-turning into the alleyway, I stared at the squat, windowless, dirty stucco building that was Boners. Large, rotting patches of mold ate through the thin layer of pink paint like it was decaying from the inside out.

I looked up at the red neon light that blinked "Boners: A Gentlemen's Paradise," with most of the vowels burned out.

Paradise, I supposed, was relative. Then again, so were gentlemen.

Cantu had once told me there were "tiers" of strip clubs. Apparently, there are expensive clubs employing beautiful young women with enough implants to float a foreign armada, there are mid-level clubs where aging strippers get put out to pasture, and then there are places like Boners, where you could have piercings, tattoos, and probably gangrene, and nobody would notice so long as you were alive, in proximity, and, of course, naked.

I rolled into the parking lot, surprised that my Jeep was the only car in front of the building. And then I saw that around the corner an array of pickups, SUVs, and minivans were practically parked on top of each other in the back lot, safe from prying eyes of wives, mothers, employers, co-workers, and roving revival ministers. And wayward obituary writers.

The building had a dismal look to it, like a three-legged dog with mange. Two bent, phallic-looking palm trees flanked the front door, undulating in a sharp burst of hot wind.

I hoped that wasn't an omen.

My heart thumped. "If Mama finds out we were here, she's going to knock us both into next Sunday," I told Marlowe, whose pointy white nose tipped toward the sky, hot on the trail of a fajita buffet somewhere inside the disreputable-looking building. Thinking about it, there was a whole list of people who'd be pissed as hell: Cantu, Logan, Tanner, my Methodist minister...

I wasn't sure what the dress code was for a strip club. I must have missed that session in Miss Mona's School for Fine Young Ladies.

I just wanted to talk to a few girls, ask some questions, flash the pictures I'd taken of the crowd, see if I could stumble over a clue. What harm could come of that?

I did a quick check in the rear-view mirror and immediately wished I hadn't. The whole search and rescue thing doesn't do a whole lot for your appearance. But really, who was I trying to impress?

"Come on, Marlowe," I said, my nerves on edge. I wasn't sure what to expect. In the movies, Bogey rarely went into strip joints, so my experience was limited.

Aside from the whole naked woman thing, there was something about a bunch of men sitting around with halfmast hard-ons, paying to see naked women, that seemed sad on both ends of the spectrum.

And thinking about it, I'd been in more than my fair share of competitions that depend on the way you look, thanks to my mother and sister. There's nothing like lining up and letting strangers judge your body against standards set by gay stylists with too much time on their hands.

Even so, I felt the old competitive edge creeping out of my bygone, baton-twirling, piano-playing, pageant-prancing past. I fluffed up my hair, adjusted my bra, and headed into Boners, ready to find Faith, kick some ass, and prove I still had it, even if I wasn't prepared to use it.

To BE HONEST, I was prepared to use it. At least some of it.

And my first chance to use it came in the form of a very large, very dark man approximately the size of Fort Worth. He lounged by the door, the neon light glinting red off his smooth, dark head. He wore black jeans and a black tee shirt that showed a lot of his biceps, which were the size of tree trunks. His arms were crossed in front of his enormous chest like interlocked branches. He wore a small gold cross on a thin gold chain—the same kind that Mia got when she went through confirmation.

The man stood in the doorway scanning the parking lot like a dark-intentioned search light.

I could see he was watching me, and as I approached, I noticed his skin was so dark I could see my reflection in his cheeks. He rolled a toothpick along his bottom lip. He was handsome in the way that alpha males are—nice to watch at the gym, but sex with a man like that would probably be like Jet Skiing in a force five hurricane.

A sane person would have turned tail and run. But sanity is not a trait that runs deep in the MacKinnon family gene pool.

I'd said I was willing to take desperate measures. This guy, I supposed, was my desperate measure.

The man's black eyes were large and seemed world-wise and world-weary. He didn't move, but I could tell he was watching me the same way a wolf watches a rabbit.

Smiling my top-shelf smile, the one with both dimples flashing, I extended my hand and said, "Cauley MacKinnon. I'd like to see some naked women."

He stood staring at me with those dark eyes like he could see all the way to the end of the earth. His gaze shifted to Marlowe, who was eyeing him back.

My spine stiffened when his gaze slid back to me.

Fight or flight… I tightened Marlowe's leash, ready to make a mad dash back to the Jeep.

And then he smiled. A brilliant flash of white, and the grin went all the way up to his eyes. "All right, blondie. You got an escort?"

"Besides the dog?"

"Yeah." Amusement sparked in his eyes, and he looked me up and down. "Club rules. Can't get in without a male escort."

"Well, shit," I said, and to my surprise, I blushed.

He grinned. It was the kind of grin like he'd heard a private joke, and it reminded me a little bit of Logan.

And as for male escorts…

I did a quick Rolodex in my head. The idea of calling Logan or Cantu didn't appeal to me, as I knew neither would approve of me being in that part of town in the middle of the night.

I could call Beckett and Jenks, who would come and probably make this little adventure more fun than a basket of kittens, but it took the two of them longer to get ready than it took God to create the earth. I could call Ethan, but that was just begging for a migraine. Plus, I wasn't in the mood to mop up drool, and I was fresh out of smelling salts.

"No other way? I just need to ask a few questions," I said, and he looked me up and down.

"Questions 'bout what?" he said. His arms were still crossed but humor still twinkled in his eyes. Apparently, I wasn't something he saw every day.

I took a deep breath and fished a card out of my purse. "Cauley MacKinnon. I'm with the *Sentinel*."

He took the card and looked at it and then nodded.

"The Obituary Babe," he said, a chuckle tickling his deep voice.

I stared at him. My card didn't say anything about obituaries.

He tilted his enormous head, sizing me up. "Could put you on the schedule for an audition."

A sudden mental picture of me bumping and grinding and rolling around on a dirty floor made me laugh out loud.

"Yeah," he said. "That's what I thought. What you really want, blondie?"

Ah, the truth. Why hadn't I thought of that? I get so caught up with Logan's clandestine ways that I forget that sometimes the best way to get information is to just ask for it.

"You know Faith Puckett?"

He stared at me some more. It wasn't that cop-eyed stare, but an assessment. I bet those dark eyes could do an automatic credit check.

"Yeah," he said. "I know her. Why do you want to know?"

"I can't find her, and I'm worried."

I fished the stack of photos from my purse, thumbed through and found the photo of the girl who'd been in the fire. I handed it to him. "A girl who looks like Faith got burned pretty bad tonight in Faith's trailer."

He stood staring at the photo and shook his head and closed his eyes. For a moment, I thought he might have been praying.

I waited.

"Name's Tiffany Parker," he said, his voice sounding gruff. "She alive?"

"Barely. The EMTs flew her to Brooke's burn unit."

He nodded, and I pressed on. "How long's Faith worked here?"

"'Bout three months."

"You know she just turned eighteen?"

He closed his eyes. "I don't hire the girls. Just look after 'em."

I nodded. "Has anyone else been here looking for her?"

A subtle change came over his face, something cold and hard. "Come on. Let's see what we find."

I noticed he hadn't answered the question.

He handed me back the photo and patted Marlowe behind the ear, and then he looked at me hard. "One thing. Don't show the girls the picture. Tell 'em what you want, but these girls got a hard life, and they don't need to see that kinda shit. This kinda thing happen to more of 'em than you think."

And then he held out his large hand. It was warm and strong, and he shook mine gently. "Deke," he said and smiled.

He swung open the door and said, "Welcome to the gentlemen's paradise. Watch your step."

I BLINKED IN THE darkness and stepped inside. I would have tripped over the step if Marlowe hadn't been in front of me. Deke waved us by a pretty, scantily clad redhead stationed at a small check-in point that reminded me of the admission gate at a dirty Disneyland. Definitely a different kind of Mr. Toad's Wild Ride.

We descended a small flight of stairs through a dark hall that opened onto an equally dark room that flashed and strobed. It was dark, but my eyes began to adjust. I wished they hadn't. Music raged through ragged speakers and drums beat in a bass so hard I could feel it in the soles of my feet. Topless young girls lounged next to men twice their age, making nice, laughing and flirting. The large room was dark and loud and throbbing with negative energy, like a beer commercial trying to convince you that you were having a good time.

The air was thick with smoke, desperation, and the kind of aloneness that seemed bottomless. Marlowe stood beside me, ears pricked, neck bristling.

Three stages were lit by soft-gelled lights, and three girls flung themselves bonelessly around poles like they were rag dolls, probably thinking deep thoughts like making mental grocery lists and figuring out what to wear to church tomorrow as they bumped, ground, and allowed middle-aged bald guys to leer at them through the amber bottoms of overpriced drinks.

I stared, trying very hard not to stare. Deke seemed amused. "Everybody's gotta do somethin', Ms. MacKinnon. Not ever'body got the same kind of options."

"Cauley," I said, and his eyebrows arched high on his dark head. "My name's Cauley."

He nodded, looking at me, and smiled.

"All right, Miz Cauley. What in hell are you doing down here by yourself?"

I shook my head. "What are all these other girls doing down here by themselves?"

"They ain't by themselves." He grinned. "They got me."

He offered me his arm.

I looked into Deke's dark eyes for a long moment, and then I looped my arm around his and said, "I'm glad of that."

I WAS SURPRISED TO see so many large-screen televisions arranged around the room, flashing every sporting event known to mankind.

I wouldn't have thought men would want to drink beer and watch television while well-endowed, naked women were simulating sex in their faces. It was, I concluded, a tribute to male attention deficit disorder.

Along one side of the club, a glass bar loomed in the darkness, a young, barely clad girl behind it mixing drinks. Against the opposite wall, a buffet was set up under red heat lamps. It smelled like day-old fajita meat, and even Marlowe lost interest.

The music changed to some kind of loud, headache-inducing hip hop, and a spotlight hit a black, sparkly curtain at the back. A woman burst from behind the curtain wearing a bandeau and a pair of black leather pants that made her look like she'd just had her butt upholstered. If she sat down, they were so tight they'd split at the seams, but that was probably the point.

Most of the men sat quietly, looking sad and lonely, trying to pretend they were having a good time. They sat hunched over, sipping their overpriced drinks and watching as women gyrated and undulated, trying to get their attention. *Hmm*, I thought. *Not so much different than an evening at the Pier. Only way creepier.* And the fact that men kept slipping money in garters so they could cop a feel of female flesh. I shook my head. These guys probably thought they were putting these girls through college.

Public service is a good thing.

Deke led me past the stage, back to a dark door that blended into a black wall and down a hall and through another door, which he opened. And then there was light.

My eyes adjusted, and then my eyebrows shot up. Six women of varying ages walked around in their altogether, naked as the day God made them. They wore a lot of makeup, and they all looked a lot older than they probably were. The room itself looked like the high-school dressing areas where we used to do quick changes for scenes in drama, except it was debauched and sagging.

The room was heady with scents of baby powder, cheap makeup, and broken dreams.

It was a small, narrow hall, closed in on each end with thin, hollow-core doors. The left wall was lined with costumes, feathers, and furs. Six large, round mirrors perched atop makeup tables at the right wall. A thirtysomething blond and a young brunette sat in metal chairs, naked except for the makeup they were applying. The young brunette had pictures of a little boy taped to her makeup mirror.

The girls had been chattering warp speed when Deke and I walked in. Their eyes lit up when they saw Deke, but the chatter slammed shut when they saw me.

Deke said, "Evenin', girls. This is Cauley MacKinnon. She's lookin' for Faith."

Nobody said anything to me. They stood there, bare as the day is long, staring at me, their faces hard with some of the best cop-eyed stares I've ever seen. These girls could've given Junior Hollis a lesson in intimidation.

I crossed my arms in front of my fully clothed chest, trying to keep my eyes at eye level, which was no easy feat. Four of the girls had breasts the size of Mia's Beetle. Tentatively, Marlowe moved forward, head down, ears flat. The faces of the girls softened as they simultaneously surged toward the dog. Marlowe, it turned out, was a cheap date.

I wasn't sure how to start, so I decided to start with Faith. Clearing my throat, I pulled out the stack of pictures, less the photo of Tiffany.

"A girl named Faith Puckett has been missing for twenty-four hours," I said. "She told me she worked here. I think she might be in trouble."

"What kind of trouble?" the brunette asked, her voice edged with suspicion.

"I'm guessing you know about the trouble with her brother, Wylie Puckett," I said, and they all nodded. I took a deep breath. "Her trailer burned down tonight, and Tiffany Parker was hurt in the fire."

A collective gasp went up in the smoke-laden air.

"Is she okay? Her face?" a thin, silver-haired girl said, and I shook my head. A hush fell over the room.

"Have any of you seen Faith or know where she might be—a friend or relative she might be staying with? A man she might have met here?"

The girls were silent, the air thick with shock.

"I have photos of people who turned out to search for her, and I was hoping y'all could take a look, see if there's anybody you recognize…"

I had their attention now, and a tall, slender black woman with large eyes and a wide mouth accepted the stack of photos, stepping over a black feather boa in a pair of five-inch metallic heels that could have been registered as lethal weapons. She cleared a spot on her makeup table and laid the photos out. The other girls crowded around her.

They whispered together as they studied the shots.

"Look, Baby, it's Josh!" a small girl with short, pink-streaked hair said, showing the black woman a photo of the farm boy.

"Her boyfriend, right?" I said.

The women flashed looks around to each other.

"We don't want him in any trouble," Baby said, and I shook my head.

"Nobody's in trouble yet. I just want to find out where she is, make sure she's okay."

More nodding in the group, and Baby said, "Yeah. Josh. He doesn't like her working here. He wants to marry her and get her away from all this glamour."

A nervous giggle bubbled up from the group like Seven and Seven on the rocks. "He loves her," Pink said. "He came in here one night all juiced on Jack Black, marched right up on the stage, threw her over his shoulder, and carried her out of here."

A simultaneous sigh sifted through the circle. Apparently, knights in shining armor are hard to come by, even when you're not wearing clothes.

I said, "You think he's capable of kidnapping her?"

Pink looked at the photo sadly. "Not if she didn't want to be. See, he's takin' over the family farm. Wants Faith to settle down, help plow fields and make babies."

I nodded. "And that doesn't sound like the high life to Faith?"

She shrugged her bare shoulders. "Faith wants to sing."

Baby shook her head. "No, darlin'. Faith wants to fly."

"Hey, wait a minute," Pink said, looking carefully at the photos. "This guy," she said, pointing into the crowd of searchers.

She narrowed her eyes. "The Beaver Retriever. Comes in here all the time," Pink said.

"He's the worst," Baby agreed. "He thinks he got it goin' on. Thinks we do this shit 'cause it's just oh-so-much fun. Thinks he's here to get a date."

Pink nodded. "We got a strict no-touchin' policy here, and he just grabs what he wants like he's checkin' produce down at the Super S."

"Don't tip for shit, either," Baby said.

I looked down at the Beaver Retriever and into the face of Junior Hollis.

County sheriff, chief perv. A real renaissance man.

I THANKED THE GIRLS and promised I'd let them know what I found out about Faith and Tiffany, and then I hurried through the staging area to get outside, where I could call Cantu and tell him what I'd found. Deke was walking me to the door when a familiar voice near the back stage called out. I turned and was stunned to see Tres Ainsworth sitting in a booth with a dark-haired woman who appeared to be naked. He was nodding his head. His man-bob hair didn't move.

Marlowe growled low in his throat.

"Excuse me," I said to Deke. "I need to talk to this guy."

"Uh-huh," Deke said, like he'd seen something in my eyes, and he escorted me over and stood, legs braced, arms crossed, as I spoke with Tres.

"Well, if it isn't Lois Lane! Come, sit, have a drink," Tres said. Jovial. Just folks. Out having a big ol' time with Daddy's money and the company card.

"Your sister's missing," I said.

"What do you mean, missing?" he said, his usual bravado faltering. "Missing as in gone? You sure she's not off with her boyfriend?"

"The one you smacked around at the Pier?"

Something cold flashed in his eyes, but it passed quickly. "You gotta look out for family, right? I'm all she's got left."

"Except her mother," I noted.

Tres snorted. "You met her mother?"

I let the comment go. "Developing talent?" I said, looking at the girl.

"What?" he said, the vodka clouding his minimal brain.

I stared at him.

"Oh, *talent*. For Incubus. Sure," he said. "Lena here has a set of pipes you wouldn't believe."

She giggled. It was one of those high-pitched, nasally giggles that sounded like nails on chalkboard. Probably had a singing voice like a drilling rig.

"You know her trailer caught fire tonight?"

"Faith's trailer?" he said, and there was so much vodka on his breath he could have fueled a flamethrower. "You're kidding," he said, setting his drink on table.

"If that's kidding, then I'm not very good at it." I pulled the pictures from my purse and laid them out on the table. He jerked back like he'd gotten a whiff of bad fish. Lena's face crumbled beneath her makeup.

"And this," I laid the picture of Tiffany on top of the pile, despite what Deke had said, "was Faith's friend. She worked here and was caught in the fire."

Tres's breath came harder. Lena made a gagging sound and held her mouth. She jumped up from the table, breasts bouncing, and made a hasty exit. Tres looked hard at the photo, his face unreadable, and something inside me wondered if he had the capacity to feel bad—to feel the full force of how horrible this crime was. I couldn't believe he let his family live in that trailer and work in this club. Surely a brother—even a stepbrother—of means could at least lend a hand, if not a safety net. He stared at the photos. Too bad they haven't invented scratch and sniff photography.

He shoved the photos away and took another hard drink.

I said, "There are searchers out looking for her tonight. By tomorrow morning, we'll have more news crews out there and the foot searchers will be out in full force. Tonight, I'm trying to find out as much as I can so we can figure out where to search or if we should search at all."

He was quiet. Deke stood at my side, big arms crossed, listening.

I gathered the pictures back into a stack.

"I didn't know," Tres said. "What do we do?" His pupils dilated to the size of manhole covers, and he seemed unsteady.

I shook my head. "I'm making a list of places she might go, people she might turn to. You think of anything, let me know."

He nodded, his eyes tearing. "She's had a hard life," he said. "I—I've tried to help her. Set her up with a record deal, bought her mama a house where she could live … "

"You want to help, now's your chance," I said, turning to leave.

"I didn't know," Tres called after us. "I didn't know!"

Lena was gone, and he sat there, alone, lights strobing off his skin in the dark.

"You think he knew?" Deke said, and I shrugged.

We walked back up the steps and out of the den of iniquity, past the receptionist and out into the moonlight.

I sucked in a breath of fresh air and turned to Deke. "How'd you know I write obituaries?"

Deke grinned. "Man came by earlier. Said to keep an eye out for you."

"Would this man be a tall, dark FBI agent?" I said.

"Wasn't that dark."

I smiled as he walked Marlowe and me to the Jeep.

When we got to the Jeep, my heart slammed into my throat.

One of my kitchen knives was jammed into the driver's seat, impaling a piece of paper.

In one deft motion, Deke whipped a snub-nose pistol out of the back of his jeans and scanned the parking lot.

I stared at the small square of paper. It was a Polaroid of me getting arrested at Faith's. The knife was stabbed through the center of my heart.

NINETEEN

DEKE ESCORTED ME BACK into the club, where we called the police. When we went back to check my Jeep, Logan was leaning against a burned-out light pole in the dark parking lot. I expected Marlowe to do his usual overjoyed routine, but he joined Logan, searching the Jeep in a search pattern, serious as a heart attack.

Tres was gone, the searchers at Faith's were calling in the second shift, and the crime geeks had taken photos and dusted for prints in and around my Jeep.

Deke had taken the lead cop into the club to look around.

I hadn't had a full night's sleep in a week, and it was beginning to catch up with me. The call of clean sheets was more than I could stand.

"Anybody know where Hollis is?" I asked Logan as he flipped his cell shut. He shook his head and reached down to scratch Marlowe's ears.

"Bugged out after the film crews left. Said he'd be back bright and early."

"When Miranda and her minions are back?"

Logan nodded. He had something on his mind, but he wasn't ready to spill.

"You find a link between this mess and El Patron?" I said.

"You mean other than the shooting on the courthouse steps and the trailers of two siblings burning to the ground?"

"You didn't answer my question."

"No," he said. "I didn't. Cauley, there's a lot going on here, and I'm asking you not to go Annie Oakley on this. And as far as we know, Faith pulled a runaway bride."

"But you don't think so."

He blew out some air. "No. I don't think so."

We stood, staring at my Jeep. "Come on," he said. "I'm going to follow you home and check your house."

The night air was stifling. The stars danced high in the dark sky, and tonight, they seemed far away.

Logan tucked a lock of hair behind my ear. I smiled, but it was a small smile. As much as I wanted him to sweep me in his arms and charge into my house, he would do as he said. Check the house, lock the doors, and get back to work.

This falling for a fed thing isn't what it's cracked up to be.

LOGAN WAS GONE. AGAIN. He'd checked the house, under beds and behind doors, and found nothing to fear but an angry calico.

I wrote a short blurb on the trailer fire and the search mission so the *Sentinel* would have the inside scoop. I called Tanner and left him a voice mail about what was going on and how I was going to be spending my Saturday.

Then I sent a stripped-down version of the facts to the local stations so the news crews would be there when we continued the search Saturday morning. Let them write their own blurbs.

On autopilot, I fed the cat, gave the dog half my ham sandwich, brushed my teeth, washed my face, and slid into bed, listening to the dry wind howl through the canyon. Muse sat at her usual perch on the headboard, waiting until the commotion died down.

As Marlowe and I had our evening territorial skirmish over the bed and who got more sheets, I wondered about Faith. I wondered where she was and if she was safe. And if she wanted to be found.

It didn't matter. We would find her, and we'd figure out the rest from there.

The sun came up, announced by an angry pounding at the door. Tying the blue silk kimono Aunt Kat sent me when she tripped around Tokyo writing *The Samurai and the Seductress,* I swung open the door and found Ethan, cheeks flushed, loaded for bear. Behind him, a young cop who'd been watching my house stood scowling.

"It's okay," I said. "He belongs here."

The cop shrugged and, still scowling, backed down the porch, watching Ethan all the way to his car.

"Why didn't you call me?" E accused, standing on the front porch, waving a stack of printouts from the news briefs I'd filed only a few hours ago. Then he got a look at the kimono and almost swallowed his tongue.

"Oh, get over it, Ethan," I said. "They're just legs."

The bright sun blazed over the horizon, burning holes into the backs of my retinas. Marlowe pranced around, doing the potty dance.

I growled. "Watch the dog. I'll put on some tea."

"I'm on potty patrol? Faith is missing and I'm watching a dog pee?"

"It builds character," I said, scuffing into the kitchen. With a huff, Ethan stood back as the dog leapt off the porch to go pee on the Bobs' rosemary bush.

Ethan and the dog bustled back in through the foyer and stood at the kitchen counter, waiting.

I pulled the tea off the stove before it was ready, jumbled some ice into two glasses, handed one to Ethan, and from the other took a good, long gulp. Because I'd been watching too many of Logan's Westerns, I had to resist the urge to wipe my mouth on the back of my robe sleeve.

I'd never seen an angry geek before, and it was a sight to behold. Ethan stood at the kitchen counter, rangy arms crossed, foot tapping. His teeth were on edge, and his skinny chest was puffed out, shoulders back, fists clenched. I wondered if he'd been watching Logan's Westerns, too. E was doing serious today: black tee shirt, black jeans, and black Converse tennis shoes, one of which was untied.

So this was why they called them code warriors.

"What's with the scratches all over your face?" I said, and his hand rose to his cheek.

"Are you aware that big orange cat is from the pit of hell?" he said, and I smiled, rolling up my sleeve to show him the mark of the feline felon on my forearm.

"I can call Burt Buggess to come get him until Logan gets back," I offered.

"The pet store guy?" He thought about it but shook his head. "I don't want Faith to worry about him. That cat is the last link she's got to her brother."

I smiled and kissed his cheek. "You're a good guy, E," I said, and he turned red right up to his roots.

Grumping at all the morning commotion, Marlowe hopped up on the couch to join Muse, who was fully involved in her pre-morning snit. Nobody believed in beauty sleep more than Muse.

"You could have called me," Ethan said.

I blew out a breath. "Ethan, there was nothing you could do. It's an official search and rescue mission, and the Dawes County cops aren't taking it too well. I was going to call you this morning and get a jump on things—see what we could do."

Ethan looked pointedly at his binary code watch. "It's been morning for half an hour."

"Technically," I said, sucking in some more caffeine.

Ethan paced the length of the living room, with Marlowe watching him, head unmoving, almond eyes shifting.

Ethan turned to me suddenly. "What are we going to do?"

"Who's we?" I said, but cringed as I heard a four-cylinder engine throw rocks in my driveway. "You called Mia?"

"You bet your sweet ass."

My sweet ass?

"Ethan," I said. "Have you been talking to Logan?"

His cheeks colored a little. "Subscribed to Netflix."

The cop in front of the house charged Mia and hustled to the door. "She's okay," I called out. He eyed her suspiciously but went back to his car.

I groaned as Mia crashed in through the front door, a woman on a mission. "What's this I hear about you going to Boners without me?" Her bright orange capri pants were so tight I was surprised she didn't succumb to the vapors. Her bright, off-the-shoulder tropical print shirt made her look like she'd escaped from a pack of Skittles. It also made it hard to take her grim expression seriously.

I sighed, my eyes watering I was so tired. "Lapse in judgment," I said.

Mia tapped the toe of her strappy orange sandal.

I sighed again.

"Here's what I know," I said, and they both sat at the kitchen table as I told them about both of the trailer fires, Cantu's call to Team Six, Hollis pulling jurisdiction over the search op, the brief but insightful stop at the strip club, and the creepy stalker photo of me stabbed through the heart.

"So why are we here? Shouldn't we be on the search site?" Ethan asked.

"There's a lot more to search and rescue than beating the bushes. We have to get information, and we have to get the word out," I said.

"So, what do we do now, *chica?*" Mia said.

"We need a list."

Before I could utter another word, Ethan had his BlackBerry out, entering in his own personal to-do list.

"Showoff," I said, and went for my pen and little red notepad. "We need recent pictures of Faith, not the cleaned-up choir girl Hollis is showing around."

Ethan said, "Done."

Mia and I stared at him.

"What?" he said. "I made stills from the video this morning. It's not like I'm stalking her or anything."

"Or anything," I said, shaking my head.

That said, I checked *Find recent photo of Faith* off my own list.

"Maybe we should make a website," Mia said.

"I'll do it," Ethan said.

I checked another item from my list. "We need to make flyers and get to the search scene before the News Boys get there," I said.

"I'll do that," Mia said. "And then what?"

I thought about that. Despite my personal opinion of Hollis, he'd been at least partially right. We needed to establish a list of suspects. We also, however, needed to establish a list of connections and a list of people and places Faith may have turned to if she hadn't met with foul play.

"Sheriff Hollis had some suppositions we should probably check out," I said, flipping the pages of my notepad, and checked my list:

1. Gangland payback: connection—Puck's murder on the courthouse steps.
2. Jealous paramours.

Ethan bristled.

"Or," I went on, "and less likely, a random twist of fate from some homicidal jerk she'd met at Boners."

I tapped the pen to my lips. "I wonder if she had life insurance or a will..." I scribbled on my list.

"Or that she'd run away on her own," Mia said.

Marlowe sat at my feet and laid his head on my lap, ears twitching as we spoke.

"All right, smart guy," I said to Marlowe. "Everyone says you're the expert on this rescue stuff. Where do we start?"

Marlowe listened, the tip of his tongue sticking out. It was cute, but not very helpful.

"Hollis said he'd called Faith's mother. He said there was no activity on credit cards, bank account, or cell phone. I found the stepbrother—he was doing dangle patrol down at the strip club."

"That is *muy repugnante!*" Mia's face twisted with disgust. "Her stepbrother was at the place where she dances? That's disgusting."

I thought Ethan's head was going to explode.

"Yeah, I thought so, too," I said.

"So what's next?" Mia said.

"When you get the flyers made, I'll take some of the flyers with me to the search site this morning." Tapping my lips with my pen, I said, "Where would I go if I were in trouble?"

"Me," Mia said.

I smiled. "Suppose you weren't available. And suppose for some reason I couldn't go to Mama's or Brynn's."

"Work?" Mia said, and I frowned.

"I spent an overlarge portion of the evening at Boners. She hasn't been there."

"Right," Mia said, still annoyed I hadn't called her for that little field trip.

"Ethan, could you double-check her bank and credit card stuff?"

"I could find pictures of Barbara Walters naked if you wanted," he said.

"Well, let's not go crazy."

Mia and Ethan set about their tasks, and I said, "There's new Pop-Tarts if you're hungry," and then headed to the back of the house where I washed my hair, shook it dry, then got dressed. I made two ham sandwiches, which I stowed in my SAR bag, grabbed a Pop-Tart and whistled for Marlowe.

"I really appreciate this. You two going to be okay? Y'all are taking a huge weight off my shoulders."

Ethan looked at me like I'd asked him if he planned to breathe today. I handed him the box of Pop-Tarts.

Mia laid her small hand on his arm. "We got it under control. And hey, *querida*, what are friends for?"

I nodded, feeling the warm rush of friendship wrap around my heart.

"Come on, boy," I said to Marlowe, breaking a Pop-Tart in half and giving the bigger half to the dog. "Let's go find Faith."

THE SEARCH SCENE WAS a disaster. News crews were out bright and early, beaming a satellite beacon for every lunatic in the tri-county area. Four private dicks showed up soliciting business, about twenty public dicks showed up from Boners, and a psychic arrived to announce that she'd had a vision that Faith had traveled to the Himalayas to teach hip rolls to Tibetan monks.

And speaking of hip rolls, the girls from Boners were out bright and early, too. Dressed in jeans and tee shirts, not looking like strippers at all, they came to help search for their friend. Olivia had the base in full-out operating mode, checking in volunteers and issuing them IDs hooked on lanyards to wear around their necks.

I had expected the trailer to look like a rectangular-shaped skeleton; instead, it looked like half of it had been blown to smithereens. The fire was still sending off the acrid smell of burned aluminum and formaldehyde, but for the most part, Faith's home was a big, black, wet mass of twisted metal.

There were no bird sounds, no late-summer insects chirring in the small, stale breeze. Somewhere in the distance, I could hear a heifer bawling for her calf.

Up the rutted, red road, I saw a familiar white Lincoln bumping along, bringing behind it a legion of boat-sized Caddies, Mercedes, Lexus, and several types of SUVs.

"Mama," I said, and grinned as the Colonel pulled up and offloaded my mother and Clairee and went to go park. Behind him, the entire leadership committee from the Charity League drove around and around, looking for parking spaces.

Warmth spread from my scalp to my toes.

Mama had a Jell-O mold. "We brought reinforcements," she said, handing me the dessert. "Where do we start?"

I looked at all the luncheon ladies jockeying for good parking and my cheeks hurt from smiling. Faith had told me she didn't have any friends—had no one to call when she was in trouble. And here they were, this unlikely lot. Neighbors, a cadre of strippers, and my mother and the Charity League.

"Every life touches someone," I said, and Mama frowned.

"Is the sun gettin' to you, darlin'?" She pressed her manicured fingers to my forehead.

"No," I said. "But I do feel warm. I love you, Mama."

"Of course you do, dear. Now go get that Jell-O mold out of the sun."

ACROSS THE FIELD BEHIND the burned-out trailer, Hollis was posing his considerable ass off for Miranda when a Porsche rolled up and Tres climbed out. He slipped off his sunglasses and squinted in the rising sun. His hair was mussed, his eyes bleary, and sheet marks dented his face. He watched as the foot searchers linked arms, preparing to do a grid search. I wasn't sure if his demeanor was from grief or from a monster Boners hangover. Or both.

He wore expensive khaki pants, a blue button-down shirt, and a pair of brown loafers that probably cost the gross national profit of Bulgaria.

He rushed over, squinting in the Saturday morning sunlight with a big dose of Friday night regret.

"Is she all right? Did you find her?" he sputtered, staring around at the commotion.

"They're sending out a new team now," I said.

"She shoulda been home by now. She's got studio time tomorrow." He rubbed his eyes with his thumb and forefinger.

"You hear from her?" I said, and Tres shook his head.

I nodded. "When was the last time you saw her?"

Tres wracked his brain. "Right after the courthouse. I offered to let her stay with me but she didn't want to leave the hospital."

Well, that was news.

"So what happens now?" he said, watching as Olivia paired some new volunteers with some Six regulars.

"This is Junior Hollis's operation, so a lot of it's up to him. He's practiced with Team Six so they're here, but it's his show."

The show was getting more characters by the moment. A white bus pulled up, offloading what looked like twenty Catholic school girls, bearing cookies and casseroles.

Tres hesitated, then squinted up at the sky, his skin tinged with a slight pallor of green, Adam's apple bobbing. "What are the odds, you know, that you'll find her?"

The real question was, alive or dead? I decided not to voice it.

I shook my head. "Each passing hour, odds go down."

He fidgeted, trying to take in the search site, trying to process the information. He shook his head. "I just didn't think… I didn't know…"

I didn't say anything.

Tres stood staring down at Marlowe, who was staring right back.

"Money," he said. "You think it would help to offer a reward?"

I shrugged. "Couldn't hurt. Talk to Hollis, and then you can probably make a public plea on television."

"How do I do that?" he said, and I pointed toward Miranda.

We needn't have worried. Across the field, Miranda had apparently honed in on the hum of Tres's Porsche, and her breasts aimed toward it like a pair of smart bombs on a GPS-marked target.

Tres was about to get Mirandized.

Miranda picked her way through the cow patties, careful not to soil her Ferragamos, her camera and sound guy in tow. This morning she was doing a gray suit—probably said "serious news" on the label. One of these days, I was going to have to get one of those. She pressed her fingers to her right ear, listening to her producer in her earbud.

"Well *hello*, Cauley," she purred on approach. "What have we here?"

I scowled. "The stuff that dreams are made of."

She aimed her million-watt smile at Tres, who lost some of his pallor. "Miranda, this is Tres Ainsworth—Faith's stepbrother. He's offering a reward."

As usual, Miranda was going to get her scoop, and I had just handed it to her on a silver platter.

Miranda tossed her big blond hair and put on her serious face. She cleared the satellite link and the red camera light clicked on. She addressed her viewers. "We're talking to Tres Ainsworth, the missing girl's brother, who has offered a reward for information leading to his sister."

Tres didn't correct the mistake in lineage.

The camera turned to Tres, and he cleared his throat. "We just want her back. We're all extremely worried about Faith. This—this disappearance—it's not like her. If anyone has information that will help us find her, I'm prepared to offer a $250,000 reward. Our brother was murdered—," he choked up, coughed twice, and cleared his throat, "Thursday morning on his way to testify against Selena Obregon and an organization called El Patron. If you have information leading to the arrest and conviction of members of that organization, there'll be a $10,000 reward per person convicted."

I stood there with my mouth open, hoping I wasn't on camera.

What the hell? I turned to Olivia and said, "Did he just put a notice out to El Patron?"

"Sounds like it." Olivia shook her head, her lips pressed together. "Like we don't have enough nuts to deal with," she said, looking pointedly at the psychic, who was holding court with Alex "Live-at-Five" Salazar.

Near the periphery of the milling crowd, a rangy man in worn blue jeans wandered the fence line like he was lost.

"Josh?" I said, and he turned to look at me. His eyes were hollow and bloodshot. His tanned face pale. His breath smelled like undiluted lighter fluid and was probably just as flammable.

"She's not here," he said. "I tried to tell them but they won't listen."

"Who won't listen?" I said.

"Cops. But she's not here."

"How do you know that, Josh?" I said, cringing away from his breath.

"Keates."

The air around me stilled, and I followed his gaze to the burned-out trailer.

"The bird?" I said, and he nodded.

"I asked the firemen. They never found the cage."

"Are you sure it didn't just burn up?"

"Did you see that cage? It was wrought iron." He blinked like there were more tears but no more moisture.

Suddenly, I was afraid for him.

"Have you had any sleep at all?" I said, and he shook his head.

"Josh, is there somewhere you can go? Can I take you somewhere?"

"I just want to find her."

I nodded, looking around as the crowd grew. All the usual suspects—except Kimmie Ray Puckett Ainsworth, who was nowhere in sight. I had called her yesterday when Faith didn't answer my call, but Mommy Dearest said she hadn't seen or heard from her.

I thought about my own mother. When I don't check in once a day, she's circling the block and calling in reinforcements. Faith told me Puck was her only family.

I had felt bad for Faith before. I felt worse for her now.

My cell beeped, and my heart quickened, hoping it was good news. It was Tanner.

"Where in the hell are you?" he yelled, and I rolled my eyes.

"Here at Blackland Ranch, the Puckett family homestead. They're getting the search teams out."

"You're not doing the search thing?" he said, and I wanted to pound the phone on something.

"No," I said. "I'm still in training. I'm managing media."

"Media?" he said. "You remember who you work for."

I stared at the phone. "I can't believe you said that!"

He was quiet. "You think they're going to find the girl?"

"Team Six is the best in the region," I said, and he grunted.

"That was a good web log you got in last night," he said. "Get Mia out there and get pictures this morning. You see the paper today?"

"I've been kind of busy."

"Yeah, well, you're lead. Front of Metro, above the fold."

"You know that's not why I'm doing this, right?" I said. "I want City Desk because I earned it, not because I was in the right place at the right time."

"Yeah, but it's a nice byproduct."

"I gotta get back—I've got a lot to do today."

"Keep me posted," he said. "And Cauley?"

"Yeah?"

"Be careful."

I shook my head. *I'll be as careful as I can.*

As the new teams gathered and proceeded into the charred field behind the house, Marlowe's fur bristled from nose to tail. He shifted from paw to paw, eager to join the hunt. "Settle down, Asta, we'll find her."

Marlowe fidgeted, suspects were running rampant, Faith's brother was dead, the Dawes County Sheriff's Department was running a sideshow, Faith's stepbrother was holding an impromptu press conference, and her own mother was a no-show.

I fished a business card out of my bag and gave it to Josh. "If you think of anything or if you need help, will you call me?"

He took the card and looked down at it like he wasn't sure what it was.

I sighed and headed back to base.

"This is why God invented antacid," I told Marlowe, handing fresh photos to Olivia, who looked like she wanted to introduce Junior Hollis's head to the inside of his lower intestines.

Marlowe stared at me with his dark almond eyes, then looked over the horizon.

"You're right," I told the dog. "The hunt isn't here."

Since we weren't actually on the search team, Marlowe and I hopped into the Jeep and headed out for other hunting grounds. We right-turned, making the slow, winding climb up Westshore Drive toward Westlake, where elaborate foliage softened the gargantuan limestone walls and all was right with the world. Westlake is an enclave that used to be west of Austin, but the city sprawled westward and surrounded it with similar high-dollar homes in a lower tax bracket.

A stranger driving through the western edge of town wouldn't notice the change in the city limits, but the zip code is the golden key to an award-winning school district, a low crime rate, and a better seat at the Charity League.

Along the neatly trimmed curbs, the buzz of Weedwackers and the hum of leaf blowers vibrated in the Saturday morning silence. Yardmen dutifully tended the bright green lawns rioting with brilliant pink hibiscus and fluffy white hydrangeas like there was no drought at all.

I'd thought about calling Information and giving Kimmie a ring, but based on what Faith had said about her relationship with her mother, I thought it best to just show up. I stared up at the Tuscan-style house that rose from the limestone cliff, looking down its wide porticos over downtown Austin. The whole affair was surrounded by a wrought-iron and limestone fence, with security cameras positioned on each pillar. An all-weather keypad was posted in front of an imposing gate.

"Well, Marlowe, some reporter I'm going to be. I had not anticipated a gate."

The dog didn't say anything.

Down the street, a small, battered white Toyota pickup pulled up to the gate. It was loaded with Weedwackers and men who looked as excited about trimming the lawn as the Colonel looks when he goes shoe shopping with Mama.

I waved at the driver. Like many immigrants, he didn't make eye contact.

I stared through the fence at the Ainsworth's lawn, which was not freshly mown and watered. "Well," I told Marlowe, "I suppose if we sit here long enough, we might stumble upon the Ainsworth gardener?"

Marlowe looked at me expectantly, probably thinking about the ham sandwiches I'd packed.

"Right. If we're going to sit here, we should have some sustenance." I revved the engine and headed back into Westlake for some iced tea.

Luckily, Marlowe is trained to search, and we found a Starbucks within snooping distance.

Armed with a venti iced tea, a slice of sugar-free banana nut loaf, and a bowl of water, we returned to our designated spy spot. I know that sugar-free does not mean it's any healthier, but delusions are easier to keep when they're chock-full of carbohydrates.

Marlowe and I sat, sharing the banana nut loaf and watching the house. When we tired of that, we watched the grass grow. Then we watched me search my face in the rear-view mirror to check for new lines or wrinkles. My birthday was looming on the horizon, and I wanted to make sure it wasn't looming on my face.

I was about to call my mother and ask her if she'd noticed a tiny line near my left eye when a small, blue Nissan pickup with a wide-faced, dark-skinned man with a thin mustache turned into the driveway.

I flipped my phone shut and climbed out of the Jeep, smiling winsomely.

"Hello," I said, bright and sunny as a kitchen garden after a spring rain. I motioned to him to roll down his window.

He sat behind the wheel, staring at me.

"I work here—this is my first day," I shouted through the window. "I totally forgot the keycode."

I smiled some more and stopped just short of batting my eyelashes.

He looked back at the Jeep, then cranked the window. It took some effort, considering his elbow kept hitting his considerable stomach.

When the window was half down, he said, "What's with the dog?"

His voice had a strong Spanish accent, and I smiled brighter. "I'm the groomer. Bringing the new dog."

The guy looked through the side-view mirror at Marlowe, who was staring back at him from the front seat of the Jeep. He shrugged, reached past me to punch in the numbers, and motioned me to follow him.

I silently repeated the numbers as I climbed back into the Jeep and followed him up the drive in case I needed them again. He pulled off to an outbuilding, and I waved. He didn't wave back.

The house was designed to impress, and it did: Tuscan turrets; wide, looming arches; a front courtyard that looked like a tropical island. I parked under a cool, leafy arbor and gave Marlowe a ham sandwich, which he promptly accepted, and he jumped into the back cargo area to enjoy it at his leisure. Hooking his leash onto the rollbar, I headed up the brick driveway toward the house.

I rang the bell, inhaling the scent of tropical flowers and listening to the sound of water trickling from the tiered fountain. The place was so green it was creating its own atmosphere, like a big terrarium. An aging Latina answered the door. She was tall and thin and hollow-faced, and wore an honest-to-God maid suit straight out of a 1930s movie, black from neck to shins, white collar and apron. She did not seem pleased to see me.

I was getting used to it.

"Good morning. My name is Cauley MacKinnon. I'm here to speak with Mrs. Ainsworth."

She didn't look like it was a good morning at all. "Mrs. Ainsworth is not taking visitors."

I nodded. "Will you at least ask her? I want to talk to her about her daughter."

There was a subtle change in her face, and for a moment I thought she might cry.

"Ah, *la buena Fe*," she said on a breath, and I smiled.

"Yes," I said. "Faith."

The woman's angular face softened, and she opened the door. Inside, the air conditioners were cranked up to Polar Ice Cap.

The ivory-colored floor was Italian marble, the cream-colored dome foyer ceiling frescoed in a pale abstract of blues and greens. A large spray of oversized white lilies presided over a marble table in the middle of the circular room, reminding me of a high-end funeral home.

The woman wrung her hands. "Is Fe all right? Have you found her?"

"We're looking," I said, coming into the foyer, which was the size of my living room. "They've got the dogs out," I pointed out the window to Marlowe, who was savoring his sandwich under the arbor. "I'm trying to find out as much as I can—any little thing that might help."

She stared at me. "How can I help?"

"Is there anyone she'd go to? Any friends or a place she feels safe?"

The woman shook her head. "This is a sad house," she said, and crossed herself, her eyes skyward. "*Pobrecito* Wylie and now Fe."

"It would really help if I could talk to Mrs. Ainsworth."

She nodded. "She's not well," she said, dipping her long fingers into her white apron pocket and fishing out a string of pale, worn beads. "*Un momento*."

I heard the clicking of sensible heels and the murmuring of liturgical prayers down the long corridor, and after a time, she returned and led me into the bowels of the big house. Her heels slapped at the stone tile as we walked down the corridor and into an office that had wide windows and high ceilings that had been decorated so tastefully that it was generic in its splendor.

The only personal possessions in the place were scatterings of photographs, all facing outward, none toward the chair where Kimmie Ray Ainsworth sat.

Appearances, apparently, were very important to her.

There were photos of Kimmie and Cullen II in various poses and places. They cavorted on a yacht, in a coliseum, and on some exotic, sandy white beach that could have been anywhere. The photos couldn't have been more than five years old, and the pair looked happy and very much in love—a lifetime from where she was now. Mama had taken Daddy's death hard, but she was living her life. Kimmie was still caught in the grasp of the ghost of her husband and the life she thought she wanted.

Kimmie Ray Puckett Ainsworth was seated behind a large, marble-topped desk like she'd been propped there. The room was swathed in ivory. Ivory carpets, ivory walls, ivory curtains. Kimmie had a fire blazing in the fireplace with a heavy glass front, so that the fire was contained and at odds with the cold room and the ongoing drought that loomed beyond the wide window.

Kimmie was probably in her early forties. She had high cheekbones like Faith, with pale skin made paler by trauma. Everything about her was drawn, her eyes large and almond-shaped, showing a little green around her very dilated pupils. Her hair was expensively cut and brushed the shoulders of her ivory silk blouse. She had probably once been very beautiful, but something inside had eaten away at her, leaving her an empty chrysalis.

I try not to make snap judgments, but I could already tell Kimmie Ray and I would never get together for a cold beer down at Deep Eddy's.

She looked at me through dark, blurry eyes. "Have you found her?" she said, and her voice was careful and small, like a breeze pushing at a heavy curtain.

Her desk was nearly bare. There was no blotter, computer, or any hint of productivity. A lovely silver tray with a martini shaker and a glass took up most of the surface.

Not looking at me, Kimmie Ray tipped the glass and drank the contents like it was milk.

"I'm with a search team working on finding your daughter. I came to see if you could help."

Behind her, the fire danced ineffectively, and in the cold room I had to suppress the urge to shiver.

Kimmie nodded. "Do you think someone has abducted her?" Her voice was careful and pronounced, but the martini betrayed her Rs and Ss.

"What would make you think so?"

"Wylie... he was... in trouble."

She was looking at the expensive area rug on the floor and blinked, very slowly. She poured herself another drink. "Would you like a drink?" she said as an afterthought.

"No, thank you," I said. "And I'm sorry for your loss."

A tear fell over her dark eyelashes and slipped down her hollow cheek.

"Do you know you're the first person who's said that to me?"

I nodded, and we sat in silence, watching the ineffective fire and the window and the single tear plop to the ivory carpet.

"You don't know what it's like to be poor," she said. "I've worked very hard to provide for my family. Sometimes things don't work out the way you thought they would."

Looking around at the photos, I hadn't noticed any family provided for outside of Kimmie Ray and Cullen, but I decided not to comment.

"Your husband was very handsome," I said. "How did you meet?"

Her eyes got soft, and her face relaxed a little. "His wife was very sick. He hired a string of nurses to care for her, but she wasn't the easiest patient. And then I came, and she seemed to like me, so I stayed."

I nodded. "Did Wylie and Faith come with you when you married?"

"Oh, yes. Tres—that's Cullen's son—was off at college. Wylie was fourteen and Faith was eleven. It was perfect." She smiled a little. "They used to run around here like demons. Cullen was sixty-two, and he tolerated them. But Pilar," she sighed. "Pilar loved them."

"Pilar is the woman who answered the door?"

Kimmie nodded.

I wasn't sure how to ask, so I took a flying leap.

"Faith said you sent her away when she was thirteen."

Kimmie's expression didn't change, but she took a big hit on her martini. "To school. I . . . we worried that she wasn't getting the right kind of education."

"Isn't the Eanes district one of the best in Texas?"

Kimmie shrugged. "They were having a hard time fitting in. The children and I aren't from this area, and it's very closed—very cliquish.

241

We were looking for more… spiritual development. New Hope Girls' Ranch. They're very good."

"And you didn't send Wylie to a different school?"

Kimmie looked out the window and didn't say anything. "I don't see how any of this could possibly help you find my daughter."

"One of the things we do in search and rescue is gather all kinds of information and see where the connections lead," I pressed, wondering how to word the next question. "Did Wylie or Faith have insurance or a will?"

There was a long silence, and I tried not to cringe at my own boldness.

"I'm very tired now," she said. She poured another drink and rang a bell on the martini tray.

I was about to get the boot. Get kicked out of enough places and you start to notice a pattern. Besides, I was starting to get a contact high off of her martini fumes.

I rose and offered her a card. "If you want to talk, I'll be here," I said.

She didn't take the card.

I set the card on the silver tray next to the martini shaker so she wouldn't miss it.

The sound of Pilar's sharp steps snapped down the hall, and then she appeared.

"Thank you for your time," I told Kimmie Ray as Pilar prodded me out the door. Behind me, ice clinked as Kimmie Ray poured herself another drink.

Down the corridor and into the foyer, Pilar opened the door, her dark eyes unreadable. There were things unsaid skittering around in the air, and I didn't know how to reach out and grab one.

I fished a card out of my purse and offered it to her.

She stood at the door, her breath audible as she looked at the card. "Pilar," I said, and she shook her head.

But she took my card and slipped it into the apron pocket where she kept her rosary.

I nodded, and she shut the door quietly behind me.

On the porch, I looked out over the rolling lawn, where the man who'd let me in was trimming branches from a low, sprawling pecan tree. Marlowe was in the driver's seat, gnawing on a big, gnarled stick. The end was freshly cut.

I smiled at the man as his chainsaw continued to spit chips of wood into the still, hot air. He shot me a wide grin.

"All right, tough guy. Scoot," I told the dog. He took his stick and, grumping low in his throat, hopped into the passenger seat.

"Where to next?" Marlowe's mouth was still full of stick, so he wasn't a lot of help.

We rolled down the driveway of the Ainsworth estate. As the gate closed behind us, I sat for a moment, looking at the street in front of us. "Right or left?"

I took a deep breath, wishing I had my father's compass. I've heard that life's a lot easier when you've got some direction.

I'm planning to try it sometime.

I pointed the Jeep back to Faith's burned-out trailer at the back of Blackland Ranch to rejoin the search. Somewhere along the way, I just might trip over a clue.

TWENTY

THE REST OF THE day was a total bust, and I manned the coms at the search site until Cantu chased me home at midnight. I hit the sack without taking a shower. The phone woke me at six.

"Hey, kid, how you holding up?"

I stretched in bed with the phone between my shoulder and ear. I figured I'd wake up with Logan one way or another. The phone was the second-best thing. A distant second, but still.

"Tired," I said, and flinched when I rolled over. "Turns out I've got muscles I didn't even know I had."

"Media went well yesterday. You do that?"

Smiling, I said, "Most of it. I tried to hit the road running. Media's got attention deficit disorder, and fifteen's the magic age."

"Magic age?"

"Media attention span shrinks exponentially if the missing kid is older than fifteen. They figure after fifteen they're a runaway. And speaking of that, how come FBI's not involved? Is this the age thing?"

"That, and we haven't been asked."

"Yeah, I don't see Junior Hollis asking for help. I think the only reason he's got Six in is because he's leading the search."

"Any word on the other girl?"

An image of the girl and the smell of burning flesh turned my stomach. "I called Brooke's burn unit. It's not good."

"I'm sorry about that, kid," he said.

"What are you doing?"

"Got a tip on Obregon. I'm on a stakeout."

"You can talk on the phone on a stakeout?"

"Yeah, but I might have to hang up real quick. If I do, no offense."

"None taken."

We were quiet for a moment, and then he said, "Are you going to the funeral today?"

"Holy hell," I swore, jumping out of bed, rolling the dog and cat on top of each other. They untangled themselves and stalked off to the living room, grumbling between themselves to make sure I knew I was being ignored.

"You okay?" Logan said, and I sighed.

"I am living with two passive-aggressive animals, and one of them is yours."

He laughed at that. When Logan laughs, it makes everything inside me settle, and no matter how bad things get, there's always hope.

"Mia and I are going. I figure if Faith is alive and able, she'll be at her brother's funeral. He's the only person she cared about."

"You've been doing your homework."

"I've been watching *To Catch a Thief.*"

"Ah, crime-busting by noir," he said, and it was my turn to smile.

He said, "Did you know there's a Cary Grant festival going on at the Paramount?"

With the phone shrugged between my shoulder and ear, I went to the closet, trying to figure out what I had that could be interpreted as funeral attire.

"I did know that. I didn't know you liked Cary Grant."

"He's okay, but I figure if I sit through that with you, you have to sit through a John Wayne retrospective at the Bob Bullock museum with me."

"That sounds fair," I said, and a small thrill zipped along my nerve endings.

"So, you're okay? No more maniacs in the closet, dead birds, or stalky photos?"

"No, but it's still early."

I chose a black linen dress that Beckett brought back from Dallas Market Days. It wasn't too short, but it had a nice enough scoop that Logan would have something to keep his mind off the funeral. I knew he felt responsible for Puck's death, even though a pair of marshals flanked Puck when he went down.

I threw the dress on the headboard, careful not to get pet fur on it. "Logan?" I said. "Are you all right?"

There was a long silence, and I knew that he was not all right.

"The family's meeting at the funeral home and then there'll be a short graveside service," he said. "I'll probably be a little late, depending on how this thing with Obregon goes."

I accepted that for an answer, because in Logan's way, it was.

"Message received," I said. "See you there."

Mia insisted on driving because she said the Jeep messed up her hair. I decided not to mention the fact that her long, dark, curly hair looked the same whether she was sitting in the salon or shooting photos in a hurricane. She arrived in her little yellow Beetle, which reminded me of a rolling yellow cupcake.

She was decked out in funeral attire Mia-style, with a short black skirt and a black jersey knit top, her smaller Nikon tucked tastefully away in her big black purse. The news never sleeps. Or mourns.

The black linen number I was wearing turned out to be hotter than I thought it would, but nobody ever said fashion was easy. If it were, everyone would do it.

Mia would take photos, and if I was lucky, I would get background for my obituary. If I was very lucky, I might run into Faith. But I kept getting the creeps. Not regular funeral creeps, but the Selena Obregon kind of creeps.

"I did your horoscope this morning," Mia chirped, passing me a cup of green tea that smelled like feet as I folded myself into her Beetle.

Jostling the tea, I buckled up. "We're going to a funeral. I don't want to know if something bad's going to happen. Something bad *already* happened—hence, the funeral."

She had pulled out of the driveway and onto Arroyo Trail when she took her hands off the wheel to dig in her purse.

"Hey!" I yelled, grabbing the steering wheel.

"No, listen. This is good news," she said, unfolding a piece of paper. "Someone important from your past will resurface."

"Well, I hope it's Faith."

"No, see, it's a man," she said, waving the page under my nose.

I groaned, thinking of Hollis and Tres and Deke—and Josh, for that matter. Not to mention Puck, who was now dead. "I've got too many new men in my life to have to put up with old ones."

"I'm just saying, *chica*, it helps to be prepared."

"These days, prepared means stocking up on pepper spray."

Mia left-turned into the parking lot so fast we nearly went on two wheels. I took a deep breath in the parking lot. "Ready?" I said.

Mia gave me the thumbs-up.

The viewing was at the Flight of Angels Funeral Home out by New Hope Church of the Second Coming.

Flight of Angels is located in an ornate limestone building with stained-glass windows and a high, arching entryway with wrought-iron, Mexican-style double Cantera doors.

Inside, the ceilings were high, the colors muted linen, the low-piled, dark red carpet meant to suppress sound and probably clean up well in high-traffic areas. Elaborately carved mahogany chairs were padded with red velvet, which matched the large table and console in the lobby.

There were three viewing rooms, two on opposite sides of the hall and a smaller room in the back. Two other funerals were in progress, and the smells of roses and lilies were giving me a headache. The muted sounds of familiar hymns drifted from under heavy mahogany and brass doors, lilting songs about amazing grace and gathering at the beautiful, beautiful river.

A solicitous old woman urged us to the back room for Puck's viewing, giving us programs. Her hair was bottle black and pulled into a bun so tight it looked like it was holding up her face. She smelled like fresh gin and the Old Testament, and had a personality that matched.

Puck's service started at three in the afternoon. Music from an organ played softly behind a red velvet curtain in the front of the small, mahogany-paneled room. In front of the curtain, three large sprays of yellow roses flanked an elaborate chrome coffin.

Kimmie Ray and Pilar were already there, sitting straight in the velvet chairs cordoned off for family. Both carried handkerchiefs they used to dab their eyes.

Kimmie wore a short black dress expensively cut and a pair of very high heels that got a lot of attention from the male mourners. Pilar, wearing a no-nonsense black cotton dress, held her hand.

I had spoken with Cantu, who reported there weren't any more leads, and that Josh was wandering the site like a zombie with a mission.

The solicitous woman from the lobby came soundlessly in, bearing a tray of cookies and punch, which she placed discretely on a corner console to enhance the viewing experience. She teetered up to Kimmie Ray and said, "I'm sorry for your loss."

Kimmie nodded and dabbed her eyes. The older woman cocked her head.

"Have we met before?" the old woman said.

Startled, Kimmie sat back a little and said, "Well, yes. I buried my husband here five years ago."

The old woman nodded, still studying Kimmie's face. "There was another one too, though, right?"

Kimmie took a deep breath and whispered, "Yes. A long time ago."

The old woman straightened her back, still eyeing her with a bird-like stare. "You got any more husbands layin' around?"

Behind her, Tres arrived, and the door soundlessly opened and shut behind him.

He stepped inside the velvet rope and bent to kiss Kimmie Ray, once on each cheek. He whispered something to her and she nodded. Then he took her hand and gave it one of those double shakes, one at the hand, the other on the elbow, with a pained look on his face. He went to hug Pilar, but she was stiff in his embrace.

"May I help you?" the funeral worker said. She'd slipped back into the room and took Tres by the elbow to seat him behind the family, which seemed to annoy him beyond all reason.

Junior Hollis stood at the back of the hall like a bulldog at the back fence.

I stared at the coffin, but I didn't want to see what was left of Puck. I made my way forward and paid my condolences to Kimmie, then sat toward the back with Mia, feeling like I'd swallowed a concrete brick. Mia squeezed my hand. "You okay, *querida*?"

"I guess. I just keep seeing him laying there on the steps in a pool of blood, and Faith, blood spattered and in shock." I sighed. "What about you? Are you okay?"

"Same thing," Mia said.

A handful of people I didn't know showed up at a quarter 'til. A couple of them were in well-made suits. They filed by, peered into the casket, and nodded to themselves. I frowned. They looked like they were just making sure he was dead. I kept craning my neck, looking for Logan.

At ten 'til, two Hispanic men came in quietly. They both wore their good jeans—the ones with no holes and no fade marks—with shiny cowboy boots, their shirts untucked. They made their way quietly to the back.

"Do we know them?" Mia whispered, and I nodded.

"Chino and Jitters. Puck's light and sound guys from the Pier."

"*Cholos,*" Mia said, and I nodded, looking at the tattoos scrawling from beneath their shirtsleeves. "There's some bad *magia negra* around here."

And then one source of the bad energy Mia felt strolled through the door.

Diego DeLeon and a pair of his cousins sauntered into the funeral home like they were comfortable with death and had seen more than their share of it. Their eyes scanned the visitors on the way up to the casket. Diego leaned over, studied Puck's body, then nodded and crossed himself. The Syndicate's front man making sure El Patron's back man was moldering in the grave. I shivered.

I stared at Diego. *Mia had predicted I'd meet a man from my past.*

He was darkly handsome, like an Abercrombie & Fitch edition of *Boys Gone Bad.* He was nearly six feet tall and dressed in a dark suit, black shirt, and black silk tie that fit so well it made me swallow hard.

His skin was the color of a double shot of bourbon. Diego knelt and said something to Kimmie Ray, gently kissed her hand, and stood.

Movement distracted me from behind, and when I turned, I noticed Chino and Jitters were gone.

I frowned, scanning the room to see if there were any other Syndicate guys skulking in the small crowd. Nobody else I recognized, nobody from El Patron, and still no Faith. I half wondered if Selena Obregon, the escaped leader of El Patron, would materialize among the floral sprays, and I shivered, looking again for Logan.

As Diego took a seat, our gazes met, and something flashed in his dark eyes. My breath caught the way it does when you stumble across a beautiful snake.

A large hand touched my shoulder from behind, and I nearly jumped out of my skin. I looked up and saw Deke. The panic subsided as he sat beside me.

Mia hit me with her elbow and whispered, "*Ay caramba!*"

"Deke," I said, "This is Mia Santiago. Mia, this is Deke. He, uh, works with Faith."

Mia's brown eyes twinkled, and Deke cranked up a smile that reminded me of spring meadows and fresh laundry. No easy feat on a guy that big.

"You all doin' okay?" he whispered in his dark velvet voice.

I shook my head.

"You seen Faith?" he said.

"Not one peep."

Nodding, he leaned back in the pew, arms crossed. Diego's guys were eyeing Deke, and he eyed them back.

Diego leveled his gaze on me, and his lips curved into a slow smile. Beside me, I felt Deke expand.

Then Logan walked in.

Our eyes locked, and I got that feeling of high-powered calm that Logan always exudes. His lips twitched into a half smile of recognition, and as soon as it was there, it was gone. His gaze swept over the room, stopping briefly on Diego and his entourage, Deke, and then Tres, Kimmie Ray, and Pilar.

Logan moved forward, taking Kimmie's hand, and he spoke softly to her. She bowed her head, nodding as the tears came again. Logan stood, turned toward the coffin, and looked down, his jaw muscle clenched, and if you didn't know any better, you'd think he was made of steel. It lasted only a moment, and then he turned, very slowly, and swept the room again. A hush fell over the small congregation. Suddenly, the room felt very cold.

Logan discretely looked down at his cell, and his face stiffened. He looked at me, a hard look that said *be careful,* and then he turned and left.

Mia whispered, "You have such interesting friends."

I'd been bugging Cantu and Logan about gang activity and the possibility of a gang war for the past two weeks. Sitting within three feet of Diego DeLeon, I realized I'd been asking the wrong people.

At that moment, a middle-aged man with proud carriage and a belly that looked like he was trying to hide a basketball pushed through the red velvet curtain and smiled a consoling smile. I wondered if they taught that smile at preacher school. He was carrying a Bible in his pudgy hand, and his hair was sprayed with so much product there was a hole opening in the ozone above him. The preacher from New Hope, I assumed.

He looked down at Puck, then out at the congregation, nodded, and said, "Are we ready?"

I looked at Mia, who shrugged.

"All right then," he said and went out the side door, where Kimmie Ray, Pilar, and Tres went for the family car. The dozen other mourners followed suit. We piled into our respective cars and joined the small funeral procession to Blackland Cemetery in Dawes County.

"Boy, they weren't kidding when they said it was a graveside service," I said, folding myself into Mia's Beetle. She slid her little round sunglasses over her small nose, popped some bubble gum into her mouth, and revved up the little motor. We peeled out of the parking lot. Once we were on the road, she tucked a small yellow rose into the Bug's dandy little dashboard bud vase.

"You stole a flower from a funeral?" I said.

"I borrowed it. They're not using it."

Mia's belief in the hereafter takes some getting used to. It also takes some keeping up with.

We joined the procession and I sat, tapping my pen to my lips.

"Anything strike you as weird back there?" I said.

"The whole thing is weird. You Anglos got a funny way of sending people off to their eternal glory."

"Well, it doesn't usually go that way," I said. "I'm trying to figure out what the deal between Tres and Josh is, and with so few people attending the funeral, why was Diego DeLeon and his Syndicate posse there? I didn't see anyone from El Patron, and we know Puck was connected to El Patron before he was killed. From what I've heard, usually *someone* from a *vato's* gang shows up at the funeral."

Mia shrugged, taking a corner so fast the G-force gave me Angelina Jolie lips.

"Who all have you talked to?" she said.

"The boyfriend, Josh, who's been inebriated since I met him at the Pier; the stepbrother, Tres, who owns her record contract; Dawes County

Sheriff Junior Hollis, who is a total ass and is in charge of the search; Deke, the bouncer, who seems to care about the girls who work at the club; about six strippers; and mama Kimmie Ray. I still have to track down the school she was sent to and why."

"You mean why they sent her and not her brother?" Mia said and took a left so sharp it nearly rolled the Beetle down the embankment. "I thought you said she went to private school for a better education."

"A better education than the Eanes district? You gotta be kidding," I said, white-knuckling the dash.

Mia shrugged. "Where did you say Kimmie met old man Ainsworth?"

I thought back to the archives I'd read.

"His wife was dying. She was a nursing assistant. Mrs. Ainsworth died, and Kimmie cleared out her closet. Old Man Cullen conveniently had a heart attack a year later. He left everything to Tres, who manages Kimmie's estate."

Mia pondered that. "How long has *la criada* been around?"

"Pilar, the housekeeper?" I shrugged. "Long enough that she seems to really care about Wylie and Faith."

"You talk to her?"

I let out a long breath. "No, I didn't. Not really."

Mia smiled serenely. "You want to know what goes on in someone's house, ask the help. People act like they're not there most of the time. And then a big family crisis comes, and they're expected to keep the whole family propped up."

"You know this from *Abuelita* Maria?" I said, and Mia nodded.

"I know from me, too. I used to help my grandmother clean houses on the weekends and after school." She looked down at her hands, no longer callused, but I remember the years when they were. Those same hands now took pictures that won the Texas Press Organization award for photography two years in a row.

I nodded. "I should have thought to ask Pilar."

There was apology in my voice, but Mia shrugged.

"You didn't know. That wasn't your experience. Just like I don't know what it's like to grow up in a house of crazy *gringas.*"

"Oh, give me a break. Your grandma is every bit as crazy as Mama and Clairee," I said, and Mia grinned.

"And you're the better for it, aren't you, *querida?*"

I squeezed her hand. "I think maybe we're both the better for it."

We arrived at the old Blackland Cemetery, where five generations of Pucketts were laid to rest among some of the original settlers of Central Texas. The cemetery showed it.

Sun-scorched weeds tangled out of control, and the drought ripped giant cracks in the earth. I wondered if it was possible for lingering spirits to drift from their dry graves for a peek at the living. Despite the heat, I shivered.

Nana MacKinnon spends an inordinate amount of time at our family plots. She goes there to picnic between Daddy and Grandpa's graves. She says it helps her see more clearly. I used to go with her right after Daddy died.

Later, I was more interested in dance lessons and drama, and my time with the living replaced my time with the dead.

Now I write obituaries for a living. Maybe if I'd sat with Nana a little longer, I could have seen that one coming.

We all filed out of our vehicles in the hundred-degree heat. Kimmie and the family flanked the minister, who smiled benevolently at us as we stood at a respectful distance. The suits all lined up behind us. I thought about Puck and his body in the box, and wondered what he would think about all this, and if he even knew what happened to him and by whom. I wondered where Logan had been called to go, knowing he would call me when he could.

Mia snapped a discrete picture, but the minister caught the lens and his smile widened. She got some crowd shots, and I noticed Diego about six feet behind me. I was trying to think of a respectful way to take a step back and hand him my card when the minister placed one hand on the coffin and lifted the Bible into the air with the other.

In a television preacher voice he boomed, "I was asked to be here today by Kimmie Ray Ainsworth, beloved mother of Wylie Ray Puckett, whom we lay to rest today. I didn't know Wylie Ray Puckett, and I don't know where he is today, but let this be a lesson to all of us."

Ah, a traditional funeral. Who knew?

I stood there, staring at the preacher. Kimmie Ray seemed to go further into shock.

"For a church called New Hope, that didn't sound very hopeful," I whispered to Mia, but her mouth was open, too.

"Did he just say Puck got what he deserved?" Mia said.

"I wonder if that preacher is from the school they sent Faith to," I whispered.

Behind me, I heard a shuffling noise, and I turned to find Diego and his *carnales* were gone.

"Mia," I whispered. "I need to go."

I sprinted around gravestones as quickly as my spike heels would carry me, trying very hard not to sweat, with Mia right behind me.

I figured God would look after Puck, and Pilar would see to Kimmie Ray. I had a gangster to catch, a cat to feed, and a girl to find.

TWENTY-ONE

KNOWING WHERE TO GET information and actually weaseling it out of someone are two different things. It was six o'clock Sunday evening and Tanner wanted something on his desk supporting or refuting a looming gang war in addition to a short on the funeral by tomorrow morning.

I'd been so caught up in finding Faith that I'd let my workload slide. But if Hollis and the crack reporters at the *Journal* were right, the two weren't mutually exclusive.

I needed to talk to Diego DeLeon. I left things badly the last time we'd met, but he didn't tear holes in my panties, leave me a dead bird, or threaten to chop off my ears at the funeral, so things were looking up.

The trick was going to be finding him. Since *carnales* usually don't take out ads in the Yellow Pages, I had Mia drop me off at home so I could make some phone calls and do a computer search on local mobsters.

I waved to the prepubescent cop who was sitting under the streetlight. He grinned and waved back, and I shook my head. The kid had honest-to-God dimples.

After doing the outdoor thing with Marlowe and letting Muse chew me out while I fed her and freshened her water, I shimmied out of my dress and slipped into an old tee shirt and shorts. My whole body sighed inside the soft cotton. I poured myself a tall bourbon and Diet Coke and flipped on the television.

CNN droned in the background about terror alerts and some arms deal going on in South America. I let it drone.

I wrote a short article on the funeral and checked my email. Mia sent the photos of the funeral, and I whizzed through them, chose three, and sent the whole shebang to the FTP site for Ethan to post to the *Sentinel* site, cc-ing a copy to Tanner.

Work for the day done, I Googled Diego DeLeon. I didn't get a phone number or address or an official confession. With a cross-reference between DeLeon and the Syndicate, I found three articles on an acquittal for money laundering two years ago, when the feds shut down a car wash that had allegedly cleaned money for under-the-table affairs at two Syndicate-owned strip clubs—Lipstick and Boners.

Oh, ick. A mafioso with a sense of humor.

I flipped on my cell and called Deke.

"Boners, gentlemen's paradise," a male voice that wasn't Deke barked into the phone. I asked for the bouncer and was informed he hadn't made it back from the funeral.

I was about to ask to leave a message when the guy said, "This is Chino." He talked around what I hoped was a big wad of bubble gum. "Somethin' I can help you wit'?"

Chino the deejay worked at Boners? That was interesting.

"Yes, I saw you at the funeral and before at the Pier, remember? You were doing lights and sound for his sister?" I said.

"Yeah," he said. "You wanted that fed to take my shirt off."

There was something sinister and suggestive in his voice, and I shuddered. "I saw Diego at the funeral today, and he told me to give him a call, but I left without getting his number."

"Uh-huh."

"He told me he's a partner at Boners," I lied, "so I thought I'd try to track him down there."

"He ain't a partner no more," Chino said, and then I was listening to a dial tone.

I stared at the phone. "Well. He obviously skipped phone etiquette in home ec," I told Marlowe. The dog raised an eyebrow but didn't comment.

I called the other club and got even less information. Some reporter I'm going to be. But what I lack in talent I make up for in persistence, and so I called and left a message for Dan Soliz at the gang unit and was told he'd be in at three tomorrow.

Hanging up, I was at a loss. "What would Bogey do?" I said to Marlowe. The dog got up and went to the kitchen and stood in front of the refrigerator.

While the fridge is not usually a font of information, it is occasionally a source of sustenance. I grazed out enough stuff to make a turkey sandwich, gave the dog half, and checked the cat's water.

Eating my half of the sandwich, the dog and I padded back down the hall to the office and fished out the file labeled Organized Crime, took it to the living room, and spread the contents on the Turkish rug.

CNN was still droning about terror alerts, so I flipped to Turner Classics, where *The Big Sleep* sizzled onscreen.

Bacall had Bogey practically panting after her. I wondered about Logan, where he was and if he was okay. I was pretty sure when he found Obregon that she would try to eat him alive. An unexpected jolt of jealousy punched me in the stomach. She was beautiful and charming, but so are some snakes.

Sighing, I sorted the clippings and interviews into two piles—one for El Patron and one for the Syndicate—flipped open a fresh sheet of paper on the legal pad, and made a flow chart, looking for connections.

I zipped through my little red notebook, glancing over the notes I'd taken during my meeting with Soliz.

The Syndicate began as a Mexican-American prison gang meant to protect Tejano prisoners from other organized gangs locked up in Folsom. Two decades later, they expanded to street crimes, including drug trafficking, extortion, and pressure rackets.

Within the past decade, the Syndicate became more organized and began ruling its areas of Austin, San Antonio, and El Paso with an iron fist.

I placed the archived articles in ascending order according to date. There was a distinct spike in execution-style killings eight years ago, but the number tapered off within a year. Following that trend, there were significantly fewer taggings and gang-related graffiti in all three cities. There were also fewer street shootouts and fewer arrests, although that didn't mean the crime wasn't still there—only that it was being controlled. The Syndicate was moving from street crime to organized crime, which meant they were probably getting some influence in local police departments, city governments, and probably even some judicial muscle.

I had a dozen articles regarding bribery between bail bondsmen and the judicial branch in El Paso, but the witnesses mysteriously came up missing.

I thought of Diego and shivered.

Shaking it off, I lined up the info on El Patron—some of which I'd gathered when I'd had my first run-in with Selena Obregon and her ear-chopping, Firestone-burning ilk. El Patron was an Argentinean outfit that came to Central Texas fully organized and running like a well-oiled machine. Their scouts and secondaries came in with smuggling, money laundering, and some insurance fraud, and were successful for a year and a half until the leadership arrived. Selena Obregon was crazy as batshit and blew the entire operation. John Fiennes, the other primary, was just as greedy a bastard. Gorgeous and hypnotic, too, but that's also what they said about Ted Bundy.

Onscreen, Bogey's voice growled along. The black-and-white movie cast amorphous shadows across the living room, making my eyelids feel heavy. I drank some bourbon and Diet Coke and, with much grumbling on his part, scooted Marlowe over on the sofa. It'd been a long day, and the morning was bringing another one hot on its heels.

I pulled the quilt over me and settled in to watch the end of the movie. My mind drifted back to Obregon, and my heart did a nervous riff against my rib cage. How had she escaped with a marshal in the bloody melee at the courthouse?

The phone rang, and I yelped.

The ringing was muffled because Muse was sprawled on the cordless, and she performed a lot of ceremonial bitching as I pulled the receiver out from under her. Muse stalked down the hall toward the bedroom.

"Hello," I said, juggling the receiver.

"Hey, kid, missed talking to you at the wake."

"Logan," I said, feeling a sharp nip of lust.

"No break-ins, no threatening letters? No photographs, no dead birds?" he said. I turned and looked back out my living room window, where the young cop was still in his cruiser, watching my house.

"Not today. Where are you?"

"Doing some paperwork at the office. I'm going out of town for a while."

"Is this one of those things where you can't tell me where you're going or when you'll be back or if you're going to be in a war zone?"

"All of the above."

"Have you got a lead on Obregon?" I said, and he was quiet. I got a terrible vision of Logan in the wilds of Argentina, dodging bullets. "Can you at least tell me if you're leaving the country?"

More silence.

I sighed. "Can you tell me if you're close?"

"Every day a little closer. How 'bout you?"

I looked down at the clutter of papers covering my living room floor. "Working on it."

"Hmm," he said. "Heard you were looking for Diego DeLeon today."

I had to stop myself from growling. "Did you talk to Deke?"

"Just warning you. You poke DeLeon with a stick, he's liable to poke back."

"Yes, I've had him take a poke at me before."

"God, you are stubborn," he said, and I could practically see him pounding his head on his desk.

I wanted to say "No, I'm not," but a sudden and unexpected bout of maturity reared its ugly head. Instead, I said, "Do you think El Patron is back from the dead? Do you think Obregon is going to reorganize?"

"She'll try. But you chop a snake at the head, the body wriggles for a while, and then it's road kill."

"As long as there's not a second snake slithering around in the bushes?"

"There's always that."

I sighed. "Is there a second snake?"

He was quiet.

"Cauley, there are going to be times when our jobs put us at cross-purposes."

I blinked, feeling like I'd just been sucker-punched. I swallowed the punch along with a big slug of bourbon and Diet Coke.

"How big are the crossed purposes?" I said.

"Only as big as you let them get."

I took a breath in and let it out slowly. "When are you leaving?"

"Early tomorrow."

I nodded to myself. "You'll be careful, right?"

I could practically hear him smile on the line. "You too, kid."

"I'm not the one heading into a war zone," I said.

He was quiet again, and then he said, "Don't be so sure."

TWENTY-TWO

"FAITH PUCKETT HAS BEEN missing for two days," Tres said into Miranda's microphone, his long hair lifting in the hot breeze. "She's eighteen years old. Eighteen and with the voice of an angel. She has her whole life ahead of her." He stopped, closed his eyes, took a deep breath through his nose, and began again. "Faith was supposed to start recording her first CD tomorrow evening." Behind him, Kimmie Ray stood holding a photo of Faith, tears streaming down her cheeks.

Cantu stood off to the side, out of camera range, leaning against a haggard-looking red oak. He nodded, encouraging them to continue.

I'd rolled out of bed before daybreak and headed for the search site to meet Mia. Marlowe was exhausted from sleeping on the sofa, and he and the cat were both in bed when I left.

As I suspected, there were fewer volunteers and less media. The big white bus brought the uniformed church kids back in, armed with cookies and Kool-Aid and a prayer circle.

"That's her stepbrother, right? What's he doing?" Mia said, sidling up to me, Nikon out and ready. She lined up her shot to get Tres in the foreground of the rising sun.

"Rescue tactics. He's putting a face and name to the missing person. If she has been kidnapped and her captor sees this broadcast, it makes her more human to her captor—repeating her name, reiterating the fact that she has a family who misses her."

Mia nodded and snapped another shot.

Tres held up a photo of Faith. It was an older shot, the way she looked before she went off to boarding school. I frowned and touched Mia's arm, shaking her off the shot. She raised a brow but lowered her camera.

"She's got so much to live for," Tres said. "Please. If you have any information, any information at all, please call this number. Any information that leads to Faith's safe return..." he looked down at his feet. "Well, we'd appreciate it."

"You mentioned a reward," Miranda said as her cameraman pushed in on the two of them.

Tres nodded and looked straight into the lens. "Any information— any at all, if it has *anything* to do with helping us find Faith and bring her home—will be rewarded."

Miranda wrapped it up and stalked off to find fresh meat.

Tres made his way toward Cantu.

"That right?" Tres said, and Cantu nodded.

"Did good."

Tres stared out over the horizon.

Behind us, Olivia cantered up to Cantu with her clipboard, spoke softly, and the two rushed back to base.

Mia moved closer to me, quietly snapping her lens cap onto her camera.

"At this rate, you people are never going to find her," Tres said. "I'm setting up a second command post at my house on the other end of the ranch."

Mia and I cast each other sideways glances.

"Tres," I said. "I know you're worried, but Cantu is very good at what he does. Team Six is the best in the region."

Tres shook his head. "It's been over two days now. Do you know how mentally fragile Faith is? I have resources you people will never have."

He scanned the field as volunteer searchers linked arms to search another area.

Tres turned to me and looked me hard in the eyes. "I want a media blitz. I want you and your photographer to come to my house this afternoon to help me get organized."

My photographer? To her credit, Mia didn't hex him right there on the spot.

"Tres, I don't know—I think you should talk to Cantu about this…"

He reached into his pocket and produced a business card, as though he hadn't given me one before.

"She's out there somewhere, and I'll find her."

I looked down at the card, feeling a little sick. He was asking me to step outside the lines. I have no problem with that, as long as I think the lines are arbitrary.

Cantu was never arbitrary.

Tres was staring back at base camp, where Cantu and an EMT were treating a young female volunteer for heat exhaustion.

I blew out a breath and slipped the card into my pocket, watching as Cantu pressed a blue cool pack on the girl's forehead. "I'll see what I can do."

Tres headed off to speak with Hollis, and I looked at Mia.

"What are you going to do?" Mia said.

I shook my head. "I don't know yet."

We gazed out over the search scene, and Mia uncapped her camera for a wide shot. Deke was there and the girls I'd spoken with at Boners. Hollis was pacing about, barking orders into his radio. The girls didn't seem impressed.

The icky deejay from the club jittered by the fence, chattering warp speed on a cell phone. Ethan was out with the foot searchers, as he'd been since the first day. Even Kimmie Ray made a brief appearance. "All the usual suspects," Mia said, framing her shot.

I shook my head. "Not all of them," I said. "Where's Josh?"

"ARE YOU ALONE?" I said to Cantu over the phone.

I was back in my office, looking at the preliminary arson reports on the two trailer fires.

"As alone as I can be with a hundred volunteers running around, passing out from the heat."

Cantu sounded tired—more tired than usual—and I was guessing Junior Hollis had a lot to do with that.

"You know anything about Tres Ainsworth going cowboy and starting up his own search op?" Cantu said.

"He's asked me to come help. I said I'd do what I could, but I was so stunned I didn't know what to say."

"Are you going?"

"Only to see what's going on."

He was quiet. "Don't go alone."

"Of course I'm not going alone. I'm taking Mia."

"Oh, that makes me feel so much better. Where's Logan?"

"Gone."

There was a long silence, and he said, "We're not getting anywhere with Boss Hogg in charge. I keep hoping Hollis will haul his fat ass out of here and let us do our job."

"Not likely," I said.

"Yeah, well, a guy can hope. When and where are you supposed to do this thing?"

"Tres's house, two o'clock, which means I might have to rearrange a meeting with Dan Soliz."

"Cauley, stay out of the gang thing," he said, and I knew from experience he was frowning with his whole face.

"My boss just got here. Gotta go," I said. "I'll let you know how it goes at the Ainsworth Palace of Dysfunction."

"What the hell are you doing here this early?" Tanner grumped, trudging down the hall with a giant cup of coffee and a stack of expense reports.

"Why does everyone keep saying that," I said, falling in behind him, armed with my little red notebook as we went into the Cage.

"And so it begins," he said, and sighed. "What've you got?"

"You got my stuff on the gang thing last night, but I'm going to go see Dan Soliz. And funny, Diego DeLeon—the head thug at the Syndicate—was at Puck's funeral. We know Puck was a soldier for El Patron. I want to talk to Soliz."

Tanner was awake now. He set his coffee and paperwork on his desk and went for a licorice whip.

"Okay," he said carefully. "What's got your engines on afterburn?"

I hopped up on his desk. "I don't know, but something. This morning at the search site, Tres Ainsworth told me he's going to branch off, start his own search operation."

Tanner dropped into his swivel chair. "What?"

"Yeah, that was my reaction, too. He wants me to help him set it up."

Tanner gnawed the red candy vine. "Your buddy Cantu know about this?"

"He does now."

Tanner shook his head, his nostrils flared like he'd just smelled a scoop. "What are you going to do?"

"Go see what's going on."

"I take it the search for the girl isn't going well."

I shook my head. "It's technically out of Cantu's jurisdiction. Dawes County's running it like a joke."

"You checking credit cards, phone calls, insurance, the will?"

"Ethan's working on it. No activity on bank or credit cards. Her cell was in the trailer fire."

"Ethan's showing a lot of interest in this."

I nodded but didn't comment.

"Any word on the girl they found in the fire?"

"They ID'd her. She's at Brooke's burn unit, still in intensive care. She's a dancer who worked with Faith. Similar build, similar hair. I only put out the general stuff because they haven't found her family for notification yet."

Tanner nodded. "They think the girl's an accident?"

"Cantu doesn't."

Still gnawing, he nodded, then got up and paced to the window. "Who else knows about the second search?"

"Mia and whoever else he's asked to help. I can't imagine it'd be that many people—it takes a near miracle to raise a search team in any kind of reasonable order, especially if you don't know what you're doing."

Tanner nodded and chewed and then nodded again. "Cauley, you're up to your ass in this thing."

My blood pressure spiked, and I could feel a scolding coming on.

"We give you a lot of leeway with the cops and with the whole search-and-rescue thing because you've got an in, and we figure it's sort of like we've got a reporter embedded in local law enforcement."

I shrugged. "Yeah, so?"

"Just don't forget whose side you're on. You're not a mouthpiece for the police department. Your job is to get all the information that's important to the public and let the public sort it out."

My jaw dropped. An uncommon bit of good sense grabbed the words that almost flew out of my mouth. It also prevented me from kicking him in the leg.

"Tanner, I'm a *volunteer* for the search unit, just like everyone else on the team except Olivia and Cantu. That crew is a good cross-section—we've got a dentist, a photographer, a CPA, and a housewife. Our District Attorney would give his left nut for a jury makeup like Team Six. I don't think any of us forget that we're volunteers."

"I knew you were going to take it that way, and that's not how I meant it," he said. "I was embedded in Afghanistan. I know how you start to depend on each other, get all buddy-buddy, watch each other's backs. I'm just telling you, forewarned is forearmed."

I gaped at him. I didn't know he'd been in Afghanistan. As far as I knew, his life started when he'd been an anchor at ESPN. You tend to forget that a journalism degree can mean a lot of things. I tried to imagine him in fatigues and a Kevlar vest, but I just couldn't picture his perfect broadcast-anchor hair getting messy in the dusty Afghani desert.

Aunt Kat always said Austin was the place to come to be who you always wanted to be or to be who you really are. I wondered now who Tanner really was.

I started to ask him about it, but he was seated at his desk, his head in his hand, looking at the reports. I was being dismissed.

I swallowed. "Okay," I said, hopping down, careful not to drag any papers with me when I went. "I'm going to go get busy."

"You know you still gotta write obituaries, right? Your inbox is getting full."

"I did half of them this morning, along with a short on the search progress."

Tanner nodded.

"I think Ainsworth is going to want a big article on his new and improved search operation."

"You probably wouldn't lose money on that bet. See what you find out, and we'll talk about it when you get back." He blew out a breath. "Where's your FBI agent in all this?"

"Gone," I said, and Tanner nodded.

"Just…" he shook his head. "Be careful."

I nodded and headed for the door.

"Cauley?"

"Yeah?"

"Fine job on getting the search stuff out on the web."

I started to say, "Who are you and what have you done with my boss?" but I figured the answer to that question could take a whole other lifetime.

TWENTY-THREE

I'D BEEN WRONG ABOUT the amount of people who knew about the new and improved amateur sleuthfest sponsored by Tres Ainsworth and his millions of dollars.

A hodgepodge of hopped-up trucks and urban assault vehicles lined the long driveway from the formidable, camera-security, wrought-iron fence to the gargantuan house.

Posted at the gate were two heavily tattooed, dark, disreputable-looking men with mean, thin lips that scowled at us as we climbed out of the car. "Great," I grumbled. Chino and Jitters.

Mia said, "*Qué?*"

"The light and sound guys from Faith's video," I whispered to Mia.

Both wore wide-waisted, low-rider jeans with chains pouring from the pockets and long-tailed, short-sleeved Mexican-style shirts over white tee shirts, attractively accessorized with thick gold necklaces and long-muzzled, intricately carved wood and black steel guns, the likes of which I'd never seen before. As we moved closer, I saw Chino was leading the show. He had an absence about him that seemed to leave a hole in the air around him. They both had elaborate tattoos and scarring that interrupted their arms, like someone had sliced skin off their biceps. I wondered if it was some sort of hazing ritual. There was a dangerous, sexual charge around them that had the little hairs on my neck at full attention. It was times like these I wondered if they still sold chastity belts.

"*Cholos,*" Mia said, and I nodded.

"Yes," I agreed. "Gangsters."

Chino grinned, revealing a desperate need for orthodontia. "*La fresa y la gringa,*" he said in a pretty decent Clint Eastwood, except I didn't think he was kidding.

"*Si,*" I said. "Whitey and the berry."

Mia jabbed me hard with her pointy little elbow, and I fought the urge to gasp and check for puncture wounds.

While getting my breath back, I looked more closely at the alpha dog peering behind the sunglasses. "Chino, right?" I said. "Remember me?"

Suddenly, he grinned a snake's smile. "I thought all us Mexicans looked alike to you."

"We keep running into each other in the most unusual places," I said.

He stared at me, and not knowing what else to do, I stared back, which was easier said than done.

After a long, uncomfortable moment, he said, "What do you want?"

"We're here to see Tres Ainsworth. He asked us to help look for Faith."

He reached behind him and extracted one of those nifty Nextel phones and buzzed the main house. "*E, Jefe,* there's a couple of *chucha cuereras* here. What do you want me to do with them?"

I couldn't hear the other end of the conversation, but Chino looked disappointed. Probably thought he'd get the go-ahead to shoot us.

Instead, he buzzed open the gate and let us in.

As we hiked up the driveway, I could feel the glint off the *pistoleros'* sunglasses starting a fire on my behind.

"What was up with those guns?" I said.

"Thompson Contender," Mia said, her voice breathy. "*Mi Tío Alejo* used to have one."

"Your uncle the drug dealer?" I said, my voice rising an octave.

"Yes. They're like the bling of weapons. I bet they had .44s in the back with their talkies."

I blinked. "Lot of help you were back there," I said. "I particularly liked the part where you choked."

"You are going to get us killed," Mia finally said, her accent heavier, her breath still coming hard. "They may look like they watch too many Robert Rodriguez movies, but those two *cholos* are not playing around. Did you see those tattoos?"

"Chino had a Virgin Mary half cut off on his bicep. I didn't look hard at the other guy," I said, feeling smaller as we walked.

"Yes, but if you look more closely, you would have seen a snake curving around a cross."

My blood froze in my left ventricle. "Like an 'S'?"

She nodded. "You think he defected from the Syndicate?"

"Jeez, I don't know, but things like that really could start a gang war."

Mia shook her head. "They looked like they were going to take us out behind the bushes and break seven of the ten commandments."

I blew out a breath and said, "My lips are zipped. That was careless of me."

She nodded but said, "It was dangerous, but you probably did the right thing. Nothing *los asquerosos* hate worse than a smart-mouth white girl."

"How is that good?"

She grinned. "They're mad at you, *amiga*, not me. If the ball drops, I got time to get away."

We continued up the drive, and I decided silence was probably not at all overrated in a situation such as this.

Despite the relative shade of the overarching trees, the sun had warmed the paved driveway so we got heat from both ends of the earth. Sweat beaded along my spine, and I really hate to sweat.

The grounds were large and well-watered, and several gardeners plodded along, shaping a row of hedges with tools that looked like deli knives. Based on the gate guards, I wondered if Tres hired trained assassins for all his housekeeping needs.

While the landscaping was incredible, the house itself was something to behold, and Mia and I had a lot of time to behold it as we trudged up the long-ass drive. It was a log home, ridiculously large and über-manly, even by Texas standards.

Cullen Wallace Ainsworth III's house was located high on a hill overlooking Blackland Creek. I wondered why Faith lived in a trailer and Tres lived in a woodland palace on neighboring plots of land.

Mia gasped as we drew closer to the house. "How many trees do you think had to die for *la mansión*?" she said, her accent swelling with anger.

"No telling. Jeez—those logs have to be at least three feet in diameter."

Mia was breathing hard, and it wasn't from exertion. She was wearing a short, swingy red skirt and a white tank, with strappy, murder-red sandals, her omnipresent camera bag bouncing off her hip. She showed no sign of exertion as we hiked up the hill. But then, she never did.

I'd decided to go conservative with a white *Sentinel* tank and a pair of khaki shorts, armed only with my mini recorder and my little red notebook. I'd opted for casual because I assumed we'd be doing at least some hiking, depending on how serious Tres was about the alternative search group. Judging from the sheer number of wheels on the pavement, I was guessing he was pretty serious.

The house rose three stories above the high limestone hill looking down on the spring-fed Blackland Creek. Wide, cedar-pillared porches sheltered all four sides of the house.

I started to knock on one of the colossal, rough-hewn doors when it swung open.

"Good afternoon, ladies. May I take your things?" The man who answered the door was small and dark like Mia, but his biceps bulged through his black polo shirt.

Mia whisked her camera and bag out of his reach, her lips curled into a formidable snarl. Probably channeling the spirits of the dead trees.

"Cauley MacKinnon and Mia Santiago. We're here to see Tres," I said. "He's expecting us."

"I bet," he said, and winked at Mia as he swaggered off in search of Tres.

"Take a deep breath," I told Mia. "We'll hit him up for a donation to Tree People on our way out."

I took her by the hand and walked through the open door and into the melee of Tres's Super Search. The little concierge could find us later.

I couldn't believe my eyes. It could have been a reality show on Fox TV. The middle of the house was a lodge that reminded me of the entrance to the Longhorn Caverns. Huge cypress beams supported the high ceiling, and windows provided a clear and commanding view of Blackland Ranch.

"Let me get this straight," Mia said. "Tres lives here, and Faith and her brother lived in rundown, rat-infested trailers?"

I nodded.

"They must really hate their stepbrother."

About a dozen men dressed in fatigues and flack jackets milled about, examining huge commissioned maps. Probably had battle plans spelled out in one-syllable, easy-to-read words.

Most carried weapons in shoulder holsters, although some opted for the old-fashioned, tried-and-true "gun tucked into the back of the pants" trick. I'd have tried it too, but I didn't have a gun, and if I did, it would ruin the side silhouette of my khakis.

From what I could tell, all of the weapons were the size and caliber to stop a herd of charging rhinos. The only thing missing was a flame-thrower. But we hadn't even made it through the foyer, so there was always hope.

There were some women there, but they seemed to be some kind of naughty catering staff—short shorts and baby tees. I could have sworn I'd seen the redhead at Boners.

Mia was snapping shots like she was auditioning for *America's Most Wanted*.

Mia has good instincts.

"Miranda," I swore, and Mia looked up.

Miranda was laughing and chatting with a very large man with a very big gun. He looked like Rambo, if Rambo had gone to prep school. He handed her a drink that looked like bourbon, and she took it, looking up at him from under her lashes. I scowled.

"Is this a search party or a hunting party?" I whispered to Mia.

"Ah, Lois Lane and the photographer," Tres said, gleaming blondly down the cavernous hallway off to the right, showing all of his very white teeth in a smile. He wore some kind of safari suit he probably had custom-made for him and new, heavy-duty hiking boots. His arms stretched out for a hug. I reached into the hug for a shake and said, "Mia."

His left brow arched. "Excuse me?"

"Mia. She's too polite to tell you her name, but I suffer no such delusions."

He looked at me for a moment, trying to decide if I was kidding, and apparently decided I was, because he took Mia's hand and kissed it. I couldn't be sure, but I'd bet this month's 401(k) deduction she'd just blasted him with some ancient Mayan curse.

"Mia, then. If you'd be so kind as to take photographs of the search team," he said. "I think it's important that the man who took Faith know what he's dealing with. Lois, I have something else in mind for you."

This time, it was Mia who cast me a warning glance. There are few things in life I enjoy more than people telling me how to do my job.

I bit my tongue because a girl was missing, his stepsister no less, and not a lot seemed to be getting done about it.

Tres led me down an arched hallway made of logs bigger around than Mia's and my butts put together. We stepped through a large door and entered what had to be his home office. I was glad Mia wasn't there to see it.

The room did all but shout *Men doing manly things here!* It was larger than my kitchen, living, and bedroom put together and was swathed in various exotic animal furs. The tiger fur by the office fireplace still had its head attached. Unconsciously, I touched my collar, making sure my head was firmly attached to my neck.

A menagerie of stuffed heads—deer and elk and some other game animals I couldn't identify—lined the upper walls close to the ceiling, where they stared grimly out into an empty eternity. Very symmetrical, not very artistic.

A stuffed bear stood upright, baring his teeth at a stuffed cougar frozen in a pounce, locked in a mortal combat that never happened in life. Beyond the bear and cougar was a large window that revealed a rugged-looking deck. Probably a place for Tres and his friends to smash beer cans on their heads and pee outdoors.

There was something Freudian about the size of the house and all the weapons and stuffed wild animals, and I had to try hard to avert my eyes from Tres's groin area to see if I was right.

"Ah, you like my mounts?" he said, catching my gaze.

"Decorating with carcasses is probably an acquired taste."

"Are you a vegetarian?" he was making himself a drink at the hand-carved Mexican bar, talking to me over the chinking ice.

"I'm a borderline vegetarian," I said. "I eat meat, but I feel bad about it."

He laughed at that and offered me a drink. I accepted it because it was polite, but more importantly, people often talk more freely when they're playing host—they're in control. Looking around at the open-mouthed animal heads peering ominously down at me, I was guessing control was important to Tres.

"Is this your family's ranch?" I said, and he nodded, pleased with himself. "But the house is new?"

"Ain't it great?" he said. "I bulldozed the old house, had this built on the same spot. Bigger and better, right?"

"Sure," I said, wanting to wash my mouth out with soap.

"Bought Kimmie a house on the hill like she always wanted. She's set for life."

"Does she know that?" I said.

"Know what?"

"That she's set for life."

"'Course she does. She's lucky, and she knows it. She's grateful for what she's got, and let me tell you, you'd be surprised how many people just don't appreciate a good thing when they've got it."

"All this and a philosopher, too," I said. "But Faith and Wylie?"

Tres's amiable smile faltered. "Hey, I tried to help them, but they don't wanna play by the rules."

"Your rules?" I said.

He looked at me like I'd spoken Swahili. Ignoring the question, he ushered me over to a brass-nailed, distressed leather chair and took his place behind the vast space of a desk constructed of a kind of wood I didn't recognize. A business-style checkbook lay on top of the desk, along with a collection of snowglobes that contained tiny worlds, tidily captured and preserved in time. The globes were lined up along the edge of the desk, much like the animal heads.

Behind him, there were photos of himself. Tres with the governor. Tres with the former governor. Tres with a past president. Tres dressed in hunting gear with a collection of German shorthaired pointers. All the photos were also lined up, perfectly spaced and aligned along the tops and bottoms like a straightedge. I was beginning to notice an anal-retentive theme.

Along the right wall, a large, custom-built gun cabinet housed what had to be at least a hundred guns of all shapes and sizes. Along the top and enclosed in individual glass cases were old flintlock pistols and shotguns that looked about two hundred years old.

I looked around and realized that everything in the office was part of a collection. Because he'd asked me here, I was guessing I was next on his acquisition list.

"I don't have a lot of confidence in Junior Hollis," he began.

That made two of us.

"I've assembled a team of some of the best hunters and trackers in the Southwest. We're going to be using state-of-the-art tracking equipment, and we're beginning our search this afternoon."

"State-of-the-art," I repeated. "You mean like night vision goggles and things?"

"Among other equipment. We have heat-seeking radar and access to all kinds of toys that Dawes County doesn't provide."

I shook my head, still blown away by the paramilitary forces loading up in the living room. "Where did you find these people? How did you scramble them so quickly?"

"They belong to the Hunters and Killers Club. We meet once a month and..." he swept his arm, indicating the animal heads, "we hunt."

I set my drink down on the desk, unsipped. I figured polite had flown out the wide window five minutes ago. "But you're not really *hunting* Faith, right?"

"Of course not. We're tracking her, but it's the same principle. These men are some of the best hunters in the world."

"So what are your plans?"

"Simple. We're gonna track her down and bring her back, and then we're gonna bring the sonovabitch who took her to justice."

I stood, and from the right rear corner of the office, I could see ten miles of countryside stretching out toward the horizon, framed in perfect symmetry through the wide pane of glass. Just below us, a large, curved swimming pool was designed to look like a creek falling into a natural pool. A cabana that probably served as both pool house and guest quarters nestled in a crook of the stream.

Farther out, a large cedar barn loomed over a cluster of smaller cedar cabins—probably for staff. Beyond the compound, a bulldozer trudged a path through a small stand of live oaks, making its way toward another outbuilding about the size of my house. Around the building, the earth was freshly moved, and building supplies lay scattered about like skeletal remains.

"Are you adding on?" I said, nodding toward the new outbuilding.

Tres nodded sadly. "That's the recording studio. I'm still making adjustments."

I remembered the card he'd given me, declaring himself the "owner" of Incubus, yet another recording company to wash ashore in the river city.

"Is Faith your only client?"

"My first."

"And you're still building?"

"Oh, we'll find her, Ms. MacKinnon."

That was the first time he hadn't called me by the nickname he'd bestowed upon me, and it sounded strange coming from his lips.

"Seems like you've got the whole thing figured out," I said. "So why am I here?"

"I need a mouthpiece for the media."

I felt a bump in my blood pressure. *Keep your cool, Cauley.*

I nodded. In a voice as calm as I could muster, I said, "You realize I'm an obituary writer, and I don't have any control over what goes into the newspaper. My editor collects stories. Ultimately, what winds up on the page is his decision."

Tres smiled. "I bet you got more influence than you think. And what about all that publicity you got for Cantu and his search team?"

"That's not publicity, that's news."

He gave an elegant shrug. "I wanna see everything you write before it goes through." He slid the big checkbook in front of him and produced an expensive pen. Leveling his gaze on me, he said, "How much?"

"Nobody but our editor reviews our copy before it's submitted," I said, fighting the color that rose hot in my cheeks. "I volunteer for Cantu's team. And if you want to pay for publicity, that's what the ad department is for."

Something flashed in his blue eyes, but it was gone as quickly as it came.

"Well, now, I pissed you off," he said. "I'm real sorry 'bout that."

I shook my head, but my stomach roiled. I was going to be sick. "No apologies necessary. I'll do what I can," I said, lying through my teeth. "In the meantime, I've got a lot of work to do. Mia has taken photos and we need to go through them to see what we're going to post on the search website."

"I'd like copies of all of those photos," he said, and I blinked.

"You'll have to take that up with Mia."

His face went hard beneath the smile he flashed me. "You bet."

I swallowed, looking into his eyes. I wondered if Faith was really missing or if she just left. I wondered if she wanted to be found.

"I appreciate your offer. I have some things I need to discuss with my boss." I didn't appreciate his offer; it made my skin crawl. But I wanted to keep this avenue of communication open. I gave him my card and flashed him my second-best smile, careful not to be added to one of his collections.

"So," I said. "You know anything about Puck's relationship with El Patron?"

He blinked. "Why would I know that?"

"Just curious. Do you know Selena Obregon?"

He smoothed his hair over his ears. "Of course not. Why would I?"

Tension stretched between us as he ushered me to the door, where Mia was already waiting for me with the short chicano major-domo who'd ushered us in.

Tres eyed Mia's camera.

"I'll email you copies of the photos," I said, bumping Mia out the door with my hip. We had a long way to travel to get to the bottom of the drive where we'd parked, and I didn't want any of that den of snipers to use our butts for target practice.

"You think *los asquerosos* are going to find her?" Mia said as we hustled down the drive.

I shook my head. "For Faith's sake, I hope they don't."

TWENTY-FOUR

I WAS WAY BEHIND on sleep by the time I got to the office. I tossed my purse under my desk and booted up my old, rickety office computer and stared at the blank screen. I had five more obits to write, but I thought I could fall asleep standing up, let alone sitting in front of a blank screen. I was tired. I knew my heart had been pounding, but I hadn't realized my adrenaline had been pumping like jet fuel. I was coming down from the pitch, and it made my blood feel like sludge oozing through my veins.

I'd called Cantu on the way back to the office and told him about the vigilantes gathering at Tres's hacienda in the hills, and then I called Dan Soliz's office and asked to reschedule my appointment for the following day. I called Olivia, who was running the third team. She had nothing new to report.

"Cauley?" Tanner came in through the front hall and motioned me into his office.

I went in behind him. My legs felt like they'd been made with a Jell-O mold that'd gone terribly wrong.

He shut the door behind me.

"You look like hell," he said.

"Thank you. I feel like hell."

"You're not hurt or anything?"

"No, just beat. It's been a long day."

He sat at his chair and listened as I told him about the search mercenaries camping out at Tres's and about the house, the over-enthusiastic security, the view from the office—including what was left of Faith's trailer—and the recording studio, which was still under construction.

Tanner fetched a licorice whip and was chewing it vigorously while he listened.

"Hunters and Killers Club, huh," he said, and I nodded.

He swiveled toward his computer and did a Lexis-Nexis search.

"The sports guy before Shiner did a piece on those headcases about three years ago," he said. "I've seen outfits like this before. Buncha middle-aged men with too much time on their hands. Paintball doesn't do it for them anymore, and they're too chicken shit to go for a real hunt."

"That sounds like this bunch. They think they're tough guys because they're armed to the teeth."

I thought about the real tough guys in my life: Logan, Cantu, my dad, and the Colonel. I shook my head. "They wouldn't know how to act if they ever got into it with a real tough guy."

Tanner nodded.

"Who you got left to talk to?"

I got out my little red notebook. "I want to talk to Pilar, the mother's housekeeper, and that minister from the funeral. And I still want to talk to Diego DeLeon and stop by the school Faith was sent off too. The Dawes County cops think Josh did it; the *Journal* thinks the Syndicate had something to do with it."

"What do you think?"

I shook my head. "I don't know. Something doesn't add up. I do know this: if I had her life, I'd sure as hell run for the hills. She doesn't seem to have any family support and no friends unless you count the strippers at Boners."

"Her brother seems to be pulling out all the stops to find her," Tanner pointed out.

"*Step*brother. Tanner, if you'd seen that place. It was like a movie set—like a John Wayne flick on steroids. Nothing about it seemed real. If she disappeared herself, I don't blame her. And if she did, I'm guessing she doesn't want to be found."

He nodded. "What are you going to do now?"

"I've got four more obits. I'm thinking about taking them home to finish. And I've got an afternoon thing with Soliz at the gang unit tomorrow, so I may need to come in late."

"What else is new?" he said, and I growled at him.

"Take the rest of the day and we'll see you tomorrow."

I looked up at his clock. "Four forty-five. You get more generous every day."

He made a lip jerk that might have been a smile. Or it could have been persistent gas. I stuck my notebook back in my pocket and headed for the door.

"Cauley," he said. "Be careful. And if you get that interview with DeLeon, take Shiner with you."

My mouth fell open. "He hasn't even darkened our door since he got on City Desk."

"Well, he'll darken it now. Don't go see DeLeon without him."

"Take Shiner, my ass," I muttered, grabbing the file folder of obits and my purse from my desk.

"I heard that," he yelled.

But he yelled it to my back, because I was already on my way down the hall and out the door.

AT HOME, I'D WRITTEN the obits, emailed them to Tanner, got myself a cold Corona with a lime, and taken a bubble bath, which would have been a lot more relaxing if the dog and cat hadn't sat in the bathroom and stared at me. Olivia would be handing the search over to Cantu by now, and Cantu told me to stay home.

Doing what I was told for a change, I slipped into the white Turkish robe Aunt Kat had sent me from Istanbul while she'd written *The Turk and the Temptress* and ordered a pizza. I called the cop parked out front that a pizza guy was coming so he wouldn't mess with my Canadian bacon. I tipped the delivery boy extra to take half of it over to the kid in the cruiser. From the window, I waved and he waved back.

I settled in on the sofa, where I shared my feast with Muse and Marlowe. I should have been going over my notes, but all I wanted to do was veg out and forget about the world whirling around outside the window. I thought about Tres and his mercenaries, Incubus, the recording studio, and Faith's ineffectual mother. I kept getting the sneaking feeling that Hollis might be right. Faith didn't want to be found.

Turner Classics was doing a Bogey and Bacall tribute, and the two simmered in the tropical setting of *To Have and Have Not*.

"Perfect," I told the dog, who, having finished his slice, was eyeing mine with his dark almond eyes. I shook my head. "Bogey's got nothin' on you, does he, boy?"

The dog looked confident, so I tore off the crust and said, "Want a pizza bone?"

He woofed, causing Muse to slink off the back of the sofa to claim her share. I tore the crust in half, and both animals looked as though they'd been transported straight to fast-food heaven.

Onscreen, Bogey was minding his own business when the island leader of the French resistance tried to recruit him to save a boatload of refugees.

At home, someone pounded at the door.

I yelped at a sudden vision of the canary guy, sneering, brandishing a steak knife and a Polaroid camera.

Outside, a young, masculine voice snapped, "Hey! Let go! I'm a friend!"

Jostling the dog and cat, I peeked through a clear piece of stained glass at the front door and found the young cop holding Ethan by the scruff of his neck. Ethan was squirming like a pup caught peeing on the carpet.

I swung open the door and shook my head. "It's okay," I said. "He's with me."

The cop looked at Ethan, then back at me, and said, "You're kidding."

"Hey!" Ethan said. "I've kissed her before."

The cop's brows rose so high they disappeared into his hairline. I shrugged. "Tequila."

The cop grinned and nodded. "Been there. You need any help, just holler," he said, and gave Ethan one more warning glare, snapped me a little salute, then headed back to his cruiser.

"Ethan, what are you doing? You look like hell."

He bustled into the house with a stack of files and a handful of mini CDs and a palm-sized computer. "I've got phone and bank records, credit card reports, insurance info, and old man Ainsworth's will. I thought maybe we could go over it—see if any of it helps."

Gazing around the living room, he spotted the box of pizza on the coffee table. "Hey, food!"

Sighing, I said, "Let's see what you got."

He grabbed a slice and, juggling sustenance and research, made for the kitchen table. I said, "There's more room on the floor."

"Won't the animals bother us?"

I looked at the puncture wounds on his neck. "Did Puck's cat bite you on the neck?"

"I tried to pry him off the curtains. That cat is the spawn of Nosferatu."

I thought of the decrepit vampire from old German horror flicks and said, "Yeah, kind of looks like him, too. I can get Bug the pet shop guy to take him until Logan gets back."

"Nah. Let's find Faith first."

I smiled. "Look's like the cat's not the only thing that bit you."

Ignoring me, Ethan spread out the papers on the rug. Muse promptly hopped onto a stack, turned around, and pawed it into a suitable nest, then curled up and sent us a smug look.

"She's wrinkling my reports," E said.

"At least she's not drawing blood."

He nodded and sighed. "Okay, here's what we've got."

Ethan had organized his research and cross-referenced it all, using a program he'd created specifically for the purpose. I trotted back to my office to get the timeline and my own file I'd created.

After deciding that no one was going to eat more pizza, Marlowe stretched out and laid his head on my lap.

Ethan and I dug into our piles of paperwork. There was nothing remarkable that I could see about the phone or bank records, and none showed activity since Faith disappeared. He pulled out a credit report.

"No loans at all. And I couldn't find any life insurance, but look—there's no health insurance, either," E said, and I frowned.

"A lot of people don't have health insurance. It's not great news, but it's not unusual, and she's eighteen. How many loans did you have when you were eighteen?"

"Did you see her teeth?"

"Well dang, Ethan, I left my dental probe at home that day."

"All of her front teeth are too even—she's had work done."

I shrugged. "So?"

"It costs almost three thousand a tooth. Where'd she get the money?"

"Her family's got money. Maybe they have a family doctor."

"Her *family* doesn't have money." He pushed a ream of paperwork under my nose. "Old man Ainsworth left half his money and all the land and holdings to Tres. The rest is in a trust monitored by a group called Lone Star Investments. Kimmie gets an allowance, but she doesn't even own the house she lives in."

I flipped through the document. "That's bizarre. I wonder why he did that?"

Ethan shrugged. "I don't know, but look at this: Kimmie Ray doesn't even own her family's ranch."

"What?" I stared at the deed he'd handed me and read aloud, "Deeded to Cullen Ainsworth II for the amount of ten dollars plus other consideration."

Ethan scowled. "Other consideration."

"This is dated seven years ago," I said, tapping my pen to my lips. I reached under Muse for a file marked *Ainsworth Family Members*. "Look," I said, thumbing through the articles until I got to the society page. "'Cullen Wallace Ainsworth II weds Kimmie Ray Puckett'— mother Puckett married into the Ainsworth empire seven years ago."

Ethan frowned. "What do you think it means?"

"It means she signed over her children's inheritance seven years ago and got married."

We sat there, staring at the documents, trying to figure out why Kimmie would do such a thing.

"Maybe she thought he'd take care of her kids?" I offered.

We were quiet.

"Do you think El Patron has anything to do with this? Like a vendetta or something?" Ethan said.

"I don't think so. Their quarrel was with Puck, and they've been off the radar in the United States since Obregon got sent to the slammer."

Ethan frowned. "But you don't know?"

"I have to believe whoever is leaving me nasty messages is connected with El Patron—everyone else stays under the radar. Who else do you know who grandstands like this?"

Ethan shook his head. "Could Puck have had a friend or something like that? Someone he confided in? I mean, we already know he was thick with El Patron and the Argentineans, so he could have been privy to the ear and panty threats. And we know he liked to brag."

"Good point," I said. "I don't know. That's something else we're going to have to check on."

Ethan swallowed hard. "Do you think someone is trying to kill her?"

"You mean do I think someone mistook Tiffany for Faith?" I said, and Ethan nodded.

I shook my head. "I don't know that either. I've got the report on Wylie's trailer fire," I said, skimming through my own paperwork. I handed Ethan the report. "Wylie's fire was an arson—kerosene and matches. Not sophisticated. Cantu said they should have a report on Faith's tomorrow."

"You sure Faith's fire is arson?"

"Yes."

"Because her brother's was arson?"

"No," I said. "Because Marlowe alerted on it when we were there."

"Alerted?"

"He's cross-trained in search and rescue and arson," I said. "He circled three times and did this weird little barking noise he does. He did it when Van Gogh tried to set my house on fire."

Marlowe lifted his head at the sound of his name. Finding no one had broken out a bag of peanut butter cookies, he laid his head back in my lap.

"Do you think someone kidnapped her?" E said, and I shook my head.

"I don't know. Tres asked me out to his house to take a look at the search op he and his hunting buddies started. I gotta tell ya, E, it was like a parody of an old Rambo flick. If she did disappear herself, I'm guessing she doesn't want to be found."

Ethan reached over and scratched Muse behind the ear. "If we find her and she doesn't want to be found, what are we going to do?"

"We have to tell people we found her. I don't think we have to tell them where."

Ethan and I were both quiet.

In the background, *To Have and Have Not* continued onscreen, casting dark, shifting shadows on the walls.

"This is one of my favorites," Ethan said.

"I thought geeks were all about *Star Trek*."

"I like to diversify my obsessions," he said.

We were quiet as we watched Bacall, playing a nightclub singer-slash-pickpocket, get slapped in the face by a Gestapo hardcase. She didn't cry, didn't even flinch, and I thought about Faith and wondered if she was more like the nightclub singer than I'd thought.

"Did you know Bogey and Bacall were married?" Ethan said.

"I did know that," I said, scratching Marlowe on his chin.

Ethan absently stroked Muse, who was in such a purring stupor that she actually slobbered. "You know they supposedly fell in love at first sight?"

I smiled, still watching the movie. Ethan was trying to say something, and I knew he'd get around to it.

"Hey," he finally said. "Do you believe in love at first sight?"

I knew he was talking about Faith. His eyes were wide, and there was pain there, pain and fear, like whatever I said next would be the key that unlocked a door he'd always hoped to find but didn't dare believe existed.

I thought of the first time I'd seen Logan, when every cell in my body seemed to leap toward him. I sighed. "Last year if you'd asked me that, I would have laughed in your face."

Ethan waited.

I looked out the front window while I scratched Marlowe between his ears. "Now," I said, "I'll have to get back to you on that."

TWENTY-FIVE

ETHAN WOUND UP SLEEPING on the sofa amid a flutter of papers. Muse, the little traitor, slept with him. Granted, she slept on his face, but still.

He hustled out of the house at the crack of dawn to go do whatever it is that computer geeks do to get ready for work, and I cleaned up the pizza mess, showered, blasted my hair, and got dressed.

Since I had an appointment to speak with Dan Soliz at the downtown cop shop, I went for a short black skirt, a fitted white shirt, and a pair of black stilettos that have been known to make men beg for mercy. I was going to need as much mercy as I could get—he'd already warned me off Diego DeLeon once. Soliz was a *two strikes and you're out* kind of guy.

I fed the cat, let the dog out, and waved at the cop sitting out in front of my house. This morning's shift was an older cop, with a bushy gray mustache and jowls that flopped over his collar. The jowls were probably a prelude to his belly.

He scowled at me when I waved, and I cranked my smile up a notch.

I was also guessing he'd screwed up big-time to have to pull pussy patrol and that he was pretty unhappy about it.

After Marlowe peed on the Bobs' rosemary bush, I headed back down the sidewalk and stopped at my walkway. The flag on my mailbox was up. I frowned, wondering if Ethan might have mailed something on his way out. But that didn't make sense. Ethan emailed or texted everything. I don't think he'd ever even seen a stamp in his short, sheltered life.

Marlowe was overjoyed at the change up in our morning routine, and danced around the mailbox like he'd hit the winning lottery numbers. As I reached for the box, I got that uneasy feeling that makes your skin crawl.

I opened door, and inside the mailbox was a Polaroid of me in my bathrobe, reaching over Ethan for a file.

"How did he get by the cop?" I said, and Cantu frowned.

My heart was still pounding, but my blood was beginning to slow down a little. A rookie crime geek was dusting my mailbox for prints, and two more were lurking around the yard, looking for dead birds, notes, knives, and chopped-off body parts.

"That fat cop? Everett Anders is a burnout," he said. "He's been busted down to beat for excessive force. Thinks pulling watch is beneath him."

"And you? Who's running the search show?"

"Hollis called it off today."

My mouth fell open. "And there's nothing you can do about it?"

"Out of our jurisdiction," he said. His voice didn't change, but I could feel the shift. He was angry, and if there ever came a time when Hollis was in a dark alley with Cantu, I didn't like the sheriff's chances.

"They aren't going to find any fingerprints, are they?"

"Pretty slim. Hasn't left any yet," he said, and I nodded.

"So," he said. "Who's the new guy?"

"Ethan?" I frowned, and he flipped out the Polaroid, which was tucked into an evidence bag. "Oh, give me a break. He's my coworker. You've seen him at the search sight. He's got it bad for Faith. We were comparing notes."

"Notes," Cantu said skeptically. "And Logan?"

"On assignment." I thought about him, picturing him on a crowded, dirty street in Argentina, and had to close my eyes a minute.

Cantu nodded. "And you? What are you up to today?"

He was looking at my shoes, and I smiled. "I'm going to weasel information out of somebody."

"Anybody I know?"

"I'll never tell," I said. "Wish me luck."

He shook his head. "Kiddo, with you, luck has nothing to do with it."

With police reports filed and cops out of my yard, I applied a fresh coat of lip-gloss and headed out for work, hoping the morning wasn't an omen about the rest of the day.

Marlowe leapt out of the house after me and jumped into the Jeep, and I was too tired to argue with him. Besides, I was on edge, and it has been my experience that Marlowe is good company when I have maniacs threatening my body parts.

We arrived at the office, and as I badged Harold the heavyset guard, he leaned over and gave Marlowe one of his powdered sugar donuts. He didn't offer me one.

I threw my purse under my desk and booted up my computer. Marlowe finished his donut and trotted down the aisle of cubicles back toward the Graphics Department in search of better sustenance.

It was eleven o'clock, and Tanner was sitting in his glass office, staring at me.

"What?" I said.

He crooked a finger. "I hear you got another message from the freaky photographer?"

"You and your damn scanner."

He sat, gnawing on a licorice whip. "Want to take the rest of the day off?"

I shook my head. "I'm sure you've heard, but the search for Faith Puckett is off. Those idiots in Dawes County have completely botched the thing, but it's not over. I've got a meeting with Soliz in a little while. I rescheduled once. I don't want to do it again."

"The report on the trailer fire," he said, handing the stack of faxes to me.

He rocked back in his chair, staring at his desk. I waited.

"You know why they called off the search?"

"Because they're idiots who didn't run it right in the first place?"

"Because they made an arrest this morning."

My breath caught. "Who?"

"Josh Lambert."

My mouth dropped open, and my brain stuttered to a complete stop.

He tossed another stack of faxes on the corner of his desk. "They picked him up last night, drunk, at that club Faith worked at. He failed a lie detector test, and this morning, he confessed."

"To what?"

"Sheriff Hollis says he's got a statement that he nabbed Faith."

I frowned. "So then where is she?"

"He wouldn't say. Hollis says he failed the polygraph."

I had to let out a long, slow breath or my head was going to explode. "Lie detectors don't count, and besides—you said yourself Josh was drunk."

"He confessed."

"Tanner, he's been inebriated since before Faith went missing. His blood alcohol content was 100-proof."

Tanner shrugged. "You know she had a restraining order out on him?"

I cringed. Apparently I'd missed the restraining order in my research. Some reporter I'm going to be.

"What about Tres and his mercenaries?" I said.

"They called off the search once Josh confessed."

"And what about Tiffany, the girl in the trailer fire?"

"They figure he did her, thinking she was Faith."

I rolled my eyes. "Tanner, Josh Lambert was the one on the scene who said the girl *wasn't* Faith."

Tanner shrugged. "You can aim for the bleachers, but you don't always get the grand slam."

One of his stupid sports analogies. I had to refrain from breaking something.

"This isn't over," I said, grabbing both of the files on my way out the door.

"It is for you," he said, and I turned and was about to say something pithy and scathing, but I stopped. Dark circles ringed his eyes like purple bruises, and he looked thinner. I hadn't noticed that before.

"Tanner," I said. "Are you okay?"

A little color tinged his cheeks, but then he turned back to his desk and the stack of reports that were waiting for him.

"I saw the dog," he said.

"He's back in Graphics, searching for Skittles."

He nodded. "You can send him in here if you want."

"He'd like that," I said. And then I shut the door quietly behind me.

Marlowe spent the rest of the morning with Tanner, who had started hiding dog biscuits in the bottom of his file cabinet back in July. The two of them had some mystical bond that transcended the biscuits, but the biscuits didn't hurt.

I checked on Ethan, who made it in to work on time, then I made some phone calls to families to finish the three obituaries in my inbox. That done, I grabbed my purse.

Tanner leaned out his door. His face was relaxed, and he looked better than I'd seen him in a while. Marlowe has that effect on people.

"You going to see Soliz?"

"Yep."

"You taking the dog?"

I nodded. "I'm going home after."

Tanner nodded and stepped aside. Marlowe trotted out of the office, tail high, with a big doggie grin on his face.

"You're spoiling him," I said, and Tanner looked pleased.

"I'll send you an email about what I find out," I said, and the dog and I trotted down the front hall, past Harold the heavyset guard and out to the parking lot, where my Jeep awaited me.

I'd arrived late that morning, so I had to park at the side of the strip center, outside the meat market, which always put Marlowe on high alert. As I was dragging him by the window display of Elgin sausage, I nearly ran right into the black Jaguar that was parked between the curb and my car.

The back door opened and a large man with skin the color of a double latte unfolded himself, straightening his tie as he stood up.

Here's the thing: the only people who wear suits in Austin are FBI agents and funeral directors. And mobsters.

"We hear you been lookin' for Diego DeLeon," he said.

Marlowe growled low in his throat.

"We're here to escort you to his office."

My heart thumped hard.

I ducked my head to look into the car, but the windows were so tinted that the only thing I could see was my own reflection.

"Come on, we'll drop off the dog."

I shook my head. "The dog comes or I don't go."

He got a pained look on his face and looked up at the sky.

There was a tap on the window, and the guy scowled.

"All right," he said, ushering me into the back seat. "Mr. DeLeon wants to see you. We'll let him sort this out."

MY HEART POUNDED AS we right-turned onto Ranch Road 2222. There were two guys in the front seat staring straight ahead. They were both broad shouldered, wore well-tailored suits, and were probably related to Diego DeLeon. Neither seemed to enjoy Marlowe poking his head over the console to growl at them.

I had my hand on his neck, but just barely. If things went south, I didn't want the dog to think these people were friends.

They had frisked me before we left and took my cell phone and my purse. I wasn't sure why they took the purse, unless they were afraid I might blind one of them with an eyebrow pencil. There was, of course, the recorder, which, in my profession, is way more dangerous than almost any other kind of weapon.

My blood pounded in my ears as we turned onto Loop One and headed downtown.

"Um, where are we going?" I said.

Thug One answered, "To see the Chairman."

I nodded. "Right. And the Chairman is Diego, right?"

They didn't answer.

Come again from a different angle. "And where would the Chairman be?"

I was picturing some white, high-walled hacienda complete with fountains and parrots and tequila with worms, when we pulled into the parking garage of a high rise next to the Frost Bank building downtown.

My heart went into overdrive.

Marlowe's growl intensified.

"Relax," Thug One said.

Right. I was sitting on the bottom floor of a parking garage with two soldiers from one of the most dangerous organized crime outfits in the southwestern United States. Nobody knew where I was; I didn't have a phone, a gun, or a clue as to what was going on.

Thug Two slid in near the elevator while Thug One opened my door. Well, if they were going to kill me, at least they were being chivalrous about it.

I'd been looking for Diego DeLeon on and off for days. I was finally here and wishing I wasn't. I wondered where Logan was. I wondered if Mia had done my horoscope today. I wondered if Marlowe was too full of Skittles to kick some serious mafia butt.

Drawing in a deep breath, I went with Thug One up the parking elevator and walked across the lobby to the glass elevator that serviced the rest of the building. The lobby was grand, as all the downtown lobbies are, with fountains and trees and flowers and piano music surrounding a bar and a restaurant.

People looked at Marlowe as they often did, but no one said a word. His orange collar meant he was an SAR dog, but most people mistook him for a service canine.

The thought of Marlowe serving anybody made me laugh a little, and it slipped out as we went up the elevator. Apparently, laughter, no matter how slight, is the wrong response to being summoned to the Chairman's office, because Thug One gaped the way some men do when they're asked to hold a wet baby.

We disembarked on the top floor, where wide windows showed the city of Austin gleaming beneath us. As we walked across the plush burgundy carpet and into the grandeur of Diego DeLeon's office, Marlowe was getting edgier.

He wasn't the only one.

The office took up almost all of the top floor, and the view was like nothing I'd ever seen. The capitol looked like it was a stone's throw away, and I felt like I could reach out and touch the Goddess of Liberty as she stood, stalwart, atop the shining dome.

The office smelled of good cigars, expensive Scotch, and fresh carpet cleaner. It was huge, and it was a wall-to-wall study in black. Black desk, black tinting on the wide windows, black and chrome furniture, and a big black and glass desk, situated so that it looked like Diego was doing a newscast in front of the capitol dome.

In a brief bit of fancy, I pictured myself at his desk, killer red shoes kicked up on the glass-topped desk, my trusty Remington Scout with clean, white paper rolled into the barrel, fresh and ready for an article that would literally stop the presses.

"Cauley," Diego said, rising to meet me, breaking me out of my truly excellent little fantasy. "We meet again. I see you brought a guest."

I narrowed my eyes. I'd known Diego in high school. He was still darkly handsome with unnaturally white teeth, but time had softened him around the edges. He wore a black suit with a monochromatic shirt and tie that probably cost more than four years of my car insurance without a deductible. Back then he had an unhealthy fixation with the *Godfather* trilogy, but he talked like a *vato*, not a Soprano. Time changes everyone, and not always for the good.

Diego waved to his second, and Thug One bowed out. I couldn't be sure, but he looked happy to be absent of my presence.

"Actually, Marlowe and I were about to see Dan Soliz about you when we got your invitation." Marlowe leaned into my leg, nearly toppling me off my killer heels.

Diego looked at me as though he was appraising a stolen gemstone, critical but appreciative. I stifled the urge to tug my skirt a little further down my thigh.

"So what is it that you want to see me about?" he said, cutting to the chase.

I blinked. I had my whole weaseling speech made out for Soliz, not for DeLeon. I hadn't gotten that far on my to-do list yet.

Because he'd jumped into the deep end, I decided I would, too. "There are a lot of people who think you had something to do with Wylie Ray Puckett's death and with Faith Puckett's disappearance. There are people who think you're going to start a territory war with Selena Obregon and what's left of El Patron."

Diego's dark gold eyes flashed and an unpleasant silence stretched across the room. Marlowe growled low in his throat. I put my hand on his neck.

Diego nodded, steepling his hands. "Why would people think that?"

I shrugged. "In a way, it makes sense. El Patron was horning in on your territory. Granted, they were doing rackets the Syndicate hasn't cashed in on."

"Yet," Diego said, and he motioned me to come sit in the sleek black leather chair in front of his desk. He swiveled around and opened a short black console that housed a stash of very expensive liquors.

He poured himself a Glenfiddich and asked if I'd like one as well.

I declined.

A slow smile spread on his full lips, and he said, "What do you think?"

I took a deep breath. "I think you didn't."

"Because they arrested a suspect?"

"No," I said. "Doesn't seem grand enough to suit your style."

He nodded and sipped his Scotch. "Would you believe me if I told you we had nothing to do with either?"

I shrugged. "I would, but I'd want to know why."

He nodded and smiled, clearly amused at his little game. "Because I already have El Patron. Selena Obregon is in the wind, and the Syndicate is absorbing the body. The rest is falling into place. Sheep will always need a leader."

Yikes.

"And as for your friend Mr. Puckett," he said.

And then he looked me in the eyes with a gaze that should have turned me straight to stone. "We have better ways of taking care of nasty business. We don't like attention. We don't shoot people on the courthouse steps. When we exert discipline, no one even knows about it. Just—*poof*—problem solved."

Diego sat back in his chair and took a long tug on his drink.

In the deafening silence, I heard the conversation Logan and I had with Puck weeks ago pounding in my ears.

"We're not staging a shootout. Hits don't go down like that," Logan said.

"How do you know? You got statistics to back it up?" Puck had said.

"Logan's right," I said. "Hits never go down like that. Nobody knows there's even been a hit until the cops find a dead body in a deserted ditch in the boondocks."

My head went light, like I didn't have enough oxygen.

I nodded, trying to get my voice back as Puck's words echoed from beyond the grave.

"So why are you telling me this?" I said. "Why not just let me keep looking for you and wait me out?"

Diego smiled. "I like you, Cauley. You are persistent, but it was only a matter of time before you started annoying me with all the questions. You got *cajones*—like how we ended things this summer. Speaking of that, have you seen Mr. Fiennes?"

"No. Have you seen Selena?"

He poured himself another drink.

"I like you because you amuse me, but make no mistake, it's not wise to annoy me."

I swallowed hard, calling up courage, resolve, and a good old-fashioned dose of complete disregard for common sense. "Have I annoyed you enough to send me a thug with a dead bird, threatening notes, and creepy photos?"

He cocked a dark brow and was quiet.

Marlowe shifted beside me, his ears half back, his almond eyes trained on DeLeon.

DeLeon sat back in his chair and steepled his hands. "Cauley, if I send you a message, you will know it was me."

He smiled and a chill settled along my skin.

"Now I've frightened you." He waved an elegant, manicured hand. "Despite what you might think, we are doing good things here. We have cleaned up the East Side. There are no more drive-by shootings. Children play in the streets. There is no more unsightly gang tagging and graffiti, no more 'You disrespect me, I'm gonna kill you and your family' bullshit. We are benevolent with our citizens. We donate to charitable causes. Who else will look after our people? The government?" He laughed bitterly. "Since I have become Chairman, we have organized. I don't wish to draw close scrutiny. Organization is the key to our future."

"The Syndicate's future or Austin's Latino future?" I said, getting my voice back.

"They're one in the same, no?"

304

They weren't one in the same, at least I hoped not. I thought about what Soliz had said about the Syndicate: blood in, blood out.

I chose not to bring it up.

"And," he said over his steepled hands. "I give you this favor. Perhaps you will do the same for me sometime."

My heart stuttered as I stared back into his lionesque eyes. He may be well dressed, handsome, and have a killer office, but Diego DeLeon had become a very dangerous man.

"Word is you've got some rogue *cholos* on your hands. And Selena Obregon may have disappeared, but she's still out there," I said. "And so is John Fiennes. El Patron may not be as leaderless as you think."

A slow smile spread across his face. "Not to worry. I have people working on those little problems as we speak."

He hit a button, and Thug One came back into the room. Diego nodded, and the guy handed me my purse. Still in a daze, I got up to leave. Marlowe pressed in close beside me.

"Cauley," Diego said. "Do you know how to shoot a gun?"

I blinked. "I took the Concealed to Carry classes."

He nodded like I'd passed some sort of test. "Do you own a gun?"

I frowned. "Someone wants to shoot me, they're going to have to bring their own gun."

He chuckled at that, but he pulled out his top drawer and produced a little .38 Smith & Wesson similar to the one Mark Ramsey had given me over the summer. The one Van Gogh had wrested from me and tried to shoot me with.

"Consider it a gift," he said, coming around the desk to give it to me. "There are dangerous men about," he said, and everything inside me went horribly still.

I'd heard those words before.

Right before I was shot at, stabbed, and nearly bled to death.

TWENTY-SIX

UNDER THE SUSPICIOUS, POWDERED-SUGAR-FOGGED gaze of Harold the heavyset guard, I got to work early and called Cantu.

I timed my call carefully—an hour before elementary school started, so he would be smack-dab in the middle of his cereal-pouring, hair-braiding, shoelace-tying, pre-school extravaganza. Up to his elbows in rugrats, he wouldn't have time to yell at me for what I had to tell him.

"Cantu," he growled when he picked up the phone. The television blared *Bob the Builder* in the background, in unison with various shrieks, cries, and something that sounded like banging on pots and pans.

"Oh," I said. "I'm sorry. Is this a bad time?"

He snarled audibly. "Just wait. Your turn will come, and then we'll see who's laughing."

The thought of that gave me a moment of slight horror, followed by an unexpected tug somewhere near my solar plexus.

"That'll be the day," I said. "I've got some stuff to tell you. Did you send the fax on Faith's fire?"

"Of course," he said. "I got nothin' better to do than leg work for you."

I smiled. "You know I appreciate this, right?"

He grumbled. "Faxed the prelim report this morning. Should be on your machine."

"Thank you," I said. "And now I've got something for you."

In the middle of his youth-infested melee, I filled him in on my misadventures with my new law-and-order-challenged friend.

"You got in a car with two of Diego DeLeon's *carnales*? Alone? Without calling me?" His voice rose in pitch with each sentence fragment, and I could practically hear him pound his head on the perennial pile of Cheerios on his kid's highchair as the oldest reprobate screamed something about flushing the hamster down the toilet.

"That kid's gonna be an exterminator," I said.

"Only exterminator around here is DeLeon. We'll talk about this later. And for God's sake, stay out of trouble," he said.

"Say hey to Arlene," I said, but he'd already disconnected.

"If I knew how to stay out of trouble, don't you think I would?" I muttered to no one.

I booted up my computer, and while it chugged and churned and sputtered to life, I got out my to-do list and checked off:

Walk dog

Feed cat

Call Cantu

Get fax

I looked up at the clock above the Cage. Eight o'clock. I smiled smugly, checking Cantu off with a flourish. Now all I had left was:

Answer email, Compare Faith's report with Puck's arson report, Call Junior Hollis re: why the hell he locked up Josh Lambert, Make appt. to talk to Josh Lambert, Face time with Tanner, Lust after Tom Logan...

I sighed. I could go ahead and check Logan off, too.

I wandered back to the fax and dug through the pile of printouts, mostly composed of useless press releases, cheap trips to Disneyland, and a couple of notes from our friendly neighborhood conspiracy theorist.

I retrieved Faith's report, refilled my iced tea in the breakroom, and headed back for my desk to compare the report to Puck's. Both Fire Scene Investigation Reports were more than twenty pages long. Both had excruciating details about contributory factors, incendiary indicators from the accelerant-detection dog, forensic lab findings, and a five-page list of additional information, which included enough firearms to give Charlton Heston multiple wet dreams. The rest of the report required massive additional doses of caffeine.

Faith's preliminary report was longer and more tedious, but in a sordid way, more interesting.

The part about the damage to Tiffany's body made my stomach slip into a queasy knot. The rest of it was almost as bad.

The words *incendiary device* jumped out at me like a rattlesnake at a gerbil farm.

The device was simple but well thought out, constructed of fertilizer, cotton, diesel fuel, and, of all things, a newspaper.

In a short, brief blight of professional narcissism, I wondered which newspaper the arsonist had used. I hoped it wasn't ours.

I placed the reports side by side and stared at them. On the surface, they looked the same.

Puck's trailer fire was arson, but it was set ablaze by a frenzied dousing of kerosene inside and out. The incendiary device wasn't identified, but the investigator surmised that it was probably common, most likely a match or cigarette.

Faith's trailer fire was arson, but the accelerant found was trace amounts of diesel fuel.

I skipped the part that detailed the condition of Tiffany's clothes, shoes, and person, although I glanced at her location inside the trailer when the fire started. Apparently, the point of origin was in the back bedroom. What was left of Tiffany was found in a pile of rubble outside the kitchen area. Her body, it appeared, had been thrown nearly twenty feet.

Taking a deep breath, I continued. There were no copious amounts of chemical fuel; however, the investigators found residue from a commonly used chemical fertilizer, with slight traces of diesel residue. The incendiary device, the investigator concluded, wasn't complicated, but it was professional and matched the MO from a string of East Austin arsons dating back eight years.

"A fertilizer bomb," I said softly, about to Google the subject when a voice said, "Who's got a bomb?"

"Jeez, E! You scared the living crap out of me."

He dropped into the swivel chair next to my desk and toed it forward so that he was squeezed in beside me.

"You got anything?" he said, and I told him what I'd found so far, ending with the arson reports.

He nodded grimly. "But Faith's report is preliminary, right?"

"Yeah, but Cantu sent it. That's enough for me."

Ethan blew out a lot of air. "Has Tiffany's family been notified?"

I nodded. "Yes. Her mother's staying at a motel near the burn center in San Antonio."

"No dad?"

"There's a dad. Hasn't spoken with her since her life started slipping downslope."

E's eyes went cold. "Maybe he's part of her slip."

We sat quietly, staring at the report as though if we stared long enough, it might change.

It didn't.

"You think the same person set both trailers on fire?" He took Jessica Alba off her paperclip perch and ran his thumb over her full head of plastic hair.

"Trick question," I said. "I think the same person's behind it, but I don't think the same person did it."

E's brows pinched into a frown.

"The first fire is sloppy. Almost like a rage. Anybody watches the Discovery Channel for an hour knows an investigator's gonna know in seconds in an arson. And anyone can get ahold of kerosene. Faith's fire was planned out. It wasn't a sophisticated incendiary device, but it does take a working knowledge of arson to pull it off without blowing yourself up. The tools take at least a day to drum up unless you've got access to the right kind of fertilizer."

"Like Josh," Ethan said. "He'd have fertilizer on the farm, right?"

"Anybody can get fertilizer," I said. "But the *kind* of fertilizer will narrow it down." I sighed. "He's in jail, so he's already at the top of Hollis's suspect list."

"Who else you think is on the list?" he said.

"Usually they start with family, friends, and boyfriends, but you have to have motive and opportunity, too."

I got out my little red notebook and started scribbling.

Ethan nodded. "Her brother's gone. You think they're looking at her mother?"

"I wouldn't doubt it. Her mother lives in a big house by herself and sent Faith off when she was just a girl. Motive could have been all kinds of mother/daughter Greek tragedy stuff, or it could be as simple as wanting her new husband and her new life, and her children wouldn't assimilate." I shook my head. "I just can't see the Cave Beetle Queen starting trailer fires."

"What about the old lady?" he said.

"Pilar?" I shook my head. "She seemed to care for Faith and Puck. Felt sorry for them, I think."

Ethan frowned. "And you don't think it's El Patron or Syndicate?"

I shook my head. "I just told you what Diego said."

"And you believe him? Just like that?"

"I believe *you* when you tell me the girls I set you up with are too geeky for you."

He stopped short of sticking his tongue out at me. "What about that sheriff—Hollis, right? I didn't like the way he looked at her that night at the Pier."

"I don't like Hollis much either, and the girls said he was a regular at the club when he wasn't raiding the place for drugs and minors."

"Yeah, but wasn't Faith a minor when she started there?"

I felt like one of those little cartoon light bulbs went off over my head. "Yes, she was." I scribbled in my notebook.

"What about friends?" E said.

"Haven't been able to track down friends. She said all she had was Puck in the whole world. And like it or not, Hollis is right about her working at Boners. It widens the suspect pool exponentially. Any one of the guys who visited the club could be a potential suspect."

Ethan's brain whirled so hard I could almost hear it. "But what about a motive? Wouldn't someone from the club have to have a motive?"

"Let's see, what are the usual motives for crime?" I said, ticking them off in my notebook. "Love, greed, revenge, envy."

"Obsession," Ethan added, and my hand stilled as I wrote.

"Don't you think Josh is obsessed with her? Obsession can be a powerful emotion," Ethan said.

"Yes," I said, looking at Ethan. "It is." As I said the words, a chill ran up my spine. I thought about Ethan and how emotionally invested he'd been with Faith since he'd met her. I knew I wasn't the only one who'd noticed. Watching Ethan, I said, "Obsession can be a real bitch."

TWENTY-SEVEN

ETHAN'S CELL WENT OFF and he scuttled back to IT to single-handedly save the cyber world, or at least the *Sentinel's* little corner of it.

I called Logan and got his voice mail. My nerves settled a little at the recorded sound of his deep Fort Worth drawl. Waiting for the beep, I wondered if he was okay and any closer to finding Selena Obregon. I worried about his safety. Not just because he was chasing a murderous femme fatale, but because this woman could charm the pants off a priest. I knew Logan thought he was keeping me safe from her, but with God as my witness, if she laid one manicured finger on him, she'd have me, my mama, and all the MacKinnons to pay. I left him a message about what was going on in my end of the world and reminded him that, though he was an FBI agent, he was also an attorney, and any information I gave him was quid pro quo.

Clicking the *off* button, I drew a deep breath and settled in to get back to work, unable to tamp down the feeling of unease slipping around my insides.

Turning to my old computer, I accessed email, which took another five minutes of chugging and churning to bring my messages onscreen. Rather than sit and swear over all the time lost to the Internet, I decided to use my time productively to access my actual paper files of stuff I'd been working on, which were available the moment I pulled them out of my messenger bag. Go figure.

I spread the papers on my desk and separated them into piles. I retrieved the notes I'd made post mortem of my interview with Diego DeLeon and looked for connections.

While I was jotting related notes, my email beeped. Fifteen death notices from area funeral homes, seventy-eight press releases from PR firms who for some unknown reason pitched me—an obituary writer—articles on everything from a chiropractor participating in a local health fair to rabies vaccination day at City Park. In retrospect, the rabies thing might actually have been sent to the right person.

I saved one of the two jokes from Mia and deleted the snippy one from Human Resources saying I'd used up my flex days.

I was about to forward Mia's joke to Ethan when my phone beeped; the caller ID said *Caller Unknown*. All the cells in my body lifted at my first thought … *Logan* …

I flipped open the phone with a whole-body smile. "Well hello, stranger," I said in my best Lauren Bacall.

There was a short, confused pause, and then a female voice said, "*Excúseme?* I must have the wrong number," in a melodic Spanish lilt.

My heart dropped and my cheeks went three shades of red over my Bacall impression. I snapped into professional mode and cleared my throat. "Um, this is Cauley MacKinnon. Is there something I can help you with?"

After a long silence, the voice came back, but it was very small. "Missus MacKinnon, I—I need to talk to you …"

My breath caught as I recognized the voice. *Pilar, Kimmie Ray's housekeeper.* Juggling the phone, I pulled out my little red notebook, steadying my voice. "Yes, yes, I'm here, Pilar."

Her voice went lower, like she was ducking for cover. "This was a mistake. I should not call you…"

"Wait," I said, "you said you needed to talk to me, and I'm listening."

Silence.

I took a deep breath. "I think Faith is in trouble, and I think you do, too. Pilar, whatever you say to me stays between you and me. You'll be covered as a journalist's confidential informant, and I swear it on my grandma MacCauley's grave."

I rarely swear on my grandma's grave. But she was one of the last of the big-shouldered broads, and I was pretty sure she wouldn't mind.

Daddy used to take me fishing, and he taught me the value of endurance—of holding back so you can reel in the big one. He also taught me there's a time for swearing—grandma's grave or not.

With my ear to the phone, I heard the woman's breath quiver. "Not here," she whispered. *"No puedo hablar aquí."*

PILAR HUNG UP.

"Arrrrggghhhh!" I said, flipping my phone shut with enough force to void my warranty.

She said she couldn't talk right now. I didn't want to scare her, and I surely didn't want to get her in trouble. So, the trick was to track her down somewhere where we could talk in private before she backed out.

She'd been calling from a cell with an unlisted number—probably one of those disposable over-the-counter jobs you can get at the gas station—so that was a bust. I Googled Pilar Hernandez. The search got me 330 sites that had nothing to do with a Latina housekeeper in Westlake.

Sighing, I flipped through my notebook, looking for clues.

What did I know about Pilar? She lived in a gated house in Westlake Hills, took care of Kimmie Ray Puckett Ainsworth—a woman who had checked out on her children and her life with a couple cases of booze several years ago—and she carried rosary beads. She also apparently cared about Wylie and Faith, the children who had been in her charge for only a few short years. I shook my head. I didn't even know Pilar's last name.

I took turns twirling my chair, thrumming my fingers, and tapping my feet dangerously near my surge protector, waiting for a brilliant thought. Nothing happened. I was about to get up to freshen my iced tea when my computer binged. *I had mail!*

From phernandez@ainsworth.com. My fingers stilled over the mouse, and then I opened it:

> Dear Ms. MacKinnon,
> I have to speak with you about los niños pobres.
> I have been reading about your search efforts for Faith.
> Please come this afternoon. Alone.

She'd given an address off of Chicon Street, an old neighborhood in the southeast quadrant of old downtown. The area was going through the growing pains that included class wars and gentrification.

I scrolled back through the email. There was an air of desperation in the short missive, and I could practically feel it pulsing on my monitor.

But meeting this afternoon? I had to wait until this afternoon?

Did this woman even know who she was talking to? I'm the girl who stands in front of the microwave and screams, "Hurry, hurry, hurry!"

A big case of the jitters grabbed me by the shoulders and shook me hard. It could have been adrenaline, the last of the five iced teas I'd packed away that morning, or a simmering combination of both.

I nearly paced the length of the aisle back to the breakroom for another glass of iced tea, but reason prevailed.

A loud *thump* sounded near the empty reception desk, and Tanner came harumphing down the hallway, arms loaded with files, a briefcase, and a humongous trough of coffee he'd bought at the gas station.

I sprinted toward him and started in on him before he hit his office. I know this is not a good thing, but I tend toward lapses in judgment when I get excited. Just ask some of my ex-boyfriends.

"You're so hot to know if the *Journal's* got a scoop on some looming gang war, and I'm happy to report that, once again, the *Journal* is wrong. There's nothing to the gang war," I said.

Tanner brandished his coffee at me like a cross warding off an over-caffeinated vampire.

He squinted at me through bloodshot eyes. "What are you doing here?" he grumbled, unlocking the Cage and shoving a stack of papers on his desk aside with the trough-o'-coffee he'd been juggling.

"I still work here, right?"

"With this staff, work is relative," he said, dropping into his office chair like he'd just run out of steam. He took a big slug of coffee and rubbed his eyes. "All right. Let me have it."

"There's nothing going on between El Patron and the Syndicate," I said.

Tanner stared at me. "And?"

"That's it."

He stared at me some more. "Your new buddy Detective Soliz told you this?"

"Well," I said, and he rolled his eyes, leaned forward, and snatched a licorice whip out of the jar. He was going to need a fresh supply soon if this kept up the way I thought it would.

"Just hear me out," I said. "I was on my way to go see Soliz when Diego DeLeon sort of offered me an invitation for an interview."

His brows rose. "You take Shiner?"

"There wasn't time. He sent a couple of his people for me."

A vein the size of a no. 2 pencil popped out on his head.

"Nothing happened. Marlowe was with me. I just had a talk with the man. The reason I couldn't find him was because I wasn't looking in the right places. I was looking for him personally, and it turns out he's incorporated."

"What in hell are you talking about?"

"He's got an office downtown and everything. I know. Shocked the hell out of me, too. But Soliz told me the Syndicate was getting organized. He wasn't kidding."

"And Diego DeLeon just crawled out of the sewer and told you they're not going to war with El Patron?"

"He said the two groups are working on an agreement to integrate."

"Integrate? Makes it sound like a corporate merger."

"For them I think it is," I said.

Tanner nodded. "He heard from Obregon?"

"No."

"And you believe him based on what?"

I shrugged. "He wasn't lying to me, Tanner."

Tanner shook his head. "You get tape on this?"

I grimaced. "They sort of took my purse, which had my recorder and cell in it."

"They took your cell? You had no way to call for help?" His left eye started to twitch. "Nothing happened, right? You're okay?"

I decided not to tell him about the gun DeLeon had given me. "Yeah," I said. "I'm fine."

"Any word on the canary killer who attacked you?" he said, and I shook my head.

"No prints. The forensics guys say they know the store the box came from, but about a bazillion people bought that kind of box. Nothing on the origin of the Polaroid."

Tanner leaned back in his chair. "How do you know DeLeon didn't do it?"

"Because I asked him."

Tanner blinked, then shook his head like I had single-handedly destroyed his last ounce of patience. Finally, he sighed. "Got enough for ink?" he said, and I nodded.

"Fine. Go write it," he growled, waving me off.

"There's more," I said, and he looked like I'd just snapped his brain stem. "I got a phone call this morning."

He stared at me. "From who?"

"I can't tell you—source insists on staying confidential—but I have a meeting this afternoon."

"Take Shiner."

I wanted to say *Screw Shiner and the horse he rode in on,* but I self-edited and said, "Tanner, the source called *me.* She's not dangerous. I've met her and I think she trusts me. If I take anyone with me, it's going to compromise the interview and you know it."

I shook my head. "She has to stay confidential, but Tanner, she's not connected—not to El Patron, and not to the Syndicate, I swear—but she could help me find out what happened to Faith."

Tanner let out a long sigh. "Remember what happened with your last confidential source," he said, and I cringed, thinking of Puck.

"That was a low blow," I said. "And technically, he was Logan's confidential informant, not mine."

Tanner pinched the bridge of his nose. "Yeah, it was a low blow. But that doesn't make it wrong. Just try to make sure nobody gets killed this time."

"You'll be sorry you said that. She's an Ainsworth insider."

Tanner got very still, and his nostrils flared the way they do when he smells a scoop—like he'd got a whiff of a big plate of red meat.

He hoisted himself out of his rolly chair and went to the big window overlooking the Hill Country, gnawing vigorously on what was left of the licorice. "Anyone else know about this?"

I shook my head. "Hence the *confidential informant* thing."

He twirled the stub of licorice between his fingers and thumb the way I'd seen him do a million times with his cigars.

He turned from the window and pointed the short whip at me. "You get tape on this, you hear?"

I shot him a salute. "You bet," I said, pivoting to rush out the door. I grabbed my purse and my flurry of papers and files and fled the scene before he could change his mind.

At home, I fed the cat, walked the dog, and settled in front of the computer with my files and concocted a short article on the possible integration of two Austin gangs, attributing Diego DeLeon's quotes to an anonymous source. Then I called Mia to ask her if she had any old file photos for the article.

"Where the hell are you?" she wanted to know.

I could hear the clattering keyboards and tech chatter from the Bull Pen.

"I went in early and left. I've got an interview this afternoon, and I need to know if you've still got old shots of tagging on the East Side."

"Of course I got tagging. It's my heritage, *chica*."

"Right," I said, and told her about my trip to the DeLeon crime headquarters, his claim of gang integration, and his boast that crime was at an all-time low on the East Side.

"Ts, ts," Mia tutted. "Report of crime may be at an all-time low, but it's still there. You know they're preying on immigrants?"

"I know a little about it. Cantu told me illegals don't report crimes against them because they're afraid of the INS, suspicious of all police, and there's a very real fear they'll be deported."

Mia snorted. "That ain't the half of it, *chica*. And yeah, I got old graffiti shots. Want me to email 'em?" She hesitated, like she was picturing the photographs in her head. "You know," she said, "some of that tagging is real art."

"I do know that. Will you email the shots to Ethan so he can get it online with the story? I want Mark the Shark Ramsey and his crack staff at the *Journal* to be able to eat our ink before noon."

Mia laughed. "Miss Competitive. So what are we going to do this afternoon?" she said.

I had to bite my tongue not to invite her to go see Pilar. Having Mia around is always a good thing. The fact that she can speak rapid-fire Spanish and knows the East Side inside out is just a bonus. But confidentiality is a touchy thing with a reluctant source.

"Just some busywork." I paused. "Mia?" I said.

"Yeah?"

"I really appreciate you getting me the tag shots."

There was a silence, and she said, "You okay, *chica?*"

I sighed. "Okay is relative these days."

THUNDERHEADS MOVED ALONG JAGGED Hill Country skyline, spattering stinging pellets of rain. I knew this kind of storm and so did Marlowe, who rode beside me under the small shelter of the Jeep's canvas. He sat, ears pricked, his dark eyes following the dark clouds that wouldn't rain.

Lightning struck, and thunder boomed so hard I could feel it all the way to my bones.

Marlowe didn't whine, but he laid his head on the dash, eyebrows twitching as he looked through the dry windshield and back at me. I put my hand on his head, and he sighed.

Texans are no strangers to drought, but each thundering boom paired with the absence of rain stings like a sharp slap to the face.

We headed down Loop One, exiting at First Street, and headed up Cesar Chavez Street and into the city's East Side.

There's no place else in Texas like Austin's East Side. It buzzes with bouncy mariachi music, vibrant color, and the spicy smells of *comida tejana* drifting like a breeze flown special delivery from Mexican food paradise.

Marlowe and I drove down the old street lined with live oaks and palm trees, past Arkie's Grill, an Austin landmark since 1948, and I heard the dog's stomach growl.

"When we get done, okay?" I told the dog, but his eyes were trained on the old restaurant.

We passed a fiesta of small, colorful houses—bright Caribbean blue, celery green, and bubble gum pink—all built before World War I, and I looked closely for addresses among the small, fenced yards that rioted with blooming yucca and palms, cheerful Mexican salvia, sunflowers, and bursts of bright native plants crowding statues of various saints.

I pulled up to the address indicated on Pilar's email. The small, red-tile-roofed, white stucco *casita* was surrounded by a gated stucco wall. The wrought-iron gate was open, so I pulled inside and parked by a birdbath.

The Jeep rattled to a stop. "What do you think?" I said to Marlowe, but I could tell his little puppy mind was still sniffing the air for pork ribs at Arkie's.

Pilar's heavy Cantera door was framed with palms, and, to the right, an arbor of shocking pink and blood-red Castilian roses shrined a statue of the Virgin of Guadalupe.

The white, tatted curtain in the front window cracked open an inch, and a faded brown eyeball peeked out.

I took a deep breath. "You're going to have to stay in the car," I said to the dog, and I swear he smirked at me.

Pilar poked her head out of the door, eyes scanning the yard. "Shut the gate, and park behind the big pampas grass," she hissed.

"Ooooh-kay," I said to no one, turning the key so that the Jeep rattled back to life. Pilar wanted me to park behind what was essentially an overgrown potted plant. You don't get much more SpyGirlz than that. I glanced around the fenced front yard, hoping the knife-wielding canary guy wasn't about to jump out from behind the palm tree.

I've been on interviews that ended up with me on the wrong end of a loaded gun, but I hadn't thought talking to an eighty-year-old woman might be one of them.

I made sure my notebook and tape recorder were in my purse and thought briefly about stashing the little .38 that Diego DeLeon had given me into the glove box. But in addition to Pilar giving me the creeps, I still had to worry about the canary guy, not to mention the fact that Selena Obregon was on the loose. Logan would catch her, I knew it as surely as I knew the earth orbited the sun, but if Pilar was spooked in her own home, I figured better safe than sorry.

Still peeking out the door, Pilar hissed, "You can bring the dog…"

I looked over at Marlowe, who seemed more than a little smug.

"All right, smarty," I said, but the dog was busy catapulting off of me and onto Pilar's brick driveway. After catching my breath from sixty pounds of dog pouncing off my solar plexus, I climbed out of the Jeep after him, careful to avoid knife-wielding maniacs and escaped homicidal femme fatales.

"Missus MacKinnon?" she said ushering us in to shut the door behind us.

"Please," I said. "Call me Cauley. This is Marlowe."

She bent to scratch Marlowe behind his ear. "I saw *el perro* in your car when you came to see Señora Ainsworth." Standing, she said, "Come." She led us through the Mexican-tiled living area and through a pair of French doors to a small walled courtyard filled with a rainforest of potted plants surrounding a little mosaic garden table. More pink and red Castilian roses rioted up the walls of the house and courtyard. They didn't smell like flower-store roses—the scent was lighter, like fruit—and it reminded me of cool sangria on a hot summer day.

Pilar herself seemed different, too; she was softer, more approachable, out of her maid's uniform. She looked elegant in black slacks with a clingy black boatneck shirt and a beautiful hand-hammered silver necklace in the shape of an intricate cross. Her long, silver hair hung in a thick braid down her back.

"Señora Hernandez," I said, and she shook her head.

"Pilar," she said, motioning to a white wrought-iron chair. "Lemonade?"

"Thank you," I said as she poured a glass for me and one for herself, then she went inside for a bowl of water for Marlowe.

I accepted the frosty glass as Marlowe lapped noisily at the water bowl Pilar gave him. I took a sip of lemonade and my eyebrows shot to my hairline. "Wow," I said, and Pilar smiled.

"Mint and Pyrate's rum," she said.

"Tasty," I said, blinking. "The Congressional Committee on Alternative Fuels know about this?"

She smiled, which deepened the lines in her face but somehow made her look younger.

"You have a lovely home," I said. "I thought you lived with Mrs. Ainsworth."

Pilar shook her head. "Tres gives Missus Kim an allowance and pays her bills. I am only there during the week now." She looked around at her courtyard with contentment. "This house has been in my family for many years, and I am happy to come home in the evenings."

I'd bet. Being trapped in that mansion with Kimmie Ray was nothing compared to the coziness and contentment here in the courtyard.

Pilar settled into a chair opposite me, looking past her roses into something I couldn't see.

"Are you any closer to finding Faith?" she said.

Guilt pricked at my insides. "No," I said. "I was hoping you could tell me something that could help."

She shook her head sadly. "I don't know. *Las cosas correctas . . .*"

"What isn't right?" I said.

She went quiet, eyes narrowed, measuring what she was about to say. "Missus MacKinnon, do you believe it is possible to love someone too much?"

I nearly choked on the high-test lemonade. Of everything I imagined her wanting to talk to me about, my opinion on the ways of love was dead last on the list.

I put the heavy glass on the table and was quiet, because I realized it wasn't really a question.

Marlowe finished his water, then went around the table and put his head in Pilar's lap. She petted him between the ears, still staring at her roses.

"My family has been with the Ainsworth family for a very long time," she said. "I used to help *mi abuela* roll tortillas for Mr. Cullen's mother. I was making the tortillas myself by the time Tres was born."

I took the mini recorder from my purse, and she stopped.

"This is nothing," I said. "I just use it to keep things straight in my head."

"No," she said. "I have been with the family a long time. Mr. Ainsworth was very good to me and my family."

Mia had told me there was a bond between families and their *criada*, so Pilar's reticence to rat out her benefactors wasn't a surprise. It was, however, a bit of a disappointment.

Nodding, I put the recorder away. "I swear I won't tell a soul where I got this information. I'm just trying to find Faith," I said, not adding that I had more than a passing interest in who broke into my house and tried to choke me to death, where Selena Obregon was, where Faith was and if she was okay, and how to get the dog away from that sorry ass Junior Hollis. Most of that Pilar would not be able to help me with, but hope springs eternal.

"Missus Adele and Mr. Cullen, Tres's *padres,* were good people. They tried many years for children, but the Holy Mother did not smile on them. And then Missus Adele got sick."

She was still stroking Marlowe, still staring absently at something I couldn't see. "She had a..." she put her hand to her chest, looking for the word, "a *mastectomía,* and for a while she got better and we all thought she was okay. And along came Tres," she said. "It was like all of their prayers were answered."

I nodded, listening and watching as her left hand, the one that wasn't petting Marlowe, clenched into a fist. It was then that I realized she was clutching her rosary.

"I don't have children," she went on. "At first, I thought Tres would be a blessing to all of us. We poured all of our love and good wishes into the boy, and he grew strong and tall. But something was wrong."

She went quiet.

"Wrong?" I prompted.

Pilar shook her head. "Cullen wanted Tres to have the best. Education, friends, opportunities. But Tres, he didn't fit in with the other boys at St. Francis Academy."

I nodded encouragingly.

"*Dado derecho,*" She made a rolling motion with her hand, which annoyed Marlowe since he'd been on the receiving end of attention from that hand. He snuggled in closer, nudging her with his pointy white nose. She smiled sadly and resumed rhythmic stroking.

"He felt entitled?" I said. "To what?"

She shrugged. "To anything he didn't have."

I nodded. "Yeah. I've known people like that," I said, thinking of my ex-husband.

Pilar took a long swallow of lemonade. "When Tres came, the whole house changed. That child was like a light in a long darkness…"

"And?"

Pilar blew out a long breath. "He got into trouble." She looked down at Marlowe, who was half out of his mind with the bliss of being petted to death.

"At school," she said. "He became a *bruto.*"

I nodded. "He got into trouble?"

"No," she said. "Tres *was* the trouble."

"How do you mean?"

Her fingers worked furiously at her rosary beads, as though if she could pray enough prayers she could erase whatever trouble Tres had caused.

She sighed. "Tres was expelled from St. Francis and was sent to Dawes High School." She shook her head. "And that is where he met Faith and Wylie and that Junior Hollis boy."

She said *Hollis boy* like she had a bad taste in her mouth.

Pilar shook her head. "Faith did not always look the way she looks now. Tres had the Puckett children over for dinner often, and I cooked for them. Large meals because they were skinny children."

I nodded encouragingly.

"But Faith—Tres was, how do you say, *golpeado violentamente?*"

"Smitten?" I said, and she shook her head.

"Yes, but more than that." Pilar sat back. "And Faith had a boyfriend—Josh Lambert—from when she was a little girl."

I nodded and took a sip of lemonade. "Do you know Josh very well?"

Pilar shook her head. "No, only that Tres *lo odió.*"

"Tres hated him? Why?"

"Because I think the girl loved Josh in a way that she could never love anyone else. First love is powerful *magia.*"

"So Josh *and* Tres had crushes on Faith?" I said, and Pilar shook her head.

"Oh, *everyone* had a crush on Faith. She had the voice and face of an angel. But the troubles came when Junior Hollis began to bother her."

"You mean like annoy her?" I said, and Pilar shook her head. "No. There was a big *alboroto* at the school. Tres said the Hollis boy shoved Faith up against a locker. Put his hand up her skirt. Josh nearly killed him and the *policía* were called."

"Josh got in trouble?"

"Both boys were *en apuro,* but both were, how do you say, reprimanded and let go."

"What did Tres do while all this was going on?" I said.

"I don't know. But I think it made Tres envious of Josh. Josh rescued Faith. I think Tres wanted to be the hero in Faith's eyes."

"A hero," I said, thinking of Tres and having to fend off a serious case of the icks. There is no parallel universe that would have Tres Ainsworth as a hero.

"Yes," Pilar said. "He wanted to be *más macho.* He started to be friends with the Hollis boy, brought him around all the time. Let him drive his father's car, smoke good cigars, do the things boys like to do."

War buddies, I thought. "How did Wylie and Faith take that?"

"Not very good. Junior Hollis was always a bad seed. Not regular bad, but ugly bad." Her dark eyes narrowed. "You can see a lot about a family from the servant's quarters. That boy used to shoot the barn cats down at the stables. He would lure them out with a bowl of chicken and just shoot them into pieces."

My stomach pitched, but I took a deep breath, pen poised over my pad. "And did he get in trouble for that?"

"Not until he shot Missus Adele's Persian cat. Do you know that cat cost more than a thousand dollars? For a cat..." She shook her head. "Missus Adele had him arrested, but Tres bailed him out. Said he could work off the cost of the cat."

I'd been scribbling like a woman possessed, but I stopped. "Pay it off? How?"

"That was the surprising thing," Pilar said. "Tres wanted Hollis to teach him how to hunt—to shoot with a gun."

I wondered if Hollis taught him how to act like a fully armed asshole, too.

"When Missus Adele got sick again, it was Tres who suggested Faith's mother come to take care of her. When Missus Adele died, Mr. Cullen married her and Faith and Wylie came to live with us. But Tres didn't like Wylie around. So he sent him away."

"So who sent Faith away to the girls' ranch?" I said.

"Mr. Cullen," Pilar said. "I think he didn't like the way Tres looked at the girl. I don't know if he did it to keep his son out of trouble or to keep the girl safe."

I nodded.

Pilar took a long swallow of lemonade. "It wasn't long after that that Mr. Cullen died."

I stared down at my notes, wondering how it all fit together. Here was a connection between Tres and Hollis. A connection between Hollis and Faith. But how did Puck fit in, and how did he go straight from the buckle of the Bible belt to the heart of El Patron?

I took a sip of lemonade, gathering my thoughts. "So where did Wylie go when Tres sent him away?"

"He always had a head for numbers. For a while, he helped Missus Adele keep the books. When Tres wanted him gone, he found him bookwork at some private business in East Austin. Soon after that, Mr. Ainsworth died."

"Is that when Tres decided to build a recording company?"

Pilar nodded. "So Faith would want to come to his house. But Wylie had saved his money and bought her a little trailer on the edge of the Puckett property. After that, we didn't see much of Wylie or Faith."

I thought about Josh, lost and confused, drowning in the bottom of a whiskey bottle.

We were quiet, and after a time, I said, "Do you know anything about the school Faith went to?"

Pilar shook her head. "I know it's at the western edge of the county. I know the Ainsworths set up some sort of endowment for the school because Tres seemed interested in it."

I looked down at my notes. "There are some people who think Josh is obsessed with Faith," I said.

Pilar stared at me and said, "I think maybe there is more than just Josh who is obsessed with her."

"Did you know that Josh had a restraining order on him?"

"Yes," Pilar said. "Tres took her down to Sheriff Hollis to fill it out."

I nodded. "Do you have any idea where Faith could be?" I said, and Pilar shook her head.

"Do you think Josh could have done something with her?"

Pilar looked out over her roses. "I think if he thought he could save her, he would."

"Even to kidnap her?"

"If he thought it would help her, I think he might."

I frowned. "Can you think of where he would keep her?"

Pilar shook her head.

I stared down at my notebook, making a little flow chart, trying to find a pattern—see how things fit together.

"Is there anything else you can tell me? Anything else I've forgotten to ask?"

Pilar shook her head.

Nodding, I rose. "Thank you very much, Pilar. I hope you don't get in trouble with Mrs. Ainsworth for talking to me."

Pilar frowned. "Oh, no. It's not Missus Kim I'm worried about. *Mi padre* used to say that a boy is a boy, two boys are half a boy, and three boys are no boy at all." She shook her head. "With Tres and Hollis, there is no need for another boy to make more trouble."

TWENTY-EIGHT

"Junior Hollis," I told Mia on my cell. She was annoyed I hadn't called her to go with me to talk to Pilar, but Mia had bigger fish to fry.

"You ever do anything about that dog of his?" she said. "'Cause I got some friends—"

Marlowe laid his head in my lap and accepted some skritching under his chin. "I called the Animal League in Dawes County, and they said they'd look into it."

"I don't like that Hollis man," Mia said, fuming after I told her about the cat killings.

"I don't like him much either," I said. "And I think killing small animals is one of the signs of being a sociopath."

"Like a serial killer?"

"I know it's not good. I wonder how a juvenile delinquent wound up being sheriff?"

"Why don't you ask him?" Mia said.

I thought about that. "Hey," I said, "can you hold on a sec?"

I switched over, dialed Information, and connected with the Dawes County Jail.

When a woman answered, I put on my sweet voice and said, "With whom do I need to speak to see Josh Lambert?"

"Sheriff," she said, smacking her lips like she was eating something delicious and messy.

"May I speak to the sheriff?"

"He ain't here right now."

"And I can't make an appointment to see Josh without speaking to the sheriff?"

"That's what I said." Again with the lip smacking.

"Is there a way to get in touch with Sheriff Hollis?"

"If there is, I don't know it," she said, making a sound like sucking on her fingers.

"May I please leave him a message?" I said, not happy about the odds of the message getting to the sheriff.

"Sure," she said.

I waited. "Do you have a pen?"

"Don't need one," she said. "Got a mind like a steel trap."

And a mouth like an open pit. I gave her my info and asked that the sheriff call me as soon as possible. She said she'd get right on it.

I clicked back over to Mia, who was scolding her cat. "I got nothing," I said. "You know what else is bothering me?"

"Peace in the Middle East?"

"What about the girl—Tiffany? Why was she at Faith's that night?"

Mia paused. "A coincidence?"

"My daddy used to say there's no such thing as coincidence. Want to go on a field trip?"

Mia popped her gum. "Is this going to involve breaking and entering?" she said, and I smiled.

Mia said, "Point me to the field."

I DIALED INFORMATION AND got Tiffany Parker's address, and I looped back to pick up Mia. We headed east toward Sunny Hollow apartments, which turned out to be not sunny at all.

"Have the cops been here?" Mia wanted to know, and I said, "Yes. I just want to see for myself."

As we approached the wrought-iron security gate, Marlowe sat up in the seat and growled.

"Yikes," Mia said as we pulled up to the gate, which was off the tracks and provided almost as much security as Cora Beth's Beauty Supply.

Leaking, old cars crowded the cracked and pitted parking lot, and small groups of young toughs leaned on the cars that could take the weight, scowling at us as we cruised by. The buildings were red brick, three-story affairs that seemed to be rotting from the inside out.

"Manager's office?" Mia said, and I shrugged.

"Doesn't look like a whole lot of managing goes on here."

I was right. No one was in the office. Information had given me Tiffany's address but not the apartment number, so we cruised by the small, cloudy swimming pool toward the community mailboxes to search for a number.

Marlowe's neck bristled as he and I climbed out of the car. His eyes narrowed, gaze searching the parking lot, and I would have laughed because he reminded me of Logan if I weren't so scared my jaws felt wired shut. I studied the mailboxes as Marlowe studied the group of teenage toughs. He growled low in his throat.

"Tiffany Parker," I read. "Box 219."

I looked toward the nearest group of buildings. Apartment 219 was close enough for a brisk walk, but the toughs were leering at Mia and me like we were hamsters at a snake farm.

Probably better to drive.

We climbed the rusting metal stairs to Tiffany's apartment on the second floor. The window was broken and would have been an easy entry if you didn't have to climb over the stair rail, scale a ledge, and risk getting second-degree glass cuts, so like a normal person I tried the door. It was locked. I looked in the crack of the jamb. No deadbolt.

Mia and I leaned against the door. The lock slipped from the socket and gave.

"Some security," Mia said, and I nodded.

"Some maintenance, too."

As we opened the door, roaches scattered like a small explosion, avoiding the dim shaft of light that preceded us in. Some of the tenants probably had the same aversion to daylight.

"Oh, ick," Mia said, and I agreed.

Even Marlowe balked in the doorway.

The three of us edged into the apartment, careful to avoid any unseen critters that might make us scream, thus calling attention to our breaking-and-entering selves. Inside, the ceiling was streaked with ugly brown water stains and the carpet reeked of mold and neglect, but Tiffany had done her best with what she had. Cast-off lace curtains lined the windows, including the broken pane with the cardboard patch. Someone, probably Tiffany, had used magic markers on the cardboard, creating a picture of a small white house with a fence and a dog, with happy puffs of smoke churning out of the chimney. In the forefront, a cartoon man and woman held a cartoon child. The drawing was pretty good in a cartoony way, but it made my heart tilt, this imaginary view Tiffany had created from her broken window.

A collection of small pewter animals in whimsical poses lined the sills.

"Looks like a little girl decorated," Mia said, and I nodded, an image of Faith's little-girl décor drifting through the back of my brain.

"I thought strippers made a lot of money," Mia said, her cute little nose wrinkling at the disreputable-looking room.

I shrugged. "If they do, they don't spend it on décor."

Mia and I moved through the living room, careful not to step on a cockroach that darted across the carpet. "What are we looking for?" Mia said.

Strangling the urge to scream, I said, "A clue as to why Tiffany was at Faith's the night the trailer blew up."

"A clue like what?"

"I don't know. Maybe we'll luck out and find a little yellow arrow that blinks *clue*."

Mia bumped me with her hip and took Marlowe's leash. He panted, his pink tongue lolling just past his teeth, and I could appreciate the sentiment. It was hot inside the apartment, which made the mold that much worse.

"Let's look so we can get out of here," Mia said. "My lungs are starting to burn."

I nodded, and we began our snoop.

The kitchen was clean, if you didn't mind the dead rat by the stove. The refrigerator was full of just-expired yogurt, milk, and some kind of organic cheese.

Down the hall and in the bedroom, the neatly made bed was home to about twenty stuffed animals. None looked like old friends from childhood, worn and bedraggled from years of love and other mishandlings. Used paperbacks crowded cheap bookcases that stretched all the way around the room.

Pink baby tees, cute little capris, and flirty dresses hung neatly in a row—it looked like the closet of a pop princess. Three suitcases sat along the back wall, behind shoes that were arranged by color. My mother would have cried tears of joy.

The bathroom was tidy. Razor on the tub rim, makeup orderly on the counter. No drugs or other contraband, just a bottle of NyQuil and some aspirin.

"You see anything?" Mia said, and I shook my head. I peeked into the toilet tank and went through the toes of shoes. Nothing.

No signs of violence. Bags, makeup, and clothing all in place, like she'd just stepped out for an afternoon. A small life interrupted.

Back in the living room, I hit the *play* button on the old answering machine and listened. Two messages from the club—one from a man wanting to know what she was doing and another from Deke, asking her to check in. He sounded worried.

No ransom messages. No one calling to claim responsibility. No messages from Faith.

I popped the tape out of the machine and stuck it in my pocket, just in case.

"Hey," Mia called from the bedroom. "Come look at this."

Mia held up a BlackBerry. Marlowe stood beside her, looking pleased.

"I found it in the zipper of the Tweety Bird doll," she said.

"I thought the cops searched this place," Mia said, staring at the small, purple device.

I nodded. "Yeah, I guess they missed it."

Mia shrugged. "Now can we get out of here?" she said. "I think one of those stuffed animals is staring back."

Animal lover extraordinaire, even Mia has her limits.

TWENTY-NINE

"It's for texting and stuff," Ethan said.

"I know that. We need a username and password. Can you get into it?"

Ethan looked at me like I'd just asked him if he could breathe.

He twisted his upper lip and went into the worst Bogart I've ever heard. "A little time, a little shpace, and we'll have this thing shinging like a canary, shweetheart."

"I've been up all night looking for connections," I said. "And I'd appreciate it if you didn't mention canaries."

It was nearly ten in the morning, and Ethan was spinning my interview chair, jittering over the possibility of a new puzzle. Marlowe had found a sunny spot in Tanner's office suspiciously close to the dog-treat drawer, while Tanner went over reports, his swivel chair angled so that he could skritch Marlowe between his ears.

"You get an appointment to see Josh?" E said, his voice noncommittal, but his thin chest puffed up like a banty rooster protecting a hen.

I scowled. "Left another message."

Ethan toed the chair some more, nodding his head, choosing his words carefully. "You think he did it?"

I shook my head. "No, I really don't."

He stopped swiveling. "Me either."

My eyebrows shot up. "Really?"

Ethan sighed. "It doesn't make sense. For one thing, he's been drunk for how long now?"

"There's that," I said, trying not to smile. Ethan was a bit of a sore loser, a natural-born gamer, and the word *defeat* has never been programmed into his hard drive.

"Kind of big of you not to blame Josh for Faith's disappearance," I said.

E shrugged. "And," he said, "I think he really does love her."

"That going to cause a problem?"

His eyes narrowed, but he swallowed hard. "I just want to find her."

I smiled. "Me too."

"So what are we going to do next?"

"You're going to find out what's on that BlackBerry, and I'm going to try to weasel a way in to see Josh."

"You need help? He is in jail, you know."

"It's the handler I'm worried about, not the handlee."

I CALLED HOLLIS'S OFFICE again and got the same response, which drew a more nasty response from me.

"Tanner," I poked my head into the Cage. "Got a minute?"

Marlowe jumped up from his prone position, a guilty look on his white, fuzzy face. "Settle down, killer," I told the dog. "I'm an equal opportunity owner."

The dog turned a circle and settled back at Tanner's feet, ever alert for a stray biscuit.

"I'm getting nowhere with Hollis. I'm trying to get in to see Josh Lambert, and the old biddy at the desk says Hollis is the only one who can give me access. He hasn't been there in more than twenty-four hours."

Sighing dramatically, Tanner pinched the bridge of his nose. "How often do *you* stay away from the office twenty-four hours?"

He had me there.

He scratched Marlowe beneath his chin. "Where are you on this?"

I told him where I'd been, who I'd questioned, and what they said. I told him about going to Tiffany's place but left out the part about how we gained access and the illegal acquisition of her BlackBerry.

"Your FBI agent any closer to finding Obregon?"

I shook my head.

Tanner sat, nodding, then leaned in for a licorice whip. "You don't think this Josh Lambert character did it?"

"I think Hollis is hassling him and, in turn, hassling me."

Tanner nodded. "I'll see what I can do."

I grinned all the way down to my toes.

Tanner leaned back in his chair, holding the licorice like a cigar. "What are you going to do?" he said.

"I want to talk to Josh and Hollis."

"And in the meantime?"

I smiled. "Keep poking."

Tanner sighed. "It's what you do best."

BACK AT MY DESK, I stared at my email inbox. I had three new obituaries to write and nearly zero interest in writing them, which made me feel terrible. Everyone deserves a decent sendoff, and I didn't know if I could do it.

Three people dead. Three obituaries to write. I thought about that.

Three people dead on my to-do list and two who were still alive.

Probably.

Faith and Tiffany.

Two young women who'd slipped through the wide gaps in the social net, left to drift in a dangerous sea on their own, some of the danger of their own making.

"Alive or dead," I said, looking at my to-do list.

There were several things that bothered me, and they all seemed to coincide. Of course, there was the big stuff. Puck dead. Faith missing. Tiffany, who looks like Faith, burned nearly to death in a trailer that belonged to Faith.

It bothered me that Hollis was caught killing small animals when he was a kid. It bothered me how Tiffany and Faith's homes were decorated so similarly.

It bothered me that Hollis wasn't around to answer my phone calls.

It bothered me that I was spinning my wheels and not getting anywhere.

It *really* bothered me that Logan was gone and I didn't know where he was, or if he was in danger ... I thought about Selena Obregon. She's as old as my mother but she's still a babe and a half. I thought about her getting her long nails into Logan, and a streak of jealousy ripped green up my spine.

At a loss, I called Dr. T.

"You find your girl?" Dr. T said.

"No, and they've called off the search. They've arrested her childhood sweetheart, and I'm trying to get an appointment to talk to him for a jailhouse interview."

She was quiet. Not the kind of shrinky quiet that makes you squirm, but the kind of quiet that felt safe, like you could talk about anything.

"I went by Tiffany Parker's apartment today," I said, and Dr. T groaned.

"By yourself?"

"No, Mia and the dog came with me."

She made a noise, signifying her disapproval, but I went on. "Something really bothered me there," I said. "Both of the girls are dancers, they look alike, and their houses are decorated almost the same—not the same stuff, but like a little girl would decorate."

"An example?" she said.

"Just lots of pinks and toys."

"I've not met either of these women, so this is based only on what you've told me and what I've read in the news. But the frou-frou girly stuff could be indicative of a number of things."

I waited, pen poised over pad.

Dr. T went on. "Is there a history of sexual abuse?" she said. "Many times, a trauma can cause a child to sort of stop emotionally developing at the point the abuse started. Or perhaps the young women in question are trying to regain their childhood, trying to rewrite history. Or it could be that they simply have bad taste."

"Well, they're strippers," I said, "but I'm trying to keep an open mind."

"You'd be surprised how many dancers suffered from some kind of childhood abuse. Physical, emotional, or sexual, often by someone in the family or a close friend of the family."

"You mean like the boyfriend?"

"I'm not saying that's what's going on here, but it's a good place to look," she said. "Most crimes against women are committed by an acquaintance, a friend, or a family member."

I sat, thinking about that.

In my silence, Dr. T said, "You sound like you don't think the boyfriend had anything to do with the disappearance or the fire."

"No," I said, "I don't."

She was quiet for a moment and then said, "Be careful, Cauley. Family secrets have a way of rattling out of the closet. You open that door, there's going to be someone who wants it closed."

"Or some*ones*," I said, and sighed.

"You hear any more from your stalker from El Patron?" she said.

"There's something that doesn't make sense about all that. If it really was about me testifying in court, why haven't they gone after anybody but me?"

"What about the dead guy?"

"Well, him too," I said. "But there are a string of people lined up to testify, including Mia. None of them have been threatened."

"Maybe it's not about the trial," she said reasonably. "Have you pissed anyone off lately?"

"Not today, but it's still early."

She chuckled at that. "Other than the trial, what do you and the Puckett guy have in common?"

I thought about Puck and his tattoos, his beer-drinking, and his redneck ways, and said, "Nothing. I don't think we have anything in common."

"Weren't you both causing trouble for a ruthless band of Argentinean mobsters?"

"Well," I said. "There's always that."

THIRTY

I SETTLED IN AND wrote the obituaries, waiting to be struck with a stroke of genius. I waited a long time.

Marlowe was in the Cage with Tanner, who seemed considerably perkier in the company of the dog, even though it appeared the dog's main job was to lie on his back, feet sticking up, tongue lolling out.

I'd called Hollis and—huge surprise—he wasn't available.

Leaning back in my chair, I had spread out the contents of my files, tapping my pen to my lips, when my gaze fell on the small paper program from Puck's funeral.

It was an expensive program, on good stationery and embossed with *New Hope Church* inscribed over an angel collapsed on a gravestone, her hand thrown over her head in grief. I thought about that preacher and his words of discomfort. Not for the first time, I wondered why Kimmie Ray sent Faith away to school and gave her son the boot not six months before Old Man Ainsworth died. I thought about the timeline.

Faith was thirteen when she left. It was about the time that Puck began his "internship" with El Patron. He would have been seventeen or eighteen.

I placed the photos I'd gathered into a timeline. Lined up in order, they showed a slow progression from a beautiful young woman into something meant to frighten and repel.

I wondered if that single act of sending Faith to the school had set off this chain of events—caused Puck to turn to El Patron for money and freedom, caused Faith to begin mutilating herself. I wondered if old man Ainsworth had anything to do with it.

I did a search on Cullen Ainsworth II and found what Pilar had already told me: that he was a bazillionaire land baron who made the bulk of his fortune from coal and oil. I also found that the first Mrs. Cullen Ainsworth II died seven years ago, and that Kimmie Ray became the second Mrs. Cullen Ainsworth six years ago. Faith was sent away the following year.

Now Puck was dead and Faith was missing. And the trouble seemed to start around the time Faith turned thirteen and was sent away to school.

A lot seemed to hinge on that period of time.

"I'll be back," I called to Tanner as I folded the program and stuffed it into my purse. I summoned Marlowe out from under Tanner's feet. The dog got up, checked the floor for stray treats, then trotted out, happy to see the leash.

"Well," I told Marlowe. "We haven't found Faith. Want to see if we can scare up some hope?"

I'D GOOGLED NEW HOPE Girls' Ranch and found that it was between Bates and Sugar Creek on a deserted stretch of County Road 963 that was literally in the middle of nowhere. Rocky limestone cliffs morphed into rocky marble and granite cliffs, and the altitude made my ears pop.

Marlowe sat in the passenger seat, the tip of his tongue sticking out, eyes dead ahead on the road.

The girls' ranch itself was a tidy, well-kept spread of land contained by an expensive, ten-foot-tall deer fence. Two rough granite pillars flanked the long asphalt drive, with an arching sign connecting them that announced, "Entering New Hope: All are welcome."

I looked over at Marlowe as we came to a stop. "I guess we're about to see if all really are welcome."

As we motored down the smooth, paved road, I wondered what I would say to the preacher. I could lie and say I had a little sister in need of some spiritual guidance and hope God didn't strike me dead for lying. Or I could tell the truth and hope New Hope wasn't code for "shoot on sight."

I looked up at the forbidding fence and thought of some of the wack-job zealots whose motto was "Praise the Lord and pass the ammunition." Probably I'd rather lie to the preacher and leave my fate to the Almighty than risk it with Brother Bob.

The buildings were laid out the same way that some of the church camps I'd spent summers in were—limestone and cedar, with a main lodge for meetings and dining, cabins for dorms, an outdoor tabernacle made of a cement slab, four metal pillars, and a metal roof, along with eight outbuildings for classes and dorms. To the left of the lodge, a half dozen girls dressed in jeans and denim shirts were on hands and knees weeding a kitchen garden. To the right, about twenty girls dressed the same way were stacking bricks and logs, probably for another building.

I sat in the Jeep outside the main lodge for a moment, conjuring the scents of campfires and s'mores and bubblegum and the sweet smell of the lake.

There were no sweet smells here. New Hope smelled like hot asphalt, old hymnals, and hard work.

I climbed out of the Jeep and knocked on rough-hewn double doors.

The hinges creaked, and a tall, strong-looking woman in her late thirties, with a long ponytail of hair the color of good cinnamon, appeared on the other side of the door. She looked at me expectantly.

"My name is Cauley MacKinnon. I'd like some information on the school," I said, smiling my innocent smile. Trustworthy. Dependable. Lying through my teeth. "My mother and father passed away recently, and my little sister is… in need of a more structured life."

The woman considered me for a moment. She wore blue jeans and a denim shirt similar to the ones the girls outside wore. Her fingers were long and callused, and in her hands was a pair of knitting needles and a shapeless, pink something or other she'd been working on.

She didn't say anything.

Instead, she reached for Marlowe, palm down. Marlowe sniffed it and gave her a lap. Sighing, she opened the enormous door and ushered me in.

The lodge was cavernous, the floor stained concrete, with a cafeteria-style kitchen on one end, an elevated stage with a piano and podium and doors that led to offices at the other. Straight across, a large marble and granite fireplace loomed in the cedar.

The woman padded across the concrete, and Marlowe and I followed her, the scents of recently devoured hotdogs and grape Kool-Aid drifting in the strange silence.

The office was small but cozy, with a plump mauve sofa, soft ivory throw rugs, and a small cherry desk. A pink plastic plaque read *Charlotte Fisher, Ph.D.* in front of a hulking, whirring Jurassic computer. Melting ice floated in a Dixie cup of grape Kool-Aid near the telephone. A window overlooking the garden and a large, pink lace embroidered cross presided over the room.

She sat behind her desk and went back to her knitting. I chose the overstuffed brocade Queen Anne in front of the desk. She reached into a jar atop a file cabinet and gave Marlowe a peanut butter cookie.

She didn't offer me any Kool-Aid.

I cleared my throat. "As I was saying... I've heard such wonderful things about this school and have a few questions before I pursue it for my sister."

Without looking up from her knitting, she said, "Ms. MacKinnon, what are you doing here?"

I blinked. "Excuse me?"

She put her knitting aside and stared at me. Then she pulled out the top drawer in her desk and produced one of the "missing" flyers Mia and Ethan had put together.

From her flyer, Faith's face stared back at me. "I saw you make the announcement on the news. We've been rotating teams of girls and staff members to volunteer for the search. We baked cookies, made casseroles, and bussed teams out to the search site until they called it off."

I did a mental head slap. *The white bus of church kids at the search site.* Some investigative reporter I'm going to be.

I didn't know what to say. I'd just lied to her and dissed her by not recognizing her and her "girls" from the search site—what could I say?

"I keep track of my girls, Ms. MacKinnon. I've been worried about Faith since she got here."

"But," I said, "I... at her brother's funeral... the minister didn't mention anything about Faith or searching for her..."

"Ah," she tutted. "You met Brother Bob. Brother Bob is what we refer to in psychiatric circles as an ass."

Guilt nipped at me with sharp little teeth. "Ms. Fisher, I'm sorry, I..."

She leaned across her desk and offered her hand. "The girls here call me Llina."

I raised my brows.

"Short for *Gallina*," she said.

I smiled at that. "They call you the Hen?" I said, rising to shake her hand.

She chuckled. "I suppose I am a bit of a hen."

She reached into the file cabinet beside her and came out with a Dixie cup. She poured me some Kool-Aid. Marlowe finished his cookie and trotted over to the desk and laid his head in Llina's lap.

"I saw that the sheriff's department made an arrest. Are you any closer to finding her?"

I sighed. "I don't know. I figure if I keep pulling at threads, something's bound to unravel."

"And I was the next thread on your list?"

"Well, Brother Bob was, but I like you better."

She smiled. It was a nice smile, an earnest smile, with straight, white teeth and crinkles around her eyes. "We're a tough school and we expect a lot of our girls. We usually get what we expect."

I accepted the Kool-Aid and took a drink. It was sweet and cold and felt like a million summer days. She offered Marlowe another cookie, which he happily took to the sofa. Marlowe would sell my soul for peanut butter.

"Our girls are required to apply for college or technical school by their junior year. Faith refused. Said she'd never make it that far. I thought it was because she was going to pursue her music."

I nodded, listening to the pain-filled undercurrent in her voice.

"For the past six years, we've been losing one or two girls, but the majority of our girls stay in touch and go on to live good, solid lives. We're like a family they never had."

"And Faith?"

"I tried to steer her toward colleges with strong music programs, but it was like she couldn't see past the ranch here at New Hope."

I sipped some Kool-Aid. "You think she was suicidal?"

Llina shook her head. "I don't know. The hair pulling and piercings started about a year and a half ago. I believe it's a form of cutting."

I nodded. "I'm familiar with the syndrome. Did something happen? Any kind of trauma that might trigger the behavior?"

"Not that I know of. She never mingled with the other girls. Considered herself other than. Like she didn't belong."

I nodded. While I had lots of friends in school, I always felt other than.

"Did she have any friends? Did anybody ever come visit?"

"Her brother came once a week. Her stepbrother came about once a month to check on the endowment."

Something inside me went very still. "Tres? Tres Ainsworth came to visit?"

"The Ainsworths endowed the school with a sizable donation about ten years ago," she said. "I supposed he was checking on his family's investment."

"Do you know when he came up with the idea to produce a CD for her?"

"On her seventeenth birthday. The studio was a surprise birthday present. The staff was thrilled for her, but that's when she started the hair pulling."

"A recording studio for her birthday?" I said. "That's a pretty big present."

Llina set her Kool-Aid down, and her face tightened around her cheekbones.

"Six months ago, Wylie bought her a little used trailer house at the edge of the Puckett family farm." She shook her head. "I had misgivings. A seventeen-year-old girl is ill-equipped to deal with this world on her own. But she said she was ready to start her music career."

She sat back in her chair and looked out a window, where the group of girls were still tending the garden. "You know, that brother of hers was all she had."

"And her mother?"

She made a derisive noise. "Her mother is ill-equipped to handle the world too. I think that woman had ideas how her life was going to be when she married Cullen Ainsworth. She spent her entire life thinking if she just had enough money, if she just had a nice house in a good neighborhood, her life would be perfect."

"A lot of us make that mistake—work so hard on the destination we miss the journey," I said. "Did she blame her children for that? For her life not working out the way she thought it would?"

She shook her head. "I don't know. But that girl was withdrawn and quiet since she got here. Startled easy, even wet the bed for a while. Classic signs of sexual abuse."

My stomach slid into a big, oily knot.

"Then we put her in the choir. She's got a voice like spring rain." A faint smile tipped the edges of her lips, like echoes of Faith's voice still drifted in her head. "She really began to bloom."

"What happened?"

Llina stared out the window. "I haven't figured it out. The school was having some financial difficulties, the board of regents signed Brother Bob on board, and the Ainsworths made another large endowment."

"In exchange for what?"

"That we keep Faith here until she was eighteen."

"Why eighteen?"

Llina shook her head. "I assumed it was so that she would go straight from here to college."

"But Faith showed no interest?"

"No."

I frowned. "And she left six months early? Did the funding stop?"

"We haven't been asked to modify our budget," she said.

"And you find that strange?"

"Very. But Tres did start asking for special favors."

"Special favors?"

"Odd things, like wanting the girls to start a voting drive. He had them folding flyers and licking envelopes."

"Any candidate in particular?" I said, but I already knew.

"That idiot Junior Hollis."

I thought about that. Tres provided an endowment to the school that housed Faith, controlled Kimmie Ray's trust fund, owned Faith's recording contract, and bought a half-interest in Boners the week Faith went to work there. Perhaps most frightening of all, he seemed to have bought himself a sheriff. A cat-killing, woman-assaulting sociopath.

"Control," I said aloud, and Llina looked at me intently. "He's narrowing her circle of friends, controlling her finances, isolating her from friends and family."

Llina nodded. "That would be a classic controlling pattern."

"And she and her stepbrother were never alone?"

"No, Brother Bob was always with—" Her voice broke, her eyes went wide. "Do you think…?"

"I hope not," I said. "But I'm afraid that's exactly what I think."

She shook her head and turned to look out the window, where the girls were cleaning their gardening tools. Her knitting needles lay still in her lap. "A lot of these girls get here in bad shape," she said. "Some were abused, some strung out, some neglected. We're like a warehouse for lost girls."

"Were you one of those girls?"

She blushed and looked back at her knitting. "Yes," she said. "I was."

I nodded. "Would she come back here if she could?"

"I don't know," she said.

"Would you tell me if Faith did come back?" I said.

"I wouldn't send the girls out on a search I knew to be fruitless," she said. "No. I suspect if Faith has disappeared of her own volition, she doesn't want to be found."

Llina resumed her knitting.

"Where did she stay when she was here?" I said.

"Dorm Two," she said, frowning. "Why?"

"Mind if I have a look?"

Llina shrugged. "It's long since been cleaned out. There's another girl bunking there."

"Did she leave anything behind when she left?"

"I have a box of things that belong to her. Would you like to see them?"

From a closet near the couch, she rummaged back behind an old badminton net and some theatrical stage props, where half a dozen similar boxes were neatly stacked. Llina came out the door dragging a box marked *For Faith*.

Llina opened the box, and Marlowe trotted over to check for food. Beneath the musty-smelling cardboard flap, I pulled out a dozen books of poetry—Yeats, Angelou, Pound, Stein, and Dickinson—and some that were not on a seventh-grade reading list: Mary Karr, Billy Collins, Sharon Olds, and Mary Oliver.

The books were slim volumes, but they felt heavy in my hand. "May I borrow these?" I said, and she looked at me, appraising. "Do you think they'll help you find her?"

"It can't hurt. I'm trying to get to know her better."

Under the books lay a half-knitted sweater balled up and given up, an old hairbrush, and a very old music box that played a haunting tune. A dozen pairs of white cotton panties, some school uniform shirts, and a cigar box of treasures: a quarter, four marbles, an interesting-looking twig, two unusual stones, and a bird's feather, probably from Keates.

At the very bottom of the box was a stack of magazines. I pulled them out and blinked.

"*Veronica's Angels*?" I said, and Llina shrugged. I picked up a pair of the cotton undies that were presumably Faith's. Something didn't make sense. The magazines were subscription, and they were addressed to Cullen Ainsworth III. Small yellow Post-its clung inside, always on a dark-haired angel dressed in the barely there. I looked more closely. The model bore a striking resemblance to Faith.

Before she started yanking her hair out.

It wasn't Faith; this woman was older, but not much. On each of the Post-its, "Angel Baby" was written in a masculine hand.

My insides went very still. I'd found my blinking yellow arrow.

Llina frowned, reading over my shoulder. "Angel Baby. That's what Tres calls Faith."

I realized some of the pages were stuck together and I let out a little yelp.

"Oh, gross!" Llina shrieked.

"I think *ick* is the correct clinical term," I said, grimacing at my hands.

"That is disgusting. Need to wash your hands?"

I gratefully absented myself to her small bathroom, where I scrubbed my hands raw, wishing I had some anti-bacterial soap, some iodine, and a big can of Raid.

"What's in the other boxes?" I said, afraid I already knew.

Llina saw it, too, and her cheeks went slightly green. "The same thing. Belongings of girls who left the school early."

She shook her head, staring at the closet, eyes wide. "I always hoped they'd find their way back."

"Have any of them? You know, found their way back?"

Llina's eyes met mine. "No," she said. "They haven't."

Slowly and deliberately, like an abyss of dread lay in the back of the closet, she opened the door, and the two of us pulled out box after box, seven in all, labeled *Asha* and *Bailey* and *Ginny*. She kept extracting boxes as I slit the tape on the box marked *Asha*.

A dark, well-worn teddy bear tumbled out, followed by a macaroni necklace and a small pink photo album. I flipped open the pages and gasped. Asha looked very much like Tiffany. And very much like Faith.

Llina looked like she might lose her lunch.

"How long has Tres Ainsworth been giving endowments to the school?" I asked.

Llina shrugged. "His father began the endowments on Tres's behalf about ten years ago, and Tres has always shown a great interest in the school and its progress."

I stared down at the beautiful, innocent young face in the photograph. "I just bet," I said.

Fury blazed in Llina's eyes, and she began to rip open the second box.

"Don't!" I said. "This could be evidence. We've got to call the police."

Llina stared at me. "You're going to call Sheriff Hollis?"

"Oh, hell no," I said, reaching for my cell. "We're calling in the cavalry."

"In Austin?" she said, and I nodded. "But aren't we out of their jurisdiction?"

"Yes," I said. "But the cop I'm calling isn't a real stickler for rules."

"What about a search warrant? Don't they need a search warrant?"

"Not if you invite them here," I said. "And not if you opened the box. I wouldn't drag me into this right now unless we absolutely have to."

I got Cantu's voice mail and left him a message about where I was and what I'd found. "As much as I hate to say this, may I take the magazines with me, too?"

Llina said, "Shouldn't the police take them?"

"Yes, they should, but they should have taken them when they started searching for her."

"Hollis," Llina growled, and I nodded.

She grabbed a paper bag out of a drawer, and with two big handfuls of tissues to keep our fingerprints off the magazines and Tres's DNA off our fingers, we placed them carefully in the bag. "I'm going to take these to a cop I know in Austin. He's a good guy, and he'll know what to do."

Llina nodded, rubbing her shoulders and looking thoroughly repelled.

I blew out a big breath and fished a card out of my purse. "I appreciate your time. And please—if you think of anything, give me a call."

"What are you going to do now?"

I thought about the sticky magazines and grossed myself out again. "I'm going to go see a man about a girl."

Llina shivered, clearly spooked. "You know, I just wanted to help the girls," she shook her head. "Be a positive influence in their lives. And then something like this happens, and you just have to think, 'Why do I even bother?' It's like trying to bail a sinking boat with a teaspoon."

I looked around the room, which was swathed in pink, a grown-up version of Faith's former home, and thought of the unfinished, balled-up pink sweater in the box. I smiled a little. "I think you had a lot more influence than you think."

THIRTY-ONE

In the Jeep, I left a text message for Cantu because I didn't want to get yelled at or given the third degree, and then I called Olivia.

"Hey," I said when she picked up. "Did y'all search Tres's property?"

"No. Turned the Lambert kid's ranch upside down, but we never made it to Tres's," Olivia said, her voice sounding like she had a sour taste in her mouth.

"No one even asked?"

"Cantu asked him to volunteer to have his ranch searched in case Faith was hiding or got lost out there in the hills—but you should have seen Ainsworth's face. Acted like we were wantin' to do a cavity search with a pair of pliers."

"And we can't search without a warrant?" I said.

"Don't have evidence to ask for a warrant."

Frustration bristled against my insides. "What about Junior Hollis? Anyone search his place?"

Olivia snorted.

"I'm going to go search Tres's property," I said as I left-turned back out on 183.

"How you gonna do that?"

"I plan to charm and beguile," I said.

Olivia snorted. "Cantu know about this?"

"Are you kidding? He'd have me locked up in the back cell at the Justice Complex."

"It'd be for your own good."

"Lots of things would be for my own good, but it doesn't always work out that way. If you don't hear from me in half an hour, will you call Cantu?"

"Honey, he's on my speed dial."

I disconnected and called Ethan. "What are you doing?" I said. "You get anything off that BlackBerry?"

"Of course. Who do you think you're talking to? I'm still working on origin, but someone texted Tiffany, said it was an emergency and that she had to get to Faith's house immediately. I've got Big Max doing a search right now for the IP. We'll be able to track the user from there."

"Who's Big Max?" I said.

"My home network."

"Oh," I said, getting a mental picture of a basement set up like a mad scientist's, only with hulking hard drives and blinking monitors. I thought about what Ethan said.

Someone texted Tiffany. So it was no coincidence she was at Faith's the night of the explosion. Someone did this on purpose. But why?

"What are you doing now?" E wanted to know, and I told him what I'd discovered at the girls' ranch.

His end of the conversation went very quiet, but I could practically feel his anger vibrating through my cell.

"Where are you heading?" he said, and I told him, "Ainsworth's."

"Wait at the gate," he said. "I'll meet you there."

"I DON'T LIKE IT," E said.

The sun warmed the sky a deep orange as it set over Ainsworth's large stone and iron security fence. I parked two blocks away behind a thicket of sage. Within moments, Ethan pulled in behind me.

I climbed out of the Jeep, careful not to totter off my fuck-me red heels so that Marlowe and I could go sit in E's Volvo and assess the situation.

My short black skirt slid up my thigh, and Ethan gawked. "You're wearing *that* to snoop around?"

I shot him a pitying look. "Trust me on this one," I said, edging my skirt further down my thigh.

"Can't we call Cantu or something?" he said, flipping open his laptop.

I shrugged. "We could, but Olivia says we don't have enough to get him a warrant, and I promise you he's going to stop us if we tell him what we're going to do."

"What are we going to do?"

"I'm going to go knock on the door."

Ethan frowned. "That's your big plan? Go knock on the door?" His fingers flew over his small keyboard, and as the computer made the wireless connection, it sounded off with a chime that sounded suspiciously like the theme to *Star Trek*.

"I've got some details that need working out. And you'll snoop around—figure out how to break into this place if we have to."

"While you go in there by yourself?" E said, still tapping the keyboard.

"Yes."

"I don't like it."

"The longer we stay down here bickering, the bigger chance we have at getting caught."

"So if we're supposed to be sneaking around, how is you knocking on the door going to help?" he said, nodding at my skirt.

"We're not snooping tonight. We're doing recon. Besides, this is my lucky black skirt."

He frowned. "How is it lucky?"

I stared at him, and he said, "Oh."

"I'm not dressed to go on an off-road search mission," I explained. "See? This way Tres won't be suspicious."

"He will, however, be distracted," Ethan said, and I hit him with my elbow.

He flipped open his cell and speed-dialed a number, setting the phone to speaker.

"Zeus, you up?"

"Here. Whatta you got?"

As they spoke, a window popped up on Ethan's screen showing a very large man with very small eyes and a prominent nose.

I stared at Ethan. "Who the hell is that?"

"Zeus. Knows everything there is to know about security."

"Whoa," the computer guy said "Who's the babe?" and I winced, realizing he could hear and see everything we were doing.

"That's just Cauley," Ethan said, and he climbed out of his car, Marlowe and I right behind him. Ethan looked up at the security cameras that swiveled slowly from their perches on the high wall.

"You see that?" he said to Zeus.

"Yeah, I see it. What a bunch of amateurs," Zeus snorted. "Hook me up, E."

"Come on," Ethan said.

I looked at the cameras. "Won't they see us?"

"We're going in against the sweep. And see the way they're angled? They won't be able to pick us up if we're pressed in close to the wall."

"What about motion detectors?" I said, and Zeus chimed in.

"The lights are set on motion detectors. See the little lenses? Everything else is on pressure and vibration."

Ethan and I, with the virtual presence of Zeus, crept in behind the watchful gaze of the swiveling camera, then pressed ourselves against the hard, rocky wall, inching our way toward the main security console, which was comprised of a keypad, a camera, and a speaker.

"Hook me in, E, we're ready for liftoff," Zeus's voice crackled through the computer speaker. The screen went blank as E hooked him in.

"Do you have a bobby pin?" he said.

"I think so," I rummaged in my purse. "Are you going to pick the lock?"

"No, I just always wanted to say that. Hey," he was looking into my purse. "Is that a gun?"

I rolled my eyes. "No, that's what I use to put on mascara."

"You never told me you had a gun."

"There's lots of things I've never told you."

He frowned, but he was looking around the perimeter. "You said there were two guys at the gate?"

"During the search, yes."

Ethan nodded, eyes flickering around the fence and the wires that snaked it. He took a closer look at the keypad, got out a little notebook, and scribbled down the make and model.

He looked up at me. "You think this guy's really taken up with those El Patron guys?"

"Tres?" I said. "Every time I start digging, I hit him or Junior Hollis or El Patron. I don't believe in coincidence."

E blew out a breath, looking up at the huge log home looming eerily on the hill. It seemed like every light in the house was on. "We need a signal—in case anything bad happens."

"Like what? You're not going to be able to see me."

"I don't know," he said. "Flick on and off some lights or something."

"All right, Ethan. If they don't tie me up and stuff a canary down my throat, I'll flick the lights. Now go."

Reluctantly, he climbed back into his car and slid down the driveway to go park on the road about a hundred feet back the way we'd come. He was outfitted for the occasion, with black jeans, a black tee shirt, and black Converse shoes. He gave me a thumbs-up and began to tiptoe back to the fence. I sighed. You gotta love geeks.

I climbed back into the Jeep and pulled up the drive so that I was in full view of the camera and could reach the intercom.

Heart pounding, I took a deep breath, gave Marlowe a quick hug, and buzzed security.

"Cauley MacKinnon to see Mr. Ainsworth," I said.

"You got an appointment?" a familiar thick Spanish accent said.

"Oh, Lord," I whispered. "Please don't let it be Chino."

I straightened my shoulders and said, "Mr. Ainsworth asked that I see him about communications. I'm here to give him a report."

There was a lot of silence, and then the gate buzzed open and I rolled up the driveway, a feeling of impending doom hanging over me like a mean little rain cloud.

Marlowe and I tumbled out of the Jeep and went to the front door, which opened almost immediately.

Oh, great. Chino. I glanced toward heaven and made a face at God.

"What do you want?" he said, eyes sliding over my chest like he'd missed lunch and was in the mood for ribs.

My heart pounded in my ears. Beside me, I felt Marlowe bristle.

When he turned to close the door, I saw the raw skin of a recently lasered tattoo of a sword wrapped with a snake. T and S. He was having it removed, but you could still see the telltale signs of the Syndicate. I thought of what Diego DeLeon had said about some of his *carnales* breaking team. I shivered.

"I have an update for Tres."

Chino leered at me, his dark eyes glittering.

My stomach rolled. I needed a pack of Rolaids, a bottle of Pepto-Bismol, and half a pound of Prozac. I thought about the gun in the bottom of my purse and felt marginally better.

Come on, Cauley, get it together…

"It's about his sister. He's going to want to hear this."

"What about his sister?" he said, and I cranked my smile up a notch. It was harder than it sounded, seeing's how my molars were grinding like a grist mill.

Chino's dark eyes slitted in suspicion, but he hustled off to find Tres, the chain jangling from his jeans pocket, his tattoos gleaming under the artificial light.

There was something malignant in the air, and Marlowe must have felt it, too, because his shoulders were stiff, his ears pricked to high alert.

After a time, Chino came back and ushered me and Marlowe back to Tres's office. Deejay, gun-toting security guard, butler. A real model citizen.

"Cauley! To what do I owe this surprise?" Tres said, pouring me a drink and motioning me to sit. I accepted the highball glass but didn't drink.

"Just here to do what I said I'd do."

He stared at me.

"Giving you a progress report on your stepsister."

I'd paired a sleeveless, tailored white shirt with the skirt, half-business, half-slutty, and it didn't go unnoticed.

Nodding, he settled in behind his enormous desk and waited, hands linked behind his head, leering at me. I thought of the *Veronica's Angels* catalogs and wanted to hurl. Beside me, Marlowe leaned hard against me, eyes trained on Tres's throat.

As cheerfully as I could manage, I placed my tape recorder on the desk and got out my little red notebook.

Tres's brows rose. "What's that for?"

I shook my head. "Just taking some notes on the progress. Don't mind it. We'll pretend like it's not even there."

He shifted in his seat, trying not to look at the recorder.

I watched him intently. "Has anyone collected the reward?" I said.

"What?"

"The reward. You know. The incentive to find Faith."

Tres shifted, still staring at me. "Sheriff Hollis found and arrested the perpetrator. He's a public servant and can't accept the reward."

"He okay with that?"

Tres shrugged. "I donated a considerable amount to his campaign, so I'm thinkin' he's okay."

I kept my face very still, but my stomach flipped and my hopes to find her alive were dwindling by the minute.

"I have some information about Faith," I said, and he blinked.

It was a small movement, but I caught it and it emboldened me, so I went on lying my ass off.

"I've been helping with the investigation—well, really just keeping up with it so Team Six can manage the media. Some things turned up."

Tres swallowed his Scotch and poured himself another. He took a long drink, then cradled the glass in his hands. Cool and collected. "What investigation? They got Lambert. He confessed. He's in jail. Case closed."

I shook my head and smiled sweetly. "This case isn't closed until we find Faith and bring her home, safe and sound."

His face showed no emotion, but he said, "Of course."

I nodded and went on. "I spoke with her friends at the club. How is it that you came to own a strip club right when Faith started working there?"

"Ms. MacKinnon—" he said.

So we were back to last-name basis again.

He shook his head. "You've seen my stepsister. You saw what she's done to herself. You see what she's doing with her life. She was determined to work at that 'club' and I was determined to protect her."

"Protect her from what? Herself?"

"If need be."

I nodded and took some notes. I noticed he tried to sneak a peek. I cleared my throat, hoping he couldn't see my pulse banging in my carotid artery. "Is that why you invested so heavily in her school?"

He shifted, half-lifting himself off his chair like he'd suddenly sprouted a hemorrhoid.

"Same reason. To protect her," he said.

I nodded and scribbled. "Any reason you said they had to keep her until she was eighteen to keep the endowment?"

"Eighteen is legal age. I hoped she'd come to some better life decisions by that time."

I smiled. "You've been watching Dr. Phil."

"What?" he said, and I shook my head.

"Any particular reason you had the girls benefiting from your endowment stuffing campaign letters for Junior Hollis's upcoming reelection?"

This time he smiled, his composure back in place. "Of course. Ms. Fisher was going to do a class on political studies. I thought it would be a good way to get hands-on knowledge from a grassroots level."

"By stuffing envelopes?"

He smiled. "I did say it was grassroots."

I nodded, flipping through my notebook for effect. I stopped at my grocery list and looked up. "Have you come across any new information about your sister's whereabouts?"

"Sheriff Hollis is workin' on it right now."

I smiled. "Yes, he's been very busy. I've been trying to talk to him and Josh Lambert, and haven't been able to get ahold of either."

Tres swallowed, trying to hide the fact that he was swallowing.

He was quiet.

"Well, if you speak with Sheriff Hollis, will you tell him I've left messages? If I don't hear from him by tomorrow, I'm going down to the jail to sit in the lobby until I get to talk to Josh."

Marlowe leaned harder against me as Tres gave me a *yeah, you go ahead and do that* smile.

"Well," I said with a laugh that came out sounding nervous. "Cantu is waiting on me. When I'm late, he comes looking for me."

I stood and gave him my card. "And if you have any more information, you'll call me?"

"You bet," he said, and stood, not taking the card.

"Oh," I said. "By the way. Have you heard any more on the girl who was burned in the fire?"

Marlowe never left my side, his eyes never left Tres.

Tres shifted. "No. Why would I?"

"She worked at your club. Thought you might be interested. I keep wondering why she was at Faith's at the exact time that a bomb went off." I said. "That's been a tough one."

"I can see how it would be." He smiled tightly, hustling me toward the front door.

He didn't seem worried, and it pissed me off. He had something to do with Faith's disappearance, and while I didn't have any proof, I was pretty sure he was the one who'd broken into my house and attacked me with a dead bird. I wanted him to sweat.

"There is some good news, though," I said, and he looked at me impatiently, still heading for the door.

"What?"

"They've found Tiffany's BlackBerry."

"Her what?"

"One of those cute portable Internet links. The cops are looking at it right now. They've been calling it her own little incendiary device."

My heart pounded like thunder as Tres and Chino escorted me and Marlowe out to my topless, doorless Jeep and stood, arms crossed, as I cranked the engine. I pulled halfway around the drive and well out of earshot. I leaned forward and fished a flashlight out of the glove compartment, then I leaned over to Marlowe and whispered, "Marlowe! Search! Search, boy!"

Marlowe looked at me once, sheer joy on his little puppy face, then he leapt out of the Jeep and into the darkness.

I screamed, careful not to scream his name, grabbed a flashlight, and took off after the dog, yelling, "Get back here, you dumb dog!"

I cringed, hoping the dog wouldn't take it personally. But he was off and in the woods, a dog on a mission. For all I knew, Marlowe thought I was yelling the key code to my office.

Teetering along behind him on my too-high heels, I followed his fluffy white tail bobbing deeper into the Ainsworth property.

Flood lights flicked on, and in moments we were bathed in artificial light.

Marlowe turned, looking at me.

"Go!" I hissed to Marlowe, and off he went, bouncing down the hill, snuffling back and forth in a perfect search pattern.

I hit a rock halfway down and fell hard on my butt, scuttling the rest of the way, bumping and scraping and scrambling to get up.

Tres and his band of *vatos* were hot on my trail, so I yanked off my shoes and ran full-out after Marlowe, yelling unintelligible things the entire way.

I winced, trying to ignore the sharp rocks and broken sticks that dug into my bare feet.

Stumbling, I caught a brief glimpse of Ethan outside the fence, still tinkering with his computer. Ethan gaped, but he stepped behind a boxbush and watched as Marlowe ran from outbuilding to outbuilding, sniffing in the search pattern until he reached the new recording studio.

Marlowe turned a circle—one, two, three—then plopped down on his haunches and did his strange little bark. Adrenaline pumped through my veins like Pilar's high-test lemonade.

Faith was here.

Marlowe knew it.

My heart kicked into fourth gear, and I was afraid I was going to have a heart attack. I wondered if Chino knew CPR. I thought about his skinny, reptilian lips. I sincerely hoped not.

I tripped again and fell into some kind of shallow pit—the kind you get when you dig a hole and there's never enough dirt to refill it. Scrambling against a rock, my skirt rode about halfway up my rear. Still panting, scrabbling for a handhold, my palm hit something small and hard and smooth.

A bone.

The breath strangled in my throat.

It was tiny and fragile, but there were others. Maybe hundreds. I thought about what Pilar had told me—about Hollis out there shooting kitties and teaching Tres to hunt.

Bile jammed the back of my throat. *Get it together, Cauley…*

I scooped up several of the bones and shoved them into the toe of my shoe. All of my internal organs felt like they were going to jump into my throat.

Scrambling to my feet, I got myself upright, then, stumbling, I rushed toward Marlowe, who was sitting, ears pricked, on perfect alert.

My heart pumped like thunder as the *cholos* caught up with me, each of them bearing their weird pistols.

I panted, struggling to get my skirt at least halfway down my thighs.

"Oh, thank you," I wheezed, holding the stitch in my side. I was panting and sweating and trying to get my breath, trying not to panic. "My dog got away and he just started running. He doesn't mind very well—"

Ah, the truth for a change.

"Ms. MacKinnon," Tres panted. "I don't care—what happened." He wheezed. "You are trespassing."

Nice to know I wasn't the only one who needed to hit the gym.

The *cholos* merely seemed amused. They didn't wheeze. They leered.

Tres glared at me. "If I catch you—out here again, there will be consequences."

Blood raced through my body, pooling in my cheeks, and I tried not to seem flushed.

All three of the *cholos* had their pistols out, and now they pointed at Marlowe.

That brought me to my senses. "Hey!" I gasped. "He's just a dog. He got away. He does that sometimes."

I winced. My feet and arms were scraped and scratched and I was very aware of the bones in the shoe I was carrying.

I panted, bending a little to catch my breath, petting Marlowe between his ears. "Dogs are like men. They run off sometimes. It's their nature."

Tres's gaze slid toward the studio. "We're all victims of our nature, aren't we, Ms. MacKinnon?" he said.

I thought about the bones in the shallow pit, and my blood ran cold.

Tres smiled a bone-chilling smile. He reached for the hem of my skirt, his fingers brushing the flesh of my upper thigh.

Fear, hot and bright, flashed through my chest. I thought about his fondness for *Veronica's Angels* and bit back the scream in my throat.

Tres leaned very close to me, his lips grazing my ear. His breath was hot and wet and coming more regularly.

I flinched. Near the studio, I caught a glimpse of something white gleaming in the moonlight. Another little bone…

Tres snapped his teeth, his finger lingering on the inside of my bare thigh. "Now see here? You've gone and torn your skirt…" His cologne surrounded me like a toxic cloud.

My heart thumped hard and I lurched away from him, nearly falling onto the tiny bone. Marlowe leapt toward me, growling at Tres.

"We have to go," I said. "Dinner with Cantu."

His jaw muscle worked hard and he glared at me.

"Just so we understand each other," he said, making a little gun sign with his thumb and forefinger. "This is private property." He let the hammer down and made a "pop" sound with his lips.

Hugging Marlowe closely to me, I nodded.

So much for my lucky skirt.

369

THIRTY-TWO

"WHAT THE HELL ARE you doing?"

"Well hello, Logan. Glad you called. I'm doing fine, thank you," I said and flopped onto the sofa with the dog and cat as I made a face at my cell phone.

"I've been trying to get ahold of you since Cantu called me. Where have you been?"

"If you talked to Cantu, then you know where I was. And I had my cell on *vibrate* because I was with Tres, and I didn't want him to get nervous."

"You have no authority to run around questioning people," he said, and I could tell he was angry, which ignited the last drop of adrenaline I had left.

"Excuse me," I said, my voice rising. "I may be an obituary writer, but I am still a journalist, and it *is* my job to interview people. And if I have half a chance in hell of getting off the Dead Beat, this is exactly the kind of thing I'm going to be doing."

He was quiet, and I knew he knew I was omitting key details of my adventures with Tres and his minions.

"Logan," I said, feeling bad about snapping at him. "You told me there would be times we would be at cross-purposes. This isn't a cross-purpose, but don't you think I'm worried about you, too? I mean, you're outside the country chasing a beautiful, deadly killer. She's like a praying mantis—she'll seduce you, then rip your head off and eat it."

"Seduce me *and* bite my head off?" he said, his voice lightening. "You're worried she's going to seduce me or that she's going to bite my head off?"

"Both," I snapped, annoyed at the streak of envy flashing up my spine.

He seemed pleased that I was worried that Selena Obregon might get him horizontal. "Okay," he said. "In the event you decide to go snooping around in dangerous places when I'm not there, you'll call Cantu, and I promise not to let Obregon bite my head."

I smiled for the first time in a long time. "Deal," I said.

"Are you any closer to finding her?" I said.

"Nearly knocking on her door."

We were quiet, the line buzzing with things unsaid.

"Logan," I said, not kidding around. "Be careful."

"Hey," he said. "I'm FBI."

I WENT AND POURED myself a Diet Coke and called Cantu, who yelled at me until he was interrupted by a kid with a runny nose.

"We'll talk about this later," he said.

"And I'll email you what I found out about Faith."

I disconnected and all of the energy that I'd been relying on left my body with a whoosh. It was late. All I wanted was a hot shower and to sleep until next week.

I waved at the cop out front. It was Bushy-Mustached Man, but I was glad just the same.

The adrenaline was gone now, replaced with ice water, and despite the heat, I felt cold and tired. Trudging down the back hall of my little bungalow, I peeled off my torn, dirty clothes and turned on the shower to let the water get hot. The dog and cat took their ceremonial seats to watch.

I never understood their fascination with water. Neither one of them liked a bath, and I suspected they wondered what I'd done to get in so much trouble that I'd need such a big bath. Apparently, I'd done a lot.

After all the hot water ran out, I toweled off and got my notepad.

I was exhausted, but I needed a plan.

I knew Faith was in that studio. Marlowe had made that clear.

I had to figure out a way to get her out without any of us winding up in that shallow grave of tiny bones.

In my bedroom, I glanced at the analog clock ticking away on the nightstand. Ten o'clock. I knew Dr. T never went to bed before eleven, so I called her. I needed advice. And I needed to talk to someone who wasn't going to flip out when I told her what I'd done—or what I needed to do.

She answered the phone on the first ring, and I said, "Hey, Dr. T, what are you doing?"

"Teaching myself to write left-handed."

That threw me. "Why?"

"Life is unpredictable. If something happens to my right arm, I want to be able to use my left."

"Oh," I said, as though it made perfect sense.

"What about you?" she said. "You make a booty call and get the wrong number?"

"I just need to talk," I said, and my voice sounded tired and defeated in my own ears.

"Tell me," she said, so I did.

I told her about the trip to the school, the icky DNA-covered magazines, the sheriff shooting cats, my encounter with Tres, and my suspicions that he was the guy who attacked me. While she didn't say anything as I spoke, I could tell she didn't approve of me going at this alone.

Dr. T sighed. "And now you think you're going to go back and get her. Just like that."

I sighed. "That's the plan."

"First," she said, "how do you know she's being held against her will?"

"I just know."

"And what if she is there? What if you find her and she doesn't want to be found?"

"That man has controlled her life since she was twelve years old. Of course she wants to be found."

"Cauley, he could be grooming her. You see it a lot in child abuse cases. Get the kid emotionally and physically dependent on you, and they think they got nowhere else to go. It's like raising and training a person to be yours—to belong to you."

I felt sick. "So you're saying if she doesn't want to leave, there's nothing I can do?"

"Not if she's eighteen and she's not being held against her will."

"But what if she doesn't know what her will is?"

"Uh-huh," Dr. T said. "How long did it take you to leave your controlling ex-husband, Dr. Dick?"

I cringed. "That was a low blow."

"But an accurate one," she said, and I had to agree.

"So what you're saying is it's taken her a long, slow slide down to get where she is today, and it's going to be a long trip back?"

"See? I always said you were a smart girl, no matter what anybody else said."

"What am I going to do?"

She was quiet for a moment. "Well, all you can do is offer her some options. She got someplace to stay awhile?"

"She can stay with me. And Mama said she could stay there until she gets on her feet."

"See? She's got two options already she didn't know she had. Give her my telephone number, tell her I'll see her and help her get this thing straightened out. Regardless, if she is in there, you know you're going to have to report it, right? And what about the bone?"

I shook my head. "You can take the girl out of the cop uniform, but you can't take the cop out of the girl."

"Huh. This girl's too old for that kinda shit. I'll make a call to the forensics lab tonight, tell them you're coming in with a bone that needs to be identified. Maybe that'll get you enough for a warrant."

"Bones," I said. "And that would be perfect."

"And what about this Ethan character? He knows he can't just charge in there on a white horse and rescue her, right? She's going to have to rescue herself."

The thought of E on a white horse made me laugh. "I'll talk to him about it."

"She's going to have to believe in herself or she's never going to get out of this cycle."

"Thank you," I said, and I felt the warm connection between us.

She sighed. "You are your father's daughter."

"And you are still his friend."

"I like to think I'm a friend to the both of you," she said, and I smiled.

"Me, too."

I DIDN'T SLEEP MUCH that night.

I spent a lot of time out on the back porch looking at the stars, wondering where Logan was and if he was thinking of me.

I wondered what he'd do if he was here. Probably stop me from breaking into Tres's property tomorrow night. Probably throw me down and make love to me until I couldn't remember my own name.

Sleepy and unable to sleep, I settled on the sofa with the dog and the cat and flipped on Turner Classics.

Gilda was in rerun, and I watched Rita Hayworth as she gyrated on the screen and wondered what it would be like to have people so obsessed with you.

I wondered who wrote the script. A good girl acting like a bad girl, trapped in a cage of her own making, although she probably didn't see it that way.

I watched as Gilda the nightclub singer warbled her heart out, all the pain and sorrow flowing out of her perfect mouth like a beautiful open wound.

I thought about Faith and her canary.

And the tiny bones in my shoe.

I felt like vomiting again.

The phone rang, and I nearly jumped out of my underwear.

I looked out the window. The cop was still there. I answered the phone and found Ethan sounding forlorn.

"Are you awake?" he said.

"Obviously."

"That BlackBerry message? I tracked it to Boners. Came from their server."

"You can't tell who sent it?"

"It's from a generic account, but I'm working on it."

"So it's still not enough for a warrant," I said.

Ethan sounded fidgety, ready to do something, but there was nothing we could do. "What are you doing now?" he said.

"Watching *Gilda* again," I said, and told him the channel so we could watch it together.

"Hey," I said. "I'm glad you called. We need to somehow get a message to Faith if we find her."

"You really sure she's there?"

"Marlowe is," I said, and Ethan snorted.

"I thought you said Marlowe was the worst search dog ever."

I frowned. "That was before he actually had to find something."

"You want to get a message to her?" Ethan said. "We aren't going to just take her?"

"Not if she doesn't want to go."

He sighed. "What do you want the message to say?"

I gave him my address, my mother's address, and Dr. T's phone number. He was quiet.

"You still want to do this?" I said.

"Yeah, you?"

"I'm ready as I'll ever be," I said. We were quiet.

"Ethan, I spoke with Dr. T tonight, and she said something you need to know. She said you can't ride in there on a white horse and save Faith. She needs to do it herself."

"I know that," he said.

"Yes, but she also has a boyfriend and a career. She's got a lot of choices to make and a lot of healing to do."

He was quiet.

"What I'm saying is, she may not choose you."

He sighed. It was a sad, resigned sigh, and he said, "I know. But I want to give her that choice."

I smiled. "You're a good guy, you know that, E?"

"Everybody says so," he said, but he sounded miserable. "I can't sleep."

"Me either."

"Want to keep the phone by the bed?" he said, and I smiled.

"Yes," I said. "I'll sleep with the phone."

After a moment, he said, "Cauley—do you think Faith's okay?"

"I don't know, Ethan. I hope so."

We disconnected and true to my word, I put the phone on the arm of the sofa in case he called again. We were both nervous, and I wondered how Logan prepared for a day like tomorrow.

Probably dusted off his Captain America uniform. Probably ate bullets for dinner.

"Marlowe," I said to the dog, who'd taken up more than his share of the sofa, "you did good tonight."

His white eyebrows moved as he stretched out even farther and laid his head in my lap.

I kissed him on his head. "You know you're going to have to stay here tomorrow, right?" I said.

I never know how much he understands, but Marlowe gave me the same look I give Tanner when he tells me I'm off a story.

Like hell I will.

THIRTY-THREE

THE SUN ROSE HOT the next day, and my nerves jangled at every sound. I took the dog and the bones to the forensic lab and checked in, as Dr. T had suggested.

"Great," I told Marlowe as we headed back to the parking garage toward the Jeep. "Now we only have eleven hours until I get myself killed."

He looked at me. I thought it was sympathy, but it could have been hunger. Usually, it's hunger.

Time trudged slowly, like I was walking under water. I thought I should be doing something to prepare. Like put bullets in the gun. Call my mother. Make out a will.

I chose the first and let the others slide.

It's times like this I wish I had nifty crime-busting accessories. Like Wonder Woman bracelets. Or super strength. Or Tom Logan.

I did a fair amount of pacing, checking and re-checking the gun Diego had given me. I counted the bullets again. The gift that keeps on giving.

All day, my body buzzed with a low-voltage shock.

I wondered if Logan and Cantu felt this way before they went on raids. I wondered if they ate their Wheaties and took a vitamin.

I didn't have Wheaties so I took a vitamin that was probably past its expiration date. Despite my better judgment, I made myself a small bourbon and Diet Coke.

Ethan arrived early, jittering like hell, which made me even more jumpy. So I gave him a bourbon and Diet Coke, too. Sometimes being with E is like babysitting—except the bourbon part.

Ethan wore black jeans and a black tee shirt that said *Code Warrior* on the front. It was a good look for him, and it was neatly accessorized with a big black bag full of stuff.

"What's in the bag?"

He grinned. "I thought you'd never ask."

He dumped the contents between us on the sofa.

"Night vision goggles, a GPS locator, a BlackBerry..."

"What's this?" I said, palming a small box with a key card.

"Belongs to Zeus. That's what we're using to get in. He says they've got the worst security system ever. It's all set up on a separate security circuit. If we bypass the main circuit, all the locks open."

"Ethan," I said. "You are a genius."

He blushed but went on. "This is the DVD of the music video I edited for her. These are some song sheets, and this..."

It was a page full of 0s and 1s. I grinned. "Is that my address and phone in binary code?"

He smiled modestly. "Yours, your mom's, the shrink's, and mine."

"That way if we get caught, we can leave it behind?" I said.

"Bingo. If Ainsworth can read binary code, we deserve to get caught. And I brought this," he said, handing me a printout.

"What's this?"

"Big Max was working on it all night. The BlackBerry message to Tiffany? It came from an alternate address from the Boners server."

"Oh, ick," I said, looking at the handle: BigDaddyTres.

I blew out a breath and looked at the clock. Two more hours to go.

We sat saying nothing, sipping our drinks, watching television, when the cat went to the jukebox and began yowling.

"All right, all right," I said, and punched in the familiar set of numbers. The forty-five clicked and whirred as it hit the turntable, and soon, Aretha was wailing about *R-E-S-P-E-C-T*. I bet Aretha wouldn't be afraid of busting into an armed structure.

"Are you going to tell anyone we're doing this?" Ethan said, his foot jittering to the beat.

"I'm going to text Cantu right before we go in."

"Text him?"

"That way he can't yell at me."

Ethan nodded and rubbed his eyes.

"You know," he said. "Hanging around you is no picnic."

I sighed. "Sadly, you're not the first person to tell me that."

THE SUN FINALLY BEGAN to set and my heart began pounding. Probably Morse code for *Stop right here before you get carved limb from limb.*

I turned to Ethan. "Go time," I said, and he nodded.

He retrieved his box of geek stuff, and I got my gun and my purse.

"You know how to shoot that thing?" he said.

"Technically, yes."

"Practically?"

"No."

Ethan looked like he wanted to strangle me.

I got my keys and opened the front door, and Marlowe leapt out of the house, nearly knocking me down on the way to the Jeep.

"I thought we weren't taking the dog."

I glared at Marlowe. "I thought so, too."

I shouldered my Team Six backpack filled with all the essentials—fruit bars, water, Faith's poetry books, the glob of pink sweater she'd been working on, and a gun. Nothing like being prepared.

I waved at the cop, and he nodded as Ethan and I pulled out of the drive.

We were quiet as Judgment Day as we made the long trip back to the ranch. Marlowe graciously shared the front seat with Ethan, while Ethan seemed to hold onto the dog for dear life.

I parked about a quarter mile away by the electrical box Ethan indicated. I got out and popped the hood. If anyone noticed, hopefully they'd think we had car trouble.

Ethan got out his bag and went to work on the box.

"Okay," he said. "Done. Now we have to get to the phone box and disconnect the cameras."

"Are you sure this is going to work?" I said, and he shrugged.

"If it doesn't, we gotta run like hell."

"Well," I said. "That's comforting."

He did his thing at the phone box, and we crept around the corner to the front gate.

"How do we know if it doesn't work?" I said.

"An alarm will go off, and people will start shooting at us."

I held my breath. Together, we took hold of the gate. Nothing happened.

"See? That's a good sign," he said. "No alarm."

There may not have been an alarm, but the gates were heavy, and it took both of us to shove it back on its tracks. Luckily, we were all kind of smallish, so we didn't have to push far.

"Wait," I said. "I'm going to go ahead and text Cantu. I'm going to add Olivia too."

"Now?"

"One or both of them will be here by the time we get to the studio and talk to Faith. If Tres and his mercenaries find us, we've already called the cavalry."

I worked my thumbs over the keys and texted where we were, the location of the studio, and the time.

Ethan nodded, and we pushed the gate again. It gave a foot.

The minute the gate made a dog-sized opening, Marlowe shot through like a streak of silver lightning.

"Marlowe!" I hissed, but I was talking to the back of a big, fluffy white tail that disappeared into the thick, wooded area to the left of Tres's house.

Marlowe made for the studio, and Ethan and I raced after him, careful not to twist an ankle or break a knee on the rocky terrain.

Marlowe beat us to the studio, where he was waiting behind the bulldozer, a smug look on his little puppy face.

"Showoff," Ethan said. He tried the door to the studio, but it didn't give.

"Dammit!" he swore. "The only lock on the whole property not on the same circuit."

"That's good news," I said. "That means she's here."

He nodded, and with newfound enthusiasm, plugged the small device into the lock and waited. Sixty seconds is a long time to wait when armed thugs might be barreling down on you, but it took that amount of time before we heard tumblers click into place.

I looked at Ethan, who looked back at me. "It could be on a different alarm system, too," he said.

I closed my eyes. "We've come this far. Open it."

Gritting my teeth, I turned the knob. Nothing happened. We let out a collective sigh of relief.

"We've only got about ten minutes before they know their security's offline," Ethan said.

My eyebrows shot up to my hairline. "You never said anything about a time limit."

Ethan shrugged impatiently. "Details," he muttered, and took off after Marlowe, who was doing his up-and-down search motion.

The dog stopped at a grate in the wall and I stood beside him, staring.

"Marlowe," I said, "are you sure?"

He turned three times and woofed.

"Nine minutes," Ethan said, setting the alarm on his watch. Taking a deep breath, we removed the grate and found a long metal vent just big enough for a body.

I cringed.

"You don't think she's in there, do you?" Ethan said. But Marlowe dove into the ductwork, a dog on a mission.

I shook my head. "The dog does."

Sighing, I shouldered my purse and shimmied into the duct after Marlowe, E grunting in behind.

It was dark. Ethan had the night vision goggles, but he was behind me, so all he got was a cartoonized, green view of my butt. Next time we'd have to think this through better.

I inched along, descending in the darkness, listening for Marlowe, who was already about five feet ahead of me. Suddenly, he yelped, and then I yelped, too. The duct came to an abrupt end, with a ladder propped at the rim of a huge hole in the duct. I missed the ladder and fell headfirst into a heap next to Marlowe, who stood staring at me.

"Ethan, wait," I yelled and rolled onto my back. Pain shot up my spine, and it got worse when Ethan fell right on top of me.

I screamed and Ethan yelped, and in the darkness, a light shone about fifty feet away.

Ethan yelled, struggling to get the goggles off and out of the light. My heart stopped as my eyes adjusted to the light.

Faith stood in a roughly arched underground doorway, staring at us. Fear shone bright in her dark eyes.

"He told me you'd come," she said, her voice detached and stiff, as though she'd forgotten how to speak. "He said you'd be here, and here you are."

"Faith," I said, but she shook her head violently.

I looked down and realized she was holding a gun.

THIRTY-FOUR

SHE HELD THE GUN on us with both hands, but her aim was shaky. To the right, I saw the big birdcage, the canary flittering around and around in circles, chirping and chittering madly. The door to the cage was open, but the bird didn't seem to notice.

"Go," she said. "Over there. On the couch."

We did as she said, and I slipped my Team Six backpack off and set it on the sofa next to me. The room was small and all white, outfitted like an efficiency apartment, with a small adjoining kitchen, and a television with a DVD player and speakers set on a cart opposite the dubious-looking sofa we were sitting on. The room was underground, with no outside-facing windows, but a door with a formidable lock stood next to a long, rectangular mirror—like the two-way mirrors you see in police stations.

I held Marlowe's collar with one hand and used the other to pat Ethan's knee. Both boys were ready to tackle her and take her home.

She looked like she desperately needed to go home—or to someone's home. Faith's hair was growing back but she looked even worse, if that was possible. Laser scars covered most of her tattoos, and her face was no longer bejeweled. Dark circles punctuated her dark eyes, and her pupils were dilated; not a good sign.

She shook her head. "I hit the security button. Tres and his *cuadrilla* will be here soon."

"Tres and his gang?" I said, my voice high, shocked that she'd set the alarm on me. I had taken her to my mother's house for dinner, for cryin' out loud. I thought I knew this girl. I shook my head. "Why would you do that? Faith, we're not here to hurt you—we just wanted to make sure you're okay. Everyone is worried about you."

"You're lying," she said. "He said you would say that. He said you would lie, and here you are, lying."

"Faith, I don't know what you've been told—just put the gun down," I said, making my voice calm and steady, the way I'd heard Cantu soothe people out of bad situations. "You don't have to do this. People are out looking for you. Whole search teams have combed the ranch—your friends from the club, the girls from your school. My mother and all her friends came out to look for you. I have pictures of people searching for you."

She faltered. "My mother?"

I blinked, trying to decide what to say that wasn't a total lie. "Your mother and Pilar are very worried about you. Your mother made a public plea on television for your safe return," I said honestly.

She made a derisive noise. "Was my mother sober?"

"Are you?" I countered, looking at the trash bin, which was full of Jack Daniel's bottles.

She took a step back, and I regrouped. "Faith," I said. "Charlotte Fisher is looking for you."

Her breath caught. "Llina?"

"She's very worried about you. The whole school is out looking for you. She thinks you're in trouble, and I think so, too."

I offered her the shapeless pink blob I'd taken from the box Charlotte had kept.

Her eyes welled with tears, and she shook her head. "I can't go back," she said. "There's too much. I've done too much."

"Faith, there are people who care about you. In your heart, you know that."

Beside me, Ethan looked at his watch. He leaned toward me and whispered, "Six minutes."

My heart pounded in my ears.

"I am alone. I have no one. I have no money. I have no options." Her voice caught on a sob. "I have nothing."

"That's not true," I said. "Everyone has options. Granted, you may not have as many as some other people, but you do have options."

Ethan unzipped his bag, and Faith yelled, "Stop! Stop or I'll shoot!"

Ethan shook his head, his voice steady and reassuring. "I brought you some things."

He laid the disk on the coffee table, along with a scrapbook he'd pieced together of photos of Faith and Wylie he'd found on the 'net.

I stared at him. "How come you didn't show me that?" I said.

He shrugged. "Some of it's from the Dead Copy file."

"Oh, jeez," I said. "If by some twist of fate we make it out of here alive, Tanner's going to kill us."

Faith stared at the photo album.

Ethan pushed the DVD into the player. Faith's breath caught as she watched Ethan's vision of her spring to life on the screen.

A tight camera angle closed in on Faith's pretty face, lingering like a loving caress.

The camera dipped slowly from her eyes to her mouth, and there was an ethereal beauty there, a poem in video.

"Two minutes," Ethan whispered, and Marlowe began to bristle.

Still watching the video love letter, Faith opened the photo album, and there was Puck, smiling back at her from a happier time.

Softly, she began to cry.

Ethan moved across the room and turned the pages to the middle of the album. A page of musical score.

She stared at it. "It's my song," she whispered.

"'Broken Wings,'" he said.

"How—?" she said, and he shook his head.

"It all boils down to math. Just like code," he said, repeating her own words.

She ran her fingers along the hand-inked musical score Ethan had drawn.

"Magic on paper," he said.

He turned the page, and her eyes went bright with tears as she ran her fingers across the binary code. "You're not alone," he said. "Friends are God's way of apologizing for the family he gave you."

She looked at him. "Did you make that up?"

"No," he said, grinning at me. "I heard it somewhere."

Her video played on in the background, the desperate lyrics set to haunting music, and we all stood, Ethan and I looking at each other. Less than a minute.

Marlowe growled low in his throat.

The dog glanced up at the trap door and then over at the door near the wall-sized mirror. I tightened my hold on his collar. Beneath my hand, I felt the dog's muscles coiled, ready to spring.

My heart thundered and a fresh surge of adrenaline pumped into my veins.

Bang!

The door beside the mirror slammed open, and Tres stormed into the room. His *cholos* dropped into the room through the vent, landing lightly on their feet.

"Well. Trespassing again," Tres said. He moved toward Faith as Chino and Jitters flanked the door. As Tres moved further into the room, the small space seemed to fill with his awful cologne.

"I warned you about trespassing."

I choked down the awful salt pooling in my mouth, trying not to gag.

"Faith is here because she wants to be here," he said. He took the gun from Faith and held it lightly, almost casually, pointing it toward the linoleum floor, tapping his thigh with the short barrel.

Faith's gaze was locked on her bare feet, all expression drained from her face.

Near the door, Chino and Jitters stared at me and Ethan like they'd just smelled raw meat. I noticed Jitters' fingers lovingly tracing the curve of his long gun's trigger. Tres laughed.

"So you found her. Big deal," he said. "Who do you think is going to find *you?*"

Faith had been holding the photo album in one hand and dropped it. The sound of the book hitting the floor echoed against the sound of her singing, still lilting through the speakers near the old television.

As though he'd just noticed the video, Tres said, "What's this?" His voice was mocking as he leered at the video lilting along on the television.

My heart pounded, and my mind flashed back to a time not so long ago, to a similar situation I'd barely survived. I took a deep breath.

"I'm not worried," I said with a good deal of false bravado. "But Cantu knows where we're at. I contacted him before we came in."

"You're trespassing." He ran a finger along Faith's cheek. "Anything unfortunate happens, I'm protecting my property."

"Faith is not your property," I seethed. "But that phone call gives him probable cause for a search."

"Not his jurisdiction," Tres said and smiled an ugly smile.

E looked at me, brows raised. Yes, we were out of Cantu's jurisdiction. I had no idea if the phone call was probable cause, but it would definitely be probable cause and someone's jurisdiction if we got killed. Probably best not to bring that up.

Tres shrugged. "This is Sheriff Junior Hollis's jurisdiction, and he's on his way over here. And even if your buddy officer Cantu happens to find you trespassing in a secure underground room, Hollis'll set him straight. I'm not doing anything wrong. Faith is here because she wants to be here—right, Faith?"

Faith was quiet but her lower lip trembled.

He tipped up her chin, and still she didn't look at him.

Rage flashed hard and sharp over his face, and he yelled, "Shut that shit off!"

Tres shoved Faith into the wall and stormed toward the DVD player, picked the black box up over his head, and smashed it onto the cement floor.

Faith and I both jumped at the shattered bits of plastic. Tres snatched the DVD out of the wreckage. Teeth clenched, he took the music in both hands and broke it.

Ethan and Marlowe vibrated with barely controlled anger, and I continued patting both of them, silently urging them not to escalate the violence.

In the corner, Keates thrashed around in his cage, eager to get out, still oblivious that the cage door was open.

Faith let out an involuntary sob.

Marlowe snarled, showing his large, white teeth, and I tightened my grip on his collar.

"She is eighteen," Tres growled. "She is *eighteen*. She is here of her own free will." His staccato words sounded like stones striking the floor, and I wondered who he was trying to convince.

Marlowe growled back.

I shrugged, swallowing the urge to throw up. "Yeah, but the door is open. Events have been set into motion, and there are things you don't have control over."

His eyes narrowed to dark, reptilian slits, and I half expected a pointy tongue to come slithering out of his thin lips.

"Those bones buried in your yard? The lab is looking at them right now. We've got Tiffany's last text message. We know the message came from the server at Boner's—the club you own—and it is currently being analyzed. We'll find out where it came from. It's just a matter of time until we find out who sent it."

Tres's eye twitched almost imperceptibly. "They can't do that," he said, his voice hitching.

"They're already half done," Ethan piped up, his chest puffing when the subject was his expertise. "You'd be surprised what a good geek can find. You know," he said, "no email, no text message, no cell phone call is ever really private, and they never go away. You just have to know where to look."

Tres's face went red, contorting with fury. "I haven't done anything wrong," he roared. "Cats and birds. It's not illegal to shoot pests on your property. And lots of people have access to my computer. You got jack shit."

"We've got enough. Cantu has those knives you stole from my kitchen and the Polaroids you took. Forensics ran the prints and we're just waiting on a match," I said.

Tres snorted. "Then you got nothing. I've never done anything wrong. My fingerprints aren't even in the system."

"Correction: you've never been *caught*. And your prints *will* be in the system as soon as Cantu gets here," I said, gaining strength as I thought of Cantu storming in at any moment and hoping it would be soon.

Tres sneered at me and slid an arm around Faith, holding her close, squeezing harder until Faith gasped and his knuckles were white.

"She's mine," Tres said. "I am making a whole new life here. She'll have a recording deal, a beautiful home—everything she ever wanted."

Except her freedom, I thought. Faith's face was frozen in a look of cold resign, and I thought of Tres's office and the animal heads staring dead-eyed from the walls, the photos of politicos and celebrities lined tidily behind his desk, the snow globes arranged in a straight line around his blotter ...

"Trophies," I said. "All your life, you've gotten everything you ever wanted and no one has ever told you no, and you've got the trophies to prove it—the heads on your wall, the photographs, the animal bones on your property. You wanted Faith, and you wanted what was left of El Patron. No one's ever told you no in your whole spoiled life." My temper flared and my voice went higher, carried by the swelling force of my anger. "You have never had to be accountable for one lousy thing in your life, and now you're scared shitless because that's all about to change."

Tres's face reddened and I went on. "What do you bet at least one of those shell casings matches the one you left with dead canary in my bedroom?"

Faith's face faded into a portrait of horror.

"Tres, you didn't," she said, her voice catching.

"Shut up!" he roared, and she cowered, but her eyes were alive now, glittering with hatred and something else I couldn't identify.

"You killed Charlotte? You killed my bird and sent her poor dead body to Cauley?"

"Yes, he did," I said. "And he didn't send the bird to me. He broke into my house and attacked me and Marlowe and the cat. I bet if he moved his hair, we'd see a chunk out of his ear about the size of a small cat's mouth."

392

Faith gasped. "You said a piece of lumber from the studio hit you during construction . . ."

"She's lying," Tres said, the first sound of panic edging his voice.

"And," I went on. "I bet if we take photos of Chino and his buddy, we could do one of two things: we could compare them to the security cameras at the courthouse. I bet with some good forensic work, we'd see it was Chino and his pal Jitters that drove the cab of shooters who killed your brother on the courthouse steps."

The men didn't move, but Faith shrunk back.

Tres shook his head. "She's lying. I love you. I'm the only one in this world who loves you." He grabbed her and shook her, like he was trying to make his words sink in. The *cholos* cast each other covert glances.

"Or," I went on, glancing over at Chino and Jitters, my gaze resting on the scarred remains of their Syndicate tattoos, "I could take the photos to Diego DeLeon. He issued me an invitation to his office a few days ago, and he told me something very interesting." I continued, gathering courage with each word. "He said that some *carnales* broke team. He said something about his displeasure with them. He said nobody leaves the Syndicate alive—something about *blood in, blood out.*"

The *cholos* didn't move but there was a perceptible shift among them. Apparently, DeLeon had means the police didn't have.

Chino's slitty eyes glittered in the near dark.

"And you," I said to Tres. "I bet a million dollars that you set the fire that nearly killed Tiffany. You sent the text that lured Tiffany to Faith's house—the text that set off the bomb. And I bet when they search your house, they're going to find that you set up the team to kill Puck."

A stillness fell about the air as I continued. "I saw you that day. You had a handkerchief over your nose and mouth, but in a million years, I'll never forget that nostril-burning cologne."

Faith made a small sound like a rabbit when it knows it's dying.

393

Nobody else seemed to notice.

Beside me, I felt Ethan shift slightly, and I closed my eyes as I realized his hand had dipped into my backpack. Cold fear froze my insides.

Ethan, don't . . . I squinted my eyes, trying not to move, trying not to draw attention to Ethan and the pistol he'd just pulled out of my backpack, trying to stop him from doing something stupid with the sheer power of my brain.

Oh, jeez, Ethan, please don't, please don't, please don't . . .

By my side, Marlowe's gaze kept lifting to the trap door.

I listened hard in the silence. Nothing.

In the heavy stillness, Chino took an audible breath in and out, and then a sharp, earsplitting *bang!* splintered the silence.

I threw myself over Marlowe. Jitters jerked to his side and fell. A horrible *crack!* rang out as his skull hit the corner of the television cart.

Blood blossomed at his shoulder from Ethan's shot, and it poured from the open wound in his head. Chino aimed his long gun at Ethan and fired, but Ethan rolled over the sofa and shot again, aiming for Chino's head. The sharp *thwang* of a ricocheting bullet echoed in the air.

Chino shot again, and Ethan yelped, falling to the floor.

I started to crawl toward Ethan, and Tres shouted, "Stop!" His voice was ear-splittingly loud in the ringing silence. "Stop or I'll kill her."

I stopped, saying a soft prayer that Ethan was going to be okay. Tres had Faith by the neck, the gun to her temple. He was backing toward the door.

"Tres, don't," I said. "You said you love her. Let her go."

He shook his head but there was something in his eyes, wild and unreachable. Jitters lay still on the floor. Chino stood, gun out, covering Tres as he and Faith moved toward the door.

"We're leaving. We haven't done anything wrong, and we're leaving," Tres said.

Panic welled in my chest. "The police may not have any evidence on your involvement yet," I said, "but your buddies here are in it up to their eyeballs. What do you bet they're the canaries when Cantu catches up with them?" Beside me, Marlowe began a low, threatening growl that was magnified in the room's tension.

Tres faltered, his chest moving as he breathed in and out.

"You keep that dog under control, or I'll kill him the way Hollis and I killed those cats," he said.

My stomach folded in on itself, and I wrapped my arms around Marlowe, trying to figure out what to do. Where the hell was Cantu? Had he not gotten my message? Could he not find us? We were in a bunker, underground, and at the back of restricted, wooded property, but he was Cantu...

Tres cocked the gun.

"Tres, don't!" I yelled.

Tres pivoted and shot Chino between the eyes.

Faith screamed and Marlowe snarled, straining against me.

A slight shock registered on Chino's face. A stream of blood oozed bright down his forehead, then dripped over his nose. He blinked twice, his gaze on Tres in disbelief. His knees buckled, and he slid down, falling onto his side. Tres aimed again and delivered two more bullets to Jitters. The *vato's* body jerked twice with the impact, then went deadly still.

"No witnesses, no problems." Tres looked up from the bodies, and a sickening smile spread over his face. "Like my mama used to say, it all comes out in the wash."

The color left Faith's face.

Behind her, the bird flung itself against the cage, shrieking like a fire alarm.

Marlowe snarled and howled like he'd gone mad, froth flinging from his fangs. I held him tighter, my body between him and Tres's gun.

"Shut that dog up," he shouted, directing his aim at me.

Bang!

Above us, the trap door slammed open, and Cantu dropped lightly on his feet near the ladder, his weapon trained on Tres's head.

Tres hesitated, then he smiled. "You wanna take a chance, pig?" He clasped Faith's face closer to his own, moving her back and forth so that Cantu didn't have a clear shot.

"Behind the couch, Cauley," Cantu ordered. A slight edge of relief caught me by surprise as I wrestled with the dog, scooting behind the sofa, heart thundering in my ears.

We scuttled in next to Ethan, who lay crumpled in a heap.

"Marlowe, rescue," I said, and the dog stopped struggling against me. He turned and woofed and curled his fluffy body gently on top of Ethan, lending his warmth. Ethan was breathing but unconscious, clearly in shock. I pressed my fingers against his neck. His pulse was thin and quick.

From behind the sofa, I saw Cantu edging toward Tres.

"Tres, this has all been a misunderstanding. Let everyone go, and we'll talk about it, just you and me, man to man." Cantu held his gun to the side, barrel to the floor. "See? We can do this peaceful and quiet, and nobody gets hurt." He laid the weapon on the floor beside his foot. What Tres couldn't see was the pistol at the small of Cantu's back.

Cantu edged forward almost infinitesimally. "See?" He spread his hands, showing that he had no weapon. "Now I know you didn't mean for any of this to happen." He crept closer. "Things just got out of hand."

He moved as he spoke, his voice calm and soothing.

"I understand. You and your girl just want to be alone..." His voice was hypnotic; without seeming to move, Cantu was within five feet of him. Tres's breathing slowed but he still had Faith in a death grip, the pistol against her cheek. At the sound of Cantu's voice, Faith's sobs receded to small, hopeless tears. Even Keates was quiet, clinging to the cage, yellow head cocking back and forth. I cradled Ethan's head in my arms, Marlowe protecting E's belly.

From behind the sofa, I saw the muscles beneath Cantu's black tee shirt tighten, and despite his peaceful voice, I knew he was about to blitz Tres like rolling black thunder.

My own muscles tensed as he advanced, and I leaned toward Ethan. "Just hold on," I whispered.

Slam!

The door by the mirror banged open, and the large body of Junior Hollis thrust into the room. "Nobody move!" he shouted.

Tres jerked toward the noise, and relief flooded into his tight face.

"Hollis!" he said. "Thank God. These people are trespassing, and this idiot detective is trying to arrest me."

He turned, smirking at Cantu and then me.

Bang!

Hollis shot him.

Tres's eyes rounded in surprise as he looked from me to Hollis.

The sound of the shot echoed in the small room, and we all froze in stunned silence.

Blood bloomed bright in the middle of Tres's chest, spattering on Faith's pale cheek.

Faith screamed.

Tres blinked and stared at Hollis, rage shimmering in his dark eyes. His grip went tighter on Faith. She sobbed, terror bright in her eyes. The fingers of his right hand loosened, and his gun clattered to the floor.

"Faith," he whispered. *"Faith…"*

And then he slid slowly to the floor, taking Faith with him.

Hollis shook his head, his big .44 still ringing from the shot.

Cantu rushed toward Tres, glaring at Hollis. He tucked Tres's pistol into his pocket and checked for a pulse. He shook his head.

I hovered closer to Marlowe and Ethan, not quite believing what I'd just seen.

Grim-faced, Cantu slid his arms under a sobbing Faith and lifted her up and away from Tres.

As he lifted, her leg caught on something.

Faith wailed as Tres's lifeless arm entangled her bare ankle. From his pocket slipped a red bandanna.

Cantu reached down to free her, but Faith shook her head. Reaching down, she slipped her small hand beneath Tres's. She held it for a moment, then let it drop back to his motionless body.

My breath caught, and a tear slid down my cheek. I rocked Ethan against me, and Marlowe looked at me, his eyes large and warm. I reached over and stroked his head.

In the silence, Hollis shook his head and clicked his teeth.

"Always figured I'd have to shoot that son of a bitch someday," he said.

THIRTY-FIVE

RED AND BLUE LIGHTS flooded the darkness around the studio and Team Six cheered as Cantu carried Faith from the underground bunker.

The crowd parted, going quiet as Cantu passed, Faith's dark head buried in Cantu's shoulder.

I followed him out. The team circled me and Marlowe, and warmth surged through me like a whole-body hug. As they surrounded Marlowe and me, tears stung the backs of my eyes, and it felt like a thousand pounds had been lifted off my chest.

Marlowe pranced through the team and practically took a bow.

I accepted hugs and pats on the back, but I watched, my throat closing, as Cantu carried Faith to one of the waiting ambulances.

Behind me, two medics emerged, bearing Ethan out on a stretcher. He was conscious but confused.

"What do you mean my bullet ricocheted? You think I shot myself and passed out at the sight of my own blood?" he said, trying to wriggle off the stretcher. "Where's Faith? Is she okay?"

The taller medic shook his head. "Just try to relax, bud. You're in shock."

"He going to be okay?" I said as they passed through the crowd. The tall medic shook his head. "Question is, are *we* going to be okay."

"Put your body in a prone position, or we're going to sedate you," he told Ethan, and E laid down.

"Faith's fine, Ethan," I said, walking next to the stretcher. "Let the docs check you, and I'll be there in a bit."

The medics lugged him into an idling ambulance and hit the lights.

Behind us, a battalion of armed officers stormed into the building, headed by a tall, bearded man I didn't recognize.

Team Six had closed ranks around me, giving each other high fives, chattering warp speed, asking questions that rang in the warm night air in a chorus of chaos.

"Thank you," I said, my voice choked with emotion. "Thank you all. We wouldn't have made it without you."

Olivia bustled through the crowd, a handler and dog in tow. "Cantu had your basic location, but Gandalf and Moreno are the ones that found you," Olivia said. Until she'd wrapped the thermal blanket around me, I hadn't realized I was shivering.

"Gandalf, you hero, you," I said, kneeling to hug the black and brown Shiloh close to me. Marlowe shoved his pointy white nose between us. "You're a hero, too, Marlowe. But we always knew that."

Gandalf yipped at Marlowe, and the two of them pranced like puppies, tails wagging. I smiled and rose.

"Thanks, Moreno," I said to Gandalf's handler. I reached in to shake his hand, but he grabbed me and hugged me hard.

I kissed him on the cheek.

"You'd do the same for me," he said, but he blushed right up to his graying hairline.

"You okay?" Dan Soliz, the gang guy, said, stepping out of the crowd.

I grinned and fell into his hug. "I think so. What are you doing here?"

"Heard El Patron might be making a comeback. Your visit got me wondering, so I've been talking to Cantu."

I nodded. "Figure anything out?"

"Getting evidence. I'd like to talk to your buddies Tres and Chino."

I shook my head, and Soliz hesitated, then nodded.

"What?" he said.

"Tres just shot Chino in cold blood," I said, "and Hollis shot Tres." Soliz frowned.

Like bloodhounds, Miranda and her media minions began showing up. Too late, several young cops began cordoning off the area with crime scene tape.

There was a commotion, and I turned to see the tall, bearded guy leading his cops out of the building. Among them, Junior Hollis was talking fast, his hands moving as he demonstrated his heroism in the face of danger.

My eyes narrowed.

If anyone was a hero in this scenario, it was Cantu. While Ethan and I were in that bunker trying to free Faith from Tres and his armed *cholos*, Cantu was calm and cool. He had the situation under control. He had been within reaching distance of Tres's gun and the whole thing would have been over. And then Hollis burst in with a hasty bullet.

A flash of blond hair caught my eye—Miranda making her way through the crowd, cameraman and producer in tow.

Then Miranda found Hollis, and he found an audience.

"Well, great," I muttered. The *Journal* would get the scoop on finding Faith. And Tanner was going to shoot me.

I sighed. Oh well. Wouldn't be the first time.

Behind me, the team of cops I didn't know came out of the building with three bodies on stretchers. My stomach pitched.

The tall, handsome bearded guy headed toward my small crowd, where he sought out Cantu, who met him halfway.

The man's hair and beard were a stunning salt-and-pepper. Beneath a blue western shirt, his shoulders were wide, and his faded blue jeans fit him well. He walked with a swagger that made me think of Logan. As the two of them came closer to me, I saw the silver star of a Texas Ranger badge.

I stared at Cantu.

"Cauley," he said. "This is David Wilkes. I've been talking to him about Dawes County."

I blinked. "You called in a Ranger?"

"Just one," Wilkes said, reaching out to shake my hand. "Jurisdiction and all."

"Oh," I said, and I could feel my face flush. Wilkes chuckled; he was probably used to striking women speechless.

"Um," I said, blinking as he gazed down at me with summer blue eyes. *Brilliant. Cauley MacKinnon, rapier wit.* Shaking myself out of my stupor, I placed my hand on Soliz's arm. "And this is Dan Soliz. He does the gang stuff with APD."

"Glad to meet you," Wilkes said, reaching in to shake Soliz's hand. "You got a big job these days."

From the corner of my eye, I saw Miranda toss her blond mane. "So," I said. "What's going to happen to Junior Hollis? He didn't have to shoot Tres. Cantu had it under control."

What I wanted to say was that I thought Hollis shot his buddy to shut him up. Honor among thieves until someone goes canary.

Wilkes nodded. "Officially he'll be on administrative leave."

"But doesn't that always happen when there's an officer-involved shooting?" I said, wanting Hollis fired or browbeaten or whatever should happen to cat-killing, bigoted, bad sheriffs.

"Yeah, it's a bureaucracy thing. But Cantu here says we got a thing or two to look into."

I smiled at Cantu, and my heart felt that familiar pull toward him. He reached forward and wiped a smudge of dirt off my cheek. "We can't arrest him just because you don't like him," Cantu said.

"Too bad. I got a list of guys that need arresting," I grumbled.

A loud, familiar barking caught my attention, and I turned. Marlowe and Gandalf had capered toward the search vehicles parked to the left, and a dog in one of the cop cars barked wildly.

Napalm. He was locked in the cop car. Again.

"Excuse me," I said to Soliz, rushing toward the dog, but Olivia beat me to it.

Alarmed, Soliz, Cantu, and Wilkes trotted along behind me.

"Damn it," Olivia growled. Napalm was tied to the adjustable bar of the headrest. His collar and leash were tight as he strained toward the window, barking for all he was worth. The leash was so tight he couldn't sit, and I swear I saw little puffs of steam coming out of Olivia's ears.

"Back up," she said.

"What?" I looked around at Cantu, Wilkes, and Soliz. They shrugged, and we did as she said.

Marlowe and Gandalf sat shifting on their paws, staring up at Napalm trapped in the back seat.

Olivia took a step back, pivoted, grunted, and then kicked up and out, hard, the weight of her short, stocky frame compacted into pure force.

The front passenger window shattered. Though the dog knew her, he snarled and snapped, choking against his short leash, his sharp white teeth flashing in the dark.

"Hey, boy, you settle down. We're just gonna get you outta here ..." Olivia cooed. She reached through the broken window and unlocked the door, her voice low and soothing as she spoke to the dog.

"Settle," she said sharply and blew in the dog's face.

Napalm blinked and went quiet, watching as she untied his leash and opened the back passenger door, letting the dog out of the stuffy car and into the fresh air.

Napalm flinched a little, looking around like he just remembered where he was. Marlowe and Gandalf pranced and bowed around him, nipping at Napalm to play.

"I'll be damned," Soliz said. "You know Hollis is going to have a cow."

"I dare Junior Hollis to have a cow with Olivia," I said, and Olivia cocked her head, looking Soliz over.

"You her friend?" she said to Soliz, nodding at me.

Soliz blinked. "Um, yes, ma'am."

"You got a dog?" she said.

Soliz shook his head.

"Happy birthday," she said, and handed him Napalm's short leash. "We got a website tells you everything you need to know 'bout takin' care of dogs. We meet on Thursdays for search and rescue."

She shuffled off with a sense of purpose.

Soliz and I watched her go.

"But I don't know anything about search and rescue," Soliz said.

"None of us did before we started," Moreno cut in. "Hell, I'm an orthodontist during the day."

Cantu nodded, still watching Olivia as she barked orders into the Team Six crowd.

"I heard she poured hot grits on her ex-husband," Cantu said.

"Yeah," I said. "I heard that, too."

Wilkes reached down to pet Napalm's big, brown, anvil-shaped head. "Well, buddy," Wilkes said to Soliz. "Looks like you got yourself a dog."

THIRTY-SIX

TRES, CHINO, AND JITTERS were dead. I knew it—I'd seen them killed with my own eyes. But something inside me couldn't quash the urge to look around every corner, peek under every piece of furniture, throw open every shower curtain.

Ethan was out of the hospital and on the mend.

The bullet nicked his left lung. Forensics established that the paramedics were right—it was his own bullet that downed him. Despite that embarrassing detail, Ethan was determined to get back to geekdom. The District Attorney's office had reviewed Ethan's shooting of Jitters Gomez and declared it self-defense, but Ethan's gaming community had branded him a hero. Thanks to his geek buddies, he'd become a YouTube sensation from the outtakes of Miranda's news clip describing how he'd shot Jitters, sparking the chain of events that had freed Faith from Tres's psychological cage. Though Ethan protested, I thought he protesteth a little too much, and he seemed to enjoy his fifteen minutes of fame.

He had his nose to the digital grindstone, saying he had a game to finish designing and an Internet conference—and, deep in his little geek heart, there was Faith. He would wait for her and would accept her decision; proof positive that life does indeed go on.

Junior Hollis was on paid administrative leave, which didn't seem fair to me. Hollis also had a lawsuit pending. Josh Lambert's parents slapped a civil suit on him and were suing the county to boot.

I knew this because Tanner assigned me the article—Page 1 of the Metro section, just below the fold. Shiner and the rest of the News Boys were still stewing about it.

The Rangers were investigating Faith's disappearance and the way that Dawes County handled it, including the shooting of Chino, Jitters, and Tres. The Rangers seemed particularly interested in Tres's death. Hollis was taking it all in stride. He'd been holding nonstop press conferences with anyone who had a microphone and a camera. Who needed a bunch of schoolgirls stuffing reelection envelopes when you were a hero with worldwide media coverage?

I suppose if I were a better person I'd have felt sorry for him. He lost his dog to Olivia and her new compadre, Soliz, and he'd lost Tres, his biggest campaign contributor. Of course, he shot Tres, so that was probably a draw. And he had the Texas Rangers breathing down his big neck. Junior Hollis would slip up sooner or later, and the law would catch up with him. Ranger Wilkes would see to it, and so would I. Patience is not my strong suit, but the payoff would be worth it.

October winds cooled the summer heat down to a balmy eighty-five degrees, and life was getting back to normal, whatever that was.

And just when I had thought things had settled down, Mia threw me a birthday party at the office the day before my birthday. I had hoped she wouldn't, because I knew Merrily would extort money from everyone from the CEO to the stock boys. I figured I had enough enemies roaming around the planet—I didn't need to grow my own.

Colorful balloons erupted from my cubicle like a crazed clown had been let loose on the office, and someone had changed my screen saver to proclaim: "28—two years 'til the Big 3-0! G-r-r-r-e-e-a-a-t!"

It didn't feel great. It felt empty.

Sure, the chocolate-covered birthday cake was delicious. Larry the heavyset guard cut a big chunk out of the corner that spelled out "Cauley" in a funky antique typewriter font and was devouring it with gusto on his way back to the security desk. Mia and Ethan pulled their rolly chairs up to my desk and were digging into the rest of the cake. Remie, our big-haired receptionist, was still out on bedrest, the latest of her pack of rugrats due any time now.

On my desk, a small stack of presents were grouped into a pile and topped with a sachet of something smelly—obviously the work of Mia. My friends had spent some thought on their gifts, and it made me smile.

Tanner gave me a week of extra vacation time, most of which I'd already burned on the search for Faith. Merrily presented me with the office gift—a Post-It dispenser with a pad of Post-Its that weren't subject to my Post-It quota. God bless her right down to her pencil-sharpening, pointy little heart.

Brynn arrived at the office, running late from her downtown PR office. She slid into the small clutch of friends and coworkers, catching her breath to join in the truly awful rendition of "Today's Your Birthday." At the end of the song and all the imaginary electric guitar playing, she brandished an unwrapped urn inscribed with the phrase "Ashes of My Ex-Husband."

My coworkers roared with laughter. I rolled my eyes as I accepted the urn and kissed Brynn's cheek. But I smiled an inside smile as I placed the urn in a prominent place near the corner of my desk, closest to the aisle.

Mia and Ethan gave me a softball-sized something wrapped in Ninja Kitty paper. Giddy, I tore off the paper and found a Magic 8 Ball much like the one in my home office.

I turned it over in my hands. Mia and Ethan had pried the little round window out of the 8 Ball and replaced the oracle's multifaceted triangle with a digital piece that spouted wisdom gleaned from Humphrey Bogart.

A big streak of sentimentality wrapped around my heart. Mia had decoupaged an image of Bogey from *Casablanca* and included a tag that spelled out "What Would Bogey Do?" over the "8" on the top of the black ball.

"You hear from Faith?" Ethan asked hopefully. He'd lost weight and was downright skinny. He delved into the cake, and I hoped he'd eat it all.

"Sort of," I said. "She's seeing Dr. T. Doc won't tell me much—patient confidentiality and all that—but she says Faith's coming along better than she'd hoped. She's living in a hotel right now, working part-time at the girl's ranch, and making small forward progress with her mother."

"Wow," Ethan said. "Has she said anything about me?"

"I don't know," I said. "Remember, patient confidentiality? I do know she's made several trips to San Antonio to spend time with Tiffany Parker."

"Oh, yeah? How do you know?"

"Because I went down to see her, too, and Tiffany told me."

"Is she all right?" He wiped chocolate off his chin.

I shook my head. "She's better, but she's a long way from being all right. She's going to have more skin grafts. But she's fighting infection and seems to get along with her bunk mate in the burn unit."

Ethan nodded. "And the housekeeper?"

"Pilar?" I smiled. "Seems Faith's been playing matchmaker. She hooked up Pilar with one of my Search buddies. So, it seems that our friend Pilar has been spending time with Faith and making time with Moreno."

Ethan looked scandalized. "Isn't he like *half* her age?"

"Yep," I said. "Ain't life grand? Makes me feel better about my own birthday."

"You hear from Logan?"

"Not for three days now," I said, staring at the office clock over Tanner's office door as though I could will time forward and he would be home safe and sound in time for my birthday.

Mia grinned. "Yeah, but I have a good feeling about that," she said, sucking the icing off a birthday candle. "Hope you didn't waste your birthday wish," she sing-songed, and stuck the candle in the penholder on my desk.

She picked up the Bogey Ball.

"Go ahead, try it," she insisted, hopping up to read the answer over my shoulder. "Ask if you're going to end up with Logan."

Something inside me cringed. I wasn't sure I wanted to know—if the answer was "No," I didn't think I could take the disappointment.

"Is Logan safe?" I asked instead. The entire office went quiet.

I shook the ball, turned it over, and read, "I don't mind a reasonable amount of trouble."

I smiled. "From *The Maltese Falcon*," I said.

Mia hopped up and down, her long hair bouncing against gravity. "He's okay!" she chirped, hugging me around the neck. "He's okay and he's coming home!"

"Mia," I said, "I think these answers are subject to interpretation."

"Yes," she said. "My interpretation, Miss Pessimist."

"You know, a pessimist is just an optimist whose heart's been run over a couple of times," Tanner said, and we stared at him.

A knock sounded at the entryway, and I looked up to find Harold escorting a good-looking guy in a suit. The guy was holding a yellow, legal-sized envelope. My heart skipped, gripped in a suffocating blanket of dread.

"No," I whispered. "Please God, no."

The guy looked through the middle of the office melee, and said, "Mike Tanner?"

"What's this about?" Tanner said, stepping forward.

The guy shrugged, handing him the envelope. "You've been served." He looked around at the balloons. "Huh," he said. "First party I ever saw before a divorce."

Tanner was quiet, and everyone froze.

He nodded, looking down at the envelope in his hands. Turning without a word, he went into the Cage and shut the door.

Wiping the chocolate off my lips, I went after him, pulling the blinds closed as the door swung shut behind me.

He stood staring at the picture of his wife in front of the jar of licorice. I could hear his breathing. I didn't know what to say, so I said the only thing I could think of.

"Tanner, I'm so sorry."

He was quiet for a time, his jaw muscle working.

"Yeah," he finally said. "Me too."

The dark circles under his eyes seemed to darken with his mood. He looked out the window onto the Hill Country, and then back at his desk.

Then he picked up the jar of licorice and smashed it against the wall.

He burrowed through the small drawer at the bottom of his desk and came out with a bottle of bourbon and an old box of cigars.

I looked up at the mangled smoke detector and sighed.

"Want one?" he said, shoving the box toward me.

"Wanna make me sick on my birthday?" I said, and he smiled a sad smile.

"Least you'd stay out of trouble," he said. Uncapping the bourbon, he reached for two coffee mugs.

"A guy can dream," I said.

THIRTY-SEVEN

"Yes, Mama, I made two," I said into the phone as I slid the last Crown Royal pecan pie into the oven. Marlowe sat, nose twitching, watching the pie progress with great interest. Muse sat on the barstool near her cookie jar, bitching her little cat blues. CNN droned in the background as my mother went over the list of items I was supposed to bring to my own birthday party. I could hear the sharp, expert snap of an eggshell breaking, and I knew she was mixing the batter for a sweet, sticky praline cake in the big, blue mixing bowl she'd had since I was a little girl.

"Have you heard from Agent Logan today?" she wanted to know, her voice moving in rhythm as she beat the egg.

"No," I said, and it came out crankier than I meant it to. I was worried about him, but I knew Mama was, too. She had been sizing up Logan for a tuxedo from the minute she'd laid eyes on him. "He called yesterday and said he had some promising leads and not to worry if I don't hear from him for a couple of days."

"Does that mean he found that awful woman?"

"I don't know," I said honestly.

"Well," Mama tutted. "He'll be home soon. We'll save him a piece of cake."

My mother. The eternal optimist.

"Your sister is flying in with the kids tomorrow morning but she has to leave early. Campaign year, you know."

I blew out a noisy breath.

"Be nice, Cauley," Mama said, and I sighed.

I didn't want to be nice. Suzanne and I never got to see each other since she married Jackson the Jerk and moved to Houston to be a senator's wife.

I sighed. "I hoped she could stay longer," I said. "Every time I see Ella and the boys they seem a foot taller."

"I know," Mama said, and a tenor of sadness betrayed her cheeriness. "Is your friend Mr. Tanner coming?"

I could see Mama, tapping her perfectly manicured nails, mentally revising the ever-increasing invitation list.

"I invited him and Mia and Brynn and Ethan," I assured her. "Anyone else you haven't thought of? The mailman busy tomorrow?"

"Ah," Mama huffed her disapproval, and I smiled. Mama loves birthdays, as long as they're not her own.

"Have you made your list yet?" she wanted to know, and I said, "No, mother, I've been making pies."

Each year on our birthdays, Mama insisted Suzanne and I make a list of new yearly goals.

That woman has got to stop watching *Oprah*.

Mama's phone beeped, and I said a silent prayer of thanks when she clicked over and said, "Your sister's on the phone. It's long-distance. See you tomorrow, sweetheart."

As I disconnected, I felt even more restless and edgy. I poured myself a big bourbon and Diet Coke and made my way to the little library in front of the house.

A master to-do list was probably a good idea. I rolled a fresh sheet of paper into Aunt Kat's old Remington Scout typewriter and stared at it as though something would magically materialize.

Most of what I wanted was to get Logan home safe and sound.

I stared out the window where storm clouds banked on the horizon. In my brown, dry yard, a dozen rain lilies lifted their delicate white blooms. The weather reports said we wouldn't get rain, but rain lilies don't lie.

I glanced at Daddy's old pocket watch. I'd propped it up on the shelf next to a compass and my spanking new Bogey Ball. Five hours and the little clock would tick me into my twenty-eighth birthday. I wondered what Bogey would do about turning twenty-eight.

I turned the ball over and shook it. "Will Logan be coming home alive and in one piece?" I asked, dreading the answer.

I turned it over and the tumbler inside read: THIS COULD BE THE START OF A BEAUTIFUL FRIENDSHIP.

"Hmm," I said to no one. Maybe Mia's 8 Ball works better than the regular kind.

And then I heard it.

On the television, the music changed the way it does when there's important news breaking and I wondered who we'd started a war with this time.

I took the drink into the living room where the starch-haired CNN anchorman said something about a gun battle on the streets of Buenos Aires in Argentina.

My heart froze. Marlowe looked at me, then at the television, and then back at me.

The anchorman pressed his ear bud as though he was getting a bad connection. "We have unofficial reports that a gun battle broke out on a backstreet in Buenos Aires this afternoon involving fugitive suspect Selena Obregon, who escaped custody with a U.S. Marshal. Reports say that at least three Americans are involved in the shooting and that one American was killed. It is unknown at this time…"

Crash.

My drink dropped to the floor, splintering into a wet, flammable mess. "No," I whispered. "No!"

Fumbling for the phone, I dialed Logan and got his voice mail. Fingers shaking, I pressed the *off* key and dialed again. The same.

Frantic, I dialed Cantu. "Have you heard from Logan?" I yelled.

"No, why?" he said.

"Turn on CNN," I said on a breath. "There was a gun battle in Argentina sometime this afternoon. and at least one American is dead!"

"What?" Cantu said, and I heard him flipping from *Blue's Clues* to the news program. My phone beeped and I switched over.

"Mama, I can't talk right now, I'm on the phone with Cantu," I snapped, and a deep drawl came over the line.

"Well, I wouldn't want to interrupt…"

"Logan?"

"Yeah, kid," he said, sounding tired. "I'm okay."

"Logan!" I yelled, ushering Marlowe into the kitchen. He woofed and whirled, jumping up and down, and I was afraid he'd land on the broken glass.

"We got her," he said.

"Someone got shot; I thought it was you," I whispered, tears stinging the backs of my eyes.

"The marshal she conned into helping her escape," he said, and there was iron in his voice.

"Oh," I said.

"Just wanted to tell you Selena's in custody, everyone but the marshal is okay, and we'll head home tomorrow."

"Jeez," I said. "And it all started with a fake obituary. This favors-for-feds thing isn't all it's cracked up to be."

"You saying you're not going to do me any more favors?"

"No. I'll just be pickier about what kind."

Logan chuckled at that. "Speaking of favors, Ethan still got that cat?" he said.

"Logan, that animal is not a cat, it's a terrorist. You sure you want him?"

"Hey," he said. "Terrorists are my specialty."

"Yeah, well, come on home and we'll see about your specialties."

"On my way home, kid."

My throat felt tight, and I swallowed back a wave of emotion. "That's the best birthday present I could ever have," I said.

"We'll see about that," he said, and heat flushed my cheeks.

"I gotta go, kid. I'll see you in a coupla days."

And then he was gone.

I hugged the phone to me, letting out a long sigh of relief, and I jumped when it beeped.

I'd forgotten Cantu was on the other line.

I clicked over. "Cantu, that was Logan! He's okay!"

"Jeez, Cauley, you gave me a heart attack. Maybe you should hook up with some nice electrical engineer or something. Not so dangerous, ya know?"

"Not on your life," I said and disconnected.

Smiling, I headed back to the kitchen to check the pies, Muse eeling figure eights through my ankles, Marlowe prancing along beside us.

Muse yowled as I opened the oven to peek, and I said, "What, cat? What do you want?"

I scowled at her. "Do any of us really know what we want?"

She scowled back at me and stalked off to the jukebox, where she leapt with no apparent difficulty, staring at me with her unblinking, yellow stare. "Fine," I told the cat. "I guess some of us do know what we want," I said, wiping my hands on a dishtowel. "You want Aretha? You got it."

The truth is, we all need a little Aretha sometimes.

I beeped the television off and hit the buttons of the jukebox, and Aretha began belting out the bliss of being a natural woman. Nodding to the beat, Marlowe and I waltzed back to the kitchen, waiting for the oven timer to ding.

I wiped some of the pie flour off my nose. Natural woman, indeed.

I was about to start wailing away when the doorbell rang.

Nobody ever rings my doorbell. A vision of armed *cholos* rushed through my head, and I shivered.

Marlowe bristled, staring at me.

I peeked through the opaque part of the stained glass, and I stood up straight, surprised.

There was Faith, standing on my front porch. Her dark hair was short and lovely, her cheeks pink and healthy. She was dressed in jeans and a jacket and was holding a large bag and a postal tube.

"Well, hello, stranger," I said, wondering what on earth she was doing at my front door.

She smiled sheepishly. "Dr. T said it was your birthday."

"Tomorrow," I said, opening the door wider so that she could come in, Marlowe and Muse peeking out from behind my legs.

"I have something," she said reaching into the bag.

I shook my head. "Faith, you didn't have to—"

"Yeah," she said, "I did."

It was a professional-looking CD. The cover was a beautiful photo of her in a white dress, her hands open, Keates fluttering up and out of her hands. My breath caught. "Faith," I said. "It's beautiful."

She shook her head. "I just—" her voice broke. Over us, the first drops of rain plopped heavily onto the porch.

"Come in before it starts pouring," I said, ushering her into the house. "This is wonderful! Let's listen ..."

"No, you can listen later," she said. "I have one for Ethan, too."

She blushed hard, and I smiled.

Thunder crashed outside the window, shaking the whole house.

"What are you doing tomorrow?" I said. "Because my mother is driving me crazy with this birthday party. Want me to call and have her set another plate?"

Mama would have a fit of joy when she saw Faith.

"I'd like that," Faith said, her cheeks going pinker. "Will Ethan be there?"

"He will now," I said, grinning. But my grin faded when I remembered that Faith already had a boyfriend. "How's Josh?" I said.

Faith sighed, her face going melancholy. "He's doing better. That Ranger from the search team worked him out of Hollis's custody. He wasn't supposed to tell me this, but the Ranger also took him to his AA meeting."

I nodded, thinking of big, burly David Wilkes taking Josh under his wing. I supose heroes come in all shapes and sizes.

"Oh," Faith said. "This was on your porch."

I frowned as she handed me a generic brown postal tube. No return address. My heart skipped a beat. The last two packages people had sent me contained loose body parts and a dead bird.

Marlowe sniffed the package, tail wagging like he'd found the last ham sandwich on earth.

Lightning struck so close that the following thunder was immediate and shook the house all the way up to the rafters. The lights dimmed and blinked off and then on.

Yikes! I hoped that wasn't an omen.

Holding my breath, I peeled off the end of the tube and pulled out a large, architectural-sized piece of paper.

Faith gasped.

I read the accompanying letter.

"What does it say?" Faith wanted to know, practically bouncing on her toes for a peek.

I shook my head in disbelief. "It says it's a star chart from the Star Registry. It says there's a star named after me."

I unfolded the document that came with it.

It spelled out the coordinates, along with my name and a handwritten note.

"So you'll never lose your way," the note said. "Happy birthday, kid. I'll be home soon."

Reading over my shoulder, Faith went into an actual swoon.

From the living room window, lightning split the horizon and the wind picked up, the rain lilies bowing in the new breeze.

The rain came hard now, pounding on the tin roof.

"Come on," I said to Faith, making my way down the short front hall.

Smiling a smile I could feel all the way down to my toes, I rolled up the star chart and placed it next to the typewriter. Faith and I stared out the library window and into the thundering rain clouds that covered the stars. The sky was dark, but I knew my star was there, waiting for the clouds to part.

I wondered where Logan was. It didn't matter. I knew he was thinking of me.

Muse hopped up on the jukebox, the tip of her tail twitching.

Thunder crashed outside the window, and the rain rushed down the roof.

Marlowe woofed, shifting from paw to paw as I punched the familiar buttons on the jukebox.

Smiling, I turned to Faith. "Hey," I said. "You like Aretha?"

THE END

ACKNOWLEDGMENTS

BEHIND THE PAGES OF every book are people who made it happen. A huge thanks to acquisitions editor Barbara Moore for believing in this series, and to senior editor Becky Zins for her brilliance, logic, and patience that passeth all understanding. A special thanks to agent Andrea Somberg for loving Cauley as much as I do. A big-haired thank-you to Kathy Patrick and Beauty and the Book for making my life more lively and for choosing *Scoop* and *Dead Copy* for her coveted book club selections. If you haven't been to Kat's Girlfriend Weekend, you don't know what you're missing.

A big thank-you to Sgt. Joe Munoz and the Austin Police Department, to John and the Williamson County Sheriff Department for their help and insight. To the Austin CPD Search and Rescue Squad, continued admiration and gratitude for doing what you do. I'm proud to be among you.

Big hugs to my family, Betty Frazier, Sherri Marcovitch, and Don Wingard, for putting up with my deadlines, and to my swim buddies Julie Ortolon, Emily McKaskle, Robyn DeHart, and Cindi Myers, for their encouragement, sympathy, and the occasional kick in the pants.

And most especially, thank you to Robert Hartmann, without whom this book would not have been possible, and for giving me the family I always dreamed of.

ABOUT THE AUTHOR

KIT FRAZIER (AUSTIN, TX) is a Mystery Guild pick of
the month and a Pulpwood Queen Reader Selection.
Kit has and garnered high praise from reviewers including *Romantic Times, Gumshoe Reviews, Blogcritics, New
Jersey Online,* and *Huntress Reviews.* Kit is the managing editor of a regional magazine and, along with her
dog, Tahoe, participates in search-and-rescue missions
with the FBI and local police. Visit Kit's website at www.
kitfrazier.com or shoot her an email at kitfrazier@
yahoo.com.

WWW.MIDNIGHTINKBOOKS.COM

From the gritty streets of New York City to sacred tombs in the Middle East, it's always midnight somewhere. Join us online at any hour for fresh new voices in mystery fiction, book club questions, author information, mystery resources, and more.

Midnight Ink promises a wild ride filled with cunning villains, conflicted heroes, hilarious hazards, mind-bending puzzles, and enough twists and turns to keep readers on the edge of their seats.

MIDNIGHT INK ORDERING INFORMATION

Order by Phone
- Call toll free within the U.S. and Canada at 1-888-NITEINK (1-888-648-3465)
- We accept VISA, MasterCard, and American Express

Order by Mail
Send the full price of your order (MN residents add 6.5% sales tax) in U.S. funds, plus postage & handling, to:

Midnight Ink
2143 Wooddale Drive, Dept. 978-0-7387-0959-8
Woodbury, MN 55125-2989

Postage & Handling
Standard (U.S., Mexico, & Canada). If your order is:
$24.99 and under, add $3.00
$25.00 and over, FREE STANDARD SHIPPING
AK, HI, PR: $15.00 for one book plus $1.00 for each additional book.

International Orders (airmail only):
$16.00 for one book plus $3.00 for each additional book

Orders are processed within two business days. Please allow for normal shipping time.
Postage and handling rates subject to change.